BODY
SCISSORS

BODY SCISSORS

A NOVEL

MICHAEL SIMON

VIKING

VIKING

Published by the Penguin Group

Penguin Group (USA) Inc., 375 Hudson Street, New York, New York 10014, U.S.A.

Penguin Group (Canada), 90 Eglinton Avenue East, Suite 700, Toronto, Ontario, Canada M4P 2Y3, Canada (a division of Pearson Penguin Canada Inc.)

Penguin Books Ltd, 80 Strand, London WC2R 0RL, England

Penguin Group Ireland, 25 St. Stephen's Green, Dublin 2, Ireland
(a division of Penguin Books Ltd)

Penguin Group Australia Ltd, 250 Camberwell Road, Camberwell, Victoria 3124, Australia
(a division of Pearson Australia Group Pty Ltd)

Penguin Books India Pvt Ltd, 11 Community Centre, Panchsheel Park,
New Delhi–110 017, India

Penguin Group (NZ), Cnr Airborne and Rosedale Roads, Albany, Auckland 1310,
New Zealand (a division of Pearson New Zealand Ltd)

Penguin Books (South Africa) (Pty) Ltd, 24 Sturdee Avenue, Rosebank,
Johannesburg 2196, South Africa

Penguin Books Ltd, Registered Offices: 80 Strand, London WC2R 0RL, England

First published in 2005 by Viking Penguin, a member of Penguin Group (USA) Inc.

10 9 8 7 6 5 4 3 2 1

LIBRARY OF CONGRESS CATALOGING IN PUBLICATION DATA
Simon, Michael, 1963–
    Body scissors : a novel / Michael Simon.
        p. cm.
    ISBN 0-670-03443-6
  1. Police—Texas—Austin—Fiction.   2. Austin (Tex.)—Fiction.   3. Jewish men—Fiction.   I. Title.
    PS3619.I5625B63 2005
    813'.6—dc22   2005042269

Printed in the United States of America

To my brother Rico
for leading the way

"Why, of course, the people don't want war . . . But, after all, it is the leaders of the country who determine the policy, and . . . the people can always be brought to the bidding of the leaders. That is easy. All you have to do is tell them they are being attacked and denounce the pacifists for lack of patriotism and exposing the country to danger. It works the same way in any country."

—Herman Goering
at the Nuremberg Trials
April 1946

". . . a stirring victory for the forces of aggression against lawlessness."

—Vice President Dan Quayle
on the alleged resolution of
the Persian Gulf War
April 1991

BODY
SCISSORS

The eighties came and went. The president who ruled over them flashed one last fatherly smile, bowed and exited the world stage to thunderous applause, with skyrocketing homeless rates, the '87 stock market crash and a hundred thousand AIDS victims at his feet. Replacing the communist boogeyman with the liberal boogeyman, he passed the reins to a new leader, the most powerful man ever to claim Texas residency as a tax dodge.

Texas, where politicians and other influence peddlers test out crimes they plan to commit nationally, faced the double-edged economic recovery of the early nineties. Quality of life eroded further than before for Texas's non-millionaires: Countryside and farmland paved themselves to make room for malls. Old neighborhoods got "renewed" for wealthier residents at a greater rate than ever. High-tech industries rolled over the northern part of town where small houses once stood, the industries spawning beehive apartment complexes and neighboring strip malls to house, feed and entertain the laborers who would build and buy the laptops, pagers and mobile phones of the new decade. Progress. Unemployment was down, at least on paper: in real life, the grunts struggled harder than they had in the depths of the recession, as rents climbed, social services were cut back and homelessness— under the "anti-camping" law—was made punishable by arrest. That's where I come in.

At street level, an economy based on self-reliance equals every man for himself. A free market cures all ills, and if it doesn't, screw the schools, screw housing, screw financial aid, don't tell us the details, just arrest everybody. Figure the twelve-year-old junkie you busted for dealing gets replaced by a new recruit before nightfall. Figure a joke among cops: "What's the best thing about crack? It lowered the price of a blow job to five bucks." Figure if your kid is lucky he goes to UT or maybe out of state; if he's not, maybe he's sleeping next to you in the back of your pickup, and dealing drugs looks better to him than flipping burgers. Figure it's the wrong time to be born unlucky.

So you're no dope, you go with the winner, you become a black conservative, a gay conservative, a poor conservative. Invite yourself to the party and sit at the back table, they'll get to you, sooner or later. Carve out a little corner for yourself, and to hell with everybody else, you've got dreams of your own. If you feel a little pang of conscience, for the friends and family you stepped on to get where you are, eat something, drink something, snort something, BUY SOMETHING! Anything. Because we need you to buy things.

And all this weaves through my mind at night as I dream my cop dreams. I'm stepping blind in this bricked-up department store, a shopping graveyard, dark and booby-trapped. My mouth is pasty dry, my eyes burn from the fumes of home-cooked crystal meth on the fire. Suddenly Rachel's with me, she's supposed to be safe and separate from this. And the building isn't gimmicked to keep people from getting in, it was easy to get in, anyone can get in: you can never leave. We can't get back the way we came. We can hardly see, save for cracks of light. My foot goes through a floorboard— Rachel cries out and grabs me. Snakes wrap my feet and I shake them off. Any step could send us plummeting through the floor. The building is crumbling, the wrong time to visit him, a trapped, wounded animal, and the wrong night to bring a date. I might feel the cold of a gun barrel at the back of my neck, or not feel it, not see the bullet coming. No sooner do I think that than suddenly he's behind us, and I whip around, draw my weapon in slo-mo and fire and my bullets spit from the chamber, one, two, three, and fall flaccidly to the ground, and he's facing us down, and I realize too late that the guy I thought I trapped, trapped me, he's the cat, I'm the mouse, I'm weak and helpless, helpless to protect Rachel or even myself, and he's smarter than me, because he's high on the best stuff, and he's motivated by greed, and greed trumps justice and greed trumps vengeance even, and greed trumps love, and I'd trade my .38 for a flashlight and a way out, making bargains I can't make, like please God, please please please God, just get her out of here alive.

PART ONE
SWEET VIRGINIA

TUESDAY
January 15, 1991

10:45 P.M.—Lamar Boulevard, Southbound

Rubin watched Jennifer as she breathed in and out through her mouth, puffing clouds on the car window, stripes of light wiping over them from the bright signs of stores and restaurants, past gas stations and convenience stores, past the gloomy horror of the State Hospital.

"Are you warm enough back there?"

"Yes, Mom," he said.

Jenny said, "Yes."

Their mother kept a woolen blanket in the back seat for these times, chilly nights on the way home from movies or restaurants or city council meetings, when the heat didn't reach the back seat. Rubin and Jennifer sat buckled up in back with the blanket pulled up over their legs as Mom drove and listened to the radio.

"*. . . was inaugurated today under the cloud of impending war, the second female governor in Texas history and the first since 'Ma' Ferguson left office in 1935. Meanwhile, the president's deadline passed for Saddam Hussein's withdrawal from Kuwait. A White House official was quoted as saying, 'Only a miracle can prevent war now.' In Austin, local churches rallied for peace . . .*"

Their mother whispered to the radio. "Talk about the meeting. Talk about the meeting."

And Jennifer turned to look at Mom, baby round cheeks, lips pursed in a curious expression, as if to ask, What's that? What's next?

But how can you explain that to a little girl? Rubin was old enough to know that something was next, and it was always bad.

"Mom?" he asked. "Is there gonna be a war?"

"Yes, baby."

"Will you be drafted?"

"No."

He turned the idea around. "Will I?"

She looked at him in the rearview mirror and smiled. He had said something cute, but he didn't know what it was. He smiled back.

She'd brought them to Threadgill's again for a late dinner. Rubin could see the hostess's face pull tight like they always did when his mother asked for a table for three. In the silence that followed, his mother kept her own polite smile: she was the customer, she was a slim, pretty lady; and, if it came to that, she was a lawyer. Mom explained all this to them a hundred times, how white people were secretly afraid of them. But they never looked afraid to him, only angry. And while she was slim and pretty and a lawyer, he was short and fat and a fourth grader and he wanted to disappear. They were always the only black people, and she was always making a stand. Easy for her.

Mom had turned from the hostess and smiled at Rubin and Jenny like she'd won, then followed the hostess's clipped steps with her own graceful ones, past the tables and the posters and the lit-up jukebox toward the back dining room.

"No, I think we'd like to sit in front," his mother said. Mom's voice wasn't very big, but the hostess heard it, and held her breath.

"Those tables are reserved."

"All of them?" In the hostess's silence, his mother winked at Rubin and marched them all toward the front of the restaurant, past the jukebox, between the tables, flashing smiles at the white families. Rubin glanced back at the entrance and caught the eye of a scuzzed-out woman in a ratty coat. The woman glared at him and scratched. Even though she had a dirty neck, a hostess was leading her to the fancy chrome counter with a smile.

Rubin took Jenny's hand and followed Mom to the very front table, in front of a bay window surrounded by old concert posters and pictures of some slutty hippie lady from the sixties. Green neon lights buzzed over the table. He helped Jenny into her chair. "That's my good little man," Mom said as she settled in. The hostess slapped three menus on the table and huffed away. A flash of wrinkled nose from Mom like they were in on some joke together. But he wasn't in on it.

Half the time, she seemed to miss it, the angry stares and the whispers. The other times she rolled in it, like, "Look how smart I am, look what I got away with!" She left the neighborhood every morning to go to work. He was stuck there, surrounded by the same white kids from the block who hated him, and he walked Jenny to school. How was he supposed to protect her from a bunch of big white kids? Sometimes six white boys would surround the two of them. He couldn't fight them. He couldn't run, not with Jenny there, and they'd catch him anyway. His skin burned as he stood through his punishment. Today his books were knocked down. Yesterday they punched him. Sometimes they'd just stand there and call him names, in front of Jenny, to remind him they were in charge, they could do anything they wanted.

There were days he'd drop Jenny off with her class and almost choke as she looked back at him, helpless, her face reading, "How can you leave me here?"

Mom was always planting time bombs and walking away, making the neighbors mad and sending him off to school, yelling at his teachers and leaving him alone with them. She didn't understand anything.

"Lemonade sound good?" his mother said, and turned to the dim-looking waitress standing over them. "And how's the fried chicken?"

"Best in the state."

His mother laughed like it was a joke and ordered two portions, three plates. When the waitress left, she said, "Always order a drink. Otherwise they'll think you're a penny-pincher and they worry about their tip. This way they might make sure no one spits in your food." She smiled at the waitress as their lemonade hit the table and Rubin looked in his glass for spit.

"So," she said, and looked right at him, something she hardly did. She never seemed to be looking at anybody. "How was my speech?"

"It was great, Mom!"

"Really?"

Jenny said, "It was really, really, really good."

"Well, thank you, baby!" Mom said, and touched Jenny's cheek.

They had sat in the back of the auditorium, Jenny coloring in her book, Rubin just waiting, taking care of Jenny. He had always been taking care.

Why did she order fried chicken? The first bite was the only one he ever enjoyed. After that he was just calming his stomach, as he felt himself get fatter. Not fat, she always said. Chubby. And he'd outgrow it. He'd be slender like his mother, not short and stumpy like his dad. He tried to remember his dad. Nothing came back except a round face and a smile. But he could have dreamed that.

Jimmy Wrightington had the locker next to Rubin's and Rubin was always nervous going there. He'd mess up on his locker combination and by the time he got it open, Wrightington would be standing there, nose turned up like a pig, calling Rubin a retard and a queer and knocking his books down. He couldn't leave them on the floor, and if he bent over to pick them up, Wrightington would kick them away. Often as not, Wrightington would punch him. People kept telling him to stand up for himself, but that just made it worse. He had a dream of going psycho on Wrightington, jamming the boy's head in a locker and slamming the door on it over and over again, and people would respect him, for kicking Jimmy Wrightington's ass, for being tough. And it would feel good, revenge. He could feel angry enough to do it, but never figured out how. He just walked away feeling angry and frightened and stupid. The feeling would stay with him all day and into the night. One day he'd fight back, be a man and kick any-one's ass who messed with Jenny, he'd be big and tough and protect her. One day he'd stand up.

He was still thinking that later on, how he'd kick someone's ass and change everything, when they climbed out of the car, sleepy Jenny grabbing his hand as they walked up the path, when Mom un-locked the front door, let Rubin and Jenny in, followed them into the quiet house, flicked on the living room light, and locked the door, still thinking how he'd smash Jimmy Wrightington's head in the locker, slam, slam, slam, when suddenly someone was saying, "Hello, Mrs. Key."

They turned around to see a nightmare-looking man, a homeless man with a dirty sweater and bad teeth, pointing a gun, a real gun, at his mother. But Jenny was in the way. The man could shoot Jenny.

This was his chance. He could leap on it from the side, knock it out of the man's hand, shoot the man dead or pound him with the gun. He waited for his mother to say something but she didn't. Rubin's heart pounded in his throat, in his ears, telling him to jump, telling him to hold still. Without taking a breath, he jumped. And as he jumped, in his moment of flight and taking action, everything like a crazy dream, he felt for the first time he could remember that he was happy, when the sound began, *Kup* . . .

It went wrong. He grabbed at the gun, clutched the man's hand as a loud blast of thunder started and didn't stop, thunder crashing in a long, slow roar, a fire ripping through Rubin's fat belly, poking, puncturing, burning through and Rubin's head crashing down on the coffee table, the thunder echoing in his ears as his mother screamed and he knew how, in one second, in one moment of stupidity, he had ruined everything.

11:30 P.M.—706 East Thirty-eighth Street

In the dirt by the door sat a half-gallon stainless-steel dog dish with three hardened king-size dog nuggets, next to a coiled dog chain and monster collar, a silent unmistakable message to potential intruders to back off, low-tech security provided by an imaginary Doberman named Wolfgang. Woofles for short. I opened the door onto an American living room, so well-kept and at the same time inviting that I was always surprised to remember it was my own. Rachel trailed me in and pushed the door closed.

I turned to her. With her going-out-to-dinner heels on, she nearly reached my height at six feet even. We squared off, Rachel staring me down with her big, dark blue eyes with a slightly Asian turn at the corner, smooth skin and chestnut brown hair brushed back from her low forehead. She moved near, a close-cut dress calculated to show off the curves of breasts and hips, to show others what they were missing, what I went home with. I kissed her, then drew back and looked into her eyes.

If I had a photo album, it would look like this: My mother, a glamour shot, taken around 1950. My parents' wedding picture, her hair piled up as she towered over my scrawny dad, the unlikely Mr. and Mrs. Reles (rhymes with "zealous"). Me as a baby, my mother cradling me, kissing my tiny hand; my dad looking on, brooding. Me at ten, in the front window of my parents' apartment in Elmira, New York, the day of my father's release from prison, as my mother packs her bag, kisses me goodbye and disappears in a blue-and-white taxi. Me at fourteen in boxing gear, at a Mafia gym in Elmira, a hard look in my eyes as I fight my way up the ranks of the Golden Gloves competition. Bleary-eyed at fifteen as my father wakes me in the middle of the night to tell me he's made an influential enemy and we're leaving the state—now! At eighteen, graduating from Austin High School, class of '71, capped and gowned, my eyes blank. In my MP uniform in Frankfurt. At the University of Texas in jeans and a T-shirt, but on the inside, wound up to my core: uptight in relaxed clothes, looking like a narc. Marrying Amy, a tiny blonde with a domestic dream, cuddled in my big arms. Being left by Amy, punching the walls of our little, empty house on Avenue F. Making rank, Sergeant Dan Reles, and no one to share it with. Appointment to Organized Crime Division. Reassigned to Homicide. With my mentor Joey Velez. With his widow, Rachel.

Rachel and I had gotten a place in the Cherrywood section of Austin. I'd pushed for a rental, even though she could have gotten us a great deal and added her commission to our bank account. She laughed off my reluctance to buy, tacked it on to the fact that, after two and a half years together, I hadn't dropped a hint about marriage. She'd dropped a few. The house itself sat on the south side of a public golf course, a run-down patch of grass and shrubbery with a few holes and no fence around it. A gesture of democracy, it allowed the poor to impersonate the space-consuming rituals of the rich. If you grew up in the area and wanted a place to get high at night or make out with your girlfriend or maybe rape someone, that was the spot. A hundred feet away, on the western border of the golf course, sat the house Rachel used to share with Joey Velez.

Senior Sergeant Joey Velez had recruited me eight years earlier to work on the Gautier case, pulling me from a low-level assignment I'd been working since I'd made sergeant. With a little help from me and a dozen others, the Gautier case targeted major and minor players of a cocaine and car-parts racket operating out of Bertrand Gautier's famous blues club, and landed them in prison; and it got Joey and me assigned to the newly founded Organized Crime Division. A political shift bounced us off the division, and Joey saved me, mentoring me onto the Homicide squad and becoming my first real friend. He was like a father to me, except that he gave useful advice. If he knew my greatest desire was to jump on his wife, Rachel, he kept his mouth shut about it. And then he died. Now, three years after he was gone, I'd still catch him whispering advice, or as often, goofy things into my ear when I was supposed to be paying attention. I tried not to listen, part of my practice of pretending to be sane. I tried not to blame Rachel for his death, for not loving him. And I tried not to blame myself, for loving his wife.

A while after Joey died, I got promoted to senior sergeant. At work, I still missed Joey, the way you'd miss your father if he died when you were young, his absence felt keenly each day. At home, I tried not to think about the fact that I was sleeping with his widow. Rachel took my promotion as a good sign. We rented this house. She got up every morning at six to stretch and aerobicize in the living room, sunlight scorching her from the east window. I would sneak peeks at her by way of the hall mirror, watch her desperately pounding against the inevitable changes of time and gravity. I kissed and treasured the occasional gray hair I spotted on her head before she found and painted it, the slight shifts in weight and shape that made her more real and human and mine.

That night we'd been out for dinner with Ray and Marissa Tierney, "old friends from Houston, lawyers both." I wasn't supposed to know from the awkward pauses and the avoided eye contact that Ray, now a criminal defense attorney, was an ex-boyfriend of Rachel's, and

Marissa his clueless wife, or that Ray had hurt Rachel bad. The bridge-night fantasy Rachel staged served multiple purposes. It convinced Rachel we'd be like other couples no matter how we'd met, no matter that we'd first kissed under the watchful eye of Joey's ghost. And it sent out a message to Ray, one I was glad to back up: cop trumps lawyer.

I left the porch light on, hung up my jacket, looked through the house and checked the locks. The carpet everywhere muffled my foot-fall, I worried, as it would muffle the steps of an intruder. I spotted Rachel wiggling her ass up the short hallway to the bedroom, wearing a black satin robe I took as a good sign.

By the time I reached the bedroom, she was lying under the blanket with the lights dimmed. I undressed and slipped in beside her. At thirty-seven, I'd kept my boxer's build—beefed up with strategically rounded shoulders—and made a pretty good appearance in spite of a hairline that had slipped a few degrees north at the temples and halted, as if to remind me who was in charge. Along with that, I showed a dozen odd scars and a boxer's nose: broken once when I was a kid and again a few years back. You should see the other guy.

Rachel slid into my arms and greeted me with a full, wet kiss, then settled in and kept still.

I asked, "Is something wrong?"

"No," she lied, "it's just . . . We're always working. We come home in time to floss and go to bed. On weekends we clean the house and play catch-up."

"We just went out tonight."

"That's what made me think of it."

I didn't want to blow the moment if it wasn't already over. Here was a woman who spent her youth coked to the rafters, cleaned up and spent the last ten years making money. She didn't know what a real home was any more than I did.

"Well . . ." I said, warding off frustration. "What do you want to do besides this?"

"I don't know," she said. Then, "What do people do?"

Between us grew a box of sad, empty space. We had decent jobs, a nice house, each other. Now what?

"Do you have Monday off?" I asked.

"Why?"

Monday was Martin Luther King Day, an optional holiday in Texas, on the same level as Rosh Hashanah, Good Friday and Confederate Heroes Day. You could take off any one of them, depending on your religion or your politics.

"We could take a long weekend, maybe go away. Do something fun."

She thought it over. "Like what?"

"Whatever. We'll think of something."

The space between us fizzled and she was pressed against me, sweetly kissing, when the cordless phone rang on her nightstand, splitting the night, and I clicked that I was the detective on call. Rachel grabbed it on the second ring as I said, "No, don't."

"Yes?" she said, as the hope drained out of her eyes. She held the receiver out to me. The base should have been on my side of the bed since I was always taking the midnight calls, but the cord from the base to the wall wouldn't reach and we should have gotten a longer cord but we didn't.

"Who?" I said.

She imitated the operator's twang. " 'Dispatch, Mrs. V.' "

I took the receiver with a standard apology written on my face. "Reles."

"*They need you at 1610 Confederate Avenue. Behind Matthews Elementary. Now.*"

"Who died?"

"*I think a kid.*"

When I reached over her to hang up, Rachel was facing the wall and smoking a cigarette.

"I'm sorry," I said.

After a while, she shook off an idea and flicked the ash in a tray by the phone.

I stood and dressed. "It could be over by the weekend. We could still go away."

And again nothing as I left the house and double-locked the door behind me.

✦

I shot down Interstate 35, veered off downtown and headed west along Sixth Street. It was quiet for the downtown barhopping street, this being a Tuesday, and the lights and siren helped. I also had the FM radio blaring and the window open, hoping to clear my head. I'd had two margaritas at the restaurant—Rachel only knew about one owing to a quick deal I worked with the hostess while Rachel was in the ladies' room, before the Tierneys arrived—and the second margarita was a double. Reformed party girl Rachel got nervous watching me have more than one drink.

I flipped channels. "*. . . Persian Gulf. Beginning at three o'clock this morning, an air assault on the city of Baghdad . . .*" Flip. Singing, "*. . . I'm all strung out on heroin, on the ou-outskirts of town.*" Off.

I turned up West Lynn, looped left around the school and turned right up tiny Confederate Avenue to see five patrol cars, two ambulances and a fire truck, the FD always the first on the scene. I parked as close as I could, adding to the spectacle, and waded through the crowd of uniforms and onlookers, my badge held high.

I said, "Homicide." Two clusters of emergency medical techs didn't blink. The five patrols spun around, four white men and one black. I said, "Talk to me."

One patrol said, "The neighbors heard shots—"

"One shot," another one said.

"Whatever, and this woman screaming bloody murder. They called 911. No one was in a rush to get outside till they were sure she was alone." I stepped into the house.

In the far corner of the front room, four white-shirted EMTs clustered around a petite black woman who was sitting upright, sobbing. They'd wrapped her in a blanket. Her skin was damp, and she was shaking. Periodically, she'd stop crying and let out a gut-wrenching scream that stopped everyone dead. A second EMT cluster kneeled on the rug around what had to be a small body.

The black patrolman said, "The woman, sir. It's Virginia Key."

I said, "Who?"

I peeked over the EMTs to get a look at the boy on the golden carpet. They had a tube in his throat and a drip in his arm, EKG beeping and the knock-and-wheeze of a breathing machine. They pumped and pounded and shocked him, watched his heart and his brain function on mobile screens. I whispered to a patrol, "How long have they been at this?"

"Since before we got here."

Virginia Key screamed out what may have been "Ruby!" and tried to get up. The techs held her down in her chair, and she broke into sobs again.

I shifted close enough to get a better look at the boy's face, round and pudgy with baby fat, black features and the frightening gray-white pallor of shock and blood loss. A baby ghost.

A thousand factors hang in the balance when EMTs try to save a life. Death, coma. Lack of oxygen to the brain can cause permanent brain damage, a living death. Maybe the bullet hit his spine. He could lose mobility, be confined to a wheelchair, lose the power to speak. His life from this random moment on could be an endless sea of suffering. Even a well-intended blood transfusion could kill him.

But scariest of all is that while we say he's "dying," while his heart and lungs and brain are pulling with everything they've got, while his crimson blood makes deepening puddles on the amber carpet, he's still 100 percent alive. He can be close to dead, near dead, but never partly dead. All that's alive in him will do anything to stay alive. And it won't give up smoothly.

Behind that cluster of technicians, under a blanket I lifted lay another body, even smaller. A baby-faced girl with a bloody bullet hole in her forehead, the very spot where she should have, just then, been getting a goodnight kiss. Whatever heroic act the EMTs pulled off with the boy, they'd still have lost one. Virginia Key sobbed.

The EMTs loaded the boy onto a stretcher, oxygen and IVs and EKGs and everything else short of a battery plugged into him. I propped the door open and stepped outside in the moonlit cold to let them pass. Another siren approached the house, a light flashing from the dashboard of the blue Chrysler of Lieutenant Miles Niederwald, my commanding officer. I moved away from the crowd and waved. Miles's car weaved up the street, bounced up the curb and onto the lawn, making me jump aside as he ripped to a halt, tearing up grass where I'd been standing.

"What the fuck?!" I shouted. "What are you doing here? Go home."

He swung his door open and struggled to his feet. The gradual shift over the last few years, from excessive drinking to an all-liquid diet, had lost Miles maybe thirty of his extra hundred pounds, making his remaining fat hang on him like a half-empty mail sack. Burst blood vessels reddened his nose and cheeks and the rims of his eyelids, the lowers hanging open as if to catch rainwater. Sparse white hair completed the picture of a decaying, sixty-five-year-old drunk. He was forty-eight. But he'd looked out for me, covered for me at the risk of looking bad himself, in my screw-up months after my partner Joey's death. There wasn't much I wouldn't do for Miles now. "We're shifting the order," he said. "Torbett's in charge. You get the next one."

"What?"

"Two-man job," he said. "You're the second man. But Torbett's in charge."

Miles looked around the front-yard crowd and eyeballed the black patrol officer, who saw Miles and nodded toward the house. A station wagon from the medical examiner's office arrived to pick up the little girl's body.

In the lit-up darkness, Torbett, the third detective on a one-detective scene, rode up the street in a somber gray Ford, driving a Sunday-straight line that put Miles's serpentine trail to shame. He pulled up to a free stretch of curb and got out, already suspicious. A blue zipper jacket and slacks took the place of the conservative suit he wore to work, twelve months a year, without fail. But this was an emergency. "What's going on?"

I looked at Miles. "I get it."

James Torbett, the department's only black detective, was transferred to Homicide three years earlier after Joey Velez died. But where Joey had been volatile and streetwise, the center of any drinking party, with a jovial smile and a boisterous laugh, Torbett was a sober, restrained, churchgoing husband and father in his early forties, the muscles of his face perpetually clenched in an attempt, I guessed, to balance opposing forces from within and without. Torbett had to be about fifty times better than any cracker to get where he got, the Jackie Robinson of the Austin Police Department. He was humorless, efficient and quietly furious. And he was clean, cleaner than anybody, cleaner than me. But he wasn't stupid. He knew the department used him where they needed him. Any other black victim or their family would get the cop on call. But Virginia Key was famous, Miles said. I'd never heard of her, most white people hadn't. But the black community in Austin loved her, or maybe hated her. Either way they'd be watching. Key got Torbett.

Inside, a dozen EMTs had trampled the house, obscuring 90 percent of any trace evidence on the scene with their own microbes: hair follicles and earwax and a thousand footprints. The destruction of evidence was supported by the overkill of five patrols. Dial 911 and you get ignored or you get an army. Outside, in the commotion, I scoped the yard, circled the house and found the back door had been jimmied, though an intruder could have punched through the glass or slipped the lock with a table knife more easily. The crowbar lay among the shrubs. I had a patrol bag it. By the time the crowd cleared and I got back inside, two EMTs had moved Mrs. Key into the kitchen and were talking to her, her sobs still echoing through the house, breaking down now like the cries of a child, weak helpless tones. Torbett had assigned two of the patrols (Officer Laurel and Officer Hardy) to check outside for footprints. He had the other three (Officers Moe, Larry and Shemp) get statements from the neighbors.

I felt around the living room floor and discovered a bullet casing, only one, that someone had kicked under the sofa. I showed it to Torbett and pocketed it for Ballistics.

Ron Wachowski, chief crime-scene technician from the Department of Public Safety and an avowed ex-liberal ("After what I've seen"), had weaved in and out of the frenzy until the wounded boy and dead girl were slid onto the stretchers and carted off in two different directions. He moved with agility for a man of sixty-five or so years, gray hair flopping over his eyes like an aged Huck Finn. He pulled Torbett and me away from the kitchen. "Wanna bring over some cadets?" he twanged. "I got a few inches of carpet nobody's stepped on yet."

"Anything?" Torbett asked.

"He came in the back way. How much he traveled around the house is a mystery, thanks to the Union army treading through. You can ask Mrs. Key if anything's missing. When they got in and shut the door he walked there, by the sofa." He pointed to a spot facing the front door from about eight feet in. "Mrs. Key was here, a few steps in from the door. The boy and girl had walked in ahead of Mom and were here and here." He pointed to two bloody splotches on the carpet by a marble coffee table. "He fired one round. The bullet went through the boy and hit the girl in the skull and stayed. The girl dropped where she stood, right in front of her mother. Look at this."

The carpet was matted with blood and footprints so it was hard to mark any one detail from the rest. Ron pointed out one original splotch of blood, not a smear or a footprint, but blood spilled on that spot. And the blood had spilled on top of a shoe, leaving an outline and a bit of tread: one left sneaker.

"Figure the boy struggled, and got shot in the process, bleeding on the shooter's foot. The boy fell to the side and cracked his head on the coffee table. The shooter bailed out the front door, the quickest way." Amid all the bloody footprints were only one set of sneaker prints. "I'll take a print, but I say those are Converse All Stars, size 7. Short strides. Little guy, or a woman, maybe five-six tops, 120 pounds."

Mrs. Key's sobs wafted in from the kitchen.

Torbett asked, "Anything else?"

"I've got some fingerprints. You'll have to check them against the patrols and EMTs and the family. Don't count on anything. And this." He held up a clear glass vial with what looked like a combination of bodily fluids in it. "He spit in the kitchen sink. If that was him."

It seemed like an unlikely spin, that a killer would leave his fluids behind in such a short visit. But we'd caught a rapist once, easier than that. After the act, he stopped in the bathroom to take a leak, lifted the toilet seat, and left his fingerprint on the underside. His thoughts were elsewhere.

"You can type him from mucus?" I asked.

"You can if there's blood in it." I looked closer.

Ron said, "The Southwest never gets a deep enough freeze to kill germs that would die in colder climates. We're a perfect petri dish for developing epidemics." He pointed out a drop of red in the yellowed phlegm. "Austin, Texas, meet tuberculosis."

We considered the potential of an infectious killer on the loose.

"On the plus side," Wachowski added, "it's only been an hour. How far could he have gone?"

11:45 P.M.—Koenig Lane

It was Mo's idea. Anything that crazy would have to be, Rainbow John thought, as he steered his Lincoln east on Koenig toward the quiet edge of town.

Normally, he didn't do his own driving, but he needed a lack of witnesses. By Mo's thinking, that would make John the only witness. It would also make, as Mo would say, "the continuation of John's stint on the planet a question for debate, rather than a foregone conclusion." But John had no choice in the matter.

Of all Mo's distributors, John seemed to be the one he called whenever he had something crappy he needed done. This time Mo got the idea to take the two craziest junkies they knew, a wiry speed freak named Vic and a strung-out heroin addict named Gaz, a limey with bad teeth, and hold them hours after they started craving, till they groaned with pain: chills, aching bones, nausea, like two kids with a bad case of the flu, side by side on a velvet sofa. Then put them in a room together in John's house, thanks a lot. Whoever comes out first gets a fix. The other walks away empty handed. Mo and Rainbow John watched through holes they'd drilled in the door. All odds on Vic, the speed freak.

The two junkies sized each other up a moment and Gaz shot for the door. Vic was on top of him, wrapped him in a half nelson and slammed him to the floor. Mo laughed gleefully. Gaz rolled backward on top of Vic, lifted himself up a few inches and slammed his hip down into Vic's groin. He rolled off but Vic held onto Gaz's arm and got up with him, slamming them both against a wall. Vic got his hands around Gaz's throat. Gaz kicked him in the gonads, then leaned forward and bit Vic's hand. Vic pulled it away and lost a bit of flesh. Mo howled. As Vic recoiled, Gaz knocked him down, then kicked him and kept on kicking him until Vic coughed blood and Mo got bored, and Rainbow John finally opened the door and dragged Gaz out.

Mo's professional distribution was mostly heroin now but he kept cocaine and a few other treats in his private stock, for himself and a few select friends. He jacked Gaz up on cocaine, highlighting the Brit's natural violence with a shot in the arm that transformed him, from sluggish to desperate to flying, a psychopathic offshoot of Mo himself. Since Gaz was Rainbow John's junkie, it was John's job to drop him off near the bitch's house, circle the block, wait, then pick him up. John's job to dispense with him. And if he didn't, Mo would hold John personally responsible, a proposition with several possible conclusions, all of them painful.

John heard the gunshot from where his Lincoln idled at the corner, saw Gaz run out the front door against orders. He pulled up close enough that Gaz dove in the back window; then the Lincoln rolled away, headlights dark, toward the bus station. There Rainbow John gave Gaz his own pants and shoes, oversized by twice, to replace Gaz's bloody ones, along with a bail of cash—fifty fifties—and a packet of Lance, meth laced with strychnine to give it a little edge. But John had laced it with more than a little strychnine. The tiny white packet had enough for two fat lines, John thought, as he drove in his overcoat, socks and boxers. If Gaz snorted one, he'd be dead, heart-attack style. Like any junkie, the minute Gaz started coming down from the coke they'd shot into him, he would snort the whole bundle.

He'd better.

12:30 A.M.—1610 Confederate Avenue

From where I stood in her living room, by the front door, I noticed that Virginia Key, sitting inside the kitchen window, didn't lift her head as the EMTs outside wheeled her son's stretcher up into the ambulance and climbed in after it, or as the ME's people slid her daughter's small body into their station wagon. They'd wiped the sweat off Mrs. Key's face. From her profile I could see she was a slender, petite, attractive woman, in spite of the shock, with straightened hair and refined features like a magazine model. Torbett absently buttoned his jacket as he approached her.

I've heard theories of yin and yang, of images and fantasies. When I first met Rachel years ago, my partner's wife, bells rang. She was the answer to all questions, the fulfillment of all dreams. Or, shrinks might argue, she was the exact shape left by the void of my parents' love, my mother who took off when I was ten, my missing pieces. The harmony created when two people's neuroses neatly complement each other's. And the skies open and the angels sing and the messiah has arrived. Or maybe the devil, the symptoms are the same.

And that's what I saw, or thought I saw, the moment James Torbett's and Virginia Key's eyes met each other's and locked.

12:45 A.M.—Mount Bonnell Overlook

Glen Bass blew tenderly into Andrea's ear, saw no effect, and tried kissing her neck instead.

That he'd managed to get her pants off again meant nothing. They'd been there a dozen times. Like the asymptote, the curved line that gets closer and closer to the axis without ever touching, their sex life progressed without ever paying off. Each day brought greater torture and greater shame in the eyes of his frat brothers, as Glen reached a point four months from a college degree without ever getting laid.

"No, no . . ."

"It's okay," he said, which seemed to be the right response.

Andrea, the blondest and the palest girl he'd ever met, nearly albino, was also the dumbest. That, and his father's money, and his BMW, didn't add up to much. But he guessed she was smart enough to be parlaying all this into marriage. He hit on a brainstorm, froze, then climbed off her and pulled his pants up. "Forget it," he said.

"I'm sorry," she said. "I don't feel well."

"You always don't feel well. What is it, your period?"

"No, I'm sick."

"I can't do this. I'm a man. I have needs."

Finally she lay back. "Okay."

Glen blinked. "You mean it?"

"I mean it. Go ahead."

Suddenly and for the first time in memory, Glen found himself flaccid. He called up the memories of a dozen nights just like this, a thousand centerfolds, entire sororities getting it on on the Fiji House pool table, rubbed himself against her and finally . . .

Sweet, sweet heaven. The Truth. The Big Reality. Conquest and manhood at once. But for a tiny yelp she was quiet, but Glen held off, had read about spots and angles, leaned himself the way articles had specified. Andrea began to hum.

"Yes," he said. "Yes. Baby."

She trembled, lightly at first, then shuddering and moaning. Glen let the restraint go, picked up steam, slammed away and finally burst into a cloud of bliss and helplessness. Then he settled down, his face against her neck.

It was then he noticed that Andrea had stopped moving.

WEDNESDAY

I spent half the night questioning Virginia Key's neighbors, chasing the cooling heat of the killer's trail. Went home for three hours' sleep, got up after Rachel, left the house, drove east on Thirty-eighth Street to I-35 and headed downtown with the windows open, a cool, wet breeze blowing through the car, ruminating on the nature of work.

Most jobs suck. You work toward a day you can retire, or a day you can make money from something you care about. In the meantime, you get up, curse God and suit up for another eight or nine hours doing something you hate for people you hate, for a tiny fraction of what they earn from your labor. I've seen people, regular people—nurses, bookkeepers, schoolteachers—go through horrible tragedies, chronic illnesses, loss of a marriage or a child, with courage and commitment, then blow their own brains out because they just couldn't go through another Wednesday.

But for some people, say, for cops, the boredom is broken up now and then by a lifeshaking trauma that makes you question any hope for man's redemption.

Christmas Eve, 1978, in Austin, our small but growing town. The birth of Christ denying any excuse to get the departmental Yid off the rolls for rookie duty in the no-man's land of no-man's lands, the night when families decide they need to be together. My blonde, Presbyterian bride Amy safely blanketed in the home of her square-jawed family, I suited up to protect America from itself. Driving through a two-storey downtown around eight in the evening, I answered a call and found two other patrols already at the scene. In a house on Nueces, two grown men, brothers, were fighting over a wishbone. Old argument, went back to childhood. Anger disproportional to the situation. The wife of one brother calls the cops while they're slugging it out. But by the time we get there, the other brother is hacked up with an electric carving knife. The first is sitting at the table, covered with blood, sucking on a wishbone. His wife is crying, "He did it! He did it!" Three kids going crazy. Christmas tree all lit up. It took three of us swinging nightsticks to take him down and lock him up. We had to drop the victim off ourselves back then, and strip the body down. Then we'd go out to eat. As it turned out, the brother we arrested was a cop.

His life was our life: dead bodies, abused kids, horror day after day, year after year after year. We sat eating our burgers, looking around the table and wondering which of us was next.

I was reviewing all this, thirteen years later, as I peeled off the interstate and turned right on Eighth Street to the municipal parking lots and the headquarters of the Austin Police Department, where the storm clouds were beginning to gather.

7:45 A.M.—2420 San Antonio Street

Clay was parked on the couch, sucking a beer and looking pissed off, same-same like always, when the doorbell rang and Luis Fuentes checked the peep and opened the door, letting in Dean the Hat and locking up behind him.

"Dino, man, *qué pasa?*" Luis made to shake Dean's hand, got no response and patted him on the shoulder so as not to look stupid.

Dean tilted back his cowboy hat, Panama white straw yellowing from the headband outward, and nodded at Clay's beer. "Where's mine?"

"Clay, man, get off your ass and get the Hat a brew."

Clay picked himself up and headed for the kitchen, grumbling. Luis picked some socks off the chair and tossed them in a corner.

"Got no respect," Dean the Hat said as he sat himself on the soft chair and settled in, scratching his neck and passing gas in commentary.

Luis added, "I tell him that all the time. 'You got no respect, man, that's Dean the Hat. Show some respect.' He don't hear it. What's the good word, man?"

Clay tossed a beer can to Luis, who caught it, opened it carefully and handed it to Dean.

"Streets are dry. Big busts in Houston." Dean swigged. His white hair and beard had turned cod-liver-oil yellow to match the hat itself, his chest bearing a crucifix big enough to have been torn from the wall of a church. Double-talk: how's business? Slow. It's always slow. Supplies down, prices up. You boys understand.

"We got a thousand," Clay blurted out.

"Shut up, man," Luis said.

"Where'd you get a thousand?"

Luis made nice. "We sold what you gave us."

"Weren't worth more'n five hundred, seven if you cut it too much. And if you did, you blow your repeat business." The Hat glared angrily at Luis, his index finger digging independently into a nostril.

Luis smiled cool. "No man, we stole some more TVs. Check this out." He picked up some laundry from the floor by the wall, revealing a thirteen-inch Zenith TV/VCR combo, flipped it on and handed Dean the remote.

"Gotta go home, get some sleep," Dean said.

"Hit MUTE," Luis said.

Dean hit MUTE, and glared at the silent screen. "Gimme this one."

"One fifty," Clay said.

"Clay, man, a little respect. This is Dean the Hat."

Clay shot a look back at Luis. Not free. Bad business.

"I can't handle a thousand," Dean said.

"You can't?"

"You need someone else." Then nothing.

Luis: "Keep the TV. It's yours."

Dean nodded. "Rainbow John. He'll find you."

As Clay disappeared down the hall after Dean, hauling the TV and cursing, Luis locked the door, threw off the chair cushions, and said, "You get all that, Milsap?"

Milsap's voice whined back through the transmitter. *"I got it. I got it."*

8:00 A.M.—HQ

In the windowless squad room, we held an informal briefing. Miles, Torbett and I had all been at the scene. We all stayed up late and got up early. Jake Lund, by virtue of always being holed up in the office, tapping the computer or talking on the phone or both, had developed a magical ability to know what anyone else knew, and had become a clearinghouse for information. A wiry sugar addict of thirty-five or so, his steel-wool hair shot in a few directions in spite of being clipped just close enough to disclose the forceps indentations on his skull, scars he'd had since the day he was pried into the world against his will. Absent: Senior Sergeant Pete Marks, a hard-nosed ex-marine, transferred off Homicide years ago for no good reason and back for the same. Present, newcomer Jeffrey Czerniak (pronounced CHER-nick), a big, thickset kid from Criminal Investigations, mentored onto the squad by Marks, working on an unrelated cold case but sucking up and listening hard. Semi-present, puffy, corpulent Able Greer. Six foot two, blubbery, and perpetually in a fresh sweat that beaded up on his pallid skin, Greer had been transferred to Homicide from a stint on Public Information: after three years of apologizing to the press, Greer's catchphrase was "I'm sorry." "I'm sorry I couldn't keep the press away." "I'm sorry I didn't find anything." He apologized when he walked in on his wife blowing the paperboy. When Saint Peter finally tallied the score, he would tell Greer how he'd wasted his life apologizing. I could guess how Greer would answer.

Five metal desks accommodated the six-man squad on the safe assumption that nothing short of genocide would get us all there at once. Amenities included a Mr. Coffee, a red vinyl couch from storage, and a new color TV/VCR with cable connection and the built-in insult that CNN knew more than we did. A bulletin board held current

"Wanted" flyers and directives: featured among these were mentions of the MLK Day march on Monday, the non-skeddo protests that would spot the week if we went to war, the suspension for this week of floating holidays. Finally, an announcement about new "cooping" places—out-of-the-way spots patrolmen liked to park for a quick on-duty nap—deemed off-limits by the department.

Torbett said, "Ron Wachowski at DPS puts him at five foot five or six, maybe 120 pounds, size 7 Converse sneakers with bloodstains. He's probably ditched them."

Miles, wearing a green blazer that hadn't buttoned closed since Nixon resigned, said "Don't be so sure."

I said, "Ballistics is just getting in. Maybe something from them by the end of the day. They have the shell but the slug is in victim number two, Jennifer Key."

Jake said, "The patrols got four clean prints that didn't belong to Mrs. Key or the kids. I'm trying to get the prints for every cop or EMT on the scene to eliminate."

Miles turned to Torbett. "Is she talking yet?"

Torbett said, "White male."

"That's it?" Miles asked.

"Would you like to talk to her, Lieutenant?" Torbett asked calmly. Miles got quiet, but fidgety. "She went through her things," Torbett went on. "There was nothing missing except a cameo brooch, her most expensive piece of jewelry. It was all he took."

"Think he knows his stuff?" I asked.

"Nothing else looked worth taking." Torbett had a photo and passed around copies, five-by-sevens, a color portrait of Virginia Key herself, looking better than she had last night. Greer and Czerniak each took one, though they weren't officially on the case. Czerniak said, "Wow!" garnering a dirty look from Torbett. The photo highlighted Mrs. Key's smooth cocoa-brown skin, round cheeks and high regal cheekbones. She wore a purple dress with a low neckline but not too low. Pinned to the dress was the brooch, nearly two inches from top to bottom, framed in gold: a neatly carved silhouette of a white, white lady.

Torbett said, "We'll have to check the pawnshops, low-rent jewelers and fences. Put it at about a thousand new." Torbett handed me a sheet of paper. "I made a list of pawnshops and jewelers who buy used. I split them up north-south. Czerniak, talk to CIB and Robbery and see if you can talk to some fences."

Czerniak turned to Miles. "Can I?" He was supposed to be helping Marks on cold cases.

Miles said, "You're a big guy. You can handle it. Lund, go with him." Jake's eyes ballooned out. "Just kiddin'. See what you can track about other burglaries in the neighborhood."

Jake had a longstanding practice of staying inside the windowless office through the shift, however long, and bought the privilege with his expertise in acquiring knowledge through electronic channels. Miles's tolerance of Jake's habit was out of character for any other CO; it was par for Miles. He had his own quirks.

Once a white-knuckler until his first drink at noon, Miles now had to drink in the morning to quiet his shakes enough that he could work. The first drink made him want more; if the drinking got out of hand, he'd be found out and fired. Every day was a struggle, making him more patient for Jake's idiosyncrasy, Jake's unwillingness to go outside and deal with the world face-to-face. And the deaths of some squad members had sent Jake into an existential tailspin that wasn't improving his social life any. "Just think of Stevie Ray Vaughan," he'd say. "Shoots dope for years, cleans up and dies in a chopper crash. You never know."

Miles had his own way of controlling the uncontrollable. He'd been glad-handing for two-plus years, making calls and fudging rules, rotating the extra three spots on the squad triple-time to hold onto what had become his unlikely core: a computer geek, a straight-arrow black churchgoer and me, a Mafia-born New York Jew. We weren't the crew you'd imagine a drunken old cracker like Miles attaching himself to, but he'd lost three key players in six months, and he wanted a few familiar faces around him as old age, the administration, up-and-comers from below and the bottle closed in on him.

"Torbett, stay in close touch with Mrs. Key. Reles, stay on top of DPS and Ballistics," Miles said. "Are we done here?" We looked at each other. "Good. Torbett, come with me."

8:30 A.M.—HQ

James Torbett followed Miles into the elevator. Miles was struggling to close the top button of his shirt, the strain on his neck reddening his face, then gave up with a "God damn it!" and just pulled his tie as tight as it would go.

"You wanna tell me what this is about, Lieutenant?" Torbett asked as a calloused hand grabbed the closing door from outside, opened it and allowed two uniforms to step in. They nodded at Miles and looked blank at Torbett, then carried on their conversation.

"Are they still drivin' around in that thing?" one man said. "Well if they're that dumb, we'll catch 'em." Miles motioned Torbett to wait.

A hand radio crackled, ". . . *Red Mustang convertible, license plate 217-RSK. Black male, five foot ten, approximately 280 pounds, gold teeth top and bottom. If you see someone fitting that description, report it to Sergeant Bill Rimmer . . .*"

They all got off on the first floor and Miles took Torbett by the arm, leading him left toward the auditorium. "I need you to talk to these people."

"What people?" Torbett asked, and stopped dead. "What is this?"

Miles, by way of answer, pushed open the auditorium door.

A hundred reporters sucked breath and swung their microphones and cameras away from the podium where Chief Cronin was standing in full dress uniform, down to the stars on his epaulettes. Lights flashed in Torbett's eyes, as Miles led him by the arm and placed him at the podium. Torbett blinked and squinted and tried to focus as reporters raised their hands like schoolchildren and shouted, "Sergeant Torbett, Sergeant Torbett!" Torbett looked at Miles, who, by way of explanation, nodded. Torbett pointed to someone in the first row. The others settled with a barely audible, "Aww!"

"Arthur Cole from the *Statesman*. Sergeant Torbett, how many officers are assigned to the Key case?"

Torbett shook his head, started to ask, "What are you talking about?" and got as far as "Wh—?" when Cronin stepped close to him and repeated, "How many officers are assigned to the case?"

Torbett shook off his own questions and zeroed in. "Uh, two."

"Two?!"

"That is, Senior Sergeant Reles and myself full time. Also Sergeant Lund . . . and, uh, Sergeant Czerniak . . . Lieutenant Niederwald is supervising."

"We thought you were supervising—"

Cronin said, "Yes, Ms. Durant."

An unusually blonde TV newswoman rose, lights hitting her hard. "Sergeant Torbett, how do you feel about the implications of an attempt on the life of a black community leader on Martin Luther King's birthday?"

The lights swung onto Torbett. "It's, uh, unclear at this time whether th—"

"Are you telling us the assault wasn't politically motivated?"

Cronin cut in, jumping in front of Torbett at the podium. "Carla, we don't know who fired the gun yet. You're asking us to tell you why?" Chuckles around the room. "Yes, in the second row."

"Donna Cullum, *Austin Chronicle*." She read from her pad. "Sergeant Torbett, do you think APD best serves justice or the black community by parading its only black detective before a press conference that he obviously hasn't even been briefed for, just because he's black?"

The room hushed. Torbett turned slowly to Chief Cronin and placed a hand over the mike, whispering, "Field that one, sir?"

9:15 A.M.—America Pawn

I show them the photo.

"Seen this brooch?"

"Nope."

"Call me if you do?"

"Yup."

I leave my card.

Repeat.

The pawnbroker has no allegiance to the police or to his sellers. If he gives up the stolen item then he's out the hundred or two he paid for it. If he doesn't, he's criminally liable for receiving stolen merchandise. But you have to keep asking these questions because that's how you find the hidden key. It's unlikely you'll find it in a neighborhood pawnshop, especially at nine the next morning. But you never know where the key is, who has your lifejacket or who has the loaded gun.

10:00 A.M.—Seton Northwest Hospital

Martin Bass stormed into the hospital with the manner of a man pulled from a war council to tend a child's skinned knee, and reached the waiting area where his hapless son Glen sat wrapped in his own arms and leaning forward and back, rhythmically. Martin stood over his son. "What the hell is going on?"

Glen looked up, pathetic, and said, "Dad?"

His father sat. "For God's sake, don't cry. Have you been here all night?" The boy's eyes made the answer obvious.

"They don't know what's wrong. They're going to do . . . an exploratory . . ."

"Surgery. All right, it's not the end of the world."

"What if . . . ?"

"Tell me, where were you when she got sick?"

"In my car."

"Were you . . . ?" Glen looked at his father, desperate. "Jesus Christ. Okay, stay calm." He looked up and down the hall, tapped his foot frantically. "In a court of law . . . could they prove . . . was there, evidence, that you . . . had sex?"

Glen's face crumpled. "What am I gonna do?"

Martin slapped him across the face. "Idiot! You're not even out of college!" Bass looked up and noted a nurse watching him. He smiled with his jaw and lowered his voice to a whisper. "What does her father do?"

"Huh?" Glen wiped his nose with his sleeve. "A dentist. I think. Why?"

"Are they here?"

Glen pointed his father to the room.

Inside, on the far bed, an older woman lay watching television with a small speaker clipped to her bedsheet. On the bed near the door, Andrea Wile lay asleep wearing a hospital gown, with a sheet pulled nearly to her chin, and her pale yellow hair spread on the pillow, framing sickly white features. All this offset by the half-full vomit pan at her side. Her parents sat in padded vinyl chairs flanking the bed. They looked up when Martin entered and said, "Dr. Wile?" Wile followed Martin into the hall and they shook hands.

"I'm Martin Bass, Glen's father."

Wile withdrew his hand. Martin went on.

"We feel awful about what happened to Andrea. Any ideas?"

What little hostility had flashed in Wile's eyes gave way to regret. He shook his head.

Martin said, "The kids are very close. I'd feel better if you let me pay for the room."

Wile squinted at the idea, jerked his head slightly. "I don't . . . the insurance covers it. Mostly. You don't need to—"

"Andrea should be in a private room."

Wile considered the notion and nodded.

"Good," Martin said, chancing a hand on Wile's shoulder. "We'll all feel better knowing she's getting the best care. I'll make a few calls."

Wile nodded, almost mouthed, "Thanks," and apparently thought better of it, as Martin led him back toward Andrea's room.

"I'm sure," Martin added, "it'll be better for Andrea if nobody speaks about her illness to the press."

10:30 A.M.—Medical Examiner's Office

I swung by Margaret Hay's office between "tain't seen its" from pawnbrokers and "call back laters" from DPS and Ballistics. I walked into the autopsy room where the iron smell of blood mixed with formaldehyde vapors, and I caught Hay at the gurney, in lab coat, gloves and plastic face shield, leaning over the tiny nude body of five-year-old Jennifer Key.

Hay matched my height at six feet, a slim, white-haired old farm-girl with a precancerous leathery complexion, lips pressed together as she struggled with a half dozen tools she'd jammed into the opening in Jennifer's forehead. Hanging on the handle of the gurney was the cane she now needed to walk on her damaged hip, at least when the barometer was high and a storm was coming. I stood back.

An autopsy is for when there's a question as to the cause of death. Here, Hay had been saddled with the job of yanking the evidence. Instead of opening the girl's head with a saw, she was trying to pluck out the bullet blind to save the girl's physical integrity for her funeral.

I tried to figure the bullet landing in her skull. When the two children were found, Jenny was behind Rubin. But if it went through his belly, it would have landed lower than her head. Unless she was crouching. Hiding behind her invincible big brother and crouching.

Hay stopped for a breath. "It's stuck," she said, without looking up or otherwise acknowledging my uninvited presence. In the autopsy room you don't ask permission to come in. More likely, you'd ask permission to leave.

"Any word on the boy?" I finally asked.

"They haven't brought him *here*," she said, and nothing else. She twisted the tools, moved around the table, shifted her arm at an unlikely angle, then asked, "You remember '89?"

Jenny's Shirley Temple cheeks seemed to puff out in sympathy as Hay jerked the girl's head around.

"Yeah, I remember '89." I had lots of memories of 1989, but none jumped out.

"You remember that little girl?"

"The drive-by?"

1989 was our first drive-by shooting, the incident that made the police own up to the longstanding presence of gangs here in Dreamville.

"You knew there were gangs here."

"I knew? Yeah, I knew."

Hay was holding me, as a representative of the department, responsible for the department's actions; I considered this about as fair as most things. The department knew there had been gangs. But "we" wouldn't admit it. Until some little innocent got caught in the crossfire.

At this point, Hay had taken a scalpel and was gingerly cutting out chunks of brain and bone from the girl's skull. She reached in with a tool I couldn't name, caught hold of something and locked on. Then she slowly pulled it out, tearing ounces of bloody tissue along with it that mounted up on the girl's forehead like a volcano. What Hay retrieved looked less like the mangled slug of a .38 and more like a hunk of bloody pulp. It clanked as she dropped it into a silver bowl.

"Take that to your friends in Ballistics."

I looked in the bowl.

Most bullets go straight into you, and failing any serious obstruction, might keep on going. Hollowpoints might take a big chunk out of you on the way out, a challenge to the finest morticians. But there's a particular kind of hollowpoint where the tip is pre-cut into six or eight pieces like a pie, and as it penetrates, the pieces spread out, clawlike, and grab everything inside you. It's a stop-and-drop bullet that makes a 9 millimeter look like an old friend. And it has a name:

The Black Talon.

12:15 P.M.—Anderson Lane

James Torbett drove between pawnshops, sensing the potential waste of time, the blind turns on the way to, maybe, finding the perpetrator. The make and model of the crowbar, the bloody phlegm in the sink, the bloody footprints, the ejected shell. But the least likely clue could be the first break.

Torbett had three jobs. The first was the real detective work, what he'd been trained for. Next he had to get through the day alive, dodge backstabbers in the department and on the street. Finally, he had to be sane when he got home to his family, the test most cops failed. The three jobs formed a delicate balance, and life often tossed curves. Today he was the mouthpiece of the press conference, the department's show Negro. Our Sergeant Torbett. He's been with us for years, like one of the family. Do that song I like.

And he'd been doing it, with all the dignity he could muster, for seventeen-plus years—since four years after a white cop clubbed his big brother Alvin on the spine for being black—Jim Torbett did it all for the privilege of being a black officer on the force, one black cop whose presence disrupted a racist machine, as he looked out for the town's unloved 30 percent.

And then there was Virginia Key, a breath of fresh air. Young, petite, with regal cheekbones and smooth dark skin. Slender and graceful, walking from a quiet rhythm inside. His heart shifted as he held her hand on the inkpad—they needed to eliminate her prints from all those found at the scene. Rolling each delicate finger on the card, an act of intimacy that made his tired eyes lose focus. How hurt and vulnerable she seemed, how she needed him to take care of her. She could barely speak, her tiny voice stammering. He'd help her talk if he could. Was there one intruder or more? Did you see the intruder? Male or female? White? Black? Hispanic? Was anything taken? All this as her son was taken off by the medics to an uncertain fate, as her daughter was rolled out under a sheet. The little girl only a year younger than Torbett's daughter Jule. It could have been Jule. He tasted the grief, his love for his youngest wrapped around the gut-wrenching misery of even the idea of her death. It made him reach out to the nearest hand and squeeze it. The nearest hand belonged to Mrs. Key.

She'd led him through the house, silently discovered the cameo missing, handed him the photograph, sat on the edge of the bed and trembled and cried.

Torbett asked, "Is there someone you can call?" She shook her head. He gave her his office and home numbers.

He thought of her as he wrote the night's report and drove home, half dreaming, and kept his face away from Nan when he walked into the bedroom, though the lights were off. He undressed and slid into bed, Nan unconsciously rolling toward him and meshing their bodies together, the harmony they'd had since year two. And he rolled away, Nan cuddling up to warm his back.

"Homicide 4."

Torbett let his foot off the brake and picked up the microphone as the traffic light turned green. "This is Homicide 4, go ahead."

"Call Mrs. Key on a land line. She wants to talk."

Torbett turned on his flashers, did a slow U-turn in the middle of Anderson Lane across two lanes of traffic and into a parking lot where he might find a pay phone, thinking about Mrs. Key and thinking about Nan, cuddled up to him last night in bed. And feeling, without thinking, the sweetness in his gut, of the grief he and Mrs. Key had shared.

1:30 P.M.—Ballistics

I passed through the open door into the expanded closet that is Ballistics, its walls lined with half the guns known to man, everything from an Uzi to a three-inch pistol made as a working accessory to a steel belt buckle. In urban life, the Uzi is an anomaly. Full automatics aren't as practical in real life as they are in Hollywood. In real life, they're too expensive.

The double microscope was presided over by Yan-Hao Wong, a Taiwanese munitions specialist who had defected to the United States decades ago. His given name was deemed unpronounceable by an earlier chief who dubbed him Eddie. Save for an occasional detail, he'd mastered English in a way I hadn't, but his accent never went anywhere. I showed him the bowl Hay gave me.

"Holy shit," he said. "Why didn't she clean it? You piss her off?"

"Hard to tell."

The bits of brain tissue voided the question of where we'd found it. From an ashtray, he fished the shell I'd found last night under Mrs.

Key's couch, and looked over a report. "Went through the boy and landed in the girl?"

I nodded. "The question is how? It's a Black Talon. It should have spread its claws and stopped."

"Come back later," he said.

I hoped he'd be able to give me more than why a stop-and-drop bullet went through Rubin Key and killed his sister, choosing one kid over another. But Rubin's fate hadn't been decided yet.

And we were facing other threats.

1:45 P.M.—1610 Confederate Avenue

Torbett called Mrs. Key from a land line.

"You called so fast," she said in her small, soft voice, like a shy child, a tone that made Torbett want to articulate her ideas for her, something he'd resisted with his daughter. Hard to believe this woman could speak before a jury.

Already he wasn't sure if he had offered to come over or if she'd asked him, only that, when they spoke on the phone, she asked him to wait an hour, that she wasn't dressed. He'd stopped at another pawnshop and a second-hand jeweler for word of her cameo, swung by HQ for a pile of burglar mug shots Czerniak had assembled, then finally arrived at Mrs. Key's house after an hour, checked with the patrol stationed in front, and knocked at her door in his raincoat, hat in hand if he'd had a hat.

She murmured, "Thank you for coming," or something similar as she closed the door behind him. The house, on the inside, looked slick and balanced, a model home. The front room geared for entertaining, not for children. He could imagine the children running into the front room as she was meeting with a friend or a client, being reminded that the living room was for company, showing their drawings or their clay creations and running back to the playroom.

And if Torbett was thinking about the children, seeing them when they weren't there, it was a cinch Virginia Key was doing the same.

She was wearing a brown dress with short sleeves that pinched at her little shoulders, black shoes and no stockings. The dress was slightly askew, and cut too low for the occasion, but losing your children wasn't the kind of thing you shopped for. Her face was pale, eyes puffy, red and half dim. She had cried herself out, at least for the moment. Her hands shook.

The neighborhood, called Clarksville, went up in the seventies, Torbett remembered. The blacks who lived there before, many of them servants, were displaced, bought out or kicked out, their dirt roads finally paved, their houses leveled and replaced with new styles. Many of the new houses were sand-colored ranches, one storey, no basement, sliding windows, very modern and at the same time, Texan. No blacks allowed. Which didn't explain why Mrs. Key was here, smack in the middle of it, sitting next to him on the couch, close enough that he could feel her warmth, serving him coffee on the marble coffee table that cracked her son's head.

What was missing was people. If someone died in Torbett's family, let alone a child, the house would be filled with family and friends, even neighbors, offering comfort and casseroles. For all he could see, she hadn't had a single visitor.

"You don't have to serve me coffee."

"Sugar?" She spoke just above a whisper.

They sipped.

"How's your son?" he asked.

She shook her head, which could have meant he was doing badly, or she couldn't talk about it or didn't want to.

Mrs. Key had placed a small, blue oval rug, probably a bathroom rug, in the awkward space by the coffee table, to cover the bloodstain. If she couldn't see it, it wasn't there. And the coffee itself probably served the same purpose, safety in ritual.

In the silence Torbett imagined his own children in a living room like this, his youngest, Jule, running in on skinny legs to show a drawing or a doll's outfit, making googly eyes at the guests. And how broken and empty he'd feel if Jule were taken from him.

The damp chill of Texas January filled the room. Virginia Key warmed her petite hands on the coffee cup.

"How long have you lived in this neighborhood?" he opened.

"Three years," she said softly, in a gentle trace of a southern drawl, a voice raspy from crying. She'd been there three years, he thought, since her children were two and six. She went on. "Just a few years out of law school. I had to scrounge for a down payment." She stopped.

"You chose an interesting neighborhood."

"The ghetto was full."

Her words packed a wallop for coming from such a tiny voice.

"I didn't mean that," he said. "I just wonder how your neighbors feel about it."

She took a breath and spoke, as if she'd memorized it in grade school. "I'll be judged, not by the color of my skin, but by the content of my character," she said.

Torbett watched her as the words, Dr. King's words, came out of her mouth in her little voice. It was hard to believe that anyone, a judge or jury, would take her seriously. And yet they were the right words. Torbett heard them.

"We've pulled together some mug shots of burglars," he said. He reached for the folio but she shook her head, she couldn't possibly. "I understand how difficult this is," he said. Her green eyes gazed at the carpet. "You can help us find the man who did this . . ."

"And put him away?"

Torbett opened his mouth twice before something came out. "That's what we do."

"I'm a defense attorney."

He searched her face. She could have been a model if not for her height. It was hard to tell what she was thinking, in her state. He wanted to protect her, help her. But there was only one way he knew how. "He wouldn't be able to do this again."

"You know from recidivism rates," she said in her tiny, breathless voice, "that prison doesn't keep people from repeating crimes. If anything it encourages them."

Torbett fought the urge to reprimand her. "Should we let him go?"

Virginia Key shook her head, looked out the window. "I'm just arguing. Old habit." She shrugged by way of apology, putting the cup down.

"You must be a very good defense attorney."

A small smile.

"Would you defend a man who . . ."

"Who I knew was guilty?" she asked, again in half a whisper. It wasn't what he meant. Everyone knew attorneys defended guilty clients every day. Then she asked, "Why do you need evidence?"

"Excuse me?"

"If you know someone is guilty?" She was leaning forward at the waist, her shoulders curled inward and her arms wrapped around her stomach. If her brain felt like arguing, her body wouldn't follow. "We need evidence to protect the defendant, and any potential defendant. It's about protecting the citizens of a free society. Everyone deserves a fair trial, even the guilty. Especially the guilty."

Torbett realized that his mouth was open, his eyes wide. He grabbed a napkin and wiped imaginary coffee traces. Virginia Key was too young for him by a decade. And cops don't marry defense attorneys.

And he was already married, he reminded himself. Happily married for seventeen years. And he had a beautiful wife and two wonderful kids. And he was happy.

He closed the folio and stood. "Thank you for the coffee. Is there a reason you asked me here today?"

"He wasn't very tall," she said. "Maybe five-five. And he smelled bad."

"Is that all?"

"He was dirty. Homeless. And he had bad teeth."

She had followed him to the front door. He opened the door awkwardly and stepped into the doorway. She stood close. Torbett said, "If you think of anything else, please call."

"I will," she said.

She lowered her eyelids and raised them again to look up at him. Her eyes were wet with tears.

2:00 P.M.—Brackenridge Hospital, Pediatric ICU

From the post I'd taken at the nurses' station I could see the duty nurse buttonholing a doctor as he came down the long hallway and explaining, I guessed, that a police detective of dubious ethnicity wanted to talk to him and wasn't leaving until he did.

The doctor, young and all business, in lab coat and necktie, sauntered over, his face painted with a particular color of irritation I'd seen before: he could be a perfectly good doctor if it weren't for all the damn patients.

"This is about the Key boy?" he asked, and glanced at the clock.

"I wonder if you can tell me his chances."

The doctor looked around for a model, a physiology diagram, a hanging skeleton, anything. Then finally he took a ballpoint and pointed to himself. "The bullet entered his abdomen here. It grazed his pelvis but didn't rupture it. He lost blood until the medics arrived and stopped the bleeding. The good news is that it didn't hit his liver or spleen. We were able to remove the necrotic tissue from his intestines and sew the healthy part back together. He'll probably lose weight, if he lives." He showed me where the exit wound was on his back, lower than the entry, he said, but not wide. The bullet hadn't spread its claws. "Then there's his skull. When he went down he hit a table, hard, causing swelling and intracranial pressure. He could come out of it just fine."

"Or?"

"Crucial questions now are whether he was deprived of oxygen—he could be facing brain damage—or whether he slips into a coma."

Crucial questions, I thought, are whether the boy will die or live, whether he'll be physically or mentally disabled, after surviving a shot with the most lethal piece of metal ever sold by mail order.

And what kind of person would use a bullet like that? Who needed someone that dead?

2:30 P.M.—Mopac Expressway, Northbound

"The great thing about living along Mopac is how easy it is to get around. Half the traffic of I-35," Rachel practiced her routine as she drove ahead of the couple toward the location. "It's a very peaceful life."

She checked the rearview mirror: the couple was still following.

"The master bedroom has its own bathroom." Subtext: Let the kids slug it out for the other toilet. Watch the phrasing.

She reached for a cigarette and realized they would see her smoke. No good. She reached for the cigarette again, discovered there was only one left in the pack. She'd opened it at ten A.M. Each fresh roll of tobacco bringing the promise of bliss, then disappointing her and leaving a bitter taste and a desire for a fresh smoke. She had taken to running into the bathroom and turning on the water first thing in the morning, to keep Dan from hearing her hack up yesterday's soot.

It started with the phone, she thought. The phone rang and Dan left and she had a Marlboro Light in her mouth before she realized it, a complex maneuver to manage unconsciously, but after all, she'd been practicing for years.

Wicked déjà vu, that was all. She was calm and comfortable, they were spending the long weekend together. And the phone rang and Dan jumped up and left. Echoing like Pavlov's bell the night three years ago when the phone rang, her husband Joey left the house and died.

She was accustomed to the sequence. A cop on call, and they were always on call. She'd dated other kinds of men, lawyers and bartenders and even dealers in the old days. They might work long hours, come home drunk or stoned, even cheat on her. But only when she was with a cop had she experienced the sequence: midafternoon or mid-lovemaking or deep in a sleep cycle, ring, and he's gone. The bell can ring at any moment and everything stops. Enough to make you jumpy.

And each ring brought up a bad memory, shook something loose, the major fears and horrors of her life. She thought of Dan in trouble, Dan hurt. The image of Joey dead in his car. And the horrible night, almost ten years ago in Houston, the night she killed that man, killed that intruder in her kitchen, in self-defense. And she'd called her cop friend Jack, and he'd brought his friend Joey Velez from Austin, and they'd told her what to tell the police on call, to keep it from sounding suspicious. And Joey held her in his big arms and made her feel safe.

But she still wasn't sure what Joey knew about what really happened that night, what he kept secret from the police as he fell in love with her. And then later, as he fell out of love, what he'd told Dan. Or anyone else.

3:00 P.M.—HQ

By midafternoon, we'd identified the make and model of the crowbar that opened Key's back door (Shark Corporation, model 21-2145, $17^3/4$ inch), eliminated all four of the sets of adult prints around the house as belonging to either Key or the uniforms and determined that no pawnbroker or jeweler in town had seen her cameo. Jake had made enough calls to determine the crowbar could have been bought pretty much anywhere. Czerniak had been pulling files on the guys who fence stolen goods, and was checking some out, when Marks bitched to Miles that he, Marks, was responsible for training Czerniak and he couldn't do that if Czerniak kept getting pulled to do other people's homework. Miles backed down.

In the squad room, Jake and Miles were fixed on the red vinyl couch in front of the color TV, watching night-vision shots of missiles flying over Baghdad, under a voice-over of the president talking about peace and how Saddam Hussein was the devil. Miles, the witness of several undeclared wars, sighed deeply and said, "Here we go." As the wall clock ticked three, he opened a file cabinet drawer, lifted out a fifth of bargain-brand whiskey and a glass and poured three fingers. Happy hour.

Jake glared at an explosion on the screen. "Cool."

Miles sipped his drink, stared it down, sipped again, then turned to me. "How's it going?"

I caught him up.

"Lean on Ballistics," he said. "That slug is your best lead." Miles was still sharp when he wanted to be, but those moments came fewer and farther between.

"What's up on this end?" I asked. He emptied the glass, filed the bottle away and led me out of the squad room to his own office across the hall. The normal frenzy of overdue paperwork was eclipsed by an onslaught of boxes. I moved some papers off the guest chair, disclosing a plaque from the Optimists Club. I picked it up. "You're in the Optimists Club?"

"I bring 'em down to earth," he said. He squeezed in behind his desk and drew out his private bottle, a slightly better brand of cheap whiskey, and I parked opposite him. The corkboard was tacked with a hundred memos and directives, blending into a blur of dos and don'ts no one could keep in order, least of all Miles. The only decoration was a five-by-seven color portrait of his daughters who, to their bad fortune, looked like him. Now thirteen and sixteen, they were his only joy and his only concern. "She's only five six," he said. He'd noticed me looking at the picture.

"Which?"

"The older. Not good enough."

I tried to make sense of his comment. "I give up."

"Lady Longhorns. They're all huge."

Miles had been hoping a basketball scholarship would somehow settle the future of at least one of his daughters, so he could drink himself to death in peace. No such luck.

"She threw me out," he said.

"Your wife?"

"Who else?" He put a glass in front of each of us, filled both halfway and downed his. I put mine in front of him and he downed that one too and put the glass back in the drawer. If anyone came in, at least they wouldn't see him drinking out of two glasses.

"You cheat on her?"

"A hundred years ago. She knew about it. I spent the last ninety-nine years making up for it. That one-night stand was the best night of her life."

"So what happened?"

He twisted his mouth and tapped his glass. She left him for drinking.

"It's worse," he said. "I owe the IRS twenty-six thousand."

"Holy shit. How'd you do that?"

"How the fuck do I know? We're trying to push the divorce through before the IRS puts a lien on my assets. She can keep the girls and the house. Maybe they'll cut me a deal, I can pay out of my salary, or my pension. Worse comes to worse, I'll cash in everything I have in retirement and pay them off."

"But then you won't have a pension."

He poured himself another drink and sipped it. "What difference does it make?"

I'd known Miles Niederwald for the better part of a decade. He'd always looked twenty years older than his real age, always battled the bottle and lost. But he'd never before said out loud that his life didn't matter, that his children and their home were worth enough that he was putting himself on the curb for pick up.

I thought about my own home, about Rachel, and about what I might have to do, or would be able to do, to keep us together.

"You could always quit," I suggested, nodding at the bottle.

He slugged one back, seemed to chew it down, and shook his head. "Too late, too late."

3:15 P.M.—Hickory Street Bar and Grill

Torbett had knocked on most of the doors on Mrs. Key's block, got shouted responses from behind peepholes like, "We gave!" Four heard the gunshot and claimed they'd called 911, though only one 911 call ever came in. When asked about Mrs. Key, all stiffened up, as if they might be accused of racism, and by extension, murder. "She's nice," was about the most they gave. One black cleaning woman answered the door and refused to talk to him at all, beyond, "You're gonna get me fired."

He headed back toward downtown, parked by Hickory Street and went in. "Just the salad bar." They nodded and left him completely alone. He piled his plate high with lettuce and vegetables—he'd be the first male in his family to live into old age, if he didn't get shot—and grabbed the day's papers piled by the cash register.

The *Statesman* yielded a mention of Key at the city council meeting last night. She had, it seemed, laid out the exact amount of money each council member had received from various developers. Yesterday's shooting hadn't made the paper's deadline.

Virginia Key the whistle-blower? Brave enough to stand up, with her little body and her little voice and her big heart. The nobodies on the city council were too busy selling out to seek revenge. And hiring a killer was out of their league. But the power brokers who *bought* the city council? Maybe.

The *Chronicle*, being a weekly, wouldn't have anything on the shooting for a week at least, but Torbett flipped through. Antiwar rallies were announced, some in conjunction with MLK Day. The biggest antiwar march was set for Saturday, separating it from the MLK march on Monday. A black state representative was quoted in "Capitol Watch" as saying, "We hope the seriousness of the war at hand, the potential carnage on both sides, will bring to Monday's march the seriousness it deserves," he said, "rather than letting it remain the picnic it's been in recent years." The article mentioned that the rep, Terrence Ludwig (D-Austin), had served two terms on the city council before running for the state legislature. And that he had been interviewed in his office at the capitol.

Torbett stuffed down as much salad as he could hold and headed there.

3:30 P.M.—Ballistics

On Miles's advice, I leaned on "Eddie" Wong.

In an automatic handgun, the firing pin hits the bullet, igniting the powder, which turns to gas, sending the bullet forward and the casing back. The ejector throws the fired casing out. So the casing carries the unique impressions of both the firing pin and the ejector. And it sits on the rug waiting for the cops, except on the rare occasions when someone looks for it between shooting and running. So with or without the bullet, the cops can match the shell to the gun. We had the bullet and the shell.

Eddie Wong had determined that the bullet was a Black Talon 9 millimeter, with a nine left twist: grooves are carved into a barrel in a spiral to send the bullet straighter and farther, like putting a spin on a football. The barrel leaves marks on the bullet. Nine left means nine grooves, counterclockwise. Black Talon 9 mm. Weapon options: One. Hi-Point 9 millimeter, Model C.

I said, "This bullet was made to expand its talons on impact, rip into the biggest, craziest psychotic and stop him in his tracks. So why did it go through a little boy and kill his sister?"

Wong held the collapsed slug in a vise, lifted something out of its tip with tweezers and said, "There's your culprit," the last word causing him serious difficulty. He doused the spec in a jar of yellowish liquid and held it up again. "Cloth. His jacket maybe, or his shirt. The bullet caught a piece of cloth in the point. So for a moment, it no good as a hollowpoint. Went right through him."

The flesh of Rubin's guts wasn't enough to make the bullet compress and spread its claws. But the bone of Jennifer's skull was. More religious people would say God had chosen Jennifer, or maybe Rubin, depending on how you looked at it. I figured God was drunk.

But there was something I didn't figure.

3:45 P.M.—Texas Capitol Building

Torbett spent what seemed like twenty minutes walking up and down the capitol's long, echoing halls. He almost passed the small office, tucked away by the fire exit, but glanced in and saw a mature black man laboring at a small steel desk, behind piles of papers and binders. Torbett stepped into the doorway. Distinguished and thickset with dusty gray hair, Ludwig looked like what Torbett's father might have become, had he lived that long. Without looking up, Ludwig nearly opened his mouth and blew out the word, "Ye-e-es?" like a low tone on a sax. The tone reminded Torbett of his own disinterested persona, what he used when asking questions. He'd based the tone on his father's.

Torbett instinctively straightened up. "Sir, I'm James Torbett with APD. I'm investigating the Key shooting."

Ludwig looked at Torbett, took some air, looked over his writing and gestured Torbett to the guest chair. As Torbett sat, Ludwig leaned back. The chair accommodated him with a creak.

"Will you be joining us for the march on Saturday?" Ludwig said.

"You mean Monday."

"Don't correct me, son. We'll be gathering at churches in East Austin and marching to the capitol, the north lawn. African Americans are underrepresented everywhere but prison and the military. We'll rally against the criminal use of American soldiers to protect oil interests."

"The department frowns on our taking part in political activities," Sergeant Torbett said.

"I'll wager the department frowns a good deal."

"Do you know Virginia Key?"

Ludwig raised an eyebrow. "An interesting beginning."

"Can you think who might be glad to see her dead?"

Ludwig mulled it over. "You know anything about her?"

"I know she's a single mother and a defense attorney. I know she lives in a white neighborhood and she spoke before the city council last night before the shooting, laying out the contributions the council members received from developers."

"So by your count," Ludwig stopped to inhale, "suspects include the mayor, mayor pro tem, five members of the city council, anyone from the half dozen developers who bought them out, and anyone from the neighborhood."

"So far, yes."

"Add to that any political rivals."

"Rivals?" Torbett asked.

"No one speaks in front of the city council every month without trying to make a name for herself. She's running for city council no matter what she says, and she won't stop there."

Torbett thought of Virginia with something that felt like pride. "She hopes to be judged not by the color of her skin but by the content—"

Ludwig suddenly turned angry and trembled. "Don't throw that in my face!"

Torbett stopped. "Sir, I—"

Ludwig held up a hand to silence Torbett. His anger seemed out of scale, but Torbett let him speak.

"People who throw that quote around do it out of context," Ludwig said. "In the sentences before Dr. King said that, he said the American Negro had been presented with a bad check, a promise that all men would be guaranteed the inalienable rights of life, liberty and the pursuit of happiness. He said America was not bankrupt. It would pay on that bad check, pay its debt to the service of America by black people. *Then* judge us by the content of our character."

Torbett felt the echo of Ludwig's voice in the tiny office. He said, "I'm sure Mrs. Key thinks in the best interests of black people."

"You see a black cause. I see Texas politics."

"I don't understand."

"Come with me."

Ludwig lifted himself up from the chair, and in heavy, authoritative steps, headed out the door and down the hall. Torbett followed him around a corner and down another hall into the thick of foot traffic. Finally Ludwig stopped in the atrium, on the circular marble floor bearing the six flags that had flown over Texas—Spain, France, Mexico, Republic of Texas, the Confederacy, and the United States— looking up four storeys of ornate balconies into the high capitol dome, a single five-pointed star at its apex. "You know how tall this building is, Mr. Torbett?"

Like everyone who had gone to public school in Texas, even in the Jim Crow years, Torbett had studied Texas history. He felt embarrassed to tell Ludwig he didn't know.

"The capitol building is 302 feet tall. The guides here will tell you that's 14 feet taller than the capitol in Washington. The Goddess of Liberty on top makes it 16 feet taller, at 318 feet. You know there was a law passed in 1930 that no one could build anything taller than the capitol?"

"I heard that." The law was revoked when skyscrapers proved profitable.

"The university tower went up in the thirties. The university guides will tell you the capitol is 311 feet, not 318. The tower is 311 feet. But the university got past the law by building it on a six foot hill, putting the tower at 317. So according to UT, they built a tower that rose higher than the capitol. According to the capitol guides, the capitol is a foot taller. You see?"

"I think so."

"Now you understand Texas politics."

4:30 P.M.—Ballistics

I waited while Eddie Wong finished two other jobs ("You think I'm just here for you? Everyone think that."), then put the shell and then the bullet under the microscope, measured their scratches, and finally hauled out the FBI General Rifling Characteristics guide, updated for 1990, thousands of pages of:

Caliber	Lands/Grooves	Twist	Lands Min.	Lands Max.	Groove Min.	Groove Max.
9 mm	6	left	.055	.065	.115	.125
9 mm	6	left	.050	.065	.115	.125

Scintillating reading.

"Two chances," he said, pointing to two rows of numbers. "Here and here. I'll try to get the slides. I'll call you."

"When?"

He let loose with a string on invectives that could have been Chinese, mixed with heavily accented English. I caught a few choice phrases like "motherfucker" and "fuckin' cops," and finally "not you fuckin' houseboy!" When he was done he breathed heavily, his face flushed, like he was waiting for me either to slug him or correct his grammar.

"Right," I said. "Call me."

I didn't wait long.

6:00 P.M.—1205 Walnut Avenue

Torbett parked the car, said a quick prayer ("Help me to be the father my children deserve . . ."), rubbed the tension out of his face with both hands and walked up the path.

Jule heard him come in. "Daddy, Daddy, you were on TV!" she sang as she climbed up into his arms.

"I was . . ."

Nan appeared from the kitchen, all smiles. "I taped it. Do you want to see?"

Torbett stood still as Jule slid down and pushed the tape back into the VCR.

The video showed him standing on the stage by the chief, looking confused in the white light, squinting like a mole. *"Sergeant Torbett, how many officers are assigned to the Key case?"*

"Wh . . ." Cronin repeated the question to him, allowing Torbett to respond, *"Uh, two."* The camera had picked up the quizzical look on his face. The question came unexpected. The whole conference came that way. They could have prepped him.

"Two?!"

"That is, Senior Sergeant Reles and myself full time. Also Sergeant Lund . . . and, uh, Sergeant Czerniak . . . Lieutenant Niederwald is supervising."

"We thought you were supervising—"

They cut back to a blonde woman in the newsroom. *"Confusion at APD and cries of tokenism from the press while the enemies of Virginia Key—"*

"Where's Guy?" Torbett asked, stopping and rewinding the tape.

Nan said, "He promised to be home by dinner."

"He hasn't seen this?"

"No." Torbett hit the RECORD button. "Jim, what are you doing?"

Jule said, "You're recording over it, Daddy."

When it was done he said, "I have to make a call," withdrew into the bedroom, closed the door and fished out the number. The machine picked up on the sixth ring. *"Please leave a message."*

"This is Sergeant Torbett—"

Mrs. Key picked up the receiver. She still sounded weak, like she had the flu, only her words gave a different notion. *"Thank God it's you."*

"Oh. Um . . ."

"Are you okay?"

"I should be asking you that."

"The phone keeps ringing."

"I can get someone there to screen your calls." Torbett wondered what made him say that, and how he could possibly make it happen.

"Did you see it?" she asked.

"The news? Are you upset?"

"Are you?"

"They said something about your enemies."

There was a knock at the bedroom door and Nan peeked in. Torbett lifted his head to ask what she wanted. She read the expression and withdrew, pulling the door shut.

Torbett asked, "Have you remembered anything?"

"No."

"Could you try?"

She sighed. *"We came into the house, I closed the door. And—"* Her voice caught.

"It's important," he said.

"He raised the gun. I was scared."

"You should be scared when someone points a gun at you."

She made a little gasp. *"He said something! I just remembered."*

"What did he say?"

"He said, 'Mrs. Key.'"

Torbett calculated. "I'll call you back." He hung up and started dialing numbers. The shooter knew her, knew her name. An enemy.

An enemy on the loose.

Torbett's complicated day suddenly seemed very simple. There was only one thought holding sway in his mind.

Get the killer. Before he gets her.

6:15 P.M.—HQ

I gave a quick look into Dispatch on my way out of the building. The lead operator saw me and waved hard, pointing to the phone. I walked over and she handed me a receiver, then hit a button.

"Reles," I said.

"It's Torbett. The shooter knew Mrs. Key."

"How do you know?"

"He called her by name. She says she never met him. I'm doubling the watch on her."

"The weapon is a Hi-Point 9 millimeter C."

"Get on it. I'm chasing her records for an old grudge, maybe someone she didn't get acquitted."

"I'll meet you."

"No, stay on the weapon."

"I'll bring Czerniak, we'll split it three ways."

"I got it."

"You want me to talk to Key. Maybe I can get something—"

"No!" Torbett blurted.

"Why the fuck not?" I asked.

"You expect her to sort this out surrounded by a bunch of crackers with guns?"

I stopped at a restaurant for a roasted chicken with vegetables to go, and headed home, circling around the public golf course, past Rachel and Joey's old place, where I'd first been a guest at their dinner table, where I'd arrived early one morning to tell Rachel her husband was dead. Where Rachel and I first made love.

I was home, finishing setting the table and laying out the meal when Rachel came home, glanced into the kitchen and went to change. Five minutes later she joined me at the table and sat down without a word. We knocked out a leg and thigh each that way and started on the wings when I said, "About last night . . ."

She waved me off. "I jolted, that's all."

"You sure?"

"Yes." Cut, chew.

"So we're cool, then."

"Of course." Chew. Sip.

"I should have told you I was on call. I forgot."

"How was your day?"

"Fine, how was yours?"

"Fine." Chew, swallow, sip.

Finally, I said, "Look, I'm sorry. It's the nature of the work. If it's driving you crazy—"

"It's not driving me crazy. Don't say that!"

"Well, what?"

She shook her head, sipped. "Déjà vu, that's all."

It was three years earlier that her husband Joey answered a call late at night, drunk, and wound up at the bottom of a cliff. Because I was his partner, I gave her the bad news. It hadn't brought us closer together.

Joey's parting gift to Rachel had been a black eye, so his passing was more of a shock to her than a loss. She was in my life today on the condition that I stop trying to make sense out of Joey's death, stop "chasing ghosts" as she put it. But he was her husband. That he flew his Chevy Caprice off a mountain pass, on purpose or not, would spook someone even as controlled and together as Rachel.

"I'm sorry," I said.

"Can't we just forget it? Seriously."

"Okay," I said. I tried out a few conversation changers in my head, nearly settled on "so how was your day," when the phone rang. I looked at her to see how much trouble I was in. She eyed the chicken bones. It rang again.

"Just get it," she said.

7:30 P.M.—Givens Park, East Twelfth Street

"This TV is bad business," Clay said, squinting over the creek, though Luis Fuentes had done all the lifting. Clay was always blowing his top, always saying the wrong thing. They had somehow convinced Dean they were ready for a bigger distributor than him, ready for someone who could give them a thousand dollars' worth of heroin. And now they were meeting the bigger distributor. Luis wasn't afraid Clay would blow their cover. People would believe they were small-time dealers. But he was sure that sooner or later, Clay would get them killed.

"Dean the Hat got a TV," Luis argued. "Rainbow John's gonna want a TV." The park was dark save for moonlight and an occasional kid looking for trouble. Vice had slammed the park's hooker traffic in waves: now it was low tide.

Clay circled a bench. "What if Vice nails him with a stolen TV?"

"Shh." Luis Fuentes made out someone approaching, but it was so dark he couldn't tell if it was one man or two. Finally the large figure split, and a single figure emerged, silhouetted in the moonlight. The second man stayed at a distance.

Luis asked, "John?"

Rainbow John, white male, Luis gauged at six foot three, 250 pounds, muscle gone to fat, ruddy, Irish complexion, maybe alcoholic. Ex-marine? Long hair. Wearing feather Stetson, tannish wool overcoat, silk suit, maybe blue or purple—hard to tell by the lighting. It didn't take too much to guess that he was armed, that he knew how to use whatever he was carrying, and that Rainbow John was a dangerous man, armed or not. Luis rethought his choice of Milsap as backup.

"I checked you guys out," John said.

"Yeah?" Luis smiled. Sweat dripped down the back of his neck.

"You're cool."

John made the gimme gesture and Luis handed over the roll, one thousand in rumpled twenties and tens. He counted it. "Five short."

"No it's not," Clay said.

John showed some teeth. "No, it's not. Over there by the garbage can. The sand is loose. I marked the spot with a straw. Go get it." He turned and walked. Beyond him, the figure in the shadows, the bodyguard, shifted stance.

"Wait a minute," Clay said. "How do we know there's anything there?"

John turned back to them. His eyes flashed wild: Clay had gone too far already. Luis said, "Be cool, man. That's Rainbow John."

Clay walked to John and faced off. "You stay here with my friend. I'll get it."

John looked away like he was laughing, then swung with a backhand left that seemed to graze Clay's face but sent him flying backward. John raised his left again. He was holding a foot of lead pipe, the end bloody, and wielding it, ready to swing again, this time for real. Clay landed and grabbed his side, a sure sign he was about to leap up, shooting.

Luis yelled, "Asshole, stay down!"

Clay held stiff, ready to spring and get them both killed. Luis moved a half step toward Rainbow John, hands up, just to draw attention without scaring him. "That's cool, man. We got burned before is all. Look, we brought you something." He gestured to the TV. Then he said to Clay, "We're all right. This is Rainbow John!"

Clay shifted on his knees, wiped the blood from his mouth. He covered the reach for his weapon like he'd bruised a rib in the tumble. John eyed the bodyguard and pointed at the TV. The guard slipped something back into his waistband and approached, a tall Latino in an overcoat. Looked the TV over, shouldered it, walked back into the distance, faced them and drew the weapon from his waistband again.

Rainbow John, still holding up the lead pipe, said to Luis: "I see this redneck again, I kill him." He took two steps, then said, "What the hell," and in three leaping strides was on Clay again, whacking him across the face with his backhand. Clay saw it coming and got his hand up in time to take the blow. Then John slammed him once in the ribs. Luis made for them but heard a click and saw the bodyguard cocking his automatic, the TV on the ground by his side.

Rainbow John wiped the bloody end of the pipe on Clay's clothes, and with a shrug to Luis that said, "No hard feelings," walked into the darkness.

7:30 P.M.—Ballistics

It was Eddie Wong on the phone. *"I found your Black Talon."*

By the time I winged it back to HQ, he had tracked the criminal use of Black Talon bullets and the Hi-Point 9 mm Model C, in Texas and elsewhere. He'd narrowed it down to the cases still open, and where the weapon wasn't found. One in Austin. He showed me two slides, Jenny Key's bullet against the file photo. The bullet markings seemed to match. Two more slides, the mark left by the firing pin.

"It's the same," I said. It looked like a little dot over a fat smile, a one-eyed happy face.

"Look again," he said. Finally I could see on one of the slides, that the dot was a little smaller, the curve of the smile a little sharper. "I look at the slides three times," he said. "Close but no cigar."

Wong had asked around and found a convenience store robbery misfiled. He'd dug up the security tape, a black and white he now pushed into his VCR. From a high angle, we saw the perpetrator as he came into the store and told the clerk to empty the cash register. Meanwhile, the perp looks up into the camera just long enough to give it a nice good shot of him, then raises his arm and shoots out the lens. I jolted like he was firing at me.

He'd left the bullet, the shell and the videotape. Bingo. The mark left by the firing pin matched the mark on the shell from Virginia Key's carpet. The claw-shaped slug matched the one that killed Jennifer Key. As it turned out, the shooter was probably figuring the camera would die and wouldn't be able to identify him: he was categorized as an emotionally disturbed person, EDP for short. They couldn't find the gun at the time of the arrest, but the video headshot allowed a positive ID, conviction, ten years in the Texas Department of Corrections plea bargained to three in Travis County Jail (helping the Bureau of Statistics soften Austin's criminal profile), released in ten months, tossed into the street, unsupervised.

I took his mug shot and found Torbett, by way of Dispatch, camped in the darkened stacks of Public Records on Eleventh Street, tracking Mrs. Key's old clients, first as public defender, and then private, and making educated guesses as to which short white male she might have pissed off and forgotten. "Add to that a bunch of city council members and their backers," Torbett said. I considered wishing him a happy Martin Luther King Day, and thought better of it.

I followed him, against his wishes, to Key's house to show her the mug shot. She thought it was the perp.

After we left Key's house, I shadowed Torbett, driving behind him as he headed out on Riverside Drive beyond the limits of what looked like town. I've heard it said that if you set foot beyond the limits of Austin, you may just find yourself in Texas. That's where I'd seen my first cow.

We reached the suspect's house and parked across the street, such as it was, a crumbling pavement off a stretch of foliage on the way to

Del Valle. If not for crack cocaine, the neighborhood would have no industry at all.

The home was part of a strip of dwellings that looked like storage units. I slid into Torbett's car to watch the windows with him.

I said, "What does Mrs. Key say lately?"

"Nothing new."

"You're not pushing her."

"She lost her daughter, Reles. She could lose her son."

Long silence. Finally I chanced, "Any possibility she's hiding something? A misdemeanor, maybe?"

Torbett breathed in. "There he is," he said, and we made for the front door.

Torbett knocked. I noticed he was carrying a Taser with him, a black item about the size of a hand radio but with two electrodes protruding from its head. It would shoot a jolt that would paralyze a normal person, if you could get close enough to hold it against him. No guarantee it would work on an EDP. Or that bullets would. "Mr. Peary?" he said. No answer. He knocked again. "Police." Nothing. Torbett backed from the door like I was supposed to shoulder it. "Yours," he said. I turned the knob and swung it open.

8:30 P.M.—2013 Maxwell Lane

Rainbow John had his driver set the TV up in the front room and leave. He poured himself a rye and settled on the couch, three remote controls sliding down next to him in the cushion. The second one worked, and the TV ran snow. He found an antenna in the closet, from the last TV. Mo had kicked in the screens of the last two, one during each of his last two visits, not counting the time he came over with the two junkies. John had stopped replacing them. He plugged the antenna into the back and the snow settled.

In the few months he'd been working for Mo, he already had this house, though it somehow still belonged to Mo. Everything somehow belonged to Mo, even the cash in John's pocket. There was no logic to it. John would have to lie about the TV, say he paid cash for it, and pray not to get caught lying. There was no standing up to Mo, no pissing him off and living to tell the tale.

Rainbow John had been a young hippie living in Austin in the sixties and early seventies. When drugs first came around, grass and pills and acid, they were shared between friends, passed around freely among like-minded youth, with a sense of fellowship and brotherhood. It was only later that somebody got the idea of making money from the exchange. It was commerce, money and greed that made drugs evil. By the early eighties, the hippie culture had fallen away. It became harder to scrape by. By then drugs had become part of his day, a joint in the morning, wake and bake. He'd party on coke or speed, needed grass or whiskey to take the edge off, Valium to sleep. All that cost money. His dumb jobs, painting houses or hauling things, paid a little. But those jobs tended not to last long.

By the mid- or late eighties he was so steeped in the world of dope that dealing wasn't even a rough transition. Hang out every night in the same bar, know everybody, and when the bartender quits they hire you. Only the dealers didn't quit. They turned up dead or in prison. One day he was buying just enough for himself, then for himself and a few friends, then a few acquaintances, then making contacts and putting the word out, then getting asked if he could handle the real thing, heroin. He could see his career arc taking shape.

But it was only in the last few months, only under Mo's rising star, that he'd become a distributor, dealing to the dealers, and that he'd achieved a level of prosperity. More money than he needed. The house. The car. The driver. The clothes. But it took a certain level of drug intake, constant ingestion of a variety of items, to ward off the notion that all this privilege was going to end one day, very suddenly.

He flipped channels. Cartoon. Cop show. Family show with a little blonde girl dressed like a whore. News. "*. . . in celebration of Martin Luther King Junior Day. No breaks are reported in the Key case. Five-year-old Jennifer Key, daughter of controversial attorney Virginia Key, a candidate for the open fifth seat on the Austin City Council, was shot to death in their Clarksville home last night by an intruder. Also wounded was her nine-year-old brother Rubin, now in a coma at Brackenridge Hospital. Mrs. Key could not be reached for comment. In sports . . ."*

John felt his stomach sink. It wasn't his idea, sending some junkie off to do a kill. Virginia Key was alive, alive and refusing comment. She wasn't even wounded. Half the state knew about it already. Anyone who had it together to watch TV.

But Bad Mo thought it was done. John would have to tell him it wasn't. And wait for the reaction.

8:45 P.M.—2350 Yellow Jacket Lane

Torbett and I stepped into Peary's apartment, one room, carpeted in brownish gray except for the linoleum area around the kitchenette. No furniture. A harsh whiff of bowel, like from a dead squirrel or cat or worse, a human, drifted through. The sink, under wooden cabinets, was piled over with dirty dishes, an army of roaches doing the samba. Stacks of empty cans. A grid of newspaper clippings on the rug, all folded in four-inch squares and paperclipped. I brushed something off my leg and realized my ankles were hopping with fleas. A white rat crawled across the counter.

Emotionally disturbed persons have a fondness for carrying edged weapons: knives, razors, other sharpened tools. In spite of the simple technology, a knife is an impact weapon, considered by many to be more devastating than a gun. What's also true is that EDPs beat any other category of offender in the number of officers they've killed with edged weapons. Something worth considering as you walk into an EDP's lair.

Besides the entrance, there was only one door and it was closed. I didn't wait for him to rush us before I drew my weapon.

"Mr. Peary?"

He came out of the bathroom, white male, mid-twenties, short, wiry, in baby blue boxers he'd been on intimate terms with for a while. "What the hell do you want?" he yelled. Then softly, "Did you hear that?"

"Yeah," Torbett said. "I heard it."

"Who the hell are you?"

Torbett's voice sang like a lullaby. "We're from the police. Are you okay?"

Peary approached us. "Stay where you are!" I shouted.

He found something interesting in our faces. Torbett asked, "We just talked to Virginia Key."

Peary rushed us. Torbett pushed the Taser against him and sent a jolt.

Peary jolted away. Then he glanced at a corner. "I hate that cat!" he said.

"Your gun. Your Hi-Point 9 millimeter Model C," Torbett asked. "You lost it. We can't find it."

Peary flashed angry again and approached Torbett. Torbett retreated as far as he could, shouting, "Get back!" and then lunged and zapped him twice. Peary took the jolts, shook them off and rushed Torbett again. I shot twice at Peary's feet. One shot missed, the second went clear through his instep as he flung his body at Torbett.

Torbett landed backward on the mildewed rug with an *oof*. Peary perched on top of him, both hands on Torbett's throat. I kicked Peary in the head as Torbett dug his nails into Peary's cuticles to make him let go, a cagey trick that doesn't work on psychotics impervious to pain. Without a clean shot, I grabbed Peary's hair with my free hand and pulled. Torbett got his arms up between Peary's hands and broke the stranglehold as I yanked Peary's hair and he yanked back. I was holding a fist of his greasy locks, some bloody at the root. Now Torbett was on top of Peary, throwing punches and kicks when he could. I was kicking Peary in the head and trying to get a good shot without killing him or hitting Torbett, when I saw Torbett was bobbing his head and I realized it was because Peary was trying to bite Torbett's face. I stopped sweating details. I pressed my shoe on Peary's mouth and fired twice.

9:30 P.M.—Austin City Limits

Rainbow John headed out and drove around town, tried four places— two clubs, a poolroom and a whorehouse—looking for Mo. He had to go somewhere. No one could stay holed up or moving all the time. Except for Mo's driver, who wasn't allowed to talk to anyone, John was probably Mo's closest contact. Dealers, and more often, their lawyers, found John when they needed to get word to Mo. But no one, not even Rainbow John, knew for sure where to find him at any given moment—that was Mo's protection. By the time anyone found him, word would get to him that someone was looking.

Most people didn't know Bad Mo by name. Half had never gotten a good look at him, or wouldn't want to. But John never had to ask more than "Is he here?" for them to know who he meant. Names weren't important. Mo never did business in front of anyone, so people didn't know for sure what he did. But his ease with money— hundreds dropped like cigarette ashes—and his air of absolute importance, narrowed down the field of imaginable possibilities.

Whenever they said "No, he ain't here" John saw them note his own face. They could say, "Some big Irishman looking for him." And his chest settled each time, a few minutes reprieve, take a pill and celebrate ten more minutes till I gotta tell him.

By the time John got to the last place he knew, he had taken a combination of speed and sedatives he hoped would keep him calm enough to give the bad news but alert enough to respond. The last place was an opulent house in West Lake Hills, in a development called Camelot, between one called Lost Creek and another named Rob Roy, off a quiet road and a private driveway. Mo had brought John there one night for what was supposed to be "a party at a friend's." The host didn't talk to John and the only other guests were whores. John suspected that the house was one of the places where Mo slept now and again, if he slept. John knew better than to ask. Mo was smart enough to keep his name off the paperwork, and not to stay there any more often than he stayed anywhere else.

The house was painted in a cheery combination of earth tones that fit in with the environment and with the neighboring houses that peeked from behind passing shrubs as John drove by. Two storeys high with a steeple on the front that gave the illusion of a third storey, the house reached out in four directions, extensions that had been added on by previous owners for bedrooms, dens and squash courts. If Mo had made any renovations they were probably of the security variety: bullet proof windows, an impenetrable basement, escape tunnels. That was the drug dealer's dilemma. He had to sleep somewhere. The country provided isolation he couldn't get in the city. Only once you were out there, you were stuck. The trick was to never be holding, be a true capitalist, let the grunts take the chances. But somewhere along the way, you had drugs on you.

The house's two-storey foyer gave way to a living room collection of mismatched marble nudes, fountains and velvet lounges that belonged in an antiques warehouse—an interior designed by a lottery winner. Rainbow John entered and walked through the front room, a party in progress. He saw a half dozen faces, the guy whose house it was, plus some whores and losers, men whose company Mo bought with drugs, laying around among the sculptures and paintings. John asked if "he" was there, took the lack of response for affirmative and passed into the dark back room.

10:00 P.M.—2350 Yellow Jacket Lane

Torbett jerked away from Peary and threw himself against the wall, holding his throat and panting. Peary lay on the carpet, twin holes leaking red from his shoulder, eyes wide as if he'd been pinned in a wrestling match, nothing more.

"Did you see that?" Peary finally said. "I have a friend who swam in the river. Can you swim?"

Torbett tried to get his breath. He wheezed, "I know you waited so long . . . 'cause you didn't want to insult me. You figured . . . I could take out that psycho by myself."

Torbett trained his weapon on Peary and I went out to my car. I made an overdue call for backup and an ambulance to bring in Peary in restraints, for medical attention and confinement at the State Hospital instead of Central Booking. They'd pump him full of antipsychotics and a few chasers to kill the side effects.

Back inside I stood a respectful distance from the downed Peary and Torbett holding him at gunpoint. "You want to look for the Hi-Point?" I asked.

Torbett didn't move. "You look for it. I'll stay here and shoot him."

11:00 P.M.—Camelot

The walls of the back room were draped with dark cloth, silk and velvet, and Bad Mo sat on a curving velvet couch between two Asian whores in silk bras and panties, patiently waiting out Mo's riff. A few others looked on from other couches as Mo cut lines on a mirror. At some point he'd let a line spill on the floor and they could dive for it, his party trick. Mo riffed in his crazy-ass Arab accent, each word individually wrapped.

"Freud discovered cocaine and got cheated out of the discovery, he did not publish first. Medical significance it has as a topical analgesic. They douse cotton in it and stuff it up the nostrils of Jewish girls and carve their oversized probosci from hawkish to porcine, their bridges turned up so high you can see into their sinuses."

Somewhere in the house was a Jacuzzi. Somewhere a big-screen TV, a pool table, a round waterbed. And Mo would always be found in the smallest room, his grotesquely pockmarked face twisted with laughter, doing lines with the friends he'd bought.

Mo eyed the woman to his right with something like concern, a brief hint he'd been human once. Then he lifted the small mirror on the palm of his left hand. With his right he held a cut straw in his right nostril between thumb and middle finger, index finger sealing the left nostril, and snorted a quarter gram's worth in one toot, what some yuppies would consider an evening. He leaned back, snorted snot, hawked it back in his throat and swallowed, reaching for water. He was in a talky mood tonight, which could go well or badly depending on just when John jumped in.

"I myself only use it for medicinal purposes, crediting it as I do," Mo's eyes flashed in John's direction and John made sure to flash back, not ruin Mo's buzz with his "gloom and doom." "Crediting it as I do with my recovery from alcoholism. Someone, another beer." He dipped his fingers into the water, dabbed some into his nostrils and snorted it back. Someone passed him a beer and he popped it and sucked half of it in a breath.

John had seen Mo in enough different moods, usually within a span of minutes, to put together some of the pieces. Mo had at least a dozen cars and always drove in the same one. He had a hundred silk suits, he'd said, but rarely changed his clothes. He claimed homes in Austin, Houston and the Virgin Islands, but rarely slept in a bed. He was hyperactive, moving constantly, and had been known to draw a weapon at the sight of his own shadow. Cocaine and his high position had made him constantly vigilant, a sleepless millionaire with five-dollar tastes.

Mo laid the mirror on his lap and withdrew, signaling the girls at his sides; they leaned forward, snorted two lines each off his lap, licked the mirror and obediently withdrew. The lights were dim enough to obscure only a few of his horrific facial scars. "Cocaine is why women love me. Am I correct, ladies? I can keep it up all night. Only I cannot come with dynamite up my anus." Mo laughed thunderously and the men across from him followed suit. For that they got the mirror and a small packet.

John settled in opposite Mo, by the two men, who eyed him suspiciously as if he'd grab the mirror. He sat up, alert but comfortable, and tried to smile admiringly at Mo's face, all but dripping with bubbled flesh. The women who he claimed loved him, were all coked-up call girls who couldn't feel any more than he could. Their romps were zombie flesh shows, more for the enjoyment of imagined viewers—if anyone would take pleasure in the spectacle of a coupling between a model and a mutant—than for the enjoyment of the participants. Coke addicts could often still perform. Sometimes they cared enough to impersonate what they'd been back when they were alive.

"Rainbow John. What brings you to this establishment?"

Rainbow John nodded toward the back.

"What? What is that?"

"Can we, uh . . ."

The light dimmed in Mo's eyes as he turned serious—or maybe worse, John would find out—then flashed a smile again. "Ladies, my friend and I need to chat. I hope you do not miss me." With that he slipped his fingers into the panties of the girl on his left and probed mightily, though she didn't seem to notice.

John followed Mo through the drapes into a kitchen, a whirring refrigerator and a sink filled with glasses. Mo faced him, as big as a house, six and a half feet with broad shoulders and an extra hundred pounds over his core of muscle. And on top of that, a psycho. John had seen him punch a hole in a man's rib cage. No time to stall.

"She's alive," John said.

11:30 P.M.—1205 Walnut Avenue

Torbett drove home sore and parked in front of the dark house. He sensed that Nan was awake when he opened the bedroom door, closed it behind him and undressed in the dark. She probably slept when he was gone, but he guessed she could sense when someone slipped a key into the steel front door.

He lowered himself to the bed and slid the covers over him and she turned toward him, pressing close. A silk nightgown was all she wore on the cool night.

How hard it must be, Torbett thought, to make a man feel so welcome when he comes home six hours late, when you must want to yell at him for leaving you alone, making you worry.

Nan kissed him, full-lipped and sweet-tongued, without a word, as if she didn't know who he was, as if they'd just met. This was her great gift. Like telling him he was so sexy, so desirable, that she'd want him even if she didn't know him. Anonymous passion, seventeen years along. Her tongue wrapped around his, her hands on his back, the silk nightgown magically riding upward, a perfect encounter between a strong man and a passionate woman. He breathed her rich smell deep as he slid inside, two perfect lovers together as if for the first time. That was the gift of his life. And buried his face in her neck thinking Virginia, sweet Virginia.

"Is something wrong?" she asked.

He'd stopped, opened his eyes wide. Nan. Not Virginia. Nan.

11:45 P.M.—Camelot

Mo didn't speak.

"The bitch. I saw her on TV."

John could hear gears crash in Mo's head. Then he felt the blows rain down on him. Though he'd anticipated the beating for over an hour, he didn't even see Mo's fists flying until they landed. Mo punched and slapped and hacked with his flattened hands at John's neck. When John backed against the fridge and held up his arms to guard himself, Mo yelled, "Do not embarrass me in front of my friends!"

"It's not my fault, it's not—"

A blow on the side of his head knocked him to the floor, where he curled up fetally, covering from the kicks until Mo finally got bored, but not tired.

"How do you know?"

"TV. He got the kids by mistake."

"Fuck, shit, fuck. She is a martyr."

John played possum. He didn't know why Mo didn't have him do the kill personally. Maybe he couldn't risk John getting caught. But John dead was less of a risk than John in custody.

Mo said, "I had one thing left in the world. One thing! And she took that." John pulled himself up to a sitting position against the counter. Mo went on. "I cannot make another attempt now."

John spat the word, "Strychnine."

"What?"

John said, "The packet I gave him. If he snorts it he's dead."

Mo seemed to notice John for the first time. "Rainbow John. You have impressed me."

Mo bent down as if to help John off the floor, grabbed him by the coat and pulled him close.

"Pray that he dies," Mo said, breathing into John's face. "Pray for your own good."

12:15 A.M.—706 East Thirty-eighth Street

Rachel shifted as I climbed into bed next to her but made no move in my direction and I didn't press the point. It gave me a chance to consider the merits of spending six or seven hours lying next to someone who hates you.

Blood still buzzing in my arms from the moment I fired the first shot, I wondered about the use of the Black Talon, the man who knew Mrs. Key by name, the time frame on Serology matching him to the phlegm in Key's sink. I thought about the little girl lying in the city morgue, and the boy fighting for his life at Brackenridge.

And I thought how I'd like to be wrapped up in Rachel's arms right now. But though I could see her across the expanse of mattress, she wasn't with me. I was alone.

12:30 A.M.—Brackenridge Hospital, Pediatric ICU

Dr. Neil Berman was on call when they brought him in, Trip Porter, seventeen, UT student, son of a prominent family. Experiencing nausea and tremors, and finally unconsciousness. Berman looked over the boy's chart, thinking that he'd never seen anything like it before. He hated to see something he'd never seen before. It could be nothing. Or it could be something brewing in the winds. Something apocalyptic. He checked the boy's reflexes.

On the Glasgow coma scale, fourteen or fifteen is awake, Berman thought as he made the notations. An hour earlier, Trip Porter had been a nine.

Now he was a three.

THURSDAY

I snapped awake with my nose pressed into Rachel's pillow, smelling her absence. Rachel had gotten up, worked out and left without my hearing her. I closed my eyes. I thought about the chase for the gun owner, the late night struggle, Torbett's near nose job. Just the kind of struggle they tried to prep me for during week one at the police academy, what they called Hell week.

September, 1977. The trainer worked us out and ran us two miles in the hot sun, then covered himself with protective gear and got us, one by one, unprotected and near collapse, to fight him. He slapped me a few times, called me a Yankee and a kike without much result. Finally he started in on my mother, her promiscuity, her standing in the world of sex professionals. It was a dumb trick but it worked: for all I knew it was true.

I pounded his gear till my fists were bloody. I knocked him down, pinned him on his back like a turtle and kicked his ribs. Finally, I jumped on his chest and bounced my weight on him until his gear compressed and he screamed for me to stop, his ribs were breaking. I owed him one for that. He taught me to turn on the rage when I was slammed, half dead. And in no time at all, in about twelve years, I learned to turn it off.

I went to the State Hospital and badged my way through a few channels, smiling innocently as if I had saved the patient in question, Mr. Peary, rather than drilling two holes in his shoulder and one in his foot. According to the nurse, he'd be up and biting squirrels again in no time.

The guard unlocked the room and I walked in with a smile. Hazy light shone through a window with a heavy steel screen. Strapped down tight and blasted on Thorazine, Peary looked bored and not much else. "Hi," I said. "How are you?"

"Do you have a cigarette?" he asked.

I borrowed one from the guard, lit it and carefully placed it in Peary's mouth, like feeding marshmallows to a lion. He sucked in a lungful.

I said, "I got into a fight." He was already looking out the wire-meshed window. He didn't seem confined, or like someone who could plan getting out. He sure didn't seem like someone who could crowbar his way into a woman's house without hurting himself, wait for her and call her by name. I fished out Virginia Key's photo, the one with the cameo. "Hey, Mr. Peary. Who's this?"

He glanced at the photograph. Nothing. When I said, "That's Virginia Key," I got about the same.

At HQ, I found Torbett sorting through a few dozen clippings from newspapers and microfilms. I read a few. Mrs. Key speaking before the city council, the state legislature. Key third in her class at Tulane Law School. Key a widow with two kids.

"Anything?" I asked.

"She never represented Peary, though he's had more than a few arrests. She doesn't know where else they could have crossed paths beside the courts, and neither do I."

"Maybe he tried to get her to represent him and she refused."

"No."

"Did she ever work the state hospital?" Public psych-hospital inmates, by law, get regular visits from an attorney. If they want, the attorney represents them before a judge when they're trying to prove sanity. These situations tend to backfire.

"Negative," he said.

"She must shake up the old guard. Any enemies?"

There was a picture of her, speaking opposite a panel of black people, young and old. And they weren't digging it. I had a hint there had to be old black activists, the NAACP crowd, and newer ones, maybe more radical. I didn't pretend to understand politics. But I guessed Virginia Key wasn't part of either crowd.

"I'm on it, Reles." He kept reading, a shut-up signal that made me want to push.

"It's funny, though," I said. "All this opposition to her, and she says she's got no enemies, no secrets, never a misdemeanor. I'm sure she's a great chick and she cares only about her kids, but Jesus Christ, is there half a chance she's afraid if she tells you something it'll leak and fuck up her career?"

Torbett blasted, "Reles, you don't know what you're talking about! Keep your damn ideas to yourself—" He cut himself off short.

I guessed the sentence was going to end with the words "white man," but I didn't ask. Torbett grabbed his raincoat and barrelled out the door. I wondered where he was headed.

9:30 A.M.—Capital Realtors

Rachel had woken early from a bad dream.

She thought she'd locked the door but there he was cornering her, upon her, the horrible man. He'd seen her at the bar, followed her home. And he was grabbing at her, telling her how worthless and stupid she was, and she tried to push him away but her arms were too weak until she ran into the kitchen and he cornered her by the sink and she could barely lift her arms, barely able to grab the knife from the dish rack, but she grabbed it and plunged it into his throat, and he groped at her anyway until she stabbed him again, in the throat, in the eye, in the empty cavern where his heart should have been, terrified of him, horrified of her actions, what she was capable of doing, and he kept grabbing at her, and she was awake.

✦

Dan lay next to her, sleeping peacefully.

The bastard was back, she thought, as she gave up on sleep and got up to get an early start, the late-night horrors that created the illusion of her relentless get-up-and-go. She wasn't so much of a power seller anymore; she was just someone who was afraid to go back to sleep. She got to the office, where she sat scanning listings and making calls as early as she dared.

Ten years dead and the bastard still haunted her dreams. Here she was with a life, a real life with a real guy. And the bastard was going to screw it up.

Joey knew everything too, or most everything. She'd played him from the first night, the night she killed the bastard, even in her tears and panic, making sure Joey fell for her, he a big bear and she a tiny Goldilocks. But Joey wasn't a bad guy, at first. He protected her, helped make sure the cops on call didn't see anything besides her killing an intruder in self-defense. No charges filed.

Other realtors and a few clients shuffled around the office. Rachel worked and tossed out smiles.

Still the dead man came back. If Dan knew anything already, he'd put it aside. What if he learned some details? It wasn't beyond him to snoop around her life. Would he leave her? And since when did she worry about a man leaving?

Would he arrest her?

Rachel grabbed a cigarette from her desk and realized she already had one in her mouth.

11:00 A.M.—Municipal Parking Lot

Torbett saw a dozen cops in riot gear loading into a van as he left for his car under the cloudy sky. The riot gear was always a setup for excess. Licensed with an official "just in case," it made ignorant patrols impervious to pain, invulnerable and battle ready. Once they knew their shell would protect them from harm, there was nothing to keep them from lashing out. They swung their clubs without mercy and without conscience.

Like the club that swung and cracked Torbett's big brother Alvin on the spine in '69, and killed him, though the death took two agonizing years. In 1971, pill-addicted Alvin drew his last handful of painkillers, and his last breath. Twenty years ago.

Torbett headed along Sixth Street to Virginia Key's place. It would be a nice break to see her.

The house sat on the corner of the tiny dead-end street, opening opposite the schoolyard. Scores of kids would pass it on the way to school. Torbett guessed its conspicuousness as the neighborhood's only black-owned house would make it a target for shaving cream, eggs, and toilet paper. Maybe rocks. A patrol car was parked across the tiny street, and another beside the house, on Robertson Street, alongside the schoolyard. Both patrols sat in the car on Confederate Avenue. Torbett parked and approached them as the driver rolled down the window.

"You two working on something?" Torbett asked.

The driver blushed. The passenger said, "Who the hell is *he?*"

Torbett leaned down to get a good look. Ruddy white boy, all full of himself.

"I'm Sergeant James Torbett. Who the hell are you?"

The passenger shifted, more angry than humbled. "Wills."

"Okay, Wills, why don't you get your fat ass in your own car where it belongs, and if you need help, radio for it."

Torbett sensed he was being watched as he made his way to the door, likely the angry patrol's eyes burning his back, a sensation he often experienced in white neighborhoods and at HQ. Three jobs: Working. Watching his back at work. And family. All at once.

Virginia was on the phone when she let him in. She mouthed, *"I'll just be a minute."*

"Mr. Hewitt," she said, her voice small but distinctive, the hoarseness half gone. "... Mr. Hewitt please don't interrupt me. Pleading *nolo contendere* is not admitting guilt ..." She sighed. "All right, we'll do it your way. Pay me my hourly rate and we'll go to trial. Figure at least twenty thousand dollars plus court costs, and at least six months in prison because the judge will hate you for tying up his court. And considering the charge, I don't think you want to go to prison." Silence. "Yes. Yes. I thought so." She hung up.

"Child molester?" Torbett asked.

"Indecent exposure," she said. She looked from spot to spot around the room as if to find something. "But he exposed himself to a child." She gave up on whatever she was looking for, and smiled sadly at Torbett. Then she cleared a pile of papers off the coffee table and looked for a place to put them, asking, "Would you like coffee? I'm sorry it's such a crazy day." She disappeared into the kitchen.

"You don't have to make coffee," he called. When she didn't answer he took off his raincoat and hung it on a hook near the door.

She came back in with two cups, napkins and a sugar bowl on a tray and set them down. "Spoons. Of course." She headed back.

"Please don't," he said. Torbett guessed she'd slipped into a manic phase. If she stood still she'd hear the absence of her children. "Can we sit down?"

"Of course," she said. He sat on the couch and she obediently parked herself near him, sitting at attention, back arched. He slid an inch away.

"Have you eaten?" he asked. The question came from nowhere.

She smiled just a bit. "I don't eat until dinner."

"Really? Why's that?"

"My parents weren't big on feeding girls. They thought boys needed food more, especially meat. Boys needed to do well in school, go to college, get good jobs. I was married before I was twenty. That's what they wanted. Then I went to college."

"Good for you."

"I couldn't do it with them around, telling me what a waste of time it was. Now I'm a lawyer and my brothers are laborers. And fat. I only eat one big meal at the end of the day. It motivates me."

Torbett let the idea hang in the air. She had been denied food. Hunger made her achieve so she opted to stay hungry. He ventured, "How is your son?"

Her professional front cracked enough that her eyes teared up. She shook her head and raised a hand, dismissing the chances of her answering the question or of his repeating it.

Torbett backed up, tested the waters. "It must be quiet here," he said.

Eyes focused on her knees, she said, "The phone's ringing off the hook."

"I mean . . ." He stopped himself. She couldn't talk about it. If it had been Torbett's children, he would have been in worse shape. Instead he said, "We have Mr. Peary in custody, the man who owned the gun. But we can't figure what he or," he coughed, "anyone else would have against you."

"Thank you," she said, staring out the front window.

"Their father?"

"He was taken from us."

"Yes. I'm sorry."

She tugged at an uncomfortable spot on her dress.

Torbett sipped the coffee. "You're becoming a public figure. You must have some enemies."

She pointed at the front door. "I have two white policemen stalking me."

Torbett smiled. "I wouldn't call it stalking. What about the city council?"

"I'm too low on their list."

"The local NAACP doesn't love you."

She half smiled at Torbett, her eyes still sad. "Do you think the NAACP put out a hit on me?"

"This is no joke, Virginia," he said. It sounded like a reprimand. Her lighthearted attitude made him angry. "The man who broke into your house wasn't after your jewelry."

Her eyes watered up again, squeezing tight as tears ran and she pressed a fist to her quaking forehead.

"I'm sorry. I'm trying to help," he said. He reached to comfort her and stopped himself, his hand stuck between advance and withdraw.

She took a napkin, blotted her eyes and wiped her nose. "I must look awful," she said.

"You don't."

But she was up and out of the room. When she came back she'd fixed her makeup. Like new. Only more beautiful, now he'd seen her cry. Like seeing her naked.

She sat again and folded her hands in her lap. "Please. Ask me anything."

He checked his pad. "I know defense attorneys will sometimes let a client stay in jail until he comes up with the money—"

She said, "I have *never* held freedom from a client," with such conviction he was afraid to question it.

He said, "Let's go over this again. Maybe we missed a detail. You came into the house."

She sighed and gave the story again. "Rubin and Jenny went in ahead of me. I locked the door. I turned on the light. I stepped into the room, there, and he was here, raising the gun."

"Where were you standing?"

She braced herself. "Just inside the door. Maybe three feet. There. Jenny was standing in front of me. Between me and . . . him. He raised the gun. Ruby jumped on him." She started to cry. "I never saw him do anything like that before."

Torbett fought the urge to comfort her. He let her pull herself together and go on.

"They fought and the gun went off."

Torbett watched her, watched her describe the worst moment of her life, cry, wipe her eyes and go on. He wondered at the empty house, what it would be like to share it with her. Her big, drenched eyes now caught his, waited for further instruction. He worked to break their gaze.

"Did he . . . did he say anything?"

"I told you. He said, 'Mrs. Key' . . ." She trailed off.

"What is it?"

"He said hello. That was it. 'Hello, Mrs. Key.'"

"He said hello. Anything else?"

"He said it funny," she said. " 'Key. Kay. Kigh. Missus Kay. Hello, Mrs. Kay. 'Ello.'" Something clicked in her eyes.

"What?"

She said, "He was English!"

Ron Wachowski told me Peary's blood sample had been sent from the State Hospital and he'd give a likely yea or nay to the Peary theory within an hour, on blood typing and a pending TB test result. A dozen jewelers and pawnbrokers promised to call me if they heard about a cameo brooch for sale. Czerniak had come up a big goose egg on guys fencing a stolen cameo, but Marks had been yanking him back to look at cold case crap so he could've missed something. Jake Lund and I pored through old burglary and B&E reports, piled high, looking for commonalities. And I read all of Torbett's articles mentioning Virginia Key, learning only that she held her opinions fearlessly and with little support.

The phone rang. "Homicide, Reles."

"It's Torbett. He was English."

"What?"

"The shooter. Mrs. Key says he was English. She's sure."

I held the receiver. "Jake, what do we have on burglary and B&E, white male, in the height range?"

He pointed to the two highest piles, a total of about two hundred suspects.

"Okay," I said. "How many of UK origin?"

He shuffled reports for five minutes while Torbett held on, then finally passed a file to me. "This."

One suspect. Multiple arrests, burglary of auto, B&E, sleeping in a public place, possession. Assault. Most recent charge probated. White male, five-five, born London, 2/29/64. Leap day. Name Gary Cruikshank.

Also known as "Gaz."

12:00 P.M.—Sunshine Motel, Houston

Gaz's head squeezed in on him, equal pressure from all directions. He ran a hand over his skull and didn't recognize it, the short dry hair. He'd cut it, he remembered, cut it with nail scissors and bleached it with Clorox. He looked at his hand. Neatly trimmed nails, clean, nothing to be ashamed of. A quick assessment told him the abscess under his arm was still horrible. It had been a needle hole once, or more than once, then a hole that didn't close. He used it again and again until he couldn't get at the vein and it got infected, a little pimple, a tender bump, then a sore, open and draining, a pustule of rotting dead flesh. His feet throbbed and burned, leaking a dozen different brands of pus in yellows and greens. Least damaged was his knob. Bit of dried blood from rolling the foreskin back, a cleaning ritual learned in childhood and somehow forgotten until last night, along with foot care, over the last few seasons. He limped to the loo— he'd lost flesh from his heel last night, peeling his sock off and washing his feet for the first time in months. Then he had a long, well-earned pee and rinsed his willy carefully.

Gray light broke through the yellowed window of the WC. Daytime. Maybe morning, maybe afternoon, but daytime all the same. Unfamiliar face in the mirror, short blond hair with splashes of green. Gaz staggered around, still groggy from the pills he'd scored to take the edge off, something he'd be careful about in the future.

He rummaged in the room. The last of his old clothing in the ash can. The remains of his old dark hair. New trousers, relatively speaking, and sweater and shoes he'd dug up from a clothing drop. New socks and Y-fronts from the chemist's.

They'd made him fight some other junkie, some speed freak, before they'd give him a fix. Rainbow John and the other bloke, Bad Mo, the boss, with the face that looked like he'd survived a house fire. Gaz could have killed the other bloke, the speed freak, killed him dead at the end of the fight. But Gaz was no killer. An East Ender, a wide boy, a bad boy, down the pub for a bit of ruckus, swinging a billiard cue and the like. But no killer. Then they gave it to him, a rush of cocaine to the armhole like nothing before. Killed the kids by accident, he did. His eyes grew hot thinking about it. It wasn't his fault, two little nippers, on the way to the grave from the offset. Saved them a life of misery, he had. But he hadn't killed the bitch. Or the speed freak. So he'd saved two, really, for the two who died. He was almost even.

It was the kid's fault, Tiny Tim off to save Mum from the invaders. Not Gaz's fault, not his fault at all.

He had leapt into the motor, he remembered, as it spun around the corner—dived through the back window. Rainbow John looked him up and down, saw the blood on his trousers and shoes, seemed satisfied, gave his own trousers and shoes to Gaz. Gaz managed to keep the gun in the back of his horrible, tatty briefs as he peeled off his gloves and changed. He was supposed to leave the gun in the house, God knew why, but he didn't, instead grabbed it tight in the flurry just to grab something, and didn't let it go until he saw the car in the distance and stashed it in his shorts.

Rainbow John dropped Gaz by the bus depot, John's enormous shoes flopping comically off Gaz's toes, John's baggy trousers cinched tight at Gaz's waist like a music hall comic's. John had given him a package when he dropped him off, twenty-five hundred dollars, American, and the instruction "Disappear." Glad to, son. And John gave him an extra packet of snow for the road—glorious, white powder, Gaz thought. Cured all his ills. Cocaine should be used to treat heroin addiction. Gaz, elevated on cocaine, ran into the dark in leaping balletic strides, his toes barely caressing the pavement. But once at the depot, paranoia kicked in. He fled at the last moment, frightened to be cornered on the bus by the pigs. Drifted south and sat by the river. Tried the Salvation Army, then bummed a ride from a trucker for the price of petrol, and rode off into the east southeast.

Arriving in Houston, he scored clean briefs, soap, nail clippers. He raided the clothing drop, or maybe the clothing drop came first. He scored a room, and some Valium. He crashed for what seemed like a day. It was light when he crashed and it was light now.

He looked around the motel room and surveyed his resources. The money. Check. The revolver? Gone. He'd flung it somewhere. The extra packet of coke John had given him for the road. Praise God. An old phone book, no one to call. Road map someone had left. Hello, then.

Houston. Population 1.8 million. Fourth largest city in the U.S. Two hundred fifty miles to Dallas, all in the wrong direction, northwest, deeper into Texas. But only fifty miles to Galveston. Coastal climate, splendid weather. Perhaps he could book passage on a freighter, make for points south, Tahiti, St. Croix, Barbados. Sip piña coladas in the shade of a palm tree.

What had happened to him was a gift, the crisis, the killing, the cocaine that cured him of heroin. He had money left, over twenty-two hundred dollars, and a new life in the offing. He'd be fine.

He just had to stay away from drugs. He considered the packet of coke, good old Charlie, a bright way to start his day. Then he slipped it into the pocket of his new trousers. Maybe later.

Lovely idea, he thought. A packet in me pocket. Like a little surprise, waiting for him.

12:30 P.M.—1610 Confederate Avenue

RAP SHEET

Suspect: Cruikshank, Gary Ian. White male. AKA Gaz
   Cruikshank.
Ht. Five ft. five in. Wt. 120 lbs. Hair lt. brown. Eyes blue.
   DOB 2/29/64 London, UK.
Immigration Status: Resident Alien.
9/1/87 Burglary of Auto. Nine months TCJ, released in
   two months.
2/29/88 B&E. Sentenced to four years Texas Dept.
   Corrections. Served at TCJ, released 7/30/88.
3/2/89 Sleeping in a Public Place. Arrested, two nights
   central booking, released, time served.
5/26/90 Possession opiates, case dismissed for lack of
   evidence.
8/26/90 Assault, probated. Travis County Adult
   Probation, East Austin Unit.

Last known employer: Milto's Restaurant. Dishwasher.
Known associates: "Brewer" Mackay, possible drug
    connection.
No Other Information.

I met Torbett at Key's house with the mug shots, Gaz Cruikshank's and four others fitting the same general description. Mrs. Key pointed out Gaz right away.

"That's him, that's definitely him."

"Are you sure?"

"That's him."

"Seen him before the shooting?"

Never, and she'd never heard the name.

If they found him, they might match his blood to what was in the phlegm in the sink. His feet would be the right size for the footprints. We'd need more.

I shot back to HQ and ordered the mug shots copied. One call to Immigration and three transfers later, I was on with Gaz Cruik-shank's caseworker. I said I was with APD and asked if she could point me to him.

"The last address I have for him is 57 Dancy Street, but he's not there anymore. He's reported in since then. But it's not against the law to be homeless."

I read her a few salient points from his rap sheet.

"I see," she said, sobered. "Were any of the sentences over five years?" They weren't. "That's why he wasn't deported. On the bright side," she joked, "if he were a citizen, he could do anything and still be a citizen."

"Uh-huh. How'd he get a green card, this career criminal?"

That made her sticky. I figured a big halo effect. Maybe she was hot for English accents.

"He was sponsored by his uncle, Dudley Cruikshank, in New York." She gave me the number. "I hope you're not judging him for his lifestyle. He does have some behavior problems, but he's got a good heart. What did he do?"

"He killed a kid," I said, and hung up.

12:45 P.M.—Wal-Mart, Houston

Still rousing himself from the Valium haze, Gaz wheeled a red plastic cart in the blinding light of the aisles, keeping the weight off his bad heel. Two shirts, button down. Toss them in. Carrying bag, keep his things in, for the trip to Galveston. Orange juice. He tore open the quart and gulped half of it, losing some down his cheek. It burned his stomach as it landed. Peanut butter cookies shaped like enormous peanuts. He swallowed four, nearly whole. They landed hard in his belly and rattled. Solid grub.

Calendars. "Excuse me, love," he asked a chunky black salesgirl with eyes on a depressing future. "What day is it?"

"Thursday."

"Thursday, the . . ."

"Seventeenth."

"Seventeenth. Thank you." She turned to go. "Seventeenth of . . ." She surveyed him up and down. "January!"

"Yes of course. That explains the chill." She huffed and withdrew. January. Houston.

In February he'd have a birthday. He'd been born on leap year day, the twenty-ninth. His parents thought they'd got away easy, only had to get him presents every fourth year. By the time they celebrated his third birthday, he'd already had it off with a girl. By his fifth he was a distant memory, if they thought of him at all.

A choir of tellys sang the news. Thousands marched on the U.S. capitol, burning an effigy of the president dressed as Rambo. Smashing visuals, Gaz thought. Known terrorists said to have entered the United States. Some ebony bird making a speech. What?

Austin. Political gadfly something or other, Virginia Key, attempted burglary, two children. Home video of the boy, maybe at age five, helping the girl, in diapers, up into a chair, and feeding her.

Gaz felt his face twisting up. Something burned behind his eyes. His face flushed hot, and a choking sob crawled up his throat. What was happening to him? The sky was crashing down. He wanted to die, needed to die at once. Let go of the cart and pulled his arms over his head.

It was Bad Mo's fault! He made Gaz do it. And the kid, watching bloody action movies, trying to save his mum, trying to wrestle the gun from Gaz. Gaz wouldn't have shot a kid, no less two. Not for anything. A bloody mass murderer, he was. He wanted to jam a spike in his arm, straight to hell on a gram of H. Kids are always the victims. Stupid and helpless against the cockeyed rule of parents, teachers and the law.

"... *recovering after surgery in Brackenridge Hospital* ..."

What? The boy was alive! Clouds opened.

"Excuse me, sir, do you need help?" A manager in a red smock.

The girl was dead, the boy alive. He might pull through, our prayers are with him, they said. The bullet killed the little girl. Not Gaz's fault, he was trying to shoot the bitch. But the boy was alive. Gaz wasn't a mass murderer. A simple accident, that was all. He pushed past the clerk and ran out into the sunlight.

He had much to do.

1:00 P.M.—HQ

I dialed Dudley Cruikshank's number. A woman with a Cockney accent answered. "*'Ello?*"

"Ma'am, I'm Sergeant Reles from the Austin Police."

Dead air. Then, "*It's Gaz, innit?*"

"I'm sorry. Yes."

"*What's 'e done now?*" She was sniffling.

"I don't suppose you've heard from him?"

Sometimes you don't get the information you're after, but you get something else. And it's volunteered. You didn't get it because you were smart enough to ask, but because you were there when someone needed to be heard, someone not used to attention.

"*My 'usband's at work. 'e's had it with Gaz. Bailed him out twice, he did. The third time, 'On your own,' he says. Can't blame him. But I bailed him meself on the sly. Family's family.*"

"How did he wind up with you?"

"Lad got in some trouble back home. Playin' music at a club. We thought 'e'd be better off 'ere."

"Music?"

"Guitar. Played like an angel. Trained at the Royal Academy. Bet you din't know that."

"No."

"Sold his guitar, last he wrote, things got so bad. Well, they finished the concert and the manager, 'e wouldn't pay them. There was a fight." Now she was crying, softly. *"Don't know how it started. Always getting into fights, our Gaz."*

I headed out on East Seventh into El Barrio, turned right on Pleasant Valley Road and into the tiny lot of Travis County Adult Probation, East Austin Unit. A surly receptionist announced me and pointed me down a long, paneled hallway to a cube of an office painted so white I could hear beams of fluorescent light ricochet off the walls. A balding, pear-shaped probation officer in his mid-twenties jumped out of his seat and shook my hand. "Wow!" he said, "a real cop! Have a seat."

I showed him the mug shot and rap sheet I had on Gary Cruikshank. Gaz.

"Burglary of auto? I didn't know half of this stuff. Mind if I make a copy?"

I said, "I was wondering if you could help *me*. Last known address, known associates, employers."

He'd pulled Cruikshank's file when I called, two overstuffed manila folders. He opened the more recent, like a book. Clipped on the left was the most recent paperwork: initialed pink cards to prove he'd been to AA meetings, urinalysis slips, supervision payment records—probationers pay for their own supervision. On the right was the log. "Let's see. He missed his last appointment. I sent him a reset."

"To where?"

He gave me an address on Annie Street, off South First. Humble white neighborhood, lots of folks just getting by. Also junkies, musicians, and often as not, junkie musicians. "Employer: Celine Salon. There's a phone number."

"Ever called it?"

He blinked at the idea, then picked up the phone and dialed. "Hi, do you have a Gary Cruikshank working there, a janitor? Oh. Did you? Never?"

He hung up, looking dejected.

"Check the front of the file. There must be a PSI report."

A pre-sentence investigation determines if an offender is a flight risk, or if he's a good candidate for probation. But now everybody is a good candidate for probation, as long as the sentence can be squeezed down to the maximum ten years. Prison overcrowding.

"It's got a few names and numbers, employer, a reference named Dondie Estamos." He furrowed his brow. "Dondie Estamos. Doesn't that mean 'Where are we'?"

On close inspection, the details that came straight from Cruikshank were all bogus. But the others weren't. I'd caught his scent.

2:00 P.M.—Elgin Hotel, Elgin Street, Houston

Drop leaned her head at an angle.

Gaz watched her eyes flagging, a bit of drool hanging from the horrid blister on her lower lip. She sat on the floor opposite him, lost in her own time zone. Slap her and in five minutes she'll scream.

He'd crossed her in the park, thought he recognized her from Austin, asked to come back to her flat. Just a room, really. Toilet in the hall, roaches on the walls, half the rooms in the building padlocked. Hospital nearby, lucky that. But he needed to be off the street, until he thought of a plan.

She snapped to as if from a nap, asking, "What do you wanna do?"

He didn't answer. Kill Bad Mo, it was the only way. Avenge the death of the little black girl.

Drop wore a hooded sweatshirt that was probably white once. She unzipped it.

Gaz counted six ribs. On each side, that made twelve. The flesh of her jubs hung against the ribs, like a pair of socks tacked up. She'd started on the jeans before he realized what she was doing, struggling to get them down to her knees before giving up and flopping against the wall, one eyebrow laboriously lifted in a half-hearted "come hither" look, an impersonation of what real prozzies do when they're impersonating interest.

"Oh," he said, realizing, but unable to find the right words. "Oh."

Her tiny bush was matted, likely from recent use, he thought. But the minimal hair, under the pale light from the window, the piss smell of the hall, the protruding bones of her pelvis, gave the effect of necrophilia. He hadn't had a girl in months. But he liked them living.

"No. God. No."

"Let's go."

"Cover up." He looked for something to throw over her. There was nothing, not even a sheet on the mattress.

"Come on, man! Don't you wanna get laid?"

"Look . . ." He reached into his pocket and plucked out a bill, a fifty. Her eyes lit on it—there was no chance to bury it and see if he could try for a five. She'd find out he had more. "Bloody hell," he said. "Take it, then."

With startling speed she'd pocketed the bill, pulled her jeans almost closed and was struggling into her hoody. Gaz leaned his head against the wall and tried to think.

He'd just close his eyes for a moment.

2:30 P.M.—HQ

I watched Torbett as he held the freshly minted copies of Gaz's mug shot. "The first seventy-two hours determine everything," he said. "And we've already spent thirty-six of them." It had taken us that long to ID the killer. He could be in Brazil by now. Torbett tossed the press phone list down on his desk.

"All of 'em?" I asked.

He said, "We could hold back. Just the local TV for the five and six o'clock news. See if we get some nibbles."

By the time he got the words out, he'd already decided. I didn't have a better idea so I shut up and headed out with a handful of copies of the mug shot.

At Gaz's last address on Annie Street, I found a house shared by four musicians running the spectrum from "professional" down to "sold my guitar for dope." They'd never seen Gaz but they'd only been there two months.

"Who owns the place?"

I phoned the landlord. *"He ran up two months back rent and disappeared."*

The rap sheet had his last job as dishwasher at Milto's Restaurant. I swung by. They remembered him. Missed shifts, broken dishes, stolen tips, fired. He left Key's home Tuesday night with a Hi-Point 9mm and a cameo brooch and we hadn't found either. Where did he go?

I borrowed the restaurant's phone. American Airlines, Southwest Airlines. No sale that night under that name. I headed for the airport anyway and dropped the mug shot with security, along with my card. I dropped the mug shot at the bus station on the way back, headed downtown, and dropped it at Amtrak. No one had seen him.

I was driving past a homeless outreach program called HOBO: Helping Our Brother Out. The doors had locked for the day—funding cuts—and a dozen brothers and sisters were setting up camp for the evening. I pulled into the New York Bagel Shop two doors down, bought a dozen and walked over.

"Anybody want a bagel?"

A few affirmative grunts, a few people in no shape for solid food. One fast-talker came up to me with a cigarette in his hand, slapped his forearm, popped the cigarette in the air and caught it in his lips.

"Is that worth a five dollar bill?" he asked.

"It's worth a bagel." I handed him one. "Anybody know an English guy named Gary? Gary Cruikshank? Goes by the name Gaz. He's a junkie."

Grunts, mumbles. I checked their faces for suspicion, deception.

"Try the Sally," the cigarette guy said.

"Yeah?"

"*They* might remember his face if they saw him. They have to look him in the eye while they're pitching the product." He winked a salesman's wink and got the last two bagels for it.

3:15 P.M.—Elgin Street, Houston

It had been raining, on and off. Drop's feet hit the wet pavement and she ran as best she could, down Elgin Street all the way to the Bel-Air. When she didn't find Two-J there she kept going toward the freeway, asked two whores and walked through Carol's. Past the freeway, she asked the bartender at the Hi-Life Bar and Grill. She followed Elgin all the way to Westheimer, went into a massage parlor and was tossed out before she got to ask anything. Her legs hurt and her feet burned and her head throbbed and her privates itched, her stomach twisted, everything ached with a desperation that required one, big, definite answer. And it was in Two-J's pocket.

He kept himself scarce on purpose, just like he'd give her a hard time when she found him. To remind her who was in charge, and just how badly she needed him.

Finally she saw him, standing outside a billiard parlor, talking to two girls. Drop stumbled up to him, wincing.

"I have . . . money." The words escaped her.

"Can't you see I'm talking to these ladies."

"But, but . . ." Drop heard herself grunt, her muscles contracting painfully.

Two-J grabbed her by the arm and pulled her around the corner before letting go. "Don't you know not to bother me when I'm talking to people?"

"Look," she whimpered, and held up the fifty.

It made him mad. "Where you get that?"

She started to answer, realized she'd best be careful. "I . . . turned a trick."

He looked her over, the sweatshirt, the fleshless torso. "No."

Drop felt her face and shoulders crumple in shame. Not worth fifty. Not twenty.

Two-J took the fifty from her hand, folded it and slipped it up his sleeve. "This is too big for you. I'll be taking it."

"No!" She grabbed his jacket. Two-J pounded the side of her head and she landed on the wet concrete.

"Bitch, don't fuck with my jacket!"

She pulled her fists to her face and keened at the injustice, all the work she did, the tricks she turned, the mooching and stealing, and here she had a fifty and even now he wouldn't give her anything. "Give me it. Give me!"

"Where'd you get this?"

"Some junkie. English."

"Rich dude? How much he got?"

She didn't know.

"Where he at?"

"My squat."

Two-J straightened his collar, waved for his car. "You give me your rich dude, you get what you need."

3:30 P.M.—Salvation Army, 4216 South Congress

The bouncer at the Sally flinched when he saw Cruikshank's mug shot and he called Sister Morris in to talk to me, leaving me to wait in a depressing schoolroom with dingy windows and cracked plaster, presided over by a portrait of Jesus looking a little on the blue-eyed and blond side.

Kindly old white-haired Sister Morris greeted me with a smile and a gentle but firm handshake. She dismissed the bouncer with a "Thank you, Brother Johnson."

"No, he can stay," I said, holding up the mug shot. "You've seen this man," I said. "Brother Johnson told me so."

She spun at Johnson who shook his head fast, to ward off punishment.

"Look, babe," I said, to knock her further off balance. "We know he was here. My question is when."

She adjusted her face to look assured, but the adjustment failed. "We don't give out that information. It's policy—"

"Like rites of confession."

"Where would the Salvation Army be if people didn't think they could find safe haven here?"

"Only you're not a priest and you didn't hear confession. What you did do was harbor a murderer." That jolted her. I held up the mug shot again. "Two kids. One dead. The other in a coma at Brackenridge right now."

She said, "Brother Johnson, please excuse us."

He left with a warning look at me, in case I was trying to get laid.

"No witnesses?" I asked.

"He was here yesterday," she said. "Before sun up. He had a package wrapped in paper. He didn't want us to see what was in it."

"A gun maybe?"

"We thought drugs, but maybe."

"When did he leave?"

"Right away. He wouldn't stay. He didn't want us taking the package."

"Any idea where he went?" She shook her head.

I dropped my card with a request to call me if he stopped in. Then I showed the mug shot around the motels and flophouses on South Congress with no result, and headed back to HQ. More bad news was waiting for me.

3:30 P.M.—Brackenridge Hospital, Pediatric ICU

Dr. Edwin Blair checked Trip Porter's chart: nausea, tremors, coma. Negative for drugs: narcotics, methamphetamine, cannabinoids. More tests pending. He stepped out into the hall and strode into the next room, Rubin Key's room, with a smile. "Hey, sport! How's it going?"

He was greeted by the even beeps of the EKG.

"Silent treatment, huh? I know you're there, I can hear you breathing."

The boy was breathing unassisted, more or less, just an oxygen tube up his nostrils. Good news. All the good news they had to go on. Blair checked his EKG rolls, reflexes and pulse. He lifted the boy's eyelids and shined a flashlight.

"Listen," he said. "My stethoscope's really cold. I keep it in the fridge so no one'll swipe it. Just tell me if it's too cold." He listened to the boy's heart, checked under the bandages and finally sat on the visitor's chair, peering through the bed's protective bars, a nine-year-old in a crib.

"What do you get," the doctor asked, "when you cross a duck with a row of the letter G? G's and quackers." Nothing. "Okay, I deserved that. Why did the chicken cross the road? I know you know that one." The EKG beeped.

He leaned in. "There's an ice-cream place not far from here that has thirty flavors, twenty you never heard of. They'll crunch in oatmeal cookies, Milk Duds, anything you want. I'll have a very pretty nurse with big boobies personally spoon the whole thing into your mouth. You just have to ask."

He waited a moment without moving.

"Your call, sport." He stood, rested his palm on Rubin's forehead. "But the longer you lay there, the worse your chances are of getting up."

3:45 P.M.—HQ

In the squad room, Torbett on the phone, Greer on the phone, his eyes flashing a silent apology at me for some imagined offense. Jake shuffling paper. Miles looking like he was less drunk than he wanted to be. "You ever see those posters," Miles said when he saw me. "The anti-drinking ones that say, 'No one ever woke up sorry for having one too few'?"

I hadn't. "Sure," I said.

"I wake up that way all the time."

Torbett hung up. "Whatcha got?"

I told him about the Salvation Army, Gaz's last address, and his last job.

Greer finished his call and said, "Got a call from the Greyhound station. Night clerk came in for her check, saw the mug shot. She sold him a ticket Tuesday night around midnight. For Dallas."

"Fuck."

He'd left town, gone to Dallas over thirty-six hours ago. He could have transferred anywhere.

"Options?" Miles asked.

"Go national?" Greer suggested.

I said, "Track down false leads from every crank in the country."

Jake, in a hillbilly voice: "Mah wife killed them kids!"

Greer looked cowed.

I said, "Backup from every corner too."

Torbett to Miles: "Can we post a reward?"

Miles said, " 'Police are offering a reward.' No numbers."

Torbett thought it over. "We go national."

In an hour we had copies of the mug shot, rap sheet and prints to every law enforcement agency in the country that had the technology to receive it. Faxes, wire services, CNN if they'd carry it. We messengered the photo and description to all the local press, and pitched it to the TV stations, the local network affiliates, like a hot story, an excuse to get their faces on nationally. *This is Bob McNeil reporting from Austin!* Gary Cruikshank, white male, five-five, 120 pounds, murderer, possibly armed and dangerous. No mention of the accent. No other information.

We'd have to search the country, even Canada. On the plus side, there's a certain ease you feel once you have a handle on things, once you know what's going on.

At least we knew he headed north.

4:00 P.M.—Elgin Hotel, Elgin Street, Houston

Gaz felt the crawling, tiny feet or claws on his neck. The horror rippled through him as he forced his eyes open, grabbing at it and flinging it across the room in a single motion, but there was nothing there.

The junkie girl, the horror show, had left him in her room and hadn't come back. It was nearly dark out. Clouds? So strange to fall asleep like that, wake up feeling almost rested. Maybe the dreams would go away too.

He checked his pockets for the money. Still there, less the fifty he'd given the girl. He'd gone through a lot in two days. The fear of being broke again was creeping up on him.

The gun? Long gone. Bugger. He'd have to get one. Or a blade. The packet? Still there. An extra packet of Charlie from Rainbow John, gift for a job well done, he thought. He had his clean clothes, the general feeling of 'not so terribly itchy as before.' Still the abscess under his arm, the foot problems. It was awful. But it would get better. He was done doping, an ex-junkie.

He unfolded the tiny packet. A bit of white powder, maybe enough for four little lines. He was feeling a little sluggish, might be in for a long night.

He looked under the mattress, opened the four rickety wooden dresser drawers one at a time. Nothing, not even a Gideon's. Finally he slid out the bottom drawer and reached in. Far in a corner, a bit of cloth. He wrapped his hand around it gently, watching for sharp edges, and pulled it out.

Blue corduroy, a rough eight-inch square. He laid it on the dresser and unrolled it. Inside a single-edged blade and a narrow hypo, a disposable. It had been used before. A metal screw-on cap from a wine bottle. Some matches. All she had in the world.

Gaz spit on the blade and wiped it on his pants. Then, carefully, so as not to disturb the paper, he cut up the coke, bit by bit, in tiny chopping motions. He licked the blade. It tasted odd. Chemical residue on the blade, he guessed, or rust. He wiped it dry and traced the coke out into four narrow rails and stared at them.

Not smack. Not what had crippled him. He'd accomplished more in thirty-six hours on coke than he had in a year on smack. He cast about for a straw, then grinned and fished out a fifty, rolled it, touched one end to the first rail of coke and sealed the left nostril and sniffed deep.

It landed in his right sinus like shards of glass, spraying and embedding in his mucus membranes. No water in the room. He snorted hard, tried to suck some gob down and swallow it. The shards settled into a gentle burn. Gaz blinked wide, looked about. Everything clear. Crystal clear. He rubbed his nostrils together. Bad idea, bad idea. Like rubbing broken glass. Bit of claret, blood, on his fingers. Snorted it back and swallowed. Best to stop. His breathing quickened as he grew accustomed to the pain. The burning would go away.

But no point in letting those other lines go to waste. He planted the rolled fifty in his left, pinched his aching right nostril and snorted again.

Both nostrils seared with an apocalyptic flame. Gaz swung around, knocking everything off the dresser. His vision went royal blue, dark night with flashes and specks of white, swimming paramecia, twitching hydra, mating slime, reproducing in twos and fours and eights, worms and snakes evolving into frogs and lizards, featherless birds squawking desperately for a meal, horrible little human fetuses with beaks and claws, kicking at the inside of his skull.

The palms of his hands were covered with blood, thick venous fluid from his nose. He pinched his nostrils and snorted again, hard. An ounce of blood and snot and Billy Whizz—speed or whatever it was, drained down from his sinus into the back of his throat and he swallowed.

There we go.

High octane pulsed from his throat upward, crazy radiance through his skull, eyes wide and alert, skin tingling, heart pounding, blood pressure soaring, a terrible, painful, pulsating edge like he'd shot gasoline, but perfect awareness, the yin and yang of low-cost stimulants.

He saw the floor, the razor blade and the hypo and the packet spread wide, the last two lines spread to the winds, mingle among dust balls and rat feces. Gone.

Gaz staggered down the hall looking for the WC, wiped his nose and washed the blood off his hands, clenching his teeth and blinking.

The girl was gone, it was a trap. Don't fall into a trap. Find Bad Mo before he finds you. He looked in the yellowed mirror, at his blinking eyes and flushed visage. He was all right, he thought as he ran down the stairs and out the fire exit, down the alley and past the garbage cans. He'd stayed away from heroin. And he hadn't used the needle.

He just had to find Mo. Find him and kill him. Before Mo found Gaz.

4:15 P.M.—Elgin Hotel, Houston

Drop led Two-J up the stairs and down the hall, past the sound of a sobbing woman, the stink of the toilets, to her room. The door was open.

"No!" she cried.

Mattress overturned, drawers pulled out, her works on the floor. He was gone.

"No, no," she said.

"Shit." Two-J turned and walked. She grabbed his jacket.

"Please," from her jaw, growling and sobbing at once. "Don't . . . please!"

He smacked her hard across the cheek. "Get off!"

She was on the floor, hanging on his legs, as he tried to walk away. "Please, please!"

"Who is the man? Who is . . ."

"You are," she cried.

"I am the man."

He raised a heavy boot and kicked her in the mouth, leaving her sobbing as he strode down the hall.

5:15 P.M.—2305 Morelos Street, Austin

Peeling off East Seventh Street on Morelos Street, in a tiny, battered, dark house, a multimillionaire sat in a windowless bathroom on the toilet seat cover, in front of a tray table, wearing rubber gloves and a breathing filter, cutting white heroin on a cracked mirror.

A portable TV, five inches diagonal and perched on the edge of the sink, showed the five o'clock news, volume low in case his driver, now sitting across the street in an inconspicuous sedan, had to sound the horn to signal intrusion and emergency flushing.

Time bends, Mo thought, as he stared down into the mirror, lines of the drug across his bubbled, damaged face. As time goes on, it passes faster. Each year is a shorter percentage of your life. So while a year is an infinite period of time to a child, it spins by for a man of advanced years. Or a man of limited years.

Which is why it is so important to make your limited time count.

He cut and blended. He should not be doing this himself. No one else was to be trusted. A hands-on supervisor like his father, always tinkering, improving the product. Planning for the future. As if there were a future. Mix in a new additive. Add strychnine to methamphetamine, you get, what was it called? Words seemed to slip from his memory. Lance, that was it. Speed with strychnine. A quicker, sharper jolt. Add too much, you get a heart attack. Add something to the heroin. Why take the risk, why lose customers? Wasn't white heroin good enough? But Americans were so stupid about buying things. Something new, something combined. They would take cocaine with their heroin and let the two drugs fight it out. Add something to it. Whatever is handy. Whatever is cheap.

A news story about Iraq. A foreign war on foreign soil. A theoretical construct. Less real to Americans than an episode of a beloved TV show.

He moved the tray table, stood and looked at his damaged face in the medicine cabinet mirror. Then he sighed with resignation as he drew the soldering iron from his pocket.

Hopelessness, of course, he thought, as he uncoiled the cord and plugged it into the outlet. The soldering iron, a piece of metal the size and shape of a pencil but with a white plastic grip, had never worked to improve his complexion. He was sure it was the defoliants the Russians had used on his own country—dusting to destroy the hiding places of "insurgents" and baking the lush greenery of his homeland to an expansive desert—that had caused his pustules in the first place. But it was only in the last few years that he had hit upon the idea of plastic surgery on himself. It barely hurt, thanks to the cocaine. And to the extent that it did hurt, it seemed an appropriate punishment, took the sting away from the loss of his family, the fact that he himself had allowed it to happen. The tip was hot. He dabbed it gently at a scar, felt the burn, pulled away, tried again.

A news story on the governor. A woman. A news story on the city council, a pending election. The bitch. He stopped working his face and looked at the television.

They showed the outside of her violated home, stock footage of her speeches. Mo felt his insides twist with anger.

Then they showed Gaz.

A mug shot, the junkie who Rainbow John had found for him. Who John had supervised and dropped off with a gun and a crowbar, and picked up. Who had missed Virginia Key and shot her children. Who made her a living martyr. And he was alive.

Mo unplugged the iron and ran water over the hot tip. He had calls to make. Several of them. Where he had people: Austin, Elgin, San Antonio, Houston. Reach out his tentacles and pull in Gaz. Quickly. And with force.

He would deal with Rainbow John later.

5:45 P.M.—Bel-Air Bar, Houston

Drop pushed the door open with all her might. Three men at the weathered wooden bar watched the news on a TV at the far end.

"He ain't here," the bartender said.

"I know," she said, taking the nearest seat. "Let me have . . . something."

She tried hard to sit up, swept her hair back from her face and placed one hand on the bar. She tongued her lip where Two-J had kicked it. She tasted blood.

"Let's see the money," he said.

"I thought," she looked at the men drinking.

"No one here wants to fuck you. Beat it."

The drinkers heard that and laughed.

Drop let one foot find the floor. Her eye caught the TV screen.

It was a picture of the junkie, the English one from her room. His hair in the picture was longer and dark, but it was him.

And they were looking for him.

7:30 P.M.—Hi-Life Bar and Grill, Houston

Two-J was sipping a tasteful cocktail with a fine lady when a couple of Philo's boys, fat boys in purple suits, walked in and started looking around. One eyeballed him and walked over.

"Mr. P. requests your company. Now."

In the back of Philo's limo, Philo sat, sweat running down his hairy white neck. Two-J slid in.

"Philo, my man. What it is!"

"Shut the door, you dumb fuckin' spook." He did. "I'm not your man. You're my man. Remember that." Philo fidgeted with his gold rings. "It's bad enough now I'm a messenger. I gotta look for you dumb niggers in half the gin joints and whorehouses in town."

Two-J made sure not to smile. Philo wasn't Two-J's man, but he was somebody's.

"The word is out," Philo said, and mopped his brow with a silk handkerchief. Even in the dimmed light, the reddish brown of his toupee didn't strike a near blow to the gray of his sideburns. "Some two-bit junkie ripped off one of the big boys for a couple grand. They want to send a message."

"So?"

"So we're supposed to keep an eye out for a short, ratty-haired junkie, a white guy. A limey."

"You're playin'."

"No, I'm not playin'."

"You're playin'."

Philo flushed angry. "I'm not playing, ya dumb coon . . ."

"I seen him."

"You what?"

"Not *seen* him. One of my junkies. White guy, she said. English. Throwing fifties around."

"Where?"

7:45 P.M.—Westheimer and Montrose, Houston

Drop's feet ached with each step but she played frogger across the street, dodging trucks and yelling "Hey!" at a cop as he stepped from the McDonald's toward his car. He spun around.

"I know the guy you're looking for."

"Who?"

"The little guy, the junkie." The cop drew a blank. It wasn't going fast enough. "Mmmmmmm! The one on TV, asshole!" The cop slid into his cruiser. "Come on, man!"

"Patrol 4030 to Central K." He was talking into the microphone.

"Go ahead, Bustos."

He grinned. "What do we have on a short guy, someone says he was on TV, we're looking for him."

Long silence, then, *"White male, five foot five. Gary Cruikshank. Longish light brown hair."*

"It was blond," Drop said.

Bustos shook his head, then thumbed the mike. "Word is we got a bleach job." Then to her, he said, "Where'd you see him?"

"Twenty bucks, man."

"We don't do things that way."

"Fuck how you do things, man! I need twenty bucks, I need it now! Give me the fuckin' money and I'll tell you where I saw him!"

Bustos stood up and opened the back door. "Get in the car."

Drop put her hands in front of her. They shook. "No. No."

"How do I know you saw him?"

"He was English!"

Bustos stopped, slid in far enough to grab the mike again. "Bustos to Central. Was he English?"

Drop held out her hand.

7:45 P.M.—HQ, Austin

I ran the photos of Gaz Cruikshank personally to the sheriff's office and DPS, to supplement what they'd gotten from us by messenger, and asked them to spread the word as far as they could. The personal touch. I contacted the state troopers. And the Dallas locals. I stalled on the FBI. But they'd jump in as soon as they realized we'd alerted every badge from here to Michigan. We might catch Gaz, but he might plant a few more Black Talons first.

Meanwhile I was about to get a blast from the past. A real blast.

7:45 P.M.—Fiesta Gardens, Austin

Rainbow John got the call. Fiesta Gardens.

Was it worth making a run for it? Who knew how far Mo's influence reached? Texas? The Southwest?

John's months of devoted service might win him leniency. Or a second chance. Or maybe a quick and painless death, something defiance would surely lose him. He had the pipe in his sleeve, a cloth latch sewn in for it specially. He thought of taking it out. No point in pissing off Bad Mo. But he couldn't get himself to walk to his death completely unarmed.

He trembled as he drove the Lincoln himself, leaving his driver behind per instructions, and smoking a joint to ward off the damp cold in the air. What the hell, he thought. He wasn't living to die old. One night was as good as another.

John parked, stubbed out the joint, stepped from the car and buttoned his overcoat, though his hands trembled. He glanced back at the Lincoln. Nice ride, he thought. He hoped he'd see it again.

Gray clouds hid the stars. John stepped among the reeds. The tiny, dark inlet seemed a fine place to die. A fitting place. Mo could dump him in the water. They'd drag him out and plant him in potter's field. No loss.

"Rainbow John!" John spun around. Mo's hulking silhouette rocked toward him in the haze of the river lights. "Allow me to look at you."

Mo grabbed John in a bear hug, pinning his arms helplessly, and released him.

"A beautiful night. Cool breeze off the black water. It does not get better than this."

"Sure, chief."

"What do you hear on the streets?"

Rainbow John said, "Man, I ain't heard nothing. Nobody's seen him. He ain't tried to score. He ain't at his regular places. I say he blew."

"You brought him to me," Mo said.

"I said he was mean and crazy—"

John saw a flash of Mo's approaching fist, a lightning jab pounding him in the mouth, and found himself on his ass in the dirt.

"Do not argue with me!" Mo snarled. The pipe had slid from John's sleeve. "What is that?"

"Nothing."

Mo reached out for it. John handed it over. "A fucking pipe," Mo said. "You were going to kill me."

"It's always in there. It slid out, see?" John tried to turn his sleeve inside out to show him the cloth latch, but instead felt the pipe slam him hard on the cheek. He toppled and saw stars. When he landed his hand came up to his swollen cheekbone. Broken.

"I told you to take care of it!" Mo shouted, his heavy boot connecting with the side of John's head and sending him rolling. "You brought him to me . . ."

John crawled away in the dark, Mo kicking him as he moved.

"You spoiled child! You lazy bourgeois. You think I wanted this life? I did this to make money, to save my family. I lost everything!"

John cried, "I'm sor—"

Mo yelled, "He killed a child. A child! He left a witness. Now every cop in America is looking for him. If they find him before we do—"

"Please," John sniveled, looking up in time to see Mo raise the lead pipe high.

8:00 P.M.—HQ

By what would have been a late dinnertime if I had dinner, I was in HQ filling out reports and calling Rachel at home and work without any luck. Torbett was making phone calls too, and visits, trying to find out what Gaz Cruikshank could have had against Virginia Key. And he was asking questions, around the city council, around the capitol, trying to find out who might consider her a nuisance, or who she had already embarrassed. Rubin Key was in a coma at Brackenridge. Jenny Key was shipped off to the undertaker's, funeral scheduled for Sunday, large crowd expected. Jake Lund was staring at the computer, doing something I couldn't pretend to understand, when the phone rang.

"Homicide, Reles."

"Let me talk to Torbett."

"Sergeant Torbett is out." I didn't bother asking to take a message.

"God damn it," he said. *"Reles, this is Jack O'Connor, Houston Homicide."*

I blinked. I'd had limited contact with O'Connor before. He was an old friend of Joey Velez's, and not quite so old a friend of Rachel's, uniting Joey and Rachel about ten years ago on the night of an unfortunate incident. The incident involved a young, hard-partying Rachel, a kitchen knife, and an intruder, in a manner that proved singularly unprofitable for the intruder. Joey took care of Rachel after the cops left, helped her clean up her act, and took her back to Austin with him. But O'Connor didn't think I was much of a friend to Joey or to Rachel, which didn't explain why he wanted to talk to me.

"What can I do for you, O'Connor?"

"*What can I do for you, you Jew fuck. I wouldn't call if I had an excuse not to. Word is all over the department, your killer, what's his name, Cruik-shank, is in Houston. He was holed up with some junkie chick in a single-room occupancy on Elgin.*"

"Are you sure?" We thought he'd headed to Dallas.

"*He was short, he was English. Short hair, crappy bleach job. And he was throwing fifties around.*"

"I'm leaving now."

"*Don't expect a reception.*"

8:00 P.M.—Fiesta Gardens

A horn honked in the distance.

"Act normal," Mo said low. He held the pipe at his side. Rainbow John wiped his face on his sleeve and saw blood.

Mo's driver, a badass mick like John, was walking in among the stones. Mo had greeted John alone. No witnesses.

"They seen him in Houston," the driver said.

"Did they apprehend him?" Mo asked. The mick shook his head. "Go back to the car."

The driver saw John in the mud and shifted. That could be me, he seemed to think. Rainbow John, Mo's greatest ally, trusted confidant, beaten to death in the mud for a bad move.

"The timing, it is unmatched," Mo said as he flung the pipe, spinning into the reeds, and pulled papers from his pockets, mostly money, twenties and higher, looking for something. A fifty hit the mud with a scrap of white paper. "We will get this cleaned up, quickly. Where is that fucking number?"

John picked up the fifty and the paper, looked at them and handed them over. "Is this it?"

"There she is. Sweet girl. Good friend. Extraordinary breasts." The words sounded peculiar with his accent. "Thank you, John," Mo said. "Where would I be without you?" Mo leaned over, cupped his hand around the front of John's throat and squeezed hard enough to cut off John's air supply.

"If this does not go smoothly, I will unravel your entrails."

John nodded. Mo went on.

"You understand I am not speaking figuratively."

Mo let go as John gasped for air. All Mo needed now was for Gaz to be dead. He'd have other concerns later. John thought about the scrap of paper. He knew what it meant, though all it had on it was a Houston phone number. And the word *Anything*.

HOUSTON

"Houston is ugly unless you're rich," my father wrote in one of the post-cards he employed to taper off our contact. *"The smog sits in a basin, gets stirred up by the rains, and settles back."*

My father raised me from the age of ten, when my mother took off. I worked out at the mob-run boxers' gym that employed him, and I ran with the bad kids. That is, until I hit five foot ten and ex-hibited a potential for leadership: elaborate supermarket beer "heists," counterattacks against other gangs, strategic displays of vengeance. Once we were hanging out in front of a pool hall when an outfit goon came out to shoo us away. He recognized me from the gym, said, "Oh. Hey," and went back in. That sealed it. After that I dictated parties and petty thefts, kept an unspoken protective shield over the three or four girls attached to the gang at any given time, and arrived home unnoticed late at night, wishing my mother was there to ask where the hell I'd been, the toughest mama's boy in Elmira.

When I was fifteen we relocated, all of a sudden, to Texas. My fa-ther, abruptly alienated from the mobsters who'd had him running their errands for years, was now hustling around 1968 Austin trying to make a living, getting involved in various "enterprises" with his new friends, and leaving me to finish raising myself. I was big and had a broken nose and a funny accent and I could fight. I carved a corner for myself quickly. I had a new gang and I always had a girlfriend. And I was always painfully alone.

The mist coated Highway 290 to a hydroplane sheen as I rolled off into Houston. By 10:15 I'd circled around the loop and found the South Central Command on Saint Emanuel, parked and went in, showing my badge to the desk sergeant behind a wooden desk that, I guessed, came with the building, some time in the last century. "I'm here for Jack O'Connor."

The wooden trim and dingy walls made the place look like a combination of an Irish saloon and an inner-city schoolroom. It buzzed with two dozen patrols and a dozen shmoes, bruised and bloody-nosed, sniffling and chattering. Three cops behind a long counter on the left answered phones, read reports and scanned security monitors.

"Hey, where's that guy they locked in his trunk?" a white-shirted badge yelled. "Is that guy still in his trunk?"

The desk sergeant gave my badge a glance and a sneer to let me know it wasn't worth the cereal box I'd fished it from. "Have a seat." He pointed his pen to three attached chairs by the far wall. In one chair sat a red-haired woman of about twenty-two, in a fuzzy pink jacket. She smiled when I joined her. I noticed that she was handcuffed to the armrest.

"What's going on here?" I asked.

"Gang initiation," she said. "You wanna take a shower?"

Someone yelled, "Hey, who's gettin' that guy outta that trunk?"

I smiled at the woman and kept the conversation going as I scanned the room. A patrol was shoving a guy with a bloody nose, the guy yelling, "Hey, I'm the victim!"

"You come here often?" I asked the woman.

"Now and then."

"What kind of place is it?"

"You'll see."

The desk sergeant yelled, "Reles!" and waved me over. I nodded at the redhead, marveling at how much of my human contact is with thieves and streetwalkers, how much more comfortable I am around them than around, say, businessmen. But thieves and hookers have a vested interest in making me comfortable.

"Two flights up on the left."

As I headed up the stairs I heard someone yell, "Is that poor bastard still in that fucking trunk?!"

10:15 P.M.—Westheimer, Houston

It had been misting on and off. Gaz finally stopped in a gas station and bought a rain poncho, green, children's size. All they had. It went down to his waist but kept his head and sweater dry.

The drug was breaking up in his nasal passages like scouring powder. He tried to ask someone where the bus depot was and found he couldn't make a whole sentence. He'd been walking for hours. He was afraid to be seen on the street, afraid to sit still, afraid to get on a bus back to Austin. Had to get back somehow, find Mo, kill him at any cost.

He scratched his scalp and found fresh crawlers. He'd shampooed, even bleached them. He'd missed these somehow. At least they were clean.

Suddenly, as Gaz walked, his prick was possessed with the greatest tumescence he'd known since secondary school. He had to stop and adjust. Steel rigidity, painful hard. He hadn't had a woody in months. Why now? Side effects of his new metabolism. He thought of ducking into a doorway for a quick wank, when a police car rolled by. Child murderer caught masturbating in public. No.

He'd seen a porn theater somewhere back, maybe a mile, but it was hard to tell where. He turned about and backtracked. He'd find it. Who would notice another hunchback abusing himself in the dark? He could even rest for a few hours. If the rain cleared he'd head back for Austin. No rest in Houston.

He could see the cinema in the distance. Adults only, three features, military discount. Keep 'em flying, mates!

The pain in his shorts was such that he let out a wince as he pushed through the door into the lobby and was greeted by a crowd of men, including a dozen coppers in blue.

Gaz dropped his jaw. A cop saw him and laughed.

"Buddy, take it outside," he said, and a few others laughed as well.

The pigs had corralled a cluster of men, businessmen and laborers, into a circle and cuffed them together. They'd busted the place and Gaz walked in on it. No one recognized him. He backed out the door and ran down the street, heart rattling in his chest, speed scraping through his veins.

And now he needed something, needed it bad, a pill, a joint, even a few drinks, something to level off. Now.

10:30 P.M.—South Central Command

Two flights up on the left, Jack O'Connor leaned back on his chair and talked on the phone. He was average height, bald, blondish, bespectacled, late forties, paunchy but solid. He hung up and said, "For the record, I think you're a rat-ass Jew fuck not fit to sniff Rachel Renier's shoes. I got bag ladies in the lockup too good for you."

"Nice town, Houston," I said. "Beautiful this time of year."

My mother (beautiful, glamorous, missing) was a gentile, a Protestant of middle-class origins, slumming in my father's world for ten years longer than she'd planned. Any Jew will tell you that means, according to Torah, that I'm no Jew: at the pragmatic core of Jewish law, as my gangster father explained it, is the notion that you can only be sure who the mother is—we'll go by her. On the other hand, because of my father's last name and his dubious standing in the community (ex-boxer, mob lackey) and because of his namesake, Abe Reles, a murderous Jewish gangster from the thirties, I was known by my father's ethnicity, the same way you'd identify a Goldberg as Jewish even if his mother was an O'Hara.

I piss off easy, but not when someone calls me a dirty Jew, or less of-ten, a kike. My father's generation of hoodlums was no more influenced by the gangsters of their childhoods—Italians like Al Capone and Lucky Luciano, Jews like Meyer Lansky and Dutch Schultz, Abe Reles and Bugsy Siegel—than they were by the films that depicted them. Capone himself watched the movie *Scarface* six times, glorying in his own de-piction by actor Paul Muni. A veteran of Yiddish theater, Muni copped his vaudeville Italian accent from that other famous Italian, Chico Marx ("Stand-a back! I'm-a shoot-a the gun!"). Capone didn't complain.

So the type of nicknames the mobsters of the forties picked up (Sid the Yid, Dago Jim) were not likely to cause insult. It didn't escape me that my dad, a frequent referee in sparring matches at the gym, was referred to as "the Jew who blows the whistle" (or sometimes just as "bagel"), or that another employee got pegged "the nigger who mops up." The words were packed with generations of violence, bit-terness and self-loathing: you heard them most from guys who hated their own lives and saw themselves as failures. But you get used to a certain level of verbal violence. Emerging into lower-middle-class so-ciety, as I did in college, made me uneasy. It's only when people break form and tell me what's on their minds, when they call me a dirty kike or a Christ killer, that they show me exactly what I'm up against. That's when I'm at ease, even at the advantage.

"He was spotted at an SRO hotel on Elgin at Ennis," O'Connor said, shuffling notes on his desk. "Fit the description but short-haired and blonded. And English. The TV report didn't include that, right?" I nodded. "We combed the area. We found a motel, the Sunshine Mo-tel on Crawford. He checked in yesterday around noon, long-haired and shaggy. Took off this afternoon around twelve thirty, clipped and blond, wearing a yellow sweater and blue slacks."

"Shouldn't be too hard to find."

"Great, Einstein. You drive."

10:45 P.M.—Elgin Hotel

Gaz thought to head back to the girl's hotel. Drop, or whatever she was called. She was a horrible, bony slag with a great herpe on her lip, but she was his only friend in town. And what the hell, she wasn't so bad. She'd offered it already.

He hacked up a cough from his guts, a bad one, and spit a big yellow grollie with blood in it. His body had been doing odd things for some time. Discolored stool, or no stool. Sores, abscesses. And now a screaming desperation for a bit of muff. A few weeks clean and he'd be right as rain.

He was nearly certain he'd found her hotel when he noticed footsteps behind him and peeked around. It was a girl, small and stout, hair half a dozen colors. Arse stretching out her skirt, top like a swimsuit under a tiny jacket. That's more like it, he thought, warmth riding up his back. He walked a few more steps and looked back again with a smile, closed lips so she wouldn't see his rotten teeth. "'Ello, darlin'," he said.

She smiled back. "Hey," she said. "Come here a secont."

Ah, Gaz thought, the subtleties of an American seduction. He turned.

"Lovely day, then, eh?"

"If you're a duck."

He looked her over. A little thick, but he wasn't picky. Much better than the stick of a junkie, Drop. Whose building, he realized, he was standing in front of. To the chunky girl he said, "You're a right stunner, you are."

"You want it?" she asked.

He nodded.

"Fifty," she said.

"Done!"

"Follow me."

As they walked, Gaz started feeling very happy. A commercial exchange, but still. "What do I call you?" he asked.

She kept her eyes in front. "Anything."

11:00 P.M.—Downtown Houston

I drove my Impala around the city as O'Connor listened to his hand radio, periodically barking directions at me. "Left, asshole!" I turned left up another dark street.

"Is there a *Mrs.* O'Connor, or is all this going to waste?"

I'd figured out over the years that O'Connor had met Rachel when she was a wild party chick in Houston, that he kept his hands off because he was married, or because he genuinely liked her, maybe loved her. I was willing to believe he was in love with her, still. I didn't know if he was married still.

We swung by the Sunshine Motel ("Naw, he ain't been back") and the SRO on Elgin. Gaz's hostess, an unnamed young woman (the desk had her down as Jane Smith), had left in a hurry, leaving the door and window open. No one saw her leave, or guessed where she went, or cared.

O'Connor directed me in and out of the wet, dark streets. Finally a McDonald's appeared on the right, a patrol parked in front. "Pull over," he said.

I pulled over behind the car. O'Connor got out and so did I.

"Stay here," he said. He walked to the driver's side, read the patrol's memo book, initialed it and came back. We got back in my car.

"Unnamed white female, five foot three, about 85 pounds, in dirty white hooded sweatshirt and jeans, fever blister on her lower lip. Tipped him off she'd seen Cruikshank, then ran. He saw her here."

"Where do junkies hang out around here?"

"Make a right, dickhead."

11:15 P.M.—Elgin Hotel

Drop was running again.

She'd been leaning her head out the window, trying to get air, calm the twitching, the shaking, the vomiting, anything. Every muscle ached.

She'd had money. Two-J took it. She tipped off the cop. He said he'd give her money if she came downtown. He'd check her for warrants and *Bam!* back in the cell she'd go. She could handle jail if they'd give her a fix but they wouldn't. She'd stood by the open window, breathed the thick wet air of the street and cried.

Just then she'd noticed a figure approaching the building, a short green poncho, hooded. The figure in the poncho looked back at a woman, a whore. She said something and he went to her, pulling his hood down to reveal crazy yellow hair. The Englishman. Drop kept to the shadows, tried to hear the exchange, couldn't, and watched as they turned and headed away.

Drop ran down the steps and pushed out the front door. She ran as best she could to the corner, saw them a block ahead and followed at a distance.

She'd nail the Englishman. She'd get money before she handed over the address. She'd get a fix.

Or she'd just kill herself.

11:45 P.M.—Washington Avenue

O'Connor and I showed Gaz Cruikshank's picture around the streets, to shelters and crack hotels and pimps, explaining the change in hair color. No one had seen him. We pulled up in front of a rotting tenement, not far from the offices of the city government. I followed O'Connor in.

"Let me guess," he said. "Thirty-eight special."

My leather jacket was closed to the chill, so he hadn't seen my gun. But he'd guessed it. "Yeah."

"Shithead. Take the safety off."

12:00 A.M.—Valhalla Apartments, Dennis Street, Houston

A dozen parking spots tucked in from the curb in front of the apartment where the bird took Gaz, his bone hard as ever, not softened since the near miss with the filth at the cinema, and surely not since hooking up with this one. Heart still pumping like a drum. The front door opened right up to the parking spaces—a parked car could block someone in. She unlocked it and led him in.

Gaz closed the door and pressed up behind her, grabbing her hips and grinding. She turned her head, corkscrewed her tongue around his and sucked till he groaned. Then she stepped away and dropped her jacket, pulled her top down around her baby fat arms and revealed small round breasts and a roll of smooth belly. Gaz ran his fingers into her blue-green-red hair and pulled her face to his. She pressed her mouth against him, grabbed him twice as hard and held him to her, lips sucking in a vacuum grip.

She slid her hand into his trousers and grabbed hold. It was still sensitive from the cleaning. He wondered if it would be bloody, and if she'd notice. And the turgidity was such that even the threat of imminent release made it worse. She rang it with her hand until his groans softened down to a desperate whimper. Horrible pain, but he'd die if she stopped.

Suddenly she slammed his back against the outer wall and pulled his trousers down, snapping the button. Her mouth was on him as it had been on his tongue, sucking blood to the surface.

"Oh, God!" he cried, punching the wall behind him. "Fuckin' 'ell! Jesus fuck! Aagh! Not so hard." She spun her tongue around him. He arched back, head banging on the wall, then pulled his hips back, thrust, thrust again, and that was that.

Life rushed through him, the torrent of a thousand wasted nights, jolts of heroin, bar fights, and before that, dirty girls from the park, sweet virgins from school, blue movies, stolen jazz mags, every seed spilled since he was a schoolboy, the energy of a thousand wanks, fucks, sucks, the bursting, rushing flood of stinging, burning, agonizing bliss, and she was still on him, he realized though he couldn't open his eyes, palsied on their own, God make it stop, please God, make it stop, but he wasn't quite done, a few more painful jolts then paralysis. "Let go, let go!" he wheezed and she wouldn't. "You're killin' me!" Until he finally slammed her head with the heel of his hand and she fell over on the rug, panting, as he slid down the wall, knees to his chest and whimpered.

When she caught her breath, she lit up a spliff, toked and passed it to him.

12:00 A.M.—Washington Avenue Hotel, Houston

As O'Connor pushed through the unlocked front doors I saw that the inside of the building had been torched. The fire department had showed in time to keep the place upright, but not habitable. It should have been knocked down for safety reasons. I stepped on crumbling wood. Charred support beams held up three floors that might tumble down on top of us with the least provocation. And still people lay around in what was probably once the lobby of a residential hotel, on bedrolls made from blankets, newspapers and cardboard. A few sat up, some slept. The first figure we reached, near what had been the front desk, was a black man of about sixty. I pegged him as potentially dangerous from his eyes and kept a strategic distance. But he was the only one I could see standing up. If anyone here knew anything, it was him.

O'Connor showed him the mug shot. He shook his head.

"Hair short and blond."

"Nope."

"How about a girl, skinny white junkie in a hooded sweatshirt, big fever blister on her lip."

"Not here."

"Put your hands on the counter," O'Connor said.

"O'Connor," I said.

O'Connor faced me. "Problem?!"

I surrendered, hands up and looking away, do what you want.

The old man said, "Man, what do you want here? Ain't nobody got nothing for you. Look around."

I said, "He's right, man. It's just a squat."

"Hands on the counter."

"Aw, man!" the older man said, but he turned around and planted his hands. O'Connor frisked him head to toe, then checked his pockets, then picked something off the ground.

"What do we have here?" It was an empty crack vial.

"Man, that ain't mine!"

I could see figures rustling in the shadows, but they weren't closing in. Yet.

O'Connor pulled out his handcuffs. "Place your hands behind your back."

I said, "What are you doing?"

"Back me up, Reles!"

"It ain't mine, man," the old man pleaded.

O'Connor had managed to get a cuff on one wrist and was having trouble with the other. He pulled out an item from his pocket, an eight-inch-long baton with his keys dangling from the end. He held it like an ice pick and pounded the end onto the man's skull. The old man cried out and fell.

I grabbed O'Connor by the arms and pulled him away. He spun out of my grip, light in his eyes and half a grin on his mouth, and swung the key end of the minibaton at my eyes. I dodged backward, the keys missing me by an inch, grabbed his other wrist and twisted it behind his back. "Drop it," I said.

O'Connor leaned his head forward, a dumb move telegraphing that he was about to swing it back hard to break my nose. I'd already had two underworld nose jobs and I didn't want a third. I dodged and caught him trying to kick off my kneecap. Dodged that and decided to go on the offensive while I still had his arm. I knocked his legs out from under him. O'Connor landed hard on his side. I heard the floor crack.

The man with one wrist cuffed had disappeared and when I looked back at O'Connor he had rolled onto his back and was pointing an oversized Magnum at my eyes.

12:15 A.M.—Dennis Street, Houston

Drop saw where they went and ran.

No time to find Two-J. She headed up and down streets, stumbling and wheezing, past apartments and crackhouses, past convenience stores. She stopped at a mailbox to dry heave, retched painfully, coughed, spat and stumbled on.

Finally she saw a black cop at a traffic light, ran up, waving her arms, and pounded on the window. He rolled it down.

"I know where that guy is, the Englishman."

"Where?"

"Twenty bucks."

"We don't do that."

She screamed, "Kiss my ass, you cocksucking prick! I sucked half the pricks on your goddamn force! I need twenty dollars and I need a fucking fix. So give me twenty dollars and I'll give you your goddamn Englishman, I'll even suck your prick but *give me twenty dollars!*"

12:15 A.M.—Washington Avenue Hotel, Houston

Most of the police literature on "what to do when someone is training an automatic on your skull while your trusty .38 is safe in its holster" stems around not getting into that situation in the first place. O'Connor was willing to pull a weapon on me. Nothing said he wouldn't use it.

The truth was, I didn't believe he intended to kill me, just that he hated me and wanted me to know it, and that he *wanted* to kill me. He got into that situation on impulse, and couldn't get out of it without losing his dignity. But the part of his mind that wanted the pleasure of shooting me might be stronger at that moment than the part of his mind that knew cops don't get to shoot other cops just for fun and try to pass it off as crossfire. It holds true with any man, especially a man with a gun: between passion and reason, there's no telling which side will win out.

"Don't do it, Jack," I said.

The fire in his eye said that only knocking off a shot or two would give him the satisfaction he needed.

"Beg me," he said. "I wanna see you squirm."

"APD knows I'm in Houston with you."

"Killed on duty."

"Slug from your weapon."

"I'll carve it out."

I realized he'd painted himself into a corner. I was attached to something bigger. Maybe a failed marriage, a typical casualty of police work, along with alcoholism and suicide. Maybe he was in love with Rachel. I'd never know. But now his dignity was at stake. He had to have an excuse not to shoot.

"Emancipation Park," I heard a woman say. We turned to her. She was sitting on a bedroll about twenty feet away.

"What?"

"Emancipation Park. Where the junkies hang out."

I turned to O'Connor. "Why didn't we start there?"

12:30 A.M.—Valhalla Apartments, Dennis Street

Gaz lay back on the rug, sucking the reefer and holding its golden smoke, tingling inside from the pasty back of his throat to the tip of his willy, flapping in the wind, his pants still around his hips, as he listened to the rain. The girl tried to pull his trousers up for him. "Leave 'em," he said. "I'm fine." He gazed at the cracked plaster on the ceiling. Sistine Chapel. God reaches out to Adam, or to Gaz. No Gazzes in the Bible. Why not?

"Wanna do a bump?" she asked. He rolled over and saw her laying out everything on the rug: rig, spoon, lighter, cotton. Baggie of something white.

"No, I'm clean," he said.

"Come on. It'll be fun."

"No, you do it."

"You don't know what this is." She dangled the baggie over his face. "It's Karachi, white heroin from the Middle East. Like a million dollars an ounce."

"What are you doing with it, then?" He watched her childlike face as she spoke.

"I fucked this guy last week," she said. "You know, just like a friend. And he gave me this as a gift. He just called, asked how I liked it. I don't usually do the stuff. I'll do it with you."

"D'you like me?" he asked.

Her eyes nearly crossed as they alighted on him. "I love you," she said. "I love everybody. No one understands that."

He ran a finger across her forehead, down her round face. He was glad to be half naked in front of her, glad to be with her.

"Come on," she said. "It'll be fun."

"No."

"I'll rig you up." She leaned over him.

"I said no."

"You can skin pop it," she said. "Shoot it under the skin, not in a vein. You get off slower but it lasts longer."

"You stupid cow, are you deaf?!" He slapped her face hard. "I said no needles! I'm off the needle for good."

The girl pouted. Lovely round cheeks. Gaz tried to make nice.

"Hey there, love. Don't be sad." He reached for her face and she pulled away, lower lip curled up, a child about to cry.

He gave her one last try. "I'm sorry, love. Look," he asked. "Can we smoke it?"

12:45 A.M.—Interstate 10, Houston

I was driving east alongside I-10 in Houston in the light rain, rolling slow into every red light to keep from hydroplaning. O'Connor rode shotgun.

"The locals hate the cops," he said. "Nothing'll change that."

After I didn't respond, he started up again, barking directions at me, yelling into his hand radio and calling me an asshole every time I stopped, started or turned. The rain picked up force.

Finally the radio squawked, *"Dispatch to 1811."*

"This is O'Connor, go ahead."

"Report of suspect with female companion, stepping into apartment building at 1200 Dennis, corner Live Oak, west end of the block, apartment one Adam on the parking lot, first door on the left, thirty minutes ago."

O'Connor clicked off the radio. "Turn here."

12:45 A.M.—Valhalla Apartments, Dennis Street

In one hand, the girl held a pie tin she'd found. With the other hand, she ran the lighter underneath. Smoke rose from the powder and Gaz sucked it up through a cardboard tube.

He heaved on the rug, just a bit, and settled back.

Thousands of tiny fingers massaged him inside and out. Waves like western mountain ranges rose and fell on his horizon, peace and tranquility starting with him and extending outward in every direction through space and time.

The girl sat by him, idly flopping his prick back and forth. When Gaz noticed her again she'd unsheathed a needle. She was framed in brown clouds, just her image in the dark, like a movie. It was all a movie.

He saw her take his hand and press it on her arm, just above the elbow. "Hold tight," she said. Then with her free hand, she jacked an air bubble into the vein in the crease of her elbow, then dropped the needle in the pie tin and held the spot Gaz had been holding.

"Watch this," she said, and traced the bubble up the inside of her arm with her index finger, almost up to the shoulder. Then she ran it back down and out the hole in her arm with a pop, and looked at him. "You try it."

Gaz leaned back and closed his eyes. Nothing could harm him. The pinch of a needle. It frightened him as a child. Now it didn't mean anything except bliss.

Bring it on, my lovely.

1:00 A.M.—Route 59

The rain was pounding as I rolled down Route 59 with the windshield wipers swishing, lights flashing, me hitting the siren in spine-jolting bursts when anyone got in my way. O'Connor cursed and barked directions, never giving me more than twenty feet's notice before shouting, "Turn! Turn!"

"Which way?"

"Left, God damn it, here! Turn left!"

I squeezed on the brakes and spun into a wild turn, Steve McQueen style, where 59 met Interstate 45 in a tangle of overpasses. I got control of the car again before I hit anything.

"Turn off! Here!"

"I heard you." And I spun right. "Are you *trying* to fuck me up?"

We swerved off the next exit, around dark corners and onto the end of Dennis Street. I could see the lamps of an apartment building far up ahead. "That's it," he yelled. "The last one on the left. Kill the lights." I did as I sped up the dark street. "Not the headlights, you asshole!"

1:15 A.M.—Valhalla Apartments, Dennis Street

Gaz felt the bubble traveling like a chunk of bone, a sharp, ambulatory agony that zoomed up the inside of his arm and traveled through his chest.

He screamed, clutching at his heart. "You've killed me!" But she was gone.

Move, he thought. Get up, get away from the pain. He rolled himself at a wall, kicked it, screamed, finally climbed to his feet, tripped on his trousers, yanked them up best he could, then opened the door and staggered out into the darkness. Someone had to help him.

1:15 A.M.—Dennis Street

Tearing up a strange city street at night in the driving rain with the lights flashing and siren screaming, you still have to watch intersections to make sure you don't get sidelined. You still have to watch for old people crossing the street. The laws of city travel don't go out the window.

But you can forget all that when you're under fire, or desperate, or someone's yelling directions at you, pressing your foot down on the accelerator with his own and calling you a dumb kike.

And that's what happened to me as I tore up the darkened street, headlights off and screeched left into the parking spot in front of apartment 1A as its door opened and a patrol car tore around the north corner doing sixty, didn't see me and crashed into my passenger side near the trunk, spinning my Impala around, a tornado spin where you lose sense of right and left, or even up and down, until the car slammed sideways against the building's outer wall.

AUSTIN

Evan Luecke kept the volume turned up on the answering machine, nights that he was on call. There was a ring, a click, silence, then, *"Dr. Luecke? This is Hal Seltzer, I'm the intern on duty tonight in ICU."*

Evan picked up. "Yes."

"Oh. Sorry. Andrea Wile? She came in Tuesday night?"

A failing of ass-licking interns. Every statement a question. "Yes." The girl had come in with her rich boyfriend. They were in his car doing the horizontal mambo. She passed out and stayed out. His father paid for her room.

"I was in twice, I checked her screens and her levels, she was stable."

"We know you did your job, son. What happened?"

"Well, sir, she seems to be, um . . . dead."

PART TWO

PANOPTICON

FRIDAY

I woke to the sound of rain on the roof and windows. A damp chill permeated the bedroom. We hadn't turned the heat on, and no house I knew in Austin was insulated. Winter hit us each year as a shock and a surprise. I pulled up the blanket and drifted back to a wet day like this, only warmer, when I played with Joey Velez on the department softball team.

The Capital City Blues were not a regular team. We gathered for one sparsely attended practice each year before our two or three games, well-attended grudge matches against DPS or the sheriff's office, calculated more to determine personal valor than more fleeting issues like skill or even physical fitness. Many was the time a bulbous law enforcement official would puff his way into first after being called out, rather than admit defeat and use it as an excuse to save himself some sweat. We had a lot of laughs.

Someone on the Texas Department of Public Safety team had gone to college. He'd read that after the French Revolution, Robespierre set about killing nobles, then the rich, then anyone who opposed him. He called his secret police the Department of Public Safety. So the Texas DPS softball team had T-shirts made up with a guillotine silk-screened on the back.

In a touching but misplaced act of faith, Coach Joey Velez decided that I should pitch. If there was any logic to this, it's that I was tall and in shape, an inspiration to the rest of the players that hard practice and teamwork might make them thinner and taller. Set aside that I could only put one pitch in three into the strike zone. No one knew when that pitch was coming, so for all they knew it could have been strategic. Set aside Joey's wife Rachel in a white cotton dress and sun hat, watching from the bleachers.

We were trailing 4–3 at the end of four innings, the point when the game would count if we'd been a real league, when, in the time it took the APD team to wobble out into the field, a blue norther blew in, storm clouds doming the field and breaking into a warm shower. The umpire, a beer-bloated alderman, stopped the game, and Joey argued. DPS shouted him down, sore loser, until he called their masculinity into question, raising a few salient points about their fondness for women's clothing and their interest in the company of visiting servicemen. Within minutes, the field was awash with fat guys tumbling in the mud, sliding into second base and beyond, sludge dripping from their cheeks as they argued each call. I think we won.

Then I opened my eyes and remembered last night, not so funny.

O'Connor had ordered the reluctant Houston PD tow-truck driver to haul me and my tailless Impala all the way back to Austin, just to get me the fuck out of town. "Set foot in Houston," O'Connor said, "and I won't be responsible."

When the patrol car rammed the right side of my trunk, my Impala spun full circle and thumped the apartment building's outer wall. My head jerked left and hit the window, not hard enough to break the glass. I climbed over a cursing O'Connor and out the passenger door, drew my weapon, took two steps, fell, got up and fell again. The patrol told me to stay where I was.

Gaz Cruikshank had been slammed against the building's front wall, his pelvis crushed in a drumbeat. I sat by dumbly as the patrol hooked a chain into my car's disabled rear axle and pulled it sideways from the wall, releasing what was left of Cruikshank, blue-faced, frothing, holding on. The EMTs laid him out as blood gushed from his nose and mouth and he shuddered and lay still.

✦

I lay in bed listening to Rachel breathe. Nerves pinched my neck and the side of my head pounded where it hit the window. Rachel's lips blew out regular puffs of sweet, thick air.

I'd sat shivering in the APD garage as they tried to figure out what to do with my car, the radio playing Stevie Ray Vaughan in mournful elegy—*"My mind is achin', oh Lord it won't stop . . ."*—a cry of pain and loneliness such that the tune saddened and comforted me at the same time. A patrol dropped me at home around four A.M. and Rachel appeared in the front window. I saw the horrified look on her face as the patrol parked, then the relief as I stepped from the car, un-aided, then screaming rage at me for scaring her, then tears, then hugs, then bed.

The clocked showed 7:30 A.M. and I realized Rachel was in bed late on purpose, also that my neck was having a spasm, an intense twist-ing pain that made amputation seem like a viable option. Rachel opened her eyes and saw me rolling my head around and stretching. She seemed to warm up at the idea of me being infirm, like it might make me more of a homebody.

"Maybe you should call someone," she said, and then, "I'm mak-ing breakfast," and hopped out of bed, silk sliding around her curves as they slalomed out the bedroom door.

I picked up the phone and dialed Torbett.

7:30 A.M.—1205 Walnut Avenue

James Torbett showered and dressed and silently entered the kitchen, avoiding Nan's eyes as she cooked and reaching around for the silver-ware to set the table.

"Morning, Daddy," Jule sang as she bounced into the kitchen, still in red pajamas.

"Morning, baby."

"Don't I get a smile?" she asked. It was a Nan question, and Jule usually got a positive reaction for it. At six, she had already been told by a great aunt that she was cuter when she was four. Since then she never passed up an opportunity for adorable points.

Torbett kissed her in lieu of a smile. It seemed to do the trick.

Guy bounded in, dressed, knapsack shouldered, reached past his mother, grabbed a handful of bacon and pretended to wipe the grease on Jule.

Nan said, "Sit down, we're eating."

"I have practice."

"We're having breakfast as a family."

Guy said, "Since when?"

Jule gasped at Guy's outright insult, his open challenge to his often-absent father's authority. Even Torbett had a flash that someone was going to get hit, not by himself, but by his own father. That was the inevitable result of back talk.

Torbett surveyed Guy, already tall, his own man at fifteen. Torbett and Nan's first blessing. But he wasn't really theirs, not from the first day. Children don't belong to parents. They belong to themselves. It was only a matter of time before Guy stopped even paying lip service to his parents' authority.

"Guy," he said. "Have a seat."

Torbett wasn't really home yet. In his mind it was still last night, when he walked into Brackenridge pediatric and asked to see Rubin Key. An obese white nurse nodded knowingly and led him into the room.

The boy lay peacefully, or so he looked. An EKG recorded a regular heartbeat. IV drip, brain electrodes. His face was baby-fat round, pumpkin round, full of hopes and dreams the way Guy's had been at that age. Torbett couldn't help but see his own son lying there in the bed, halfway to heaven, for the accident of getting in the way of a bullet, everything Torbett had worked to prevent. A random accident, but one that seemed to happen more to black kids than to white ones.

A white-coated physician, nametagged Dr. Blair, tall, fiftyish, glasses, comb-over, entered and stood by Torbett. "Any questions?" he asked, with a studied comforting smile.

"How's he doing?"

"Well, considering. Vital signs normal. Brain function normal. There's no reason to think he won't make a full recovery."

"Why is he in a coma?"

"He has some brain swelling. But don't trouble yourself."

The doctor checked the monitors, made marks on the clipboard at the foot of the boy's bed. Without looking up, the doctor asked, "How is Mrs. Key doing?" but not like he meant it.

"Hard to say."

"We'd be glad to answer any of her questions."

"Excuse me?"

"If she wants to know anything about the boy's condition, we'd be glad to." The doctor nodded as he spoke, a mockery of compassion: "I'm sure she's having a difficult time."

"She hasn't been here?" Torbett demanded.

"Once. The first day. Not since then," he said, now with undisguised hostility, "not even during surgery. This is his second visit, Mr. Key."

"I'm not Mr. Key."

The doctor stood straight. The hostility broke from his face, leaving confusion. "I don't understand."

Torbett walked out, saying, "Neither do I."

At home, Torbett had refused Nan's affection. She'd always read his moods and he was usually in the mood when she was. He was obviously not tired, no more distracted than usual, when she warmed up to him. Torbett worried. Maybe she noticed that he wasn't even affectionate: if he'd warmed up to her without making love, that would have been fine. Maybe he seemed distant, not able to respond to her, even verbally. Maybe she was testing him. And the truth, the reason he had failed the test, was not, as Nan might have expected, that he was sleeping with Virginia Key. The truth was that Virginia Key was all he could think about.

Everyone was settled at the breakfast table when the phone rang and the kids chorused, "It's for Dad!"

7:45 A.M.—706 East Thirty-eighth Street

I told Torbett about my night, the Houston fiasco, the accident, Gaz Cruikshank's death. Torbett had asked around the city council, was pretty sure no council member had it together to put out a hit, and that the stakes weren't that high.

"So we're done?" he asked. "I'd like to be done with this."

I chewed on it. Something felt wrong. "Maybe. Every crime has a willing offender, a viable target—"

"Yeah, yeah, a perceived guardian. Finish this before my kids leave home."

"We have the offender, Cruikshank. Say the target is Key's house, the guardian is Key."

"Sure."

"Only he knew Key by name. And she didn't know him before the incident, not his name, not his photo. So the target was Key."

"Unless he learned her name from papers lying around the house."

"Last thing on his mind."

"Explain the missing cameo."

"I can't. He didn't have it on him when he died. O'Connor promised he'd check Houston pawnshops for it but he was lying."

"So?"

"So Mrs. Key insists no one in the world had anything against her, except some petty rivalries at the city council level."

Torbett inhaled. "So it seems."

"Hear me out. Let's say she's right. Gary Cruikshank was just a junkie who broke into her house looking for something he could sell fast for dope. And maybe he broke into her house randomly, the only black-owned house in a white, white neighborhood, got her name off her phone bill so he could address her politely. And he had a gun with a stop-and-drop bullet in it but he didn't plan on using it."

"Reles—"

"And we don't believe her, we go ahead asking questions and piss-ing people off, and we're wrong and we look like idiots, no story here."

"*Yes?*"

"Or let's say she's wrong. Maybe Virginia Key has pissed off all of the city council and half the state legislature and some of their back-ers, which you do when you're ambitious. They don't like her politics or they see her as a threat to their careers. And somebody finally took up a collection and put a contract out on her. But we file the case, things get quiet and whoever put that Hi-Point in that junkie's hand comes back to finish the job, RIP Virginia Key."

Long silence. Then he said, *"I'll call you later."*

8:20 A.M.—1100 Guadalupe Street

Virginia Key's cleaning woman told Torbett that Mrs. Key had gone to her office, she couldn't put it off any longer, and gave him the address. He drove there, parked in the county courthouse lot, rode up an an-cient elevator in his raincoat to a modern hallway and found the door, VIRGINIA KEY PC, propped open. In Key's waiting room, a short, chunky white woman dodged men with lights, cameras and a boom mike, all jamming the inner office doorway. Torbett caught the ex-change on a pair of monitors, one showing each speaker.

"Mrs. Key," a dark-haired, female newscaster asked, "you've lost your daughter, your son lies in a coma fighting for his life . . ."

Mrs. Key swallowed hard at that.

". . . And yet here you are back in your office two days after this horrible attack."

"This is a very important time," Mrs. Key said. "Young people, men and women, are going bravely off to protect us in the Middle East—"

The light man whispered to the boom man, "And the city council's up for reelection."

Anchorwoman Lyda Collins turned to the crew. "Can we not have so much chatter in the background."

Mrs. Key said, into the camera, "Bonnie, make sure the outer door is closed."

"Yes, ma'am." The chunky little secretary noticed Torbett, submitted when she saw his badge and closed the outer door.

Collins said to Mrs. Key, "Just take it from 'protect us in the Middle East'."

"Our work here is too important to stop because of my personal tragedy."

"And your daughter?"

"My daughter was a brave soldier." She seemed to choke back a cry. "She would have wanted me to go on."

"Monday is, of course, Martin Luther King Day."

She spoke softly, with reverence. "It heartens me to know that the city will be coming together to celebrate the spirit of Dr. King."

"Do you feel that it's important not to miss the King Day celebration for you in particular, because of your rumored run for the city coun—"

"I think it's important to remember, as Dr. King said, that people should be judged not by the color of their skin, but by the content of their character."

Torbett felt his stomach twist. He stepped back to maintain balance and leaned on the secretary's desk. The mail had been opened, unfolded, envelopes stapled to the back of each document. They lay in a sloppy pile. Payments, letters, phone bill, and—he moved the pile with his fingertip—a bank statement.

Collins dropped the idea and instead said, "Mrs. Key, I think you are the bravest woman in Texas." They leaned forward and held each other's hands. Collins turned to the camera. "This is Lyda Collins. Back to you, Jim."

Torbett thought the bank statement looked odd, the style of printing, the layout. On closer look it bore the letterhead Magna Vista Asset Management Ltd—no period after the abbreviation—PO Box 3307, Road Town, Tortola, BVI. BVI?

The cameraman said, "Got it. We okay on sound?"

"All set."

Torbett clutched the statement as they shifted out of the doorway and stuffed it into his raincoat pocket.

They loaded up, coiled power cords and hauled their equipment out of the office. Mrs. Key followed Collins out of the inner office, chatting politely and shaking hands. When she saw Torbett she lit up a sad smile, a child after a ballet recital, as if asking, Did you see it? Was I good?

8:30 A.M.—706 East Thirty-eighth Street

I stood in the kitchen archway watching the choreographed movements of Rachel wrapped in my plaid flannel robe, making French toast. For some cooks, the act of preparing food has a dynamic of frenzy: every component has to be ready at the exact same moment as two others, so the best-planned culinary acts are marked by a constant game of catch-up. But with Rachel, the meal preparation looked like a synchronized performance, each phase unfolding in perfect rhythm: the eggs soaked the bread just in time for the butter to get hot, just hot enough, as the coffee percolated and the bacon sizzled. She moved them in a gliding motion to the table, in a predetermined order as if they'd been waiting for her cue.

The truth is, none of it was very good. The coffee could be strong and watery at the same time. The bread was cold and hard in spots. And while the bacon might be perfectly crisp on one side, even charred, raw spots brought the fear of trichinosis. I didn't know if anyone actually taught her to cook or if she'd just seen it done, but she'd been reared with other skills. The artistry of Rachel's cooking was the beauty of the preparation, the dance. And like Rachel, it always looked perfect. What caught me by the heart was that Rachel, ex-party girl turned high-powered real estate broker, would do this for me. Not daily, of course. Not even regularly. But that she would go to the trouble to make a meal for me, when it was so unnatural to her. And that she did it with the skills she had, mostly logistical and visual: she could do something complex and look great doing it.

I sugared down the coffee and syruped up the French toast, waited till she was sitting across from me so she could see in my face how grateful I was, how much I appreciated her efforts, even before I sampled them. So she could see how everything between us would work out. We were just digging in when the wall phone rang.

I reached for it. "Yeah?"

"Dan, it's Ron Wachowski. I'm at Fiesta Gardens. You might want to come down here."

8:45 A.M.—Brackenridge Hospital, Pediatric ICU

A nurse told Dr. Blair about the call and he took it where he stood in Trip Porter's room, watching the beeps on the comatose young man's EKG. "Blair."

"Dr. Blair, this is Evan Luecke over at Seton Northwest. We had a girl come in Tuesday night, nausea and tremors and then a coma. Seen anything like that lately?"

"I'm looking at it right now."

"Caucasian? UT student? Comes from money?"

Blair shifted on his feet. "What's going on?"

"I've been calling around town. I count six of these, all in comas, so they can't tell us if they know each other. I'll venture they do. No drugs, no testable illnesses. And one just died."

Blair wheezed. "Ideas?"

"Try sexually transmitted. We tested them for everything—"

Blair said, "So did I."

"—but then, when AIDS first appeared, we didn't have a test for that."

"Something new?"

"Christ, I hope not. The university police are talking to the families, trying to figure out when the students were together. Maybe they were exposed to something. The families are very clear that their children aren't homosexuals or drug addicts. And they want everyone to know that."

"Have you called the Center for Disease Control?"

"I'm waiting for the first girl's autopsy report. She just went off to the medical examiner. I'll keep you posted. One more thing. The parents asked that we keep the whole thing very quiet."

"Keep it quiet?" Blair asked. "Are you fucking kidding me?"

9:00 A.M.—706 East Thirty-eighth Street

Rachel Renier, formerly Velez, formerly Renier, sat at the table and smoked. Rain drummed the window.

She'd woken suddenly in the middle of the night when the patrol car pulled up in front of the house, as suddenly as if it had plowed through the wall. Instinct of a cop's wife. But she wasn't a cop's wife. She had to remind herself of that.

She ran to the window and saw the patrol get out of the car, and her heart dropped. Then Dan, alive. A fraction of a second of relief, and then fury. He did it again. How could he keep doing that, making her think he'd died? She'd grabbed him, wanted to clutch him till they both gasped for air. But all she could feel was hurt.

They lay on the bed, miles apart.

Not easy for a girl like her, she thought. Not easy for a disco girl, a party girl, who went through her youth making sure never to think ten minutes ahead, or a minute behind. Not easy for her to live in a house with just one man, the same one, and let him see her in the daylight. And worry if he'll even come home. She played domestic when she could. Today she was even making French toast, special breakfast for his long night and his injury. An "all is forgiven" breakfast. You went out hunting, killed the bad guy, came home wounded. Fine. Let's eat and take a long weekend.

She watched the digits on the clock tick to 9:10. Officially ten minutes late. First time ever. Unofficially, an hour or two past her typical show-up time. She was entitled. One more cigarette, then she'd shower. For sure. She just couldn't move.

He took a phone call during breakfast, hung up and sat back down. After they cleaned up she was ready to take him to the doctor when he said he was going to HQ, would she drop him off?

The bad guy's dead, she'd told him. You're hurt. Let's start the long weekend. You can follow up on Tuesday.

I have to go, he'd said. Would you please drive me.

Finally, she told him to call a cab. And she sat alone in the kitchen.

He didn't know what she went through. What it was like to play a tough career woman all day, to be so brash and forceful that people thought you knew what you were doing. To hold back old hurt and new hurt, old terrors and new fears, without ever taking a drink. Day after day, year after year after year.

Suddenly all his jumping up and leaving at the ring of the phone was making her crazy, terrified, neurotic. She didn't know if she could live with a cop anymore. Especially one who she loved.

9:30 A.M.—Fiesta Gardens

The taxi weaved among the narrow paved strips through the greenery that flanked the river called Town Lake, separating Austin central and south, and dropped me by the inlet at Fiesta Gardens. I followed the trail: DPS van, DPS patrol car, traffic cones, footprints, Wachowski and two assistants in galoshes. Mud on my black cop-Oxfords.

Wachowski greeted me with a toothy smile. "Guess why the crime scene hasn't been destroyed."

I guessed, "The scientists got here first."

He led me to a spot in the reeds. "Gentleman out for a six A.M. stroll noticed this among the reeds." He showed me a basin with a foot of lead pipe, bloody at one threaded end. "Note that both ends are threaded. My guess is we'll have trouble finding prints. Partials, maybe. And we should be able to match the blood if you find a victim."

"No victim?"

He looked around, palms up. "Do you see one?"

A mist floated over the tiny lagoon, powered by a gentle gust from the river beyond it. I looked into the lagoon.

"If I killed someone here," Wachowski said, "I'd probably toss him into that water."

I followed his gaze over the tiny inlet out to the cool expanse of the river.

"So we put out two boats and dragged the area," he said, "and we didn't find a body. But you'll never guess what we did find." A tech handed him what looked like a plastic tool box. He opened it. Inside was a Hi-Point 9 millimeter Model C. "Is this it?" I asked.

"We'll get what we can get from it, then forward it to Mr. Wong. He can verify for you."

Odds said we had the right gun, the one Gaz Cruikshank used on Jenny and Rubin Key.

"So," Wachowski said. "I guess your work is done."

9:30 A.M.—5 Nob Hill Circle

Martin Bass and his core office staff were operating out of his home, the best way to keep normal business operations going and still maintain some level of privacy around the abnormal. Four phones operated, faxes rolled in and out. He kept his focus above the din. Messages shouted to him. Oil prices up. Stocks down. Readjust. He stepped out into the hall to call his lawyers, closing the door behind him, and saw his son Glen standing in the front hallway looking guilty and weak.

"What are you doing here? You should be at school."

Glen's face half crumpled, on its way to tears. "She's dead."

"What?"

"Andrea's dead. What am I gonna do?"

Martin's brain spun. He'd paid for the girl's private room and the best care. He could offer to pay for the funeral, but that might look like admitting responsibility. Who would believe Glen could kill someone with his prick? But still, word would get out.

Martin closed in on his son, grabbing the boy by the collar of his jacket. "Straighten up! Be a man! There are worse things than this."

Glen looked doubtful.

Martin went on. "Did you rape her?"

"No!"

"You're sure? They can prove force."

"She said yes."

"Was she on drugs?"

"No. Jesus!"

"Then it's not your responsibility." The boy looked like he hadn't slept. "Go upstairs. Shower. Put on some clean clothes. Go back to school. Act sad, but not guilty." He slapped Glen's shoulder. The boy nearly fell over. "For God's sake, don't act guilty!"

"Yes, sir."

"Now go."

Martin turned and headed back to the den. But something, the absence of movement behind him, made him stop and look back at Glen.

The boy had begun to tremble, visibly from down the hall. And just before he hit the floor he cried out, "Dad?"

10:00 A.M.—Medical Examiner's Office

I watched Margaret Hay twist the stripped remains of Gaz Cruikshank, and shout details to an assistant who dutifully recorded them on a clipboard. "Pinpoint pupils. Fresh needle mark, left arm." I stood guiltily at a distance. O'Connor had shipped the body up in the middle of the night. It arrived at Hay's office with a delivery bill. He was our corpse and O'Connor, who'd suffered a concussion in the car accident, wanted him out of Houston. I'd caused enough trouble. My own head throbbed and my neck spasmed.

"Floating ribs cracked. Pelvis crushed. Feet badly decayed, fungal. Missing flesh. He tried to clean them. Abscess left armpit. Likely from needle use."

Once she stripped his skin and spread his ribs, she got a look at his lungs. "Tuberculosis, all right."

She did the usual cutting and weighing, drew some fluids, then bagged his giblets again and tossed them back into his chest cavity. She peeled off her gloves, washed up, handed me a breathing filter, and made notes on a clipboard as one assistant wheeled out Gaz while the other wheeled in the next contestant.

You think you get used to things, getting jumped, seeing murder victims, naked dead bodies rolling in and out of the cutting room. Then one catches you off guard and you find yourself speechless, dumb, stumped.

The gurney bore a young woman, maybe twenty, slender, shapely, with alabaster skin and yellow-white hair. An angel.

"You want me to introduce you?" Hay said, yanking me out of my reverie.

"Who is she?"

"College girl. Nausea, shakes, coma, death. We don't think it's contagious, but wash up after you leave anyway."

I turned away from the girl, turned my thoughts back to Gaz. "Any way to tell what killed him? Whether it was the drugs or the car?"

She raised her shoulders slow, like she was stretching her old spine. "He was crushed," she said.

"He was frothing when he died. Blood but also foam. I thought maybe drugs. Maybe he was OD'ing or something." She didn't answer. "Never mind." I made for the door.

"Reles," she said.

I stopped. She tapped the girl's head with the handle end of her scalpel.

"First rule of forensic medicine," she said. "Dead is dead."

10:30 A.M.—Medical Examiner's Office

Margaret Hay, ME, pulled on fresh gloves and looked over the girl's file. Andrea Wile. DOB 1/13/71. DOD 1/18/91. Hospital reports. Negatives for narcotics, HIV, hepatitis, syphilis et al.

Nausea, tremors, coma, death.

Word from Seton Northwest: doctor stumped. Six other patients with same symptoms.

Six.

She looked over hospital reports from each, looked for similarities, differences, gaps.

Hay took a scalpel and sliced from one shoulder diagonally down to the sternum, then the other, then a vertical line down to the pubis. She peeled the flaps back.

Guessing time. Carbon monoxide? Negative. Would have turned the victim's blood and tissues cherry red. Ditto for cyanide.

Strychnine? Wouldn't have produced tremors but violent convulsions, almost immediate rigor mortis after death, body frozen in a convulsed position. Eyes wide as if in agony and terror.

She took out the liver, spleen, adrenals. Stomach and pancreas. A thought.

Heavy metals? Gastrointestinal complaints, vomiting. Tremors? Sure. Coma. Eventually.

After she washed up, Hay picked up the phone and dialed.

"Toxicology."

"This is Margaret Hay. I'm sending over some fluids from an Andrea Wile."

"Yes, ma'am."

"Test them for metals. Arsenic, copper, mercury."

"Will do."

"And listen. Half a dozen people around town seem to have the same ailment. So if you could hurry that through."

Hay hung up and dialed Dr. Luecke at Seton. He should test them for metals, on the odd chance they were poisoned. Maybe he could treat them in time. Metal poisoning is so unusual that people don't even think to test for it. How would they have been exposed? From a bad meal? A science lab?

And how long would it take them to find out?

10:30 A.M.—HQ

When Torbett got to the squad room, Greer was working on a cold case, with help from the kid, Czerniak. Absent: Jake Lund. He'd probably ducked out for a shower. Television on, now a constant companion to their daily work, though the volume was often down, to be turned up for news shows. Other offices had a monitor for every channel.

Mrs. Key was in a manic phase, he was sure, gabbing about business, the thing she was good at. He tried to warn her about the danger to herself, still. She turned it around, telling him he worried too much. It wasn't that she had no sense at all, or that she wasn't crestfallen about her kids. It was that she was shell-shocked. That's why she hadn't been to the hospital. And she was alone, except for Torbett. He hadn't seen one friend at the house, not one.

Torbett recognized a face on the TV screen—a tall distinguished man with white hair—alongside a photo of Gaz Cruikshank, and turned up the volume.

"We're here with university president Bill Oliver, now chair of the non-profit Austin Area Reclamation Organization . . ."

Bill Oliver, Torbett remembered, had been a sneeze away from the governor's office when he dropped out of the race inexplicably, leaving it to be slugged out between a law-and-order cracker in a ten-gallon hat, and a dubious liberal, a woman with no real commitment beyond getting elected. The cowboy had refused to shake the lady's hand after a debate, acknowledged his trysts with prostitutes, made a lighthearted joke about rape, and as pundits put it, generally knocked himself out before she got her gloves on.

The newsman was, for some reason, asking Oliver about Cruik-shank. The death report had been released, a necessary follow-up to the release of Cruikshank's photo.

"I've spoken with the board at AARO," he pronounced it *"arrow." "And we're horribly dismayed that a man like this was even allowed to enter the country. In one act of cruel, racist violence, Gary Cruikshank risked setting back the accomplishments of the last hundred years."*

Across the bottom of the screen: "DOW RISES 115 POINTS . . . IRAQI MISSILES HIT ISRAEL . . . PRESIDENT TELLS COUNTRY TO PREPARE FOR LONG WAR AND MANY CASUALTIES . . ."

"And yet AARO supports sending jobs overseas. Are you endorsing—"

"We're under a nonprofit 510-C3. We don't endorse candidates. What AARO does is to provide ways that private leaders can assist Austin's city government in the problems it faces . . ."

A marriage of government and private industry. Texas politics.

The camera showed a photo of key AARO members, Oliver along with powerful-looking white men, bankers and politicians. A few younger men, brash and full of potential. And a few women, including the governor. And one face that was black. Virginia Key.

Torbett grabbed his coat and headed out in the rain, found his car, drove in and out of the remnants of morning traffic and badged into the capitol lot, parked, then ran up and down the steps, down the long hall to the far end and the inconspicuous doorway of Representative Terrence Ludwig, D-Austin.

Ludwig looked up from his notes to see Torbett dripping rain in his doorway. The congressman didn't seem surprised to see him.

10:45 A.M.—APD Auto Shop

At the sharpest mountain curve of 2222, just before the house on the bluff, is a row of yardstick crosses painted white, marking the final leap of each soul who took the curve too fast. One of those souls belonged to Joey Velez.

Joey's chariot to the stars was his beloved broad white 1975 Chevy Caprice with red vinyl seats and a three-on-the-tree gearshift. I'd often driven with him in the car as he mentored me onto Homicide and after. After he died, my sleep was broken many times with nightmares of me taking that final ride with him.

I waited in the APD body shop for the prognosis on my Impala ("Not good"), and the limping head mechanic asked someone which of the loaners was in shape for active use: The Green Monster? No brakes. Uncle Ike? Busted radiator. Elvis? Yeah, Elvis is ready.

A chill moved through me as they drove Elvis up, given the name because there had been an Elvis sighting in it, and handed me the keys. Elvis was a 1975 white Chevy Caprice, identical to Joey's down to the three-on-the-tree gearshift and the red vinyl seats.

The concrete floor seemed to dip and I lost my balance, a certain side effect of last night's accident.

I signed the papers and drove out into the rain.

11:00 A.M.—Texas Capitol Building

"College isn't for everybody. Trade school is perfectly respectable, maybe the best possible avenue for some African American . . ."

Torbett and Terrence Ludwig stood in the dusty, windowless equipment-rental room, watching the tape on a monitor on a rolling table.

Torbett said, "She could be right."

"Mm-hmm," Ludwig said and fast-forwarded. "Here it is."

"... is this: equal opportunity laws have been a hindrance to black progress and they always will be." Ludwig froze the frame on Key, mouth half open, eyes sliding to her right.

"Ever study rhetoric?" Ludwig asked.

"No, sir."

"I can let you stay and watch the whole tape. Look at the structure of the seduction."

"Seduction?"

"First she lays out issues of college, practical issues. Then she says college isn't for everybody. But she leaves out that the opportunity to go to college should be for everybody. What she's saying is that because college isn't for everybody, not everyone needs the option of college."

"She didn't say that."

"Mm-hmm. Then while you're debating the pros and cons, the arguability of her arguments, she's got you, you're engaged. And she's turning up the heat. By the time she's up to 'equal opportunity is bad for black people'—black is white, night is day—you're already willing to give her the benefit of the doubt. In a way she presented something debatable as fact, then presented something insane as debatable. That's how we move the center to the right. When she engaged you in dialogue, when she got you to reconsider what you already know to be true, that's when the seed took root."

"You don't believe—"

"That a foxy little number with a mousey voice could be so smart? I watched you watch that tape, boy. Little Ginny Key, all hot and defenseless. 'She needs me to take care of her.' You think she doesn't know that?"

Torbett tried to breathe deeply. "You don't share her politics. And maybe I don't."

"I think the question you want to be asking yourself is, does she believe them herself? Or is she just in it for her career?"

Ludwig went on. "I know someone in the state lege who's a psychologist. You can look up who it is. She suspects Mrs. Key is suffering from narcissistic personality disorder, which is what it sounds like. Not just that you're in love with yourself, but that you don't quite believe other people count. You can't imagine that other people have feelings or needs. You have no guilt because you don't feel obligated by your part of any agreement. And the disorder is difficult to treat, my colleague says, because you're perfectly happy the way you are. As long as you get what you want."

Torbett was trying not to yell, wondering why he was so angry he had to hold it back. "Suppose you're right. And suppose you've warned me, raised my suspicions?"

"A narcissist is a good con artist: she loves a suspicious mark. There's always some element of doubt. It's her job to get you to put that doubt aside, to listen to some other voice inside you. Greed, or ambition." Torbett considered these, until Ludwig added, "Or desire?"

Torbett noticed the silence. He'd been holding his breath.

Ludwig popped out the video. "Joining us for the march tomorrow?"

11:45 A.M.—Seton Northwest Hospital

Martin Bass left his wife at home, nursing herself through her son Glen's unexplained illness with a box of tissues and a bottle of Remy, and drove himself and Glen to the hospital. Glen was rushed through emergency, x-rayed and blood-tested. Now he was lying in an examination room, waiting. Martin stepped out to call the office, to estimate how many thousands his missed two hours of work had cost him. As he headed back toward the room, Martin saw Glen's doctor, Dr. Luecke, a squat, silver-haired Dutchman with glasses and no chin, sitting on a white bench in the hall, leaning his head against the wall and staring. Martin realized he'd never before seen a doctor in a state of rest.

"Doctor?" he asked. "Is something wrong?"

Luecke broke out of his dream, saw Martin and smiled with a bit of fatigue, then patted the bench next to him.

"We're testing your son's blood," Luecke said. "Along with everyone else's. The catch is that we don't know what to test for, so we have to run each possible test. Now, for example, we're testing for heavy metals—arsenic, lead. But anything would be dissipated in his blood. And we're only guessing because we don't know what he might have been exposed to, or how."

"Neither do I."

"Well," Luecke said, staring at the opposite wall again, "somebody's hiding something."

Martin sat silently. A quack earning a measly eighty thousand a year was accusing his son of something, God knew what. Luecke finally said, without looking at him, "Ever been in the service? Vietnam, that would have been your era."

"My number never came up."

The doctor looked Martin up and down, smiled and looked away. Child of the rich.

"I was in Korea," Luecke said, without pride. "What I remember most is people dying around me. One day it would be one person. Then no one for days, or weeks. Then five at once, then nobody. Very unpredictable."

"I see," Martin said.

"No you don't. You should have been here when AIDS first hit. People would get sick, cancers, diseases no one had seen for centuries, illnesses only cats and birds normally get. And the numbers grew, exponentially. One, then six, then thirty, then a hundred."

Martin felt himself growing angry. He kept quiet.

Luecke went on. "We poked and prodded them. We drew blood and ran tests. Walked around in masks and space suits. Some hospitals turned them away. They died in the streets. We had no funding. And bit by bit we learned. But by then there were too many."

Finally Martin burst out, "Why are you telling me this?!"

Luecke glanced back at him, not as if Martin had yelled, but as if Luecke had just noticed him. "Just making conversation."

Martin stood, cursed and stormed into the examination room. Glen jolted at the sight of him. "Tell me how you feel," Martin said.

Glen seemed to have lost weight in the two hours he'd been at the hospital. His skin was pale, he clutched a pan of vomit on a shelf by his bed and he looked frightened.

Martin closed the door and walked to the bed.

"You'll be fine!" he insisted. Glen jolted at the words, nodded, but didn't seem reassured. "Look," Martin said, "if this goes public, it'll kill your mother." Glen nodded. Suddenly the boy's weakness seemed, to Martin, like someone politely agreeing to die.

Martin went on. "But . . . I know everyone. I can call someone who can call the surgeon general. That's two phone calls away from a state of emergency. You're not some poor faggot lying in the street. You're the son of Martin Bass." He leaned closer, more threatening, he knew, than comforting. "We don't have any time. I'll make that call today." He leaned close enough to whisper, instead hissing his words emphatically. "But god damn it, you better be telling me everything!"

12:00 P.M.—East Seventh Street

I scanned Gaz Cruikshank's rap sheet.

Figuring out a suspect's actions from his standard modus operandi is like trying to find a killer from his profile. The information you have might be very helpful. Or misleading. Or incomplete. Or just wrong.

People who knew Gaz said he was a junkie. All he cared about was getting high. He was fine unless he needed dope. Then he was crazy. Before dope, his aunt said, he was getting into fights all the time. So he was violent by temperament.

Maybe he just needed a fix when he broke into Virginia Key's house and shot her kids. Or maybe she pissed him off.

A few phone calls got me that Brewer Mackay, Gaz's possible drug connection listed on the rap sheet, was paroled and free. I found him at his home off East Seventh, terrorizing his girlfriend: from outside I could hear her screaming and him yelling, "Bitch!" My pounding at the door interrupted them. He yanked the door open, shouting, "What?" and saw my badge. His girlfriend, sporting a rising black eye, stopped crying suddenly. She was a slight young woman, maybe twenty, wispy brown hair, sleepy eyes. She could strip at a club that played to pedophiles dodging prosecution. They both stood frozen, impressed with the police department's efficiency in responding to a domestic disturbance call no one had made.

"Brewer Mackay?" I asked as I pocketed the badge and walked in. He nodded. "Miss, do you need assistance?" She shook her head. No, it's always like this. I said, "Why don't you go clean yourself up."

She disappeared.

I swung a left backhand at him just to keep his hands busy. My left isn't worth much anymore. When he blocked it, I pounded his ribs with my right, maybe a hairline fracture's worth. He wheezed and hit the wall. I cornered him, cocked my right fist and held it high. He covered his face.

"Take your hands down," I said. "Take your hands down."

"But . . ."

"Just do it."

He lowered his hand. I jabbed his left eye. He grabbed it and cried out.

"Take your hands down."

"Why?" he whimpered.

"Because I said so." He lowered his hands slowly. I clocked the same eye again. He cried out in pain and frustration.

In spite of spending most of my life in Texas (words like "y'all" and "fixin'" were solidly a part of my vocabulary—words with no northern equivalent), I still had a New York accent I kept on a thread of a leash. I couldn't make it disappear but I could let it loose, drop the final r's, twist the vowels. On occasion, I'd offset that by speaking from the top of my vocabulary, my high speech contrasting my working-class diction. The upshot could be very disorienting, an articulate goon.

I said, "See, dat's what it means to use disproportional force. Why did you take your hand down?"

"Y-you told me to."

"You knew I would hit you. Why did you do it?"

"You're a cop."

"So my authority as a cop was significant enough to get you to lower your guard, even against your own better interests."

Long pause. Nod.

"So," I said, "having already assured your cooperation, I then punched you in the eye. Twice. Totally unnecessary." He nodded. I let the accent alone. "That's what you did to your girlfriend. Understand?" He nodded. "Good." He lowered his hands. I jabbed him in the nose. He went down, bleeding into his hands. Then I got close to him. "Don't hit that nice girl again."

I walked around the room, mobster style. He wiped his bloody nose with a sleeve.

I said, "House smells of grass."

"It's my girlfriend's. I'm clean."

"That makes her a criminal. You know you're not supposed to associate with criminals. Condition of parole."

Finally he said, "What? I don't get it."

"Gary Cruikshank. Gaz."

Long silence, then he said, "Who?"

"Long pause for you to remember you don't know him. You deal to him."

"I don't deal anymore. I'm clean."

"You told the court you didn't deal at all." No answer. I didn't really know that he'd pled innocent, but it was a safe guess. "Good, I'm glad you're an ex-not-dealer. I know you dealt to Gaz. Here's the thing. Gaz killed a kid. By accident. He was out to kill a woman named Virginia Key. That's what I say. Other people say he was robbing her house, he was a junkie, it was an accident."

"He *was* a junkie."

"How do you know?" No answer. "So he comes in with a badass automatic. Not some zip gun he bought in a pawn shop. And he knows her name. I say he was out to kill her. And I want to know why."

He was sitting up now, cowering like a battered bride. "How would I know?"

I shrugged it off. "Probably you don't. Thing is, not a lot of people are tied to Gaz on paper. And I caught you committing a felony."

Nothing. "I need to know who might have put a killing tool in that loser's hand. Who's important that might know Gaz."

"The fuck would I know?" He climbed to his feet. "I ain't seen him in months."

"You let a client go to another dealer? Who?"

Dead silence. Bingo.

"You're under arrest for aggravated assault. Sorry about the bruises, but you put up a fight. And you're about to put up a worse one."

He guarded his face. "No, wait!" he said.

I waited.

12:00 P.M.—HQ

Torbett was on the line with the Texas Bar Association, tracking connections.

Virginia Ann Key, née Albertson. Graduated Tulane Law, third in class, public defender, then private practice, criminal defense. Never represented Gary Cruikshank.

"Who did?"

Another long wait. Torbett reached into his jacket pocket and took out the crumpled document he'd taken, a bank statement. Magna Vista Asset Management Ltd, PO Box 3307, Road Town, Tortola, BVI. Account for Westpark Ltd, Virginia Key executor. Jake Lund was tapping on the computer.

"Lund," Torbett said. "What's BVI?"

"What do you mean?"

"In an address. BVI." Still nothing. "A bank statement."

Lund's head leaned back, lightbulb. "Right, BVI, British Virgin Islands. Offshore banking."

"Come again?"

"Tax free, get it? In case you get paid in cash."

The deposits were hefty, some of them. Ten thousand, fifty thousand, and in one case, a hundred thousand.

The man at the Texas Bar came back on the line. *"Two men represented Cruikshank. Alan Anderton and Leo Park. They share an office on*

*East Sixth by the bail bondsmen and the day laborers. One or the other cov-
ered all his Austin court scenes."*

"Any connection between them and Key?"

"Not that I can see. You wanna hear complaints?"

"Complaints?"

*"Standard stuff. Overcharging usually. Yeah, here, overcharged for hours
rendered, something about withholding services from a client in jail."*

Torbett asked, "Anderton and Park?"

*"No, Key. Looks like this one client was in jail, he owed her money, she
wouldn't continue representing him until he paid up. Standard. But he says
she had paperwork of his, old testimonies and transcripts he'd already paid
for, and she wouldn't release those either until he paid up. Nothing big."*

Nothing big, Torbett thought. Except that she swore she'd never
held liberty over a client. Swore it like life and death.

12:15 P.M.—Seton Northwest Hospital

Dr. Luecke was seated at his desk when he heard a tentative knock at
the door. "Come in," he said.

The door opened and Martin Bass stepped in, suddenly smaller,
mumbling, apologetic.

"Yes?" Luecke asked.

"You, you talked about, what Glen was exposed to. And how."

"Yes."

"His girlf—the girl. He said it was her idea."

"I don't understand."

Bass said something but Luecke couldn't make it out.

"I'm sorry, Mr. Bass, I didn't catch that."

Bass was mumbling, pulling on his eyebrow, hiding his face. Finally he choked it out.

"Heroin."

Luecke nodded. Bass added, "White. White heroin."

"White heroin?"

"That's what he said. Promise me you won't let this get out."

Luecke rose and gave Bass a reassuring hand on the shoulder. "Go home," he said. He led Bass out to the hall and closed the door. He thought about the victim's parents and their desire for secrecy. And he thought about what it would cost. Then he sat at his desk, pulled out a list of phone numbers and dialed. They answered on the third ring.

"APD."

"Can you tell me," Luecke asked, "who's in charge of Narcotics?"

12:30 P.M.—700 Tillery Street

On the far reaches of East Seventh Street, past the slave market and the interstate, past the black college and the H-E-B supermarket and the storefront churches and liquor stores and hair salons and white-owned gun shops, on a side street in a once-hopeful neighborhood, sat a tiny strip mall, bricks painted over in what must have been a dozen cheerful colors hoping to bring in local trade, finishing off in a dull green that probably looked good in the paint store. The windows were boarded from the inside, darkened glass panels all cracked or broken. A monument to sadness and a reminder of despair. The fog and drizzle added to the misery.

Mackay had slid down in my passenger seat. "Keep driving, that's it," he said.

I passed the corner of Lyons Road and took the second right on Neal, looping around.

"Came in a few months ago, but they fuckin' *swept*. Put the local dealers out of the neighborhood. All the junkies go there, shoot there. No one holds."

"How do you get in?"

"I got close to it one day and they shot at me!" He sniffed. Blood was still running from his nose. His left eye had swollen in a permanent wink. "Some kids hanging out in back like they just got out of school. Maybe a secret passageway or something. I guess they check the junkies out before they let 'em in."

"Okay, get out." I pulled over.

"No, man, someone'll see me!"

"Just tell them you were helping a cop."

"Fuck. Fuck fuck fuck." He opened the door, rolled out low, closed it without a sound and ran. I made a right on Cherico, another right on Lyons and parked where I could see the back of the strip mall between two houses, the whiteness of my Caprice mocking the notion of a stakeout.

A green Crown Victoria was parked a house ahead of me. I thought it was empty, and then I saw movement, maybe two people making out. I zipped up my jacket and walked over. I could make out one big figure in a dark blue raincoat and baseball cap, lounging, maybe propped up on his elbow. I approached the window and he was up, pointing an automatic at me through the driver's window and looking scared. He shouted behind the glass. "Reles?"

I answered. "Milsap?"

12:45 P.M.—South Lamar Boulevard

Mo sat in the front passenger seat of his Cadillac as his driver kept the vehicle moving on the wet roads. No tint on the windows, too suspicious. No driving in back like the president, ditto.

Anything had not called, and Mo was not sleeping. Harder each day to sit still. Why had she not called? Surely she would have called if she had not found Gaz. Just as surely she would have called if she had finished him. Something went wrong.

"Anything" was not her name. It was her vocation. Anything for a price. Absolutely anything. To Mo, that meant finding a man and liberating the air from his lungs. The police might just pay her to talk.

She could be in the Houston lockup right now, talking.

Mo needed Gaz dead and publicly scapegoated, before he could get another shot at Virginia Key, before he could even get near her. Key would pay for what she did to him, to his sister.

His mobile phone rang.

"Yes."

"It's me."

Philo, Mo's own Jew. Crass, loud, hairy, and disposable.

"Speak quickly and efficiently."

"A little bird told me a few things."

Philo was known for having friends among the police. "A bird of the blue persuasion?"

"Huh? Oh, yeah. Your English friend passed away in an unfortunate accident."

Mo leaned back. She was to be paid at the motel at 3:30 the day after she finished the job. But she was supposed to tell him it was finished. Mo said, "Meet her at our meeting place at 3:30."

"Her? You mean what's-her-name?"

"Yes."

"All right!"

"Bring five thousand."

"Sure. Um . . ."

"What is it?"

"Will I get it back? Not that you need to. I just mean, am I laying it out, or . . . Forget it. No problem."

"What else?"

"A cop from Austin was down here looking for the Brit. My contact thinks this Austin guy is maybe too smart to call it a day. Or too stupid."

"Interesting. What is his name?"

"Reles."

Mo rolled the name on his tongue. Reles. Reles. It sounded familiar.

1:00 P.M.—Lyons Road

"Ready?" Milsap grunted, slouching down to reach the lever, with the steering wheel crushing his ample gut. "Now!" We kicked forward and slid the front seat back. Milsap let out a breath. "It jerked forward when I parked. I couldn't get it back. Shit detail. I got the day sittin' in the goddamn rain to fix it."

Milsap and I sat together in his car as the rain pounded the hood. We watched the abandoned back of the strip mall he confirmed was a shooting gallery.

Sergeant Carl Milsap was a regular on the Homicide squad until he got busted for corruption, suspended, and reinstated for a sudden lack of evidence, a development broadly attributed to his connections in a certain prominent white-sheeted fraternity. He was punished for his felonious acts with suspension and fines, the administration's protection, ultimately, of its investment in him. This came as a blow to Carter Serio in Internal Affairs, who alone bore the notion that cops who commit felonies should be charged with felonies. The administration was more traditional.

Short, fat, stupid and corrupt, his cowboy boots stained with misfired tobacco juice, Milsap was the model of Texas law enforcement. His body and ruby cheeks bulged outward balloon-style without sagging, as if he'd suddenly put on an extra eighty pounds that day. He was stupid enough to argue with a recorded message and lose. Only the death of his corrupt, slightly less-stupid mentor kept him from greater financial success or a career in license plate manufacturing. Jeffries, Milsap's partner, was killed some time back in the line of duty, more or less. Died with his boots on. We'd hated each other famously, Jeffries and I, and Jeffries's allies, an inbred subdepartmental network of cross burners and sister fuckers, couldn't be blamed for looking at me when Jeffries turned up gutted. Milsap was demoted to Criminal Investigations and recently appointed to Narcotics, though his presence there was only tolerated, hence the shit detail, watching the back of a shooting gallery in the January rain.

"Freezing my goddamn balls off," he muttered. " 'You're doin' great, Milsap!' " he said in a mocking voice, the voice of his new squad.

I laid out the Key case, the Black Talon bullet, the dead killer, the dubious motive.

"Why here?" he said.

"The shooter's old dealer says he lost business to this place. I'm grasping at straws here," I admitted. "But this is a guy with very few connections. Who runs the place?"

He shook his head. "I'm just watching."

"You don't know whose place it is?"

"I ain't Homicide no more. I'm Narcotics." It sounded like a vow he didn't believe yet.

"We're on the same department. We're supposed to help each other, aren't we?"

Dirty look, long silence. Then, "Vice is slamming the shit outta South Congress, trying to clean it up for good."

"Right." Anyone who read the papers knew that. In response to community outcry, they were busting whores and johns by the van load, hoping to drive business away. Periodically a teacher or a bureaucrat would be busted on his night off and publicly humiliated in the papers. The pros would change neighborhoods, or move to Houston or Dallas, then head back here when other crackdowns drove them away from their new haunts.

Milsap said, "I heard they hauled in a bunch an hour ago from a massage parlor, rainy day crowd."

"So?"

"Dozen or so hookers, gotta be a few hopheads in the batch. You can show the mug shot around."

"That's it? That's your idea?"

He yelled, "I told you! I'm Narcotics."

"Great! Whose fucking shooting gallery is it?"

He clenched his teeth at the windshield. I opened the door and let the rain in. "Wait a minute, wait a minute," he said. I waited but I didn't close the door. "We'll both go."

I got in my new car and followed Milsap back to the municipal lot. He'd use a visit to Central Booking to justify leaving a bogus stakeout if they called him on it, if they cared. We went into Central Booking, dripping with rain as we checked our weapons. The holding tank held a dozen or so hookers sporting raincoats or rain-streaked mascara, sneezing and scratching themselves, waiting for the one phone, collect calls only. Glass separated them from a dozen or so johns of every stripe, college kids and laborers and suits, linked together only by their total humiliation and the threat that today, for some, would be the day their lives fell apart.

Aguinaldo from the sheriff's office, the innkeepers of Central Booking, flipped on the loudspeaker in the women's tank. I slapped Gaz Cruikshank's mug shot against the glass and spoke into the microphone. "Who knows this guy?"

They looked up, scanned it, went back to waiting. One skinny young woman, long black hair, wicked black circles under her eyes like a pair of shiners, stared.

"You," I said. "You know him?"

She drifted toward the photo. "He's English," she said.

"Yeah, he's English. Where do you know him from?"

Long, long silence.

I said, "Miss?"

"Rainbow John. He's a dealer."

I let go of the microphone, turned to Aguinaldo. "Put it down this woman cooperated with the police."

Milsap said, "Stupid Milsap."

"You know Rainbow John?"

"No," he said.

"I'll check it out."

"I'm Narcotics," he said for the third time. I think he was starting to believe it. "*I'll* check it out."

Back in the squad room, I asked Jake about Rainbow John. Jake told me about another KA of Cruikshank's he'd discovered in an old arrest report, a partner in crime, one Tom Shookster.

"Why didn't the rap sheet have this?" I asked.

"Computers only know what you tell 'em."

"Sure," I said, "defend the computer."

Shookster's temporary residence: Travis County Jail. Likely to be at home.

1:45 P.M.—United Bank, Guadalupe Street

Torbett stepped into a bank at the foot of the Drag and waited for someone in customer service, a young brown-haired white woman in a navy blue skirt-suit, a bow around her collar and a deliberate smile, How can I help you Mr. Black Man?

When they sat he introduced himself. "I'm trying to find out about offshore banking. This, for instance."

She looked at the bank statement. "Westpark Limited. British? Oh, British Virgin Islands. I see. So . . ." She scanned the document. "Virginia Key is the executor of Westpark Limited, but see," she pointed out a detail in a cluster of smaller print at the bottom, "the account is in trust for another company, Eastpark Limited."

"What does that mean?"

"Honestly?" She looked around to see if anyone was listening. The nice-nice smile dropped from her face. Torbett noticed the shift. "It means crap. Someone's hiding tax money in two companies that probably don't exist. Find out who's behind those fake companies, and you'll find your tax evader." She handed the statement back and smiled, all perky again. "You might start with Ms. Key."

2:00 P.M.—Travis County Jail

The county jail cells with their Plexiglas walls, were set up panopticon style—fanning out from the guards' booth where I stood so that every cell was in full view, and any prisoner might be observed at any time. The French judicial system determined long ago that the potential of constant observation, and the impossibility of determining whether you were being watched or not, was a more effective, humane and efficient form of punishment than, say, mutilation or torture. To date, we haven't found a form of punishment that discourages crime.

The one exception to visibility at TCJ was the shower, ensuring that the prisoners would be in full view of the guard, except while they were being raped. Call it a Texan respect for privacy.

When the guard opened the outer door, all the prisoners glommed to the Plexiglas walls of their cells, save for one guy who only looked up, a fist bouncing merrily under his blanket. Their lives consisted of waiting. Any intruder was a potential visitor, lawyer, release. The guard led me along the wall of cells. One prisoner, a head-shaved biker-type the size of a truck, glared angrily, eyes following me as I passed. We got up to Shookster's cell. "Wanna go in?" the guard asked. Shookster stood an awkward six foot five. The greatest potential threat was that I'd be standing in front of him when he fell over. He backed to the wall when I entered, afraid I'd been let in to work him over.

"You were arrested with Gaz Cruikshank last May?"

"This is crazy," he said, as if my statement were one in a series. "That charge was thrown out. Lack of evidence. I gotta get out of here."

"Why?"

"Do you see these guys? They'll chew me up."

I realized Shookster was not in a league with Cruikshank, not a bar fighter, just a loser trying to get out of jail before he got gang-banged.

"What are you in for now?" I asked.

"What I'm telling you. That old possession charge. They picked me up on a dead charge from six months ago."

"If it's true the charge has been dismissed, I'll see what I can do. How'd you know Gaz?"

"Roommates."

"Tell me about him."

He was pacing caged-animal rhythms against a three-foot stretch of the back wall. "I don't know anything. He answered an ad, paid cash. Seemed kind of laid back. He was there a month before I figured out he was a doper. It was catching up with him, I guess."

"He ever talk about old grudges, people he wanted to get back at?"

"How would I know? He'd lie on the couch for days. Then he'd be gone. Sometimes he looked banged up, like from a fight."

"You ever fight with him?"

"He tried to borrow money once and I didn't have any. He looked like he was gonna punch me out but he just smashed this lamp and stormed out. That was the last time I saw him. Are you gonna get me out of here?"

On my way out I passed the glaring prisoner again, the biker guy. He watched me walk, then suddenly he drummed his palms on the window till it rumbled. "Hey!" he shouted. "Hey!" I stopped and looked at him, then kept going. He drummed again, shouting, "Velez! VELEZ!"

I felt the blood drain from my face. I knew where I'd seen him.

Joey Velez had mentored me onto the Homicide squad after I helped him on the Gautier case. But the case took months of surveillance, all led by Joey. The truck-sized guy in this cell had been the bouncer at Gautier's blues club.

"Yeah, you know me," the bouncer yelled from his Plexiglas cell. I turned my back on him. "Hey! *Hey!*"

Bueno, mazel tov, amigo, I heard Joey say. The phrase drifted back to me as the guard locked the cell block behind me, what I said to my new mentor the day we met, when he told me he'd never met a Jewish cop before. And he said it back to me whenever he got the chance. *Bueno, mazel tov, amigo.*

Our first laugh together and the last thing he said to me before he died.

2:15 P.M.—Guadalupe at Nineteenth

Torbett got two dollars in change at a convenience store and stood at a pay phone outside. He thought about Virginia Key, that he had been somehow taken in, but he wasn't sure how or why. She was a widow, a sad widow, small and alone, losing her children.

He phoned Brackenridge and asked how Rubin was doing. The same, they said. Did they have a birth certificate on file? A few transfers. Rubin Albertson Key, born New Orleans, May 5, 1981, son of Harold Louis Key and Virginia Ann Albertson Key. Phone call to IRS, Harold Key, married to Virginia Ann Key. DOB June 19, 1954. No date of death on file. Call to Social Security, born June 19, 1954, Baton Rouge, Louisiana. No DOD on file. Last employment date June 1986. Profession: accountant.

Torbett called DPS. Rap sheet on Harold Louis Key? Transfer, wait, computers. Bingo, one arrest, July 1986, New Orleans, embezzlement, serving ten years at the United States Penitentiary at Pollock, Louisiana.

He phoned Dispatch, asked them to locate Harold Key at Pollock and arrange a call. Then he headed for HQ.

2:30 P.M.—HQ

Jake Lund greeted me when I got back to the squad room. His work area was piled with papers, reports, a videotape and a box of Raisinets. Marks and Czerniak were sorting through some old newspapers looking for something. They gave me a dirty look and a smile, respectively. TV on, CNN flashing silently.

I said, "Jake, man, you ever leave this place?"

He blinked and held up a videocassette. "Greyhound sent this." He pushed it into the VCR.

On the TV, computer graphics gave way to fuzzy black and white, overhead, oblique angle. Support columns. Screen stamped Tuesday, 1/15/91, 11:55:03 P.M. and counting. "Here he is." Marks and Czerniak looked on, the automatic effect of a TV screen in any room.

A small, shaggy figure in baggy sweater and oversized pants appeared, disappeared behind a column, walked in clipped steps to the window, paid for a ticket, took it and left. Jake fast-forwarded. Gaz reappeared, looked around, slid close to the window, drew a weapon. Jake hit PAUSE.

"There's our Hi-Point."

Marks asked, "Does he use it?"

Jake started the tape. Someone came in, Gaz fumbled with the gun and disappeared.

Jake hit STOP and said, "The end."

Czerniak said, "You'd think they'd have sent it sooner."

"Word came from Serology," Jake said. "That was his blood type in the sink, all right. And Hay says a big positive on tuberculosis, right? So that was him. Miles says case closed, do the paperwork, get on some cold cases."

"Goddamned right," Marks growled.

I gestured Jake into the hall. When we were out of Marks's earshot I said, "Miles isn't around right now."

He grinned. "What's up?"

"Have you seen this guy's rap sheet? Burglary of auto? B&E? Sleeping in a public place? One arrest for assault, probated. Junkie, petty thief, no weapons, ever. Barroom fights. And he used her name. But she says she didn't know him. Maybe she's lying, but why? And why an expensive automatic and why Black Talons unless someone wanted Virginia Key deader than dead?"

"Maybe he really hated her?"

"Great. Why?"

Jake popped a Raisinet and chewed it thoughtfully.

"What?" I said.

"You think I'm crazy, right?"

"You ever leave here in the daytime?"

By way of response, he bowed his head and looked up at me, half smiling, ashamed.

"Yeah," I said. "I think you're crazy."

"So you won't be offended by what I say. You ID'd with the killer. You killed him, you feel guilty, now you're trying to make it up to him by getting him off the hook. Acquitted, post mortem." The phone rang in the squad room. He popped another candy and turned to the door. "What do I know? Crazy Jake."

The door opened and Czerniak looked at me. "It's for you."

I went in and took the phone. "Reles." Marks pretended he hadn't been listening at the door.

"Dan, it's Ron Wachowski. You might want to come over here."

2:45 P.M.—HQ

Torbett stopped at Dispatch, found the switchboard operator who was helping him and waited while she put the call through to the federal prison at Pollock. She handed him a headset.

"Hello?"

"Harold Louis Key?"

"Who is this?"

"James Torbett, Austin Police. Are you married to Virginia Key?"

"Is that what this is about? We were married, yes."

Point one: Virginia Key was no widow. Point two: Harold Key was well spoken, likely educated and indisputably alive.

"Sir, your wife, uh, ex-wife?"

"Yes."

". . . is involved in an investigation and we're wondering if you'll answer some questions."

"Ha! Sure, I've got time."

"You're divorced?"

"Three years back. But I wasn't there. You can check the records."

"Can you tell me why you were divorced?"

"Long story." Torbett didn't interrupt. *"Okay,"* he sighed. *"I was an accountant for a dentist, an office of dentists. Ginny had this great idea about me juggling their money, drawing on the interest. She swore it was legal, or marginally legal, like a questionable tax deduction. We had two babies and she was in school and we were broke. We needed money for her tuition and the doctor. Upshot, we paid her tuition, the doctor, we pulled together I guess it was a hundred and twenty K."* He took a breath and let it out. *"One day I was at work, two federal agents showed up, cuffed me in front of my bosses, bang, I'm in jail. Ginny said I should leave her out of the story, just to make sure one of us is free to take care of the kids. The lawyer told me to do it. But here's the catch: she paid the lawyer. And the judge said I'd get a shorter sentence if I turned over the money but I didn't have the money, she said it went to the lawyer."* He was building up steam. *"The judge didn't believe me! He thought I was going to prison to keep my nest egg. And I watched this lawyer clown in the courtroom and I was thinking, a hundred and twenty thousand for this? And I saw how he looked at her, and I didn't get it till later."*

"Get what?" Torbett asked.

"He was in love with her! Same reason I'm here. I bet she didn't pay him a dime. Two months later I'm in Pollock Federal trying to pull together the appeal, but she stopped taking my calls, you know we can only call collect. And she sent me a letter saying she can't pay my lawyer, she doesn't have the money, I got myself into this." He roared, *"I got myself! Next thing, I get the papers, she's divorcing me. Guess what grounds. Unreasonable cruelty. She sent me to prison and I'm cruel!"*

Torbett realized the man had been thinking about the turn of events day and night, for some time.

The man snarled, *"Icing on the cake? I can't see the kids. I can't talk to them and I can't write them. Why? She told the judge I sexually molested them. My own kids! Of course I wasn't in court for the divorce, I didn't have a lawyer, so there was no one to say, when did he sexually molest them? How? Did they see a doctor? Is there evidence? Police report? What did the children say? Nothing. Torbett, that's your name, right? You have kids?"*

Torbett weighed the possible pitfalls of answering, and said, "Yes."

"What would you do if someone messed with them? The truth."

Torbett didn't answer.

Harold Key answered for him. *"You'd kill him, wouldn't you?"* Again Torbett didn't answer. But he didn't argue. *"Me too, Torbett. My kids are everything to me. I know I sound crazy. I am crazy. I've been in here four years! But I wasn't crazy when I was with my kids. My best moment was my years as a father. Best thing I ever did."*

Torbett said, "She told us you were dead."

"Why'd you take her word?"

Torbett considered the question. Harold Key went on. *"Is that what she tells my kids?"*

Bam! It hit Torbett like a two-by-four. Harold Key didn't know. Torbett realized the line was silent. Then, *"Torbett?"*

"Mr. Key, have you been following the news?"

"No. Why?"

Torbett thought the story was likely to have limited play outside the state. And if the man had family, they sure weren't in touch with Virginia. Torbett took a deep breath.

"Mr. Key. I have some very bad news."

2:45 P.M.—706 East Thirty-eighth Street

Bad Mo parked around the corner on Greenway, made sure the house was dark, had no cars parked near it, then casually strode up the front walk. His breath shortened and he felt himself wheeze. Just scoping the opposition. He needed to learn what he was dealing with, this Reles, partner of the late Joey Velez. There was much to do, and so little time.

He slipped his hand into the mailbox.

Southwestern Bell, for Daniel Reles. Catalogue for Dan Reles. Auto insurance something for Rachel Renier. Girlfriend. Hmm.

Then something from Austin Police Department, benefits, only not for Reles. Addressed to Mrs. Rachel Velez.

Mrs. Velez, Mo thought. The discovery of a potential trump card. *Interesting.*

3:00 P.M.—Department of Public Safety Crime Lab, Koenig Lane

Highway 290 rolled into Austin and humbled itself, narrowing as it passed the airport, then crossed I-35 and Airport Boulevard and became Koenig Lane. As it headed west it would become Allandale Road and Farm-to-Market Road 2222, which snaked out of town and up through the hills. The airport, like the roads, was too small to accommodate the town's awkward growth. The combination of its short runways, its ever-increasing air traffic and the thick trail of plane flights descending over the middle of town, was widely described as a disaster waiting to happen. Tenants tanning themselves on the roofs of small apartment complexes on Fifty-first Street could make out the faces of passengers in the airplanes' small windows and wave at them. The passengers would wave back, slack jawed.

The lot on Lamar Boulevard across Koenig Lane from DPS, had been a drive-in movie theater since the fifties, closing in 1970 due to changes in the culture, to sit dormant and finally be replaced in the mid seventies by a strip mall, a more suitable companion to the multiple-building complex of the Texas Department of Public Safety. I had borrowed my father's yellow Dodge convertible one night in high school, during the drive-in's final months, to take Kathleen Welishar to a horror double feature. I was about to capitalize on my ability to protect Kathleen from sluggish monsters when my dad tapped at the window, sending her into sudden hysterics and said he needed the car "to move something." He had rented an abandoned

filling station and was using it to fence unfenceable goods, in this
case a U-Haul full of stolen coffins. We dropped Kathleen at home
before going to get the trailer. She ignored me in the halls at school
after that, turning away as I passed, with the special kind of hurt
most women save for the guy who stood them up on prom night.
Thanks, Pop.

Ron Wachowski greeted me in the hall at DPS, with more exuberance
than was typical for someone of sixty-plus years, the bouncing step of
a man fascinated with science, in love with his job. Something I
didn't see often.
    "Boy, they really hate you in Houston," he said. "What did you do?"
    "What do you hear?"
    He handed me an incident report.

WHILE ON PATROL ON THE 3500 BLOCK OF ELGIN STREET I AN-
SWERED AN URGENT CALL FOR BACKUP AT DENNIS AND LIVE OAK. I
TURNED ON MY FLASHERS AND PROCEEDED QUICKLY DOWN ELGIN
AND TURNED RIGHT ON LIVE OAK AND RIGHT ON DENNIS. AS I
STRAIGHTENED OUT OF THE TURN I REALIZED THAT A VEHICLE
FROM THE ONCOMING LANE WAS TURNING LEFT ACROSS MY PATH.
THE VEHICLE'S HEADLIGHTS WERE OFF. I SWERVED LEFT TO AVOID
AN ACCIDENT, MINIMIZING DAMAGE BUT KNOCKING THE TAIL END
OF THE CAR. THE VEHICLE, A BROWN 1983 CHEVROLET IMPALA,
TEXAS LICENSE 251-VKV, SPUN AND HIT THE BUILDING, CRUSHING A
PEDESTRIAN AGAINST THE WALL. PEDESTRIAN WAS LATER IDENTI-
FIED AS SUSPECT GARY CRUIKSHANK.

I RADIOED FOR ADDITIONAL BACKUP AND MEDICAL ASSISTANCE,
MAKING NO ATTEMPT TO DISLODGE CRUIKSHANK FROM HIS POSI-
TION. THE DRIVER OF THE OTHER VEHICLE, VISITING AUSTIN PO-
LICE DETECTIVE RELES, EMERGED FROM THE PASSENGER SIDE OF
THE VEHICLE, CLIMBING OVER THE PASSENGER, WHO I RECOG-
NIZED AS HOMICIDE SERGEANT JACK O'CONNOR. RELES FELL
TWICE, THE SECOND TIME ANSWERING MY DIRECTIVE TO STAY

DOWN. I ENTERED APARTMENT 1A, THE DOOR THE VICTIM HAD EX-
ITED, WITH WEAPON DRAWN. IT WAS A ONE-ROOM APARTMENT,
UNFURNISHED. I KICKED OPEN THE BATHROOM DOOR. THE BATH-
ROOM WAS EMPTY. A SLIDING WINDOW ON THE WEST WALL OF THE
LARGER ROOM WAS WIDE OPEN AND THE SCREEN HAD BEEN
PUSHED OUT. I SURMISED THAT A SECOND PERSON WAS PRESENT
WHO HAD ESCAPED DURING THE ACCIDENT. I DUSTED FOR PRINTS.
NEGATIVE. IN THE CENTER OF THE CARPET SAT A SHALLOW ALU-
MINUM PAN HOLDING A BURNT SUBSTANCE. ALSO ON THE CARPET
WHAT APPEARED TO BE THE REMAINS OF A MARIJUANA CIGARETTE,
A HYPODERMIC NEEDLE, A DISPOSABLE CIGARETTE LIGHTER. THESE
WERE SECURED AND PASSED ON TO DEPARTMENT OF PUBLIC
SAFETY CRIME LAB, AUSTIN.

"We're statewide, don't you know," Wachowski grinned. "We get
orders from everywhere."

"So someone was in there with him?"

He handed me a bundle of related reports. "A witness, female, said
Gaz went in there with a woman, but no description of that woman,
and the witness vanished and was never identified."

"We were looking for her."

"She was right about the location, though." He led me into the lab,
a classroom-sized operation with butcher block sinks, Bunsen burners, fish tanks pumped full of smoke, everything tagged DO NOT
TOUCH.

He showed me a small tray, a few crumbled dry leaves. Not enough
to roll a joint. Next to it a half dozen test tubes, a clump of the stuff in
each, each liquid a different color. "We're testing it," he said.

"I'll save you some trouble," I said. "If you set it on fire, you'll get
high."

He smiled paternally. "Look at this." He had a pie plate with a
strip of something burned in the middle. "Look closely." Part of it
wasn't burned, a whitish powder. "Angel dust?" I asked.

"Light purple tint," he said. "The tests will just confirm. Either
that's raspberry Kool-Aid, or it's Karachi."

"What's that?"

"White heroin from Pakistan. Expensive white heroin. Very pure, very potent, much more addictive than brown heroin. You can't shoot it because it won't break down. You have to snort it or smoke it."

"So why the hypo?"

He led me to the tanks, each with a cover weighted down on top, an exhaust tube and a tiny hotplate inside, cooking something invisible. "We cook superglue. The fumes seal onto the moisture and we get the clearest prints." He had the hypo, the lighter and even the rolling paper from the joint. "You can see a little remnant of the print on the rolling paper, not enough to get a partial. But it's his."

"How do you know?"

He lifted the lid, picked up the hypo with his gloved hand. "He never touched the hypo. We're playing with the few drops of blood but I wouldn't expect anything. What's interesting is that it hasn't been used. I mean, there was nothing in the syringe, no drugs, no fluid, no blood—they hadn't drawn back. Nothing. Air. But there was blood on the needle tip. It had been injected, and not by him."

He held up the hypo. "See? Nothing. If there were prints they'd show. At least a smudge. I say she shot him with air, trying to kill him. Popular myth. It would have to be a lot of air, more than this syringe would fit. She could have caused him pain, though. But she left in a hurry, she didn't have time to wipe anything clean, let alone sterile. No prints anywhere. If there are any, they're probably his. Traces of talcum, though."

"Talcum?"

"She was wearing rubber gloves."

3:30 P.M.—Starlight Motel, Houston

Anything had bleached her hair peroxide yellow in memory of the Brit, sweet and dreamy with an accent. Give her a Brit any day.

She was kerchiefed just the same, had watched the motel all day to make sure it wasn't under prying eyes. She saw Mo's man arrive—a car salesman in a limo, red hairpiece on gray sideburns. He hit the desk and walked around to find the room. She waited five minutes, shouldered her vinyl bag and walked around the building the long way, avoiding the limo driver and the motel clerk. As she passed the doors along the far wall, one opened and he appeared, shiny suit and all. He stepped back to allow her in.

"It's a pleasure," he growled as she closed the door, glanced into the doorless closet and the bathroom to make sure there were only two of them. There was no furniture in the room save the bed. He wore tinted glasses; thick black hair crawled out of his ears.

"Let's see it," she said. He leered. "The money."

He reached under the bed and pulled out a paper bag, dumping its contents on the bedspread. Twenties and tens, old, crumpled, nonsequential. She counted with an eye on him. Five thousand even. She stuffed it into her bag and shouldered the bag.

"You know I ran into some trouble last night?" she said. She held her bag on her left shoulder, right hand in jacket pocket. Straight razor, sharpest metal in the world. She could whip it open and slice off a man's hand before he had a chance to bleed.

"What kind of trouble?" he asked. She watched him closely.

Maybe Mo had set her up. Someone had. But if he set her up, would he send the money? Maybe. Maybe she was supposed to be dead or in jail. And he sent the money in case she wasn't.

Or maybe he learned she was alive. The Brit's death was in the news. If she'd been killed or arrested, the news would have covered that too.

"What did you hear?" she asked.

"All's I know is, he's happy."

Mo had set her up, the timing was too right on the cops pulling up just as she was finishing the job. This guy, the hairpiece, was playing dumb since the Brit was dead and she was alive.

Hairpiece was walking toward her, closing in.

"What is it?" she asked.

"The big guy said once you had a nice way of sealing a deal."

Anything sighed. She liked Mo, in spite of his face. He was a poet. Always riffing. Not this loser.

But add the five grand to the two she'd picked off the Brit when he was dozing, and it had been a pretty good deal. Except for when she almost got nailed by the pigs. Hairy Boy unzipped and laid his flabby cock in her free left hand. Her right still clutched the razor. She considered her options.

Interstate 10 East. New Orleans? Miami? I-45 North to Dallas, then where? Vegas? Chicago? Too much competition. Highway 290 back to Austin. She'd enjoyed Austin. Too small, though, and she could be recognized. Hairy groaned and started clutching at her tits.

She could slip into Austin, kill Mo, and slip out. Bad business to leave him alive, after how friendly she'd been and how he'd screwed her over. He was hard to find, though. It wouldn't be easy. Hairy was working up a flopping sweat, grabbing at her crotch. She tightened her grip. He built his speed.

Maybe Mo hadn't set her up. He had no motive. And the cops could have been after the Brit. Or someone could have been watching them. There was something between guilt and innocence.

Wherever she went, there would be work. There was always work. It kept her going.

Kill Mo. Don't kill Mo.

Hairy built up to a frenzy, sweating on her neck as he nuzzled her with his heavy five o'clock shadow, the wool of his hairpiece scratching at her ear.

Kill Mo. Don't kill him. And to kill him, she'd have to find him first. And he might not have set her up at all.

But his messenger was right here.

She could always compromise.

4:00 P.M.—HQ

Gaz Cruikshank died with a lungful of Karachi—the smoke of white heroin cooked in a pie plate—and an armload of air. Neither of them killed him. I did.

That Wachowski had determined a woman shot Gaz with air and that she was wearing rubber gloves, set up the scenario that she had planned to kill him, got interrupted and split. And I couldn't search her out in Houston. Jack O'Connor would have me shot on sight.

Milsap was sitting in the Narcotics squad room when I walked in. With him were two other cops he introduced, eventually, as Clay and Fuentes, both younger and sharper-looking than Milsap by a decade. Clay, thin and ruddy with a drooping mustache and longish hair slicked back, bore a few serious abrasions on his face. Someone had worked him over. None of the men looked glad to see me.

"Karachi," I said. "White heroin. What do you know about it?"

A few eyebrows jumped. The three looked at each other to decide if I deserved the intelligence.

I said, "I can handle it."

Fuentes said, "From Pakistan."

"That's the only place they make it?" I asked.

Fuentes said, "White is in the refining. They could leave it like tar, not clean, but very strong. Easier to get through customs. Or they can process it to brown powder, or white. White's the best: the cleanest, the most potent, the most addictive. And the most expensive. Figure three thousand dollars an ounce. Where'd you see it?"

"Houston," I said. "Any idea where it could have come from?"

Fuentes said, "We can make some calls."

I said, "Don't mention my name. Milsap, you ever find that Rainbow John?" We all looked at him.

"No," he said. "I ain't heard nothing."

"Any of you guys know a dealer named Rainbow John? He's supposed to have dealt to this killer, Cruikshank."

They drew blanks.

4:00 P.M.—Starlight Motel, Houston

Anything held her position against the wall as Hairy Boy pounded against her, yelping with each thrust, and finally cried out as he shot it against the wall behind her, his left hand locked onto her right tit like a vise, sweat flooding onto her neck and shoulder. She slipped the razor from her pocket, flipped it open and sliced into his stomach.

Hairy pulled back, saw the ruby red flushing out of his gut, drenching his slashed shirt and his half-flaccid cock. First the horror appeared on his face, and the hurt. She should have let him zip up first. Then he screamed.

She swung the blade again. She just meant to slash his cheek. But he flinched and she slashed his neck. He grabbed it, blood spurting out. He might get help in time. But she'd have to split. She made for the door.

"Send him a message for me," she said. That was dumb. This was the message. Don't fuck me over.

"Help me," he shrieked. "Help me!" Blood poured thick from his neck and his belly. He clutched them both. "Please." He ran after her, missed her, hit the wall.

She stood at the door. If he lived, he'd come after her. Mo wouldn't mind if this one died. Might not notice. But he'd be mad if he had to deal with someone mutilated. People are sticky about that.

She walked closer to him. He was leaned over, clutching his throat as blood dribbled heavily between his fingers. He whimpered in rhythm, like when he had her against the wall. Only this time it was fear. Would she help him? Hurt him? He was at her mercy.

Of course she would help him.

"Move your hand," she said. He bore his neck.

She raised the blade again and brought it down, slashing through flesh and arteries. A torrent of blood flowed before he hit the ground.

She cleaned the blade and left it, sealed her clothes in plastic she kept in her vinyl shoulder bag for such occasions. She'd burn them right away. She wiped down the vinyl shoulder bag and herself with alcohol she carried, put on new clothes and shoes, also in the bag. Always a change of everything, her mother used to say. You never know.

She stepped out, watching for blood puddles, closing the door and again dodging the front desk and Hairy's limo.

When she drove up to the entrance ramp, she stopped the car to adjust her mirrors and peel off the kerchief. Then she hit the highway and picked up some speed on the way out of town. The clear air whipping through her newly blonde hair made her think, and reconsider. He wasn't so bad, the hairy guy. She should have given him another chance, such a sad puppy. She felt a twinge of regret as she looked down the stretch of Highway 290 toward Austin.

She felt so sorry for them all.

6:30 P.M.—Lyons Road, Austin

I sat next to Milsap in his Crown Victoria in the dark, rubbing my hands together to fight off the bone-chilling dampness. "Can't you turn the heat on?"

"Drain the battery," he said.

He'd taken me along on a few "interviews," Milsap style. The department had long since stripped him of his brass knuckles—he swore they weren't his—reducing his interrogation techniques to bare fists and pistol-whipping, which were rougher on his hands. I wasn't sure how he'd chosen the subjects to interview, an assortment of pimps, burglars and generic badasses. But I was sure that, given the way he worked them over, if they knew Rainbow John, they'd have said as much.

The rain had stopped but everything was still wet and cold, and now dark, save for light from the lampposts. I scratched ideas on a piece of an envelope, a diagramming technique my partner Joey taught me years earlier. I could hear his voice: "out of your head, onto the paper where you can see it." In Austin: junkies, to Rainbow John, to who? In Houston: junkies up to street dealers up to distributors up to . . . who? Who would traffic three-thousand-dollar-an-ounce white heroin into Houston? The street junkies wouldn't pay for it. Rich dopers usually chose coke, or maybe that was an urban myth. Heroin carried a working-class stigma.

"We need to find that woman who was in the room with him," I said. "Without help from HPD. And we need to find this guy," I pointed to the gap in my diagram. "Mr. Big, the guy who brought the dope into Texas."

"Why?"

"Because I haven't got anything else. Maybe we can find Mr. Big without setting foot in Houston."

Milsap was screwing with a telephoto lens on his camera, too delicate work for his fat fingers.

A young guy, what my father would call a square from Delaware, with a barbershop haircut and a windbreaker, carried a gym bag along the back of the strip mall.

"Carl!" I said.

He responded, "Milsap."

"What?"

"Reles, Milsap. Simple respect."

I pointed. Milsap saw the kid in time to snap pictures of him approaching the boarded door: snap picture, wind film, pounding the door, snap, wind, waiting, and as the door opened inward, walking through, snap, wind, last picture, rewind to top of roll.

"Now we wait," he said, like that was a novelty.

After about five minutes, Dobie Gillis exited with his gym bag and headed the opposite way, down Tillery. Milsap put the Crown Victoria into gear, backed up into a drunken three-point turn and headed the opposite way on Lyons.

"Are you crazy?" I said. "Follow him."

"They'll see us."

"They'll see you doing this Steve McQueen shit."

He made a right on Springdale, past a sign that said, "East Austin welcomes APD! New Substation to be completed May 1991." Turned right on Seventh and again on Tillery, and pulled up face to face with the shmoe.

I jumped out of the car and showed my badge. "Police. Drop the bag on the ground."

He turned and ran, fast. I followed, shouting, "Stop or I'll shoot" with breath I couldn't spare. He was in someone's yard, hopping a four-foot fence like it was a coffee table, gym bag still in hand. I got over the fence, losing distance. I fired into the air. It was cloudy and dark and I couldn't risk shooting him from far away. I poured on the speed but I couldn't beat him for endurance. I followed him through another yard and out onto Cherico. I chanced a shot at the sidewalk behind him. *Blam!* Concrete chips shot up and hit him in the back. He stopped.

"Keep your hands out to the sides and lower the bag to the ground.

Good. Now put your hands behind your neck and link your fingers. Don't turn around. Don't turn around!"

I made it close to him, holstered my gun, pulled my cuffs and linked one around his right wrist. His left elbow hit my jaw and sent me a step backward. He swung around with his right and belted me across the mouth, the cuffs scraping across for an after-shot. Milsap nowhere. I ducked and grabbed his left leg and yanked it from under him, a trick that works on guys afraid to fall. He went down but kicked with his right leg as he did, landing it square in my gut.

Before I knew it, the kid was on top of me landing blows all over my face. I threw my weight and rolled on top of him but not before he got both hands around my throat, a death grip I wasn't willing to test. I pushed my arms up between his, knocked his grip loose and then punched my thumbs hard into his eyes.

7:00 P.M.—1205 Walnut Avenue

". . . through Jesus Christ our Lord, Amen."

"Amen."

"And they're off," Guy said and grabbed two chicken legs and thighs off the serving plate in one sweeping motion and passed the platter back to Nan.

"One piece at a time," Torbett was saying to Guy too late, but Nan nudged him under the table. "Eat what you want."

Jule said, "May I have some juice pleeeeeze," stretching it out for cuteness.

That nine years had passed between births of the Torbett children was a frequent subject for public comment. That there had been a second child in between, who lived long enough to be named War-ren, was the detail left from the discussion. Each day of the life of Jule, the child who followed, seemed precious, a gift, and one easily withdrawn.

Chatter overlaid chatter. Basketball had replaced football. Barbie dolls were replacing teddy bears. Everyone ate well and everyone was together. Torbett wondered when this had become a special occasion. But he knew whose fault it was.

The kids seemed especially excited. Just a Friday dinner, a rainy Friday. Usually Guy was getting ready to go out. Evenings had degenerated into a movie or a video for the parents and Jule. But today had a novelty: Dad was home when they got back from school.

Torbett had bailed straight from Dispatch, after he'd talked to Harold Key, told him his son was shot and his daughter was dead. Key cried out in a wail to tear the sky. The woman he once loved, perhaps, had stolen his freedom and his children. And, as far as he was concerned, she'd gotten them shot. Torbett headed home to see if he still had a home, if it hadn't disappeared in his distraction. He'd spent days thinking about Virginia Key. Meanwhile Jule was growing from a little girl into a girl—she was choosing dresses more often than pants, and Guy was growing from a boy into a man. He'd had two girlfriends in the last year. Torbett was sure Guy had sex with the second. Torbett had taken him aside, talked to him about sex and birth control and condoms, a hell of a lot more guidance than his own father had given. Guy casually reassured Torbett, "nothing to worry about, Dad," as he'd reassured him about drugs. Part of being a man was being your own man, Guy had gotten that part down. Torbett hoped he got the part about drugs and condoms too.

Nan was jubilant to see Torbett home at midafternoon, home when he should have been working, instead of the other way around. And if any of their lovemaking seemed like overcompensation, if he seemed to be making something up to her, to be extra attentive, she didn't complain. The children got big hugs when they came home, which Guy tolerated with a smile, shocked to see Dad in the house at three when no one was sick. Guy seemed vaguely suspicious of just how happy and relaxed his parents looked at that point in the afternoon.

Monday, first thing, Torbett would talk to the district attorney's office. There'd be an indictment for Virginia Key. But he couldn't do that now, not when she'd just lost her daughter. Even if the boy made it. He'd have to wait. But there would be an indictment and she'd turn over the money and Mr. Key would be released. She had the money and Torbett had the bank statement to prove it.

A jolt of pain shot through him. He'd seized the document illegally. You couldn't build a prosecution on it: fruit of the poisoned tree. He could have the DA subpoena her financial records. He could cite plain view—the bank statement was sitting on her desk. But it was sitting under another document. Arguable. They could win or lose. He couldn't get rid of the document without admitting his offense or committing another one. He'd screwed up. He'd have to fix it somehow. Harold Key *would* be reunited with his son. If the boy survived. Torbett would call the DA first thing Monday.

Nan put her fork down and announced, "I know something we can all do together tomorrow." Total silence, and Guy laughed, to Jule's confusion. A six-year-old would constantly forgive and forget the missed family engagements, the broken hearts. Teenagers had given up trust.

"Listen to your mother," Torbett said, but the words sounded foolish.

"We're going to an antiwar protest," she declared.

Torbett watched her, amazed.

"What?!" Guy said, half smiling.

"What's an antiwar protest?" Jule asked.

"There's a war in Iraq. We think it's wrong. We're protesting. Tomorrow."

"Mom!" Guy seemed impressed, even shocked at his mother's audacity, her first antiestablishment action, and her willingness, her desire, to make it a family event, like going to church or grandma's house.

Nan had amazed Torbett again. She had waited until they were all together, until an "up" moment. Then she sprang her genius on them. The protest was outright rebellion, political rebellion, nothing Guy could claim was hokey or old-fashioned. It hadn't escaped Guy, Torbett knew, that he would soon be old enough to have to register for the draft. Nor had it escaped them that older boys from the neighborhood, several of them, had sought futures in the military. Some would be going to Iraq.

It was a protest. It was important. It was antiestablishment. And they'd be doing it as a family.

Guy laughed. "No, I can't, I'm busy tomorrow," and focused on his dinner, a busy man, too busy to be publicly associated with this crowd.

Nan kept on. "What's more important than this?" She looked around the table, held her hand, palm down, over the green beans. "Who's in?" Torbett, Jule and Guy looked at each other, for instructions they hadn't received. One thing was clear: Jule would do nothing if Guy didn't do it first, so things had operated on the subject of big brothers since the beginning of time. Eyes went to Guy.

Guy looked around, saw he was in the spotlight, he'd take responsibility if he ruined his mother's plan. And he still needed two and a half years of room and board. He let his fork clank to the plate.

"I'm in," he said, placing his hand down, with noticeable discomfort, on his mother's.

"I'm in," Jule giggled and leaned forward to reach the others. Nan turned to Torbett.

He had said in the past that the department frowned on officer participation in partisan politics. The words always felt dirty in his mouth, and they all knew it.

"What's up, Dad," Guy asked, holding the cards now. "Does the department frown?"

Torbett clapped his hand on top. They all raised their hands with a roar and whooped, high-fived.

"We're radicals!" Guy said.

"We're a family!" Nan said.

Torbett looked at his wife, his children. For one moment they were all on the same page. In his life, as son and brother, husband and father, it had never been better than this.

They'd go together as a family, Torbett thought, warmed and vaguely frightened. What's the worst thing that could happen?

9:00 P.M.—Central Booking

The young man I'd arrested, ID'd as Airman First Class Kenneth Kemp, currently stationed at Bergstrom Air Force Base, received medical attention, his left eye heavily bandaged, right bruised and scratched, but not severely damaged owing to the weakness of my left hand. He sat in the glass-walled interrogation room cuffed to the table, stiff jawed and righteous like he was standing up to the Communists.

"Who did you meet with?" I asked.

"Kenneth Kemp, Airman First Class, serial number oh-seven—"

"You're not a prisoner of war, shithead, you're a dope dealer." No response. "How much money was in the bag? I put it at about fifty thousand, but that's just an estimate. We have people counting and analyzing it right now. I wonder if they'll find traces of heroin on it. Snorters, you know?" He looked worried, then stiffened up again. "To tell the truth, we were expecting you to come out with dope, not money. Money in the bag means you went in with dope, which is much more interesting."

I knew planes were flying out of Bergstrom every day, taking young men and, thanks to the women's movement, young women, off to the Persian Gulf. I also knew those planes were coming back, though many of the men and women wouldn't. Empty planes, free transportation, heroin coming back from the Middle East. It was making sense.

"I plead the Fifth."

"On what grounds?" Nothing. "How's Pakistan?" Quizzical look. A guard opened the door and handed me a slip of paper and disappeared. The paper read, in pencil, *Bergstrom brass to governor: Military incident. Kemp and evidence to be turned over to MPs. Now. Milsap.*

Kemp must have seen the shock on my face because his good eye was probing me.

"I can't believe it," I said.

He stayed mum.

I went on. "Bergstrom says they hope you can afford an attorney. You're on your own."

"What?!"

"But we have a public defender. Old Clem. He'll get you a fair trial, don't worry about that."

"That fuck!" He was red faced and shaking, now, struggling against the cuff.

"Who?"

"He—"

Kemp stopped short as the guard appeared again, opening the door for Milsap who walked in with a nod to each of us and unlocked Kemp's cuff. He was followed in by an air force lieutenant in full dress—sky blue but with a storm blowing in—and two MPs. They locked their own cuffs on Kemp and led him out.

"What is this?" I asked. "This man was arrested for a felony. He resisted arrest and assaulted an officer."

He handed me a document, signed by the lieutenant governor, a general named Knobloch, and at the bottom, APD Chief Cronin. "This man is our responsibility."

Ten minutes later we were outside the loading dock, waving Kemp, his fifty grand, and his military escort goodbye. And Kemp was smiling.

And the chain of events didn't seem to surprise Milsap at all.

9:30 P.M.—Camelot

Mo lay on the basement couch staring at the TV screen, when his phone rang. He turned it on, coughed and said, "Speak."

"*Is this . . .*" The voice trailed off. A man's voice.

"Who is calling?"

"*Is this . . . Mo?*"

"I am hanging up."

"*I'm . . . I work for Philo.*"

Mo listened. He could hear the man breathing, short breaths, as if a long one might kill him. The man went on.

"*I dropped him off. It was supposed to be ten minutes. I went up an hour later. He was dead.*"

Mo didn't respond. He felt himself shift.

The driver went on. "*I didn't know what to do. There was blood everywhere. His dick was out. I ran back to the car. I think I threw up. Then I went back. I got his wallet and his phone. What should I do?*"

Mo gazed into the glare of the screen. Anything had left Philo's dick hanging out of his trousers. Almost her signature. But she had killed him. Why? There was no grudge between her and Philo. It was a message for Mo. Something had gone wrong in Houston. That was why she did not call. And she blamed Mo. She would come for him next. Or he would have to go after her.

In the meantime, his cough was worse. The tumors were growing in his throat, and elsewhere. His skin left him unrecognizable. He'd die horribly in a prison hospital. He hung up the phone.

Or he could wait for her. It made sense, the moment he first thought it. The plan had been conceived and settled on, the perfect solution to all his problems. He would die in the arms of a beautiful woman, as Philo had. He had things to take care of first, but then he would wait for her. Suddenly he felt an urgency to be with her. Like after basic training, when he ran for the brothel near Bergstrom. He longed for her, sweet Anything, for their moment together. Their magnificent final moment.

Philo did not know how lucky he was.

10:00 P.M.—HQ

I ducked past the first-floor elevators, waiting for them to open so I could breeze by as if I'd just come from the stairs. Taped onto the brick wall, a memo with a tone of desperation said that Saturday's antiwar protest was now expected to draw a bigger-than-anticipated crowd, and just about begged officers who would be off-duty to come in, in exchange for overtime pay or comp time. The situation didn't yet warrant ordering them in on their day off.

The door pinged open and I saw the backs of three men walking out toward the exit: the unmistakable expanse of Milsap's back, alongside Clay and Fuentes.

"Hey, guys!" I said, catching up.

"Reles!" Fuentes said. "Heard about your hard luck. Man, that fly-boy gave you a working over."

My face was bruised from the fight, but I'd had worse. "Yeah, I got some good shots in, though. Carl fill you in?" I asked. Milsap tightened his jaw. "Man, it's like that UT football star with the DWI. Hear about him? He gets released and the cop who busted him got fired. I mean, the football player didn't have fifty grand on him and didn't beat up the arresting officer, but still. Tough break all around, huh, *Carl?*"

Milsap ground his molars as we passed through the outer doors. He managed a nod.

"But, you know," I went on, "Carl said the whole thing looked kind of suspicious."

Clay asked, "Did you?" His voice was tinged with threat.

"No!" Milsap insisted.

"Sure you did," I said. We crossed the southbound frontage road in the fog, toward the parking lot under the overpass. "All that military brass fishing out this little airman. Big military deals. Too bad you guys can't get into that, huh?"

Clay's already dark demeanor darkened. "Try fighting the military," he said.

"Tell me about it! Hey, Carl, don't forget what we talked about."

"What?" Clay asked, all suspicion.

"You know. That thing."

"What's that, *Carl,*" Fuentes asked.

Milsap's tongue caught in his throat.

"Basketball season, man!" I said. "Carl's gonna teach me how to choose a winner, aren't you, Carl?"

Milsap said, "I said I would, didn't I?" His face was losing color.

I remembered something I'd forgotten in my office and wished them goodnight.

Jake Lund was in the Homicide squad room. I said, "Jake, what do you know about Karachi?"

"Heard of it."

"See what you can find." I heard footsteps in the hall. "Listen, Milsap's gonna come in here. Don't leave the room, no matter what."

Milsap walked in. "I wanna talk to you—" He stopped when he saw a witness.

Jake said, "Milsap!"

"Lund."

I said, "What's up, Carl?"

Milsap stared at Jake who smiled back at him, innocently.

Milsap finally turned to me. "Narco," he said.

"I'll be right down." I promised Jake a box of jawbreakers for his trouble, and waited five minutes before following Milsap, carefully, to his new squad room.

Milsap was standing alone in the Narcotics office as I pushed in and locked the door behind me. "What's up, Carl?"

"Don't Carl me, you Jew bastard. You tryin' to get me killed?"

I hid a grin. "I was just trying to figure out who was bullshitting me, you or your whole squad. I can see it was the whole squad. Someone let you in on some secret and they don't trust you to keep it."

"Sure they trust me."

"You're so fuckin' stupid, Milsap. You're supposed to say, 'What secret? There ain't no secret.' "

"Shit."

"Here's what I get. Tell me where I'm wrong. Sergeant Jewboy gets in Narco's way. I'm tracking this shooter, I find the place he buys his drugs. I stumble into some big investigation, maybe around that shooting gallery, if it *is* a shooting gallery. You don't want me fucking it up, so you misdirect me, taking me around to a bunch of shakedowns, carefully chosen stooges you could ask about Rainbow John in front of me, and they wouldn't know anything. Then you brought me back to your stakeout but you didn't figure we'd catch anything. We did and you didn't help me take the guy down, hoped he'd get away. When we brought him in, combat training and all, you alerted the Bergstrom brass and they picked him up. That's why you weren't surprised when he got sprung."

"That ain't true," he blustered.

"Which part?"

He got stuck, realized he'd admitted I wasn't far off.

"Fuck this," I said. "You think I won't rat you out to Internal Affairs, you're wrong."

He followed me toward the door. "It ain't like that," he said.

"Like what? You could've cracked a fifty-grand heroin deal. Years of graft and extortion, and you almost did something right. You almost acted like a real cop. But you sold out. You cut a deal with Bergstrom brass. Now you're in the heroin business." I opened the door.

"No, no, no," he said.

"You've outdone yourself, Milsap. I always figured you for petty crime. I figured at your core you were a cop. I was wrong. You're a fuckin' international drug lord."

He pulled me back in, slammed the door shut and locked it. "No," he said. "We know what's up with Bergstrom. Jurisdiction. We can't get on the base, so we can't get evidence. Anyone we bust, they cut loose. They say they'll discipline they're own. Bullshit."

"So?"

"I know Rainbow John. He's nobody, just a distributor."

"For who?"

"Shit. I'm *building* something here, Reles," he pleaded. "You're gonna fuck it all up!"

"Not if you work with me," I lied. He weighed my statement a moment, and without a better option, pretended to believe me.

He unlocked a file cabinet, pulled a thin file labeled CONFIDENTIAL and dropped it on a desk.

The file included an old black-and-white photo, foggy surveillance shot, of the biggest heroin man in town, maybe in Texas.

Milsap said, "We think he came from Houston. Came with a vengence. But HPD's no help. And all we got is this one picture."

Most of the time you're slugging along, plowing through mug shots and old phone books, trying hard just to give a shit. Maybe you catch the fucker, maybe you even get a conviction. He's out in a few years and in the meantime another hundred fuckers are out there gutting anyone who looks at them funny, hanging out in bus stations, chewing up runaway teens and spitting them out. And the rich get richer, and you wonder what's the point of handing out minor convictions like parking tickets. And then something big crosses your path and you go, *Bingo!*

I held Mr. Big's photo in my fingers. I knew that face. And I knew where I'd seen it.

SATURDAY

My sleep that night was so stormy you could barely call it sleep. A jumble of images and convoluted thoughts with a backbeat of teethgrinding as I faded in and out of consciousness, trying to get double duty out of the third shift by sleeping and sorting details at the same time.

The bouncer in the cell at TCJ, pounding on the Plexi, shouting "Velez! Velez!" I turn around and I'm Velez, the student become the teacher, the son now the father.

I'm in a clapboard eastside bar with red light, hepatitis-dirty glasses and a jukebox playing Sam and Dave. I ask a bartender something about Joey and he mentions "the other one."

"What other one?"

"The other cop Velez got killed with."

"There wasn't any other cop. There was just Joey."

He got irritated. "Who was that other cop Velez was with all the time?"

"That was me," I said.

"Oh." But he wasn't convinced and I wondered if he was right, if I had gone over that cliff with Joey. Then half awake again, I wondered who else besides me might have been traveling around with him.

I tell Joey's temptress wife Rachel that her husband is dead, her loveless marriage over. I blame her.

Now we're in the house, she and I, our house together, only it's my par-ents' apartment in Elmira, New York, but it's on the first floor, a thousand points of entry, and someone's breaking in. I can't find my weapon and I can't lift my arms to fight, even create a barrier between her and harm and she fizzles, gets smaller and smaller until she's so small I hold her in my hand, tiny and broken in half, and then dead. I force my eyes open.

The sun was shining in the windows, a clear day, when I scoped the house and found the telltale signs of Rachel gone to work early—cigarette ashes in three separate ashtrays, coffee cup in the sink—though it was Saturday and we had promised to spend the long weekend together. I figured she did this not out of spite, but as an an-ticipatory strike against the solid chance I'd do the same thing an hour later: I'd make apologies and promises and head off for a job that I hated but that must seem, day to day, to be more important in my life than she was. I was impressed that she could slip out of the house without breaking my paper-light sleep. I decided to call her later, when she got settled in at the office, to make nice.

The bouncer at the county jail, the one I knew from my first case with Joey all those years ago, reminded me about Joey and made me think about him, despite the fact that I'd promised Rachel I wouldn't. I was done chasing ghosts. If I had any thoughts about Joey I would force them out of my mind.

But then Milsap showed me the surveillance photo of the man called "Bad Mo," the presumed new controller of the bulk of Austin's heroin market and the subject of the largest of Narco's new investiga-tions. They had only scraps of information on Bad Mo, or scraps Mil-sap knew about. I knew something they didn't.

I burrowed into my hall closet, past the off-season jackets, under Rachel's less-loved shoes and the bottle of white wine we kept for the someday when we'd invite dinner guests, and I pulled out the card-board box with Joey's stuff. Among the issues Rachel and I never dis-cussed was the weirdness of keeping the box in the home we shared, his widow and his best friend—a reminder of what felt like our betrayal of him. But we were his survivors. We couldn't dump the record of his professional life.

The box summed up his legacy as far as we knew it: papers and commendations, a brochure called "Buying Rental Property" bearing his notes on a real-estate venture Rachel and I had never gotten to the bottom of ("*Seized property on Ulit: 150G. Less 80 is 70G. Ten units at $200/mo*") and a large manila envelope, which I plucked.

Two years earlier, a powerful man named Bill Oliver tried to blackmail me into silence and succeeded, showing me the surveillance photograph I pulled from this envelope, a black-and-white of my dead partner with a drug runner. If Joey had been on duty, I would have known about it. Partners know each other's business, unless someone has something to hide. I knew Joey's mood swings had been wild in his last days. I knew from Rachel that his finances had improved without explanation. And I knew from Oliver that the pockmarked man Joey shot pool with in the photo was named Mohammed Rashid Nadiri. Bad Mo.

I took the photo and buried the box again under the wine and old shoes. I was shaken by wild dreams, a stormy night's sleep, the natural result of working eighteen- and sometimes twenty-four-hour shifts. I would rest, relax when the case was over. And I would keep my promise to Rachel, stop chasing ghosts, stop trying to figure out the details of Joey's death.

But to do that, I would have to find Bad Mo.

7:30 A.M.—Interstate 35, Southbound

Anything had rolled her beat-up blue Corolla off Highway 290 and up Route 6 to Waco, where she killed the evening drinking in a honky-tonk and fucking a cowboy. Not having a home, a place to stash her clothes outside of her car (which she chose for its similarity to every other car), had never bothered her. One bed was as good as another. The same held true for cowboys.

By morning she was rolling down I-35 toward Austin. If anybody asked, she was coming from Dallas. But they wouldn't, she thought. Until she saw the flashing lights in her rearview. She pulled over. She checked the mirror. Leftover makeup. Only one way to play it. Jilted by her man. She pulled onto the narrow shoulder and a DPS cracker in boots walked up to the window, aviator shades and all.

"Miss, do you know how fast you were going?"

"Was I speeding?"

"You were going thirty-five. Have you been drinking?"

"Last night. I guess I overdid it."

"Step out of the car."

8:00 A.M.—HQ

Jake Lund greeted me with a grin and a pile of printouts when I hit the squad room, the photo of Joey and Nadiri folded loosely in my jacket pocket. "Karachi," he said, handing me the pile.

"What are you doing here? It's Saturday."

"I could ask you the same."

"What's this?"

He took the papers, tossed back a swig of a Dr Pepper and flipped pages. "The city of Karachi is in Pakistan, on the coast of the Arabian Sea. Major port of trade. But this starts in Afghanistan. In the seventies, Afghanistan is under a dictatorship. This dictator, he plays ball with the CIA. In '79, a bunch of Soviet 'advisors' in Afghanistan get killed, the Soviets send in the Red Army, occupy the country. You with me?"

I pretended I was.

"Well," he leaned back in his chair, "the CIA thought it would be cool to suck the Soviets dry the way we'd been sucked in Vietnam, and make them look stupid in the bargain. Cagey. So through the eighties, the CIA arms anyone in Afghanistan who'll fight the Russians. It cost us about six billion dollars, but the CIA argued it was worth it for what it cost the Russians. Cold War economics.

"Anyway," he went on, "ten years go by and about a million dead, lots of them civilians, but what the fuck, the Agency says, they weren't

Americans. And when it's over, sixty percent of the heroin sold in the U.S. is from Afghanistan."

"How?"

"Beats the shit outta me. But if I'm any judge of the CIA, they opened the market themselves, figuring they'd found a perfect way to fund their arming of Afghan rebels. But Russia is leaning on the heroin trade in Afghanistan, so a lot of the big operators shifted to Pakistan, where they could operate freely." He finished with a flourish of the hands, like a magician. "*Hence* Karachi."

I considered Nadiri. "So," I said, "if there's a big drug dealer in Texas who was born in Afghanistan—"

"In the U.S. a while?"

"The file didn't say."

"What file?"

"A file that doesn't exist."

Jake popped an M&M. "Right. Probably he was one of a bunch of Afghan nationals in the U.S. already, fluent in English and American culture, and with lots of contacts."

I thought about the airman and his bag of heroin money. "Maybe contacts in the air force."

Everything inside me spun around and whirled upward, cyclone style.

Jake said, "What gives?"

"This conversation never happened."

"I'm deaf and dumb."

"Run a check on a Mohammed Rashid Nadiri. Local, federal. If that doesn't work, try immigration. And the armed forces." I stepped away and turned back. "And get me the phone records for 3809 Peck Avenue, Austin, for March 8 and 9, 1988."

"That's three years ago. Why?"

"I need to know what happened to Joey Velez."

9:00 A.M.—1205 Walnut Avenue

Torbett guessed it was for psychological effect, but Nan made more breakfast than a family of four could eat on their hungriest day. Biscuits and gravy. Hand-sliced bacon and scrambled eggs *and* French toast and a pitcher of fresh-squeezed orange juice. Squeezing it must have nearly taken her arm off. When she finally let everyone in the kitchen to see the spread that covered the table, Jule gasped, "This is better than Denny's!"

Nan said, "That's what I was going for!"

Torbett ate and watched the children and felt like a rich man.

Stomachs filled ("I can't move. I can't move. I'm dying!"), table cleared, dishes done, break for final preparation. Shouting from different rooms.

"Dad, do you have an army jacket?"

"No."

"Didn't you save one from 'Nam?"

"Mommy, where are my Mary Janes?"

"Wear your sneakers. We'll be walking a lot."

"I want my Mary Janes!"

Torbett put on slacks, a button-down shirt and a spring jacket, and caught himself in the mirror. He looked like a marine on leave. An old marine. He still didn't know how civilians dressed.

With silent regrets, he concealed his firearm and holster under the jacket and zipped up.

"Hey, Dad!" Guy's grinning face appeared in the doorway. "Is this what it was like in the sixties?"

Torbett remembered first hearing about Vietnam, not knowing where it was, somewhere on the flipside of the planet. And dutifully marching into the sphincter of a jet to get there, some notion that things would be better when he got back, once he'd proven himself in battle, his willingness to go to war for a country that didn't always allow him entry to public restrooms. Years later he read how black inductees had fallen for the same trick in World War One. Today, Guy wasn't far from draft age. He could fall for the same trick. Is this what it was like in the sixties?

"Every inch of it," he said.

Jule yelled, "Are we supposed to make signs?" No answer. Jule again: "Does this mean Monday is canceled?"

"No, honey," her mother said. "Monday is for Dr. King. Today is about the war."

Torbett was pretty sure Jule didn't get it, but there were no more questions.

Nan announced, "Everyone go to the bathroom. It's going to be a long day."

They were to meet in a church parking lot and walk along MLK toward downtown and the capitol. Torbett imagined Jule getting tired before the march kicked off, Guy griping, the inevitable crankiness of a day of togetherness. He allowed himself one long sigh. "Okay, everyone," he announced as the last bathroom shift finished. "Let's move 'em out!"

It was exactly that moment when the phone rang.

10:00 A.M.—HQ

Ron Wachowski called me from his home. A DPS officer had pulled over a young woman in a blue Corolla, and in a random search, found a clump of raspberry white powder in a fold of her purse. Pending tests, Wachowski guessed, it was Karachi.

I met the arresting officer at Central Booking. He'd brought the woman into a separate room for questioning. Caucasian female, bottle blonde, about five foot two, chunky, early to midtwenties. Last night's makeup smeared her eyes. Delaware license called her Debbie Kubasik. A DPS tech standing in for Wachowski joined us.

I told her my name and asked the regular questions, name, address, job. Her boyfriend had dumped her, she said, and she was driving down from Dallas.

"Is that where you got the heroin?"

She dropped her head.

The tech said, "They don't have it in Dallas." That may have been true. More likely, no one had seen it there yet.

She said, "My boyfriend brought it from Chicago."

I looked at the tech. He nodded.

I said, "What's your boyfriend's name?" No answer. "Fine," I said. "Protect the guy who dumped you. You better love him a lot, because you're going to prison for him." I turned to the DPS patrol. "Book her." The girl gasped. I could see tears in her eyes. One of those moments when I wanted to be the one setting someone free, instead of locking her up. "Call me if you remember his name."

As I stepped out into the sunshine in front of HQ, onto the brick expanse that fronted the interstate, I saw a dozen or so people watching as Miles was interviewed for the TV news. Miles's size and shape next to the square-jawed interviewer didn't buy him credibility. I stood behind Miles at an angle so I could hear him but he couldn't see me. He was wearing his good suit, one that fit him just fine once, and a clean shirt which no longer closed around or beneath his many chins.

"Lieutenant Niederwald, how many men do you have mobilized for today's event?"

"We have three hundred men today, uniform and plainclothes."

"Don't you think that's excessive, considering that turnout for the entire event isn't expected to be that high?"

"What are your numbers, 'cause we ain't got none yet."

I stifled a laugh. If Chief Cronin was trying out Miles for mouthpiece, he hadn't researched the issue. No one told him that Miles had long surrendered his practice of staying sober till lunch.

"Is there any connection between the police presence here and the Key shooting?"

"The perpetrator of that incident is no longer at large."

"And yet still people wonder if the police are moderate enough in their approach to be charged with keeping order at an event such as this protest."

Miles tightened his spine and grabbed the only line he could find: "APD has one of the strictest use-of-force policies in the country. There's consequences for anyone violating departmental policy."

"The NAACP and other groups have filed complaints that force is used disproportionately against suspects who are African American or Latin—"

I caught his face turning red a half second before he burst out.

"God damn it, we got the damn killer! What the hell do you want?"

The interviewer's face lit up. My lungs collapsed.

Miles tried to backtrack. "I mean, I mean people always say we're rougher on black people than we are on regular . . . white folks. I mean . . . That's not the way it is. The killer was white. If they resist, they resist, that ups the ante."

The interviewer looked amazed at her good fortune. "So are you saying—"

Some woman from Public Information stepped in front of Miles. "I think the best way to express this . . ."

I jumped into the melee, grabbed Miles by both arms and pulled him inside the lobby. When he realized who had him he said, "That's it, right? I'm fucked?"

10:15 A.M.—APD Administration, Fifth Floor

Torbett took the elevator up to five.

He didn't change out of his Saturday clothes. After answering the call and giving his family the bad news, he didn't dare suit up in office clothes at home before leaving them in the lurch. Nan followed him outside and closed the door. She felt like they were working toward opposite ends, she said. She was staying home like an old-fashioned mom, not her style, but it was the only way to keep the family together, give the kids a sense they were coming home to something. And for all her work, he was working against her, going to the office on Saturday, when they had something planned, something important. Why was he always on call?

"This is important," he said.

Guy walked out the front door and slammed it, then crossed the lawn and headed down the block.

"Guy," his mother shouted, "where are you going? Guy?"

There was nothing to say. She was right. But he had to go. When he saw her in his rearview mirror, he wondered if she'd be there when he got home. Women will only take so much.

Meanwhile the document from Virginia Key's desk sat folded in his pants pocket. He couldn't leave it at home for fear Nan would ask about it and he'd have to explain it or lie. He couldn't use it officially because of the illegal seizure. And what was more, he couldn't deny to himself that, in the impulse of placing the document in his pocket, where it would now sit until the end of time, that he wasn't trying to unearth evidence against Virginia Key but to hide it.

The elevator door opened onto the carpeted Fifth Floor. A mature receptionist granted him a cheekbones-only smile, announced him by phone and pointed to the chair where he would wait, magazine-less, for a strategic fifteen minutes on the dot, to remind him who was in charge; then Miss Elderly buzzed him in.

Chief Cronin sat behind the desk in full dress uniform, waist-length jacket with four stars on each epaulette, paperwork in small, neat piles on his expansive desk, his oversized leather chair flanked by portraits of John Wayne and Arnold Palmer. "Sergeant. Have a seat."

Torbett noticed that the man seemed to have aged five years in the two or so since taking office, his Nordic features crunching and compressing away from his bald pate, wrinkles deepening, eyebrows perpetually lowered in a partial squint, something Torbett had caught himself doing and had to deliberately undo when he arrived home each night. He used the same action now only without rubbing his face, relaxing his eyebrows as best he could, to hide his suspicion as he sat before the chief.

"Torbett. Jim. How long have you been with the department?"

"My file is in front of you, sir."

Cronin forced a chuckle. "So it is. How's that, um, Key case going?"

"Sergeant Reles tracked the perpetrator to Houston on Thursday. The perpetrator was killed in a car accident. Reles and two Houston officers sustained minor injuries. You probably read all that in the reports."

"Anything questionable about the accident?"

"No."

"Good. We understand there's going to be some kind of protest starting in your neighborhood today."

Torbett lifted his chin. Of course his address was in his file. The department knew most things. He had just forgotten that the department would use what it knew. "*My* neighborhood?"

"They're rounding up now at the church parking lot on Chestnut and MLK. The plan is to travel along MLK to Congress, then to walk down to the capitol for a rally."

"Yes?"

"Don't play dumb, Torbett."

"I know of the rally, sir."

"We want you to be there."

The chief spoke with a midwestern crispness, law and order before right or wrong.

"I don't understand."

"It's no secret that I'm not pleased about your comportment at the press conference Wednesday—"

"I'm not the public information officer—"

Cronin burst. "I don't want to argue about this!" Torbett sensed the document in his pocket. "I allowed this march. What I need you to do is go there and keep it under control. Mollify the protesters."

Torbett felt his eyebrows tighten. "Mollify?"

"Since those Key kids got shot, word is out, come to Austin. People are coming in from all over the state, Louisiana . . . in droves. I'm getting calls from the highway patrol. This event has potential for crisis, both in terms of injuries and potential harm to the community."

Torbett opted not to add, *and public relations.* Instead he said, "Why me? Sir."

The obvious answer had something to do with color, and Cronin dodged it. "You're smart, Torbett. You can make 'sir' sound like an insult."

"I've served this department faithfully for seventeen years."

"And been rewarded for it."

Torbett sat up straight, weighed his words. "It's my job to uphold the law. Not to violate people's constitutional right to free assembly."

Cronin's eyes refocused. He flipped through Torbett's file. "On Wednesday night you were involved in an altercation with a suspect named Arthur Peary. Resisting arrest?"

"He attacked me."

"Was that before or after you used the Taser?"

Torbett checked his breathing. "I used the Taser when he approached me in a threatening manner—"

"A threatening manner? And when did you shoot him?"

It almost wasn't worth answering. The cards were stacked. "Sergeant Reles fired the shots after the suspect attacked me. He did that in attempt to protect my life."

Cronin nodded. "Torbett, you're a family man. Probably your family is accustomed to a certain level of comfort."

Torbett felt the punch. He'd been foolish to stand up to the chief. He should have known the threat when he walked in. *Play ball or I'll fire you on trumped-up charges.*

Choose your battles, Torbett thought. *And don't try to battle the chief with career-wrecking documents in your pants pocket.* It was Virginia Key who had put those documents there, with her innocent eyes and her mousey voice. Virginia who he'd tried to protect. And because of her, he couldn't stand up to the chief, risk mediation in an open forum. Torbett stood up and straightened his jacket.

"Where do I report? Sir."

11:00 A.M.—2013 Maxwell Lane

Rainbow John was smoking a joint in front of the TV when the phone rang.

"Yeah?"

"This is blah blah Anderton of Anderton and Park." A lawyer.

"Yeah."

"We were asked to call you by a Miss Debbie Kubasik." Woman's

name, not familiar. It sounded bogus, but John found a pen and wrote it down. *"She suggested we call you about getting in touch with a certain gentleman who might be able to help her with bail or my fee. She has the resources but not where she can get them right now. She said the officer holding her was Sergeant Reles."* He spelled the name.

"All right."

"One last point. She asked that your friend do anything necessary to secure her release. And she wanted to make sure we emphasized that word. Anything."

11:15 A.M.—HQ

I got Miles upstairs and started pouring coffee into him. A call would come, maybe not until Monday, but maybe now, and he had to be in good shape when it came.

"Offensive is bad," I said. "You don't bitch about the interviewer and you don't complain that Public Info put you in front of a camera. Got it?"

"I got it."

"Defensive is bad. You acknowledge that you fucked up, you used the wrong words. You don't grovel."

Jake tossed in, "Were you drinking?"

"I had one drink!"

I said, "No. You didn't drink before the interview. You had a few drinks last night. You have any Valium?"

"At home."

"Push comes to shove, you took a Valium this morning because you were nervous about the interview."

He sipped his coffee with resignation. He seemed less ready to fight than to surrender. "Jake says you and Torbett are still on Virginia Key."

"He said that?" I turned to Jake.

"He's my CO, man," Jake said. "He raised me. What could I do?"

Miles's eyes wandered the room, looking for something worth focusing on. "She'll be speaking at that thing today."

"I guess."

He said, "If you're right, if someone besides that Brit was in on it?"

"Yeah?"

"Suppose it's a grudge, like you said. The Black Talon bullet. Deader than dead. Suppose he cares more about doing it, especially after he fucked up once, than he does about getting away? Maybe he's some Klan fuck who thinks he'll be a hero."

"Okay."

"Then he wouldn't mind witnesses."

I thought about it, then bolted from the room. Miles still had it.

11:45 A.M.—First Austin Baptist Church, Chestnut Avenue and MLK

At HQ, I took the surveillance photo of Joey and Mo Nadiri shooting pool, covered Joey's half and ran off fifty copies. Then I called Torbett at home, got no answer, ditto at Key's, and tried Dispatch, who said Torbett was at a church parking lot, working the march.

By the time I got there the crowd was overflowing into Chestnut Avenue and the vacant lot across the street, over a thousand people, white and black, under a banner of NO BLOOD FOR OIL. Yesterday's rain clouds had cleared, the sun shined and we were looking at an afternoon high of 62 degrees, God smiling on the peace march. Martin Luther King Jr. Boulevard had been sliced in half, auto traffic now packing a single lane bound in each direction, as the other two lanes filled with bodies. East of Chestnut Avenue sat over a dozen patrol cars and some police vans, the modern equivalent of the old Black Mariah; fully a hundred patrols, some in riot gear, stood around sucking their guts in and spoiling for action. I found Torbett arguing with a patrol sergeant, one of the breed of stone-faced ex-military ghouls who can take a promotion but can't let go of the uniform. The cracks in the patrol sergeant's face shifted slightly but didn't give, and Torbett finally tossed up his hands and stormed away. I chased him.

"What was that about?"

He glanced quickly at me, then plodded on, his head swiveling, and joined a group of half a dozen men and women, including two with clergy collars. I took these for the parade organizers. I kept at a distance as he spoke to them, but a few shot dirty looks back at me. Finally he headed back in my direction and breezed by me. I followed chase.

"It's not helping me to be seen with you," he said.

"Jews and blacks have a lot in common."

"That may be," he said. "But your people came here for a better life. And they came by choice." He walked on. "Schleider, the patrol sergeant. He has some kind of 'plan' I'm not supposed to know about. I'm supposed to mollify the marchers. All the marchers want is to march."

"Where's Virginia Key?"

He stopped. "She's speaking today. Why?"

"Whoever tried to kill her fucked up once. But at the podium she's a sitting duck."

"A thousand witnesses," he said.

"Fuckload of good that did JFK."

I handed him the photocopies of Bad Mo.

"What's this?"

"Maybe nothing. Big dealer. Gaz Cruikshank's only known associate with money. Just a hunch."

"What do you want me to do?"

"Pass these to the patrols. Have them keep an eye out for him."

"Those are Schleider's boys. They won't hear it from me."

I took the bundle back and handed him one copy, then headed off to find Schleider. I'd traveled a few steps when Torbett called, "Reles!"

"Yeah."

"Who's in the other half of this picture?"

I jolted. I should have had an answer ready. "That's . . . separate," I said.

Torbett added, "But equal?"

Schleider was leaning on a patrol car. He'd donned his aviator shades and crossed his ankles. I walked close enough that he had to wave away the patrols surrounding him. "Homicide, right?" he said. "I saw you with that Torbett."

I squinted at the sky. "Boy don't have the sense God gave geese."

He showed his tobacco-yellow teeth. "What can I do for you?"

I gave him the bundle. "We have intelligence this man is an out-side agitator. Planning to create havoc, maybe pin it on the police. Armed and dangerous."

Schleider surveyed Mo's pockmarked face. "A-rab?"

"You guessed it."

He nodded. Done.

12:00 P.M.—2013 Maxwell Lane

When he heard the car door close, Mo clicked awake, still restful, but did not open his eyes where he lay, in the back seat of his Caddy. A long silence from the front seat. Finally, he heard Rainbow John ask tentatively, "Is he . . . sleeping?!"

"It has happened, Rainbow John," Mo said. "And soon I will know a bliss which is complete and total."

"Oh," Rainbow John said. "Cool."

There was no point in explaining. Mo knew where he would be in, perhaps, a matter of hours. Sweet Anything would come to him, send him to paradise with her smooth hands, free his soul from his body. But he had to stay mobile until he finished the crucial business, the bitch. He had barely grieved for his parents, put everything he had into saving his sister. It all caught him when she died, three deaths in one. And one person to take the blame. Virginia Key.

"Rainbow John," he said, "what good news have you brought me?"

"I didn't understand it. These lawyers called, they said this chick is in the lockup. That this cop, Reles, is holding her." John gave the woman's name, unfamiliar. Debbie Kubasik.

"How does this concern me?"

"She said you should do anything to get her out. And they made sure to use that word. *Anything.*"

Mo felt his spine seize and his face burn, as he leaned his head back and cried out in frustration and grief. Reles has found Anything, arrested her. Kept him from his promised destiny. They had stolen everything from him, his parents, his brothers, his sister, and now even his death. His world would bust apart, settled in pieces, and then congealed into a single, final idea that made him grow strong again:

He would have his revenge.

12:15 P.M.—Casa Rosa Apartments, East Twelfth Street

I drove east thinking about all the leads I'd dropped in the months after Joey's death, when depression and liquor fogged my thinking and Miles's concern for Rachel's pension and life insurance obstructed my curiosity. My standing in the department was too shaky, back then, for me to keep plugging against Miles's wishes. But now Miles was the one in dutch with the Fifth Floor, thanks to his liquid diet and his poor interviewing skills. And I was the grown-up.

I thought about the Joey/Nadiri photo.

Joey had very few friends in Austin, that I knew of, who weren't on the force. One, apparently, was Nadiri. The photo showed the two of them shooting pool in a whorehouse.

Joey had one other non-cop friend who worked, occasionally, in that same whorehouse. And she lived just a few blocks away, if she hadn't moved.

By the faded pink stucco of Casa Rosa Apartments on East Twelfth, I headed up the iron outside staircase and knocked on number 11, interrupted its rumblings into a sudden silence. I pounded the door with my palm.

"I'm busy!" a woman's voice called out.

I shouted, "Police!"

A man's voice said, "Shit!"

In a few seconds the door opened. Vita, green eyes blazing, long black hair tipped in crayon red, held a kimono over her ample brown breasts. "You!"

"Did I interrupt?"

She headed for the bedroom, shouting, "It's okay, it's just a friend." I followed her to see a bland-looking nobody half in a gray suit, one leg out the window. He froze when he saw me.

"Haven't I seen you?" I asked. "In the papers?"

He tried to draw his head, turtle style, into his collar. I was pretty sure he was some low-level bureaucrat, water company, electric company. A blurb in the police blotter would be it for him.

"Please," he muttered. "Please!"

"Who are you kidding?" she asked me. "You're just like him."

"Second storey, pal," I said. "Pull your pants on and go."

He left the front way. Vita slammed the door. "Thanks a lot, asshole! I'll never see him again." Her kimono had breezed wide open and she took a moment to hold the lapels out before crossing and tying them shut. She wanted to remind me who held the cards. She'd been a friend, of some sort, to Joey Velez. After that, she and I had a drunken moment together one night that cost me a lot and could have cost me more. The years since my last peek had been kind. Her tannish skin had smoothed, if anything. Full, brown-tipped breasts, soft pubic hair and hips unpinched by the burden of undergarments. She said, "You think it's easy making a living, with you assholes busting everything that walks?"

"You could get a job."

"Yeah," she asked, lighting a cigarette. "Are the pigs hiring?"

"You been keeping your little ear to the ground?"

"No," she sneered. "Just my little knees. Last week I got busted at the supermarket. Shopping. Two weeks ago coming home, two patrol cops stopped me, felt my tits, and dumped the condoms out of my purse."

"I'm sorry," I said. "Maybe I can talk to somebody."

"Good-hearted cop."

"How well did you know Joey Velez?"

She took a deep drag. "Take a guess."

I held up the photo. "You ever see him with this guy?"

She didn't look at the shot, instead swung open the front door and let the cool air and light in.

I stepped out the door and turned toward her. I don't know if I was waiting for her to answer the question or open her robe again. Or what I would have done if she had.

I said, "This is for Joey." I held up the picture again. She looked at it.

"No," she said, "I never saw him. Tell you something about your friend, though," she said. "He always paid."

I took out my money and peeled off a twenty. She stared at me. I peeled off another. She took them both.

She put one hand on the knot in her sash. Then she slammed the door.

I went home, dropped the Joey/Nadiri photo on the coffee table. Then I hauled out Joey's cardboard box, flipped through some of it and dialed Rachel at work. The receptionist patched me through, which meant Rachel didn't have a client, but she kept me holding for two minutes anyway. I deserved it. I looked at Joey's notes: *Seized property on Ulit: 150G. Less 80 is 70G.*

Rachel finally picked up. *"Hi."*

"You left early," I said. "We were gonna spend the day together, the weekend."

"We were?"

I glanced at the box, and the assorted Joey papers, and the Joey/Nadiri photo on the coffee table. If she'd walked in on this, I'd be single.

"I'm sorry," I said, which beat conceding that I would have canceled out on her today if she hadn't canceled first.

"For what?"

"For everything. For being a lousy boyfriend."

"That's not very specific."

"You know what I mean." Silence. "Listen, I was wondering if we could have dinner tonight, someplace nice."

Pause. *"Yes, that would be fine."* Her official voice.

"Yeah, okay. Have your secretary put it in your schedule."

"Is it worth it?" The doorbell rang. *"Who's that?"* I peeked through the front window. Carter Serio, Internal Affairs. At my front door.

"No one," I said. "Salesman." The bell rang again. I waved at Serio through the window, showed him the phone and my index finger, one minute. It wasn't the finger I had in mind. To Rachel. "I'm sorry for canceling, I'm sorry for canceling again. I'll be there tonight unless someone gets killed."

Another silence, and a settlement: *"Most I can ask."*

We rang off and I opened the door. I knew from experience that Serio, half a foot shorter than me and nearly gray but still heavy and powerful, could take me down without too much effort. I leaned in the doorway: he'd have to tackle me if he wanted entry. He held a bale of photocopies a quarter-inch thick.

"Sorry, man," I said, "I was on with my girlfriend."

"Anyone I know?"

I was used to cracks about my living with Joey's wife. "You saw I have a phone."

"Funny thing about that. Did you know we can get phone records, as long as we get a subpoena signed by the judge? But you do know that, because you've got Jake Lund calling around, trying to get a judge on a Saturday. Mind if I come in?"

He tried to step past me and I shifted in front of him, very casual, not defensive. I had Joey's stuff on the rug, and a photo of Joey with Nadiri on the coffee table. I raised my chin and my chest and tried to act territorial, not like I was hiding something.

"I know Jake didn't tell you what I was up to," I grinned, sparring all friendly. Jake was more likely to give something away, say, to Miles out of devotion, than to Serio out of rank. "So you've got something set up with the judge's office or maybe even Southwestern Bell to call you if anyone snoops around internally."

"Good man, that Jake," he said, stepping back so he wouldn't seem so short. "Nice place. Own or rent?"

"It's my day off, Lieutenant. I'll swing by on Monday if you wanna shoot the shit."

"You got me wrong, Reles. I'm glad you're on the Velez case again. I'll help you. It's my job to find out what happened, not to make the department look good."

"Well, thanks." I stepped back and grabbed the doorknob, preparing for a smooth closing maneuver. "If I need anything I'll get in touch with you."

"I know that Thursday night you killed a suspect in Houston under very peculiar circumstances."

My breath caught. I said, "I was in the presence of a Houston detective and a Houston patrol. The two vehicles collided. My vehicle—"

"Mm-hmm. And last night you and Milsap, your old pal, brought in a service man with a bag of cash, and he was cleared in an hour. Even *I* can't get to the bottom of that."

I deadpanned it. I wanted to hear what he had to say but I didn't want to owe him for it.

He said, "The release orders came from Bergstrom by way of the governor's office. No explanation. The military is beyond my authority."

I took in a breath to say something, but let it out. I was stumped too. I opened the door again.

"Look, Reles," he said. "I know I'm a ballbuster. That's my job. You and me, we're not like these other guys. A bunch of Aggie dropouts with badges and guns, doing whatever the hell they want. I'm not trying to fire you. Shit, you saw how hard it was to get rid of Milsap. But not cooperating with Internal Affairs, that alone is a serious violation."

I rolled along with it, gave a theatrical sigh and started. "The guy who died in Houston, Gary Cruikshank, positive ID on him as the shooter in the Key case. Milsap helped me track him. Cruikshank was a junkie. So I was helping Milsap at that shooting gallery they've been keeping an eye on. We took down the kid, GI Joe. Don't ask me why they sprung him."

It was a collection of half-truths about Serio's size and he mulled it over. "I suppose Milsap's account will confirm this?" I shrugged. Why not? Serio wouldn't get anything out of Milsap or Narco. Narco had become a department of its own, gassed up on balls and adrenaline, only tossing Serio its rejects now and again. He came to me as a last resort.

"If it means anything," I said, "the names on the release order were the lieutenant governor, Chief Cronin and a general named Knobloch."

He nodded. "One more name than I had."

"Let me know if you find out anything about it?" I asked, good-natured.

He nodded. "Let me know what you find on Velez."

"You know I will." We shook hands, not exactly enemies. He handed me the bale of copies and I closed the door on his back.

1:45 P.M.—First Austin Baptist Church, Chestnut Avenue and MLK

By one thirty, Torbett guessed the crowd had swelled to two thousand, spilling a block down Chestnut and filling the empty lot across the little street. Groups gradually took their places behind banners which stretched back for blocks along MLK: individual church banners, NAACP, Concerned Mothers, Doctors for Racial and Economic Justice, War Resisters League. They'd brought sandwiches and soda and shared them freely, meeting and greeting old friends and complete strangers as if they were friends. If Nan and the kids were there, or at least Nan and Jule, he hadn't seen them. The sky was mostly clear, cloud cover high, and the air had warmed up, a pleasant break from yesterday's rain and fog and damp chill. Everyone looked celebratory, except Schleider's patrols.

The traffic had been blocked on MLK much too early and it was clogged on both ends, two lanes not enough to allow for Saturday excursions. Horns beeped and occasional epithets were hurled, "Go back to Russia," "Arabs die" and such. But Torbett had hopes it would finish out smoothly.

Torbett assembled the organizers: a housewife, four clergymen (two black, two white), some white college girls, two of the local NAACP—all in all about a dozen of the nicest protesters he'd ever met. They reviewed the parade route: MLK to Congress Avenue to the capitol, what could be simpler?

"Can anyone tell me," he asked, "where Virginia Key is right now?"

Most of the black faces grimaced. "She's at the capitol," one woman said. "She insisted on speaking."

Another said, "Terrible what happened to those babies."

General muttered assent. Torbett thanked them all for their help and cooperation.

"Please understand," said an older black clergyman whose name had flown from Torbett's head. He spoke with a Jamaican lilt. "This is a protest, but a nonviolent protest. You will have no trouble with the marchers today, Brother Torbett."

"That's good," Torbett said.

The reverend nodded at a row of Schleider's sour faced men. Like the traffic, they had been allowed to stagnate too long.

The reverend added, "I only hope those pigs have such a fine overseer as yourself."

1:45 P.M.—706 East Thirty-eighth Street

I sifted through the reports Serio had handed me, a bail of them, copies of computer printouts, letter size, printed on the horizontal, dotted lines across the printing.

AUSTIN POLICE INFORMATION NETWORK   PAGE 7,808

INCIDENTS MORE THAN 2 YEARS OLDER THAN CURRENT YEAR

INCIDENT REPORT

INCIDENT NO=88-03-09-H-0015   TYPE=3500 *DECEASED PERSON

REPORTED DATE=MARCH 9, 1988   REPORTED TIME=0150

DISPATCH=2893 DODY MARTHA NELL

ORIGINAL=XSUPPLEMENT PAGE 1

NARRATIVE 3/9/88   REPORTING OFFICER 1027 RYDLE, HOWARD,

BAKER SECTOR

I ANSWERED A CALL TO THE MOUNTAIN PASS OF FM 2222 (CAT MOUNTAIN). WHEN I ARRIVED, FIRE TRUCKS HAD ALREADY ARRIVED AND BLOCKED THE ENTIRE SOUTHBOUND TWO LANES. ONE FIREFIGHTER WAS DIRECTING TRAFFIC. I PARKED SOUTH OF THEM AND SET UP CONES AND FLARES DIVIDING THE TWO NORTHBOUND LANES FOR NORTH AND SOUTHBOUND TRAFFIC.

Scanning down.

ORIGINAL=ZSUPPLEMENTAL   PAGE 2

NARRATIVE 3/9/88   REPORTING OFFICER 3939 MALAO, RONALD

RESPONDING TO A CALL TO CAT MOUNTAIN PASS OF FM 2222. OFFICER RYDLE HAD SET UP CONES AND WAS DIRECTING TRAFFIC. TWO FIRE TRUCKS BLOCKED THE SOUTHBOUND LANES. WITH NO WATER

SUPPLY, FIREFIGHTERS STOOD BY THE EDGE. WHAT APPEARED TO BE ONE VEHICLE HAD GONE OVER THE CLIFF AND CRASHED IN FLAMES, APPROXIMATELY ONE HUNDRED FEET BELOW. HELICOPTERS . . .

Scanning.

. . . UNTIL THE FIRE WAS OUT. SERGEANT RELES APPEARED INTOXICATED, STUMBLED DOWN THE HILL. THE VEHICLE BY THEN HAD BEEN IDENTIFIED AS BELONGING TO HOMICIDE SENIOR SERGEANT JOSE VELEZ . . .

. . . SUN HAD COME UP. WHEN THE FIRE TRUCKS LEFT I CHECKED THE ROAD FOR SKID MARKS AND AT FIRST DIDN'T FIND ANY, LEADING ME TO BELIEVE THAT THE VICTIM HAD BEEN ASLEEP AT THE WHEEL. BUT CUTTING DIAGONALLY ACROSS THE NORTHBOUND LANE, I DISCOVERED SKID MARKS APPROXIMATELY EIGHTEEN INCHES IN LENGTH, ENDING SUDDENLY, SUGGESTING THE VICTIM HAD SWERVED OFF COURSE AND JAMMED ON HIS BRAKES. THEN HE EITHER RELEASED THEM OR THEY GAVE OUT. I PHOTOGRAPHED THE TREADS AND TURNED THE FILM OVER TO LIEUTENANT NIEDERWALD, HOMICIDE DIVISION . . .

The freaky element of this was that most of the cars that drove off 2222 had done it on the way south, heading back home after a day or evening of drinking at the lake. Joey was headed north. He had to cut across the southbound lanes to go over the cliff. But it was dark, a twisting road and he was already drunk.

Serio attached a list of phone calls, records from Southwestern Bell, calls that Joey and Rachel's house had received on the day he died, March 8 going into March 9, 1988. One was Rachel's dentist. Two couples who could have been Rachel's clients, or friends I didn't know. To find out, I could read her phone book, or sniff around her old business records, if she kept them, or ask her, if I felt like telling her I'd broken my promise to let dead husbands lie. I could contact them directly if I had a plan for covering up who I was, and for making sure they didn't get back to Rachel. I put the idea aside.

The last call, at 11:38 P.M., was from a pay phone downtown. It didn't take much to figure that was the call Joey was answering when he went out and died.

I gave the Joey/Nadiri photo a long look, reminding myself where it had been taken: in a whorehouse I shouldn't have recognized, called Heaven's Gate. The place was owned by university president Bill Oliver, though we couldn't prove it. Oliver came from an oil family, and seemed to be using the university gig and the academic credibility it gave him to bridge the gap between the public and private sectors, both of which he would, one day, own. I also had a hunch the candid photo was not an accident. Oliver had given me the photo, but the chances of his giving me any details about the photo or its subjects were about nil: while the brothel was disclosed to be a cop playground, the thrust of its trade was on the rich and powerful side. I was among those who believed Oliver used his candid photography system to capture them as they romped, and blackmail them later to build and maintain his power. But that's just me talking.

I felt like I was slipping back into the craziness of those months, the months that followed Joey's death. That ended when I hooked up with Rachel and promised to stop wondering about Joey. And here I was spinning the events of his death around in my head again. It pissed me off because it never went anywhere. And it made me feel guilty. Also I was supposed to be on the Key case. But if I found out what happened to Joey, and why, well, then I wouldn't be curious anymore. Rachel didn't have to know.

I didn't know much about Nadiri. Homeless junkie Gaz Cruikshank shot the Key kids, with a gun he couldn't have afforded. Gaz died leaving a pie pan of cooked Karachi, heroin from Pakistan. Nadiri was the likely bigwig for Karachi traffic in Texas, or at least in Austin, and he was the likely source for general heroin sales to Gaz and thousands like him. Nadiri was Gaz's only human connection with money. And Narco had been after Nadiri, or said they had, for a while.

By the time I got back to Homicide, Miles was gone. "The call never came," Jake said. Jake was alternately watching CNN, tapping the computer and reading a newspaper. "He looked at the empty coffeepot and said, 'Sobered up for nothin'!' Then he split."

"Jake, listen. About those phone records from Joey's house. I want more. I want you to find out what you can about Joey's last few months."

"You were there, man."

"I'm not so sure. Rachel said once they only had a few hundred in a checking account, but I have some notes that he was putting down eighty grand on a seized ten-unit property on Ulit."

"Seized foreclosed, or seized DA's office?"

"Try the DA first. I want to know if he put that money down and where it is."

"And where it came from?"

Jake looked at me like he'd just figured out some unfortunate truth about Santa Claus.

"Yeah, well," I said, "let's just figure out a piece of this at a time. Bank records, IRS."

"Yeah, okay."

"You get anything on that Nadiri?"

"A little," he said. "No rap sheet, though. Either he's good or he's connected."

"Figure both."

"INS says he emigrated from Afghanistan in '80, joined the air force the same year. Released in '82."

"Any connection to a General Knobloch? He might not have been a general then."

"Sorry, doc. Out of my league."

"You know anything about Afghanistan?"

"Besides what I told you? No. But I know who would." He picked up his newspaper, turned a few pages and flipped the paper down on his desk.

Under a photo of a bespectacled man, bald on top with his remaining hair grown down to his shoulders, read the small headline, "Activist Runs for City Council." The copy began, *Vying for the vacated fifth seat on the city council, known activist Bob Temple, the author of several articles on the U.S. military presence in the Middle East . . ."*

I picked up the phone.

2:00 P.M.—706 East Thirty-eighth Street

With no real work to do, Rachel headed home for a change of clothes and a cigarette and maybe lunch. She wasn't surprised that Dan's car was already gone when she got there. It would have been unpolitic to see him right away after their call. But it would have been nice.

She slipped out of her semicasual Saturday "I'm just in the office to catch up" clothes and was about to go wash up when the phone rang. She picked up in the living room.

"Hello?"

"Excuse me, madam. Is Daniel Reles at home?" A man's deep voice, foreign accent, maybe Indian.

"No. You can call him at the office."

"I would prefer not to. I have information which may be of interest."

Christ, she thought. Did the business have to come home? She looked around, found a pencil and paper on the end table.

"Okay, go ahead."

"I am a friend of Joey Velez."

Rachel's writing hand froze.

"Hello?" he said. *"Are you there?"*

She answered in clipped tones. "Your name and number please."

"I have information which may be of great use to him. I will call back."

"Who is this?" Rachel tried to control her breathing.

"Why, Mrs. Velez. You are so very short tempered. I can see why Mr. Velez had such trouble with you."

She tried her most authoritative voice, but her throat tightened and it sounded, to her, nearly like crying. "Who is this?!"

"I speak of a matter of interest to your current gentleman friend. It is of no importance to you." He hung up.

Rachel's hand shook as she placed the phone in the cradle.

That's what the dream was about, she thought. Her past was coming back. Joey had told someone. And now that someone was going to tell Dan.

2:45 P.M.—Magnolia Café, South Congress Avenue

I headed down Congress, checking my rearview mirror. I'd been getting the strange sensation of being watched, maybe followed. I shifted lane to lane. There were a dozen cars behind me. None took an interest.

I'd laid off the Magnolia Café for a while, a hippie joint with an assortment of art for sale, a community bulletin board, entrees of the vegetarian and near-vegetarian variety, and a hip but unconditional welcome to anyone, even cops, twenty-four hours a day. I'd worn out my welcome with the night manager, a childhood friend of Joey's, but he wasn't on duty or didn't work there anymore when I showed up that day to meet Bob Temple, and it seemed like the right spot for the meeting.

Temple, in an army jacket and baggy jeans, his body thickening with middle age, shook my hand suspiciously at the door and we found a booth. The padded vinyl seats sparkled red, and clear plastic covered a batik print—an image of Don Quixote fighting a windmill—that wrapped the tabletop. Temple had clipped his hair short for the city council campaign. He hadn't bought a suit. We both ordered without glancing at the menus. Then he said, "You want to know about Afghanistan."

I said, "I want insight."

"Why should I help you?"

"Bring a killer to justice."

"Your job, not mine."

"Then what?" I asked.

"A story."

"Are you a reporter?"

He said, "The people who run for city council, they start like me. Leftists. Idealists. Nobodies. But the corporations developing Austin—the people who developed Barton Springs, the Blacklands, the hill country—they drop money on these candidates. Ten thousand, fifteen thousand, for nothing. To the corporations, it's pocket change. But to the candidates, that's a whole small-town campaign. By the time they get into office, they've sold out already."

I said, "Including Virginia Key?"

He grinned. Several people were after the same seat. Key had the most name recognition, good or bad. It made her the likely favorite. "The donations are public record. I've turned down three offers already."

"You're a moral man."

He spoke calmly. "I don't care that you don't believe that. If I took the money and turned on them, they'd have me killed. For these little donations, they have the city council in their pockets. That's why, if you look at the record, the city council has always sold the city out, always let the developers move in and do pretty much whatever they wanted, even if it made the water unswimmable or undrinkable. The council always sells out, and not to the highest bidder, either. To the first."

"So?" I said.

"When you get your killer, I get a story I can break in the *Chronicle*. If it's hot enough, maybe the *Statesman*. Then I'm a muckraker who gets results."

"And free publicity," I added.

"And with luck, the city gets one new council member who hasn't already been bought."

A waiter dropped Temple's whole-wheat pancakes and my burger.

"Sold," I said. "Talk to me. Military profiteering in Afghanistan."

He doused his pancakes with butter and syrup, stuffed a mouthful and said, "Macro and micro. Macro: a U.S. president employs his army to protect the oil interests of his rich friends. Kuwait is a tiny country with oil under every grain of sand. We can't have that in Iraqi hands. But China marched into Tibet and you didn't see us complaining. Tibet is Kuwait without oil."

"Okay," I said. "Micro: some guy stashing a load of heroin in the back of a cargo plane."

"Lots of it, sure. The micro is part of the macro. Don't fool yourself that the world is just, and some random bad guy comes out of nowhere who wants to ruin everything."

"Don't worry about it."

"There's always been lots of profiteering, by individuals and groups at every level, even in W.W. Two, the good war. And in a different way since then. NSC 68."

I chewed. "Am I supposed to know what that is?"

"To defense contractors, the Second World War meant wealth beyond their wildest dreams. They weren't about to give up their source of income just because the war ended. God knows how this went down, but on April 14, 1950, National Security Council Memo 68 proposed an intensive buildup of political, military and economic strength for what was called the Free World. What it meant was the U.S. economy would stay on a wartime footing even in peacetime. But to get Americans to go along with it, with an ever-increasing amount of their tax dollars spent on defense rather than, say, schools, they'd have to be convinced that there was a threat against them. That worked when we had the Soviet Union, but now we don't. So we have Iraq."

I'd heard crazier things before and seen them prove out. So NSC 68 set up half a century of fat military contracts and kickbacks and more. Fair enough. "A little more micro," I said. "What if I have a guy, an Afghani, who's dealing drugs in the U.S.?"

He smiled. "We backed the insurgents in Afghanistan, armed them against the Soviets. But there was no way they could win. Now the Soviets are gone, they don't even exist. And all these different Afghani factions are shooting at each other. With American weapons. The country is reduced to rubble."

"So . . ."

"So," he said, wiping up buttery syrup with some pancake. "Out of the rubble you have a bunch of people with nothing to lose. And a range of opportunists. Scroungers, thieves, pimps. And, of course, drug dealers. They know where the money is. It's right here in the U.S."

I thought about Nadiri, working his contacts in the United States and Pakistan and the air force, slowly building his empire.

"P.S.," Temple added. "You're a street-level cop. You think of heroin in grams and ounces."

"So?"

"Think in metric tons."

2:45 P.M.—First Austin Baptist Church, Chestnut Avenue and MLK

Torbett had watched the marchers straggle into place, and noted that the two blocked-off traffic lanes couldn't contain the gathering throng, which now stretched four blocks in each direction, fore and aft. People waited curbside for the opportunity, when the march kicked off and space cleared, to join their group and march in solidarity. Signs and banners bobbed, chants of "Hell no, we won't go, not to die for Texaco!" When the go-ahead came after two o'clock, and the whistles finally blew, first at the front, then by the leaders of each group all down the line, an enormous cheer swelled up and the crowd began to march.

The first groups moved. Others, Torbett could see from his distance by the church, took tentative steps forward and then stopped short, to wait for a traffic jam that would surely clear up soon. For several minutes the crowd on the sidewalks siphoned in and filled any gaps allowed by the march as it stretched out—a tentative beginning but a beginning just the same. Torbett scanned the line and the banners, hoping he'd catch Nan and Jule among them.

By 2:45 the line stretched forward to I-35 and beyond. Stragglers at the end stood a few feet ahead of where they'd started. Save for a better turnout than anyone anticipated, this end, Torbett thought, was going well. He figured he'd head to the front of the march and make sure that was settled. And he'd check on Virginia Key. It was his job.

He'd been distracted, checked-out, all week, dreaming about a new life with a new woman, one he didn't know. His life with Nan was hard and complicated. His life with Virginia Key would be simple and perfect, he'd dreamed. But no life was perfect. It just looked that way from the outside. He'd have to clear his head, shift gears, come back to his family again. And hope that it wasn't too late.

Torbett found his car, drove down Chestnut to Fourteenth to I-35, up the frontage road and under the highway to Fifteenth, west, past the Erwin Center and into the capitol grounds, to Congress Avenue, where the march would turn left. He parked and looked down the barren stretch of Congress toward the capitol, where he saw a group of about fifty people wandering southward. Half the march should have reached that point, he thought, not a tiny cluster. He walked back up to MLK and looked east. Three blocks away, another hundred or so approached. He walked east to greet them.

"What happened?" Torbett asked.

A brown girl of about twenty said, "They busted the organizers. All of them."

Someone else said, "They blocked off the street at I-35. They're only letting a few through at a time."

Torbett ran the rest of the way to I-35. He could see from where he stood that there was very little traffic backed up on the frontage roads, north and south, which meant the cars were being let through almost without interruption. He jogged across the shadowed pass under the highway. Schleider's patrols had blocked the march east of MLK. The marchers were stopped by barricades on the traffic side, the fence along the cemetery and barricades at the front and back. They stood penned in like cattle.

Torbett badged a patrol. "This is a licensed march. Why aren't these people being allowed through?"

"Get to the side of the road."

Torbett held his badge higher. "Hey!"

The patrol did a double take at the badge and Torbett's black face. "Sorry. Orders."

The crowd cried out, argued with the cops, asked questions like, "When are you gonna let us through?" and got answers like, "You wanna make this easy or hard?" Cop answers.

Torbett said, "Last order from a higher ranking officer. Open this barricade now."

"Can't do that, sir."

Torbett slipped his badge back into his breast pocket. The crowd from the east surged forward and shoved the barricade. Torbett saw a line of patrols form along the barricade. The patrols braced their batons with both hands and shoved against the crowd.

3:30 P.M.—Congress Avenue

I headed back up from the Magnolia when my regular mirror checks
yielded something. A tan-colored sedan, maybe a Duster, appeared a
few lengths behind me. Another car cut it off, but each time I checked,
it was there again. I pulled into the right lane, slowed down and
waited for it to pass, but it disappeared, somehow dropping back into
the spotty traffic. Paranoia? I turned off at Riverside, up Lamar and
over the bridge, then east on Fifth and up Congress again through
downtown, and badged my way onto the capitol grounds. The capitol
area was set up for a rally, but I only saw a tiny crowd there. A few
people meandered south in their direction. I parked by the Texas attorney general's office, went in and found Logan's cubicle.

Logan was a longtime acquaintance I'd hit up often for easy information. His willingness to find records for me on cue had faded when
he realized my gratitude wasn't going to make him a cop. I chanced
that an unscheduled visit would have a greater potency than a phone
call and I appeared behind him.

"Logan?"

He spun around, sandy brown hair, aviator glasses of a previous
decade and a mustache trimmed to army regulation, but I couldn't
guess which army. His eyes scored blank.

I said, "Dan Reles."

"Reles! Dan!" He stood and shook my hand. "What gives?"

"I wanted to see where it all happens."

He gestured to his penned-in desk with a sweep of the arm that the
carpeted half-walls cut short.

"Far out," I said. "Bust any good whorehouses lately?"

"You kiddin'? South Congress sweeps. Vice slams the place with
busts but I'm the one that puts it all together." He pointed to a stack
of pages. "That's the porn theater on South Congress and Annie. It's
mine!"

"You bastard," I said. "Joey Velez used to tell me stories about Vice.
He'd bust those places, but without the AG they'd open right back up."

Joey had been on Vice before Homicide, and he'd probably told me stories about it, but the truth was, I couldn't think of any just then.

"What do you need?" he asked with a trace of fatigue. It was a Texas phrase that seemed geared to lower the listener's expectations.

"Mohammed Rashid Nadiri. AKA Bad Mo."

He walked between cubicles, hauled open a file drawer, sifted through, closed it, tried two more drawers, excused himself and came back five minutes later.

"We don't have a file on him," he said, "but I was sure I heard the name. I ran him for involvement. One incident, no details, which is screwy." He handed me a page from a computer printer: no address and a prominent collection of blanks. "I guess he's down as a witness. You probably heard all about the Gautier case, right?"

3:30 P.M.—Martin Luther King Jr. Boulevard

Torbett crossed traffic to the north side of MLK, ran the block to Comal Street where the first block of marchers had been penned in at the rear with metal barricades like bicycle racks. Another set of cops and barricades held back the second group, allowing the occasional trickle of traffic down tiny Comal Street to flow across MLK unimpeded.

Torbett identified himself to a patrol directing traffic and crossed over to the gap between the barricades. A row of patrols stood along each barricade, preventing people from going forward or back or even home.

"Where's Schleider?" Torbett demanded.

"Our orders come from Cronin."

"Who's in charge here?"

The patrol spun his head, then pointed out a thick-necked wrestler, a senior patrol, at the side of the street along the cemetery, talking into a hand radio. Torbett made his way through the patrols. The marchers shouted, chanted, blew whistles. Some of the patrols stood stoically, others mopped sweat from their brows, pointed, shouted. Suddenly the metal barricades rattled. In the first group, a tide from the crowd ahead was pushing back toward Comal and East

Austin, and the few suckers against the barricades were bearing the brunt.

"Let us out!" someone screamed. The shouts were taking on a hysterical tint. Torbett had lost the senior patrol in his sights.

"Jim!" a woman's voice shrieked from the hell side of the barricade. Torbett spun around to see a patrol raising his club at Nan, and Jule looking on helplessly.

3:45 P.M.—Congress Avenue

I cut south out of the capitol complex and headed down Congress when I spotted the tan Duster in my rearview again. The downtown traffic was heavy enough that there were four or five cars between us at any moment, but I could see him. I pulled left, then hit my flashers and did a U-turn into the northbound lane. I slowed down as I approached him but a light turned green ahead and he pulled away with the traffic. I caught a blur of red hair. I tried to pull another U and follow, but cars zoomed past as I tried to cut in, flashers and all, and by the time I headed south again he was gone.

All of which added up to the possibility that I was out of my nut again, a Grade-A paranoiac who thought he was important enough to follow. Besides, I was in a new car now, the white Caprice. Who even knew I had a new car, who might want to have me followed?

The answer came. APD, Internal Affairs, that's who. Carter Serio.

I parked on Tenth Street at Guadalupe and babbled my way into the county jail which, like most things, is easier to get into than to leave. In minutes I was on the cell block I'd visited the day before, spying the figure of the bald, truck-sized biker who'd greeted me yesterday, the one who'd been the bouncer at Gautier's blues club when Joey and I busted it years earlier.

I knew from Logan that Mo Nadiri was on record as having "involvement" with the Gautier case, an operation which involved exchanging parts from stolen cars for money, using that money to buy cocaine which would be out on the street the same day, to be exchanged for even more money. It was the department's first organized-crime bust, and since it qualified as racketeering, the RICO Act allowed for the arrest of everyone involved. As one of a select group avoiding arrest, Nadiri should rate at least a file at the AG's office: either it was restricted and Logan didn't have the access, or someone, maybe Narco, had studiously kept everything they had on Nadiri to themselves. I couldn't ask Joey because he was dead. Gautier was in federal prison, and I was pressed for time. But Gautier's former employee was a captive audience.

The biker rose, along with all the other prisoners, when I entered the cell block. I saw that Shookster, Gaz's old roommate, had left an empty cell. I hoped that was good news. The bouncer saw me stop by his cell, realized who I'd come to see. "Sure," he said. "*Now* you wanna talk."

I slapped the picture of Joey and Nadiri against the glass. He looked closely at it, then nodded. "What are you gonna give me?" he asked. "Shorter time?"

"What'd you get?" I said.

"Two years for possession, an eighth of an ounce of Sense."

Kids walked through the halls of their high school with that much. Sensimelia kicked the shit out of most marijuana but it didn't warrant two years, not at that quantity.

"You won't do five months."

He snarled, hands against the glass. "I'm a repeat offender!" he shouted. "'Cause of Gautier. I did two years hard in the fed for that. And they never *pinned* anything on me."

"Help me and I'll talk to the DA."

He calculated, then shook his head. I walked away.

"Wait a minute!" He waved me back to the window. My promise wasn't worth much, but the microscopic possibility of shorter time weighed out against the threat of serving a full two years, day by day. And he needed to talk, to be heard, as much as I needed to hear him.

"I got screwed," he said. "I didn't do anything but keep the peace. I saw a lot, same as any bouncer. I was there the first time your friend got high." He spotted whatever interest I gave away. The Plexiglas prevented an exchange of cigarettes or cash so he went on. "It makes sense to me now, knowing he was a cop. Everyone is passing this mirror around, doing lines. It got up to your friend. He says, no thanks. It looks suspicious. Who turns down free blow? So they start razzing him and he breaks down and does it. Took to it, I guess. Who doesn't?"

"What about this other guy?" I asked, pointing to Nadiri in the photo.

"I don't know his name."

"Nadiri? Mo?" I offered.

He shrugged. "Gautier's personal connection. Nothing big. He was hardly ever at the club and he never mixed. Whatever else was going through the club, cars or coke and whatever, I don't think it had anything to do with him. He wasn't there when the busts went down."

I wondered if Nadiri was like the young hoods who took over KGB fortunes when the Soviet Union collapsed in '89. Maybe Nadiri had pocketed some of Gautier's assets, with the promise of returning them whenever Gautier saw freedom again.

"You ever see these two together?" I asked.

"Gautier usually met Frankenstein," he meant Nadiri and his lunar complexion, "alone. There were private parties I heard about. Gautier was always in the middle of everything. If someone was introduced, he was doing the introducing."

I put in a call to the DA's office, in the bouncer's defense.

His story meant Joey had been using coke, at least a little, when we met. And that Joey had known Nadiri as long as he knew me, since Nadiri was a small-timer.

And for all I knew, that Joey was more devoted to Nadiri than he was to me. Or to the police.

I was Joey's partner. I was supposed to know all about his life, and I didn't. I headed north to find the person who was supposed to know all about his death.

3:45 P.M.—Martin Luther King Jr. Boulevard

All the events of those seconds flashed to Torbett like snapshots to be observed and analyzed later, all snapped during the long drawn-out moment of the nightstick swinging down. The image of Nan spotting him from the other side of the barricades. The desperate, terrified plea in Nan's face. Jule's mouth opening in a cry of infantile horror. Torbett himself in flight as he leapt on the patrol and grabbed the baton with one hand as it swung down, steering it away from Nan and kicking the patrol's feet from under him. Other patrols wheeling around at the unfamiliar, black intruder; the words "He's a cop! He's a cop!" hanging in the air; the slow dawn of Torbett's awareness as he reached in his breast pocket for his badge, that you don't do that in front of a white cop when he's scared; and the unmistakable, protracted *cra-a-ack* of a weighted nightstick on Torbett's spine just as he pulled the badge into daylight.

In the drawn-out sound of the crack, and as he hit the pavement, it made sense to him, that somewhere in the last three seconds he had made a fatal mistake that would change the course of his life and his family's—that none of this would have happened, that Nan wouldn't have thought of this outing, if she didn't have to compensate for Jim's absence and distraction, if he hadn't always been at work, if he hadn't spent that last week falling in love with Virginia Key.

5:00 P.M.—Deer Ridge Circle

I radioed Dispatch from the road as I headed north on Mopac, and had them plug me through to Homicide. Jake answered. "Got anything for me?" I asked. I was afraid of what he would have found out about Joey and his finances.

"Yeah, the DA seized a ten-unit property on Ulit in late '87 and yeah, it was for sale, but no, Joey didn't put anything down on it. Factor in today is Saturday and I had to make a lot of calls just to get that. Whether he stashed money somewhere, I don't know yet. Where are you?"

"Deer Ridge Circle," I said, turning on to Dr. Hay's street in the ghost of Joey's Caprice, as the sun set. "Go home."

I pulled over on the left in front of Hay's house, so she could see me in the driver's seat from inside, and I waited about ten minutes. I thought of the police report on Joey's death, the skid marks starting and stopping, as if he'd hit the brakes and they'd given out. Hay came outside in a sweater and jeans. She looked spooked first, at seeing a replica of the car our friend Joey had died in. Also angry. But mostly spooked. She didn't speak.

I said, "Tell me how Joey Velez died."

In the yellow light of Margaret Hay's cluttered den, I stood under the accusing scrutiny of a calico cat, as Hay ransacked her desk and some old boxes and finally pulled out a few rumpled sheets of paper.

"Normally I don't bring things home," she said, smoothing out the sheets. "But there were too many people who wanted this information to go away."

All the documentation on Joey's death had gotten lost in the shuffle long ago, a tribute to the department's commitment to burying Joey a hero, rather than a drunk driver, which he was, or a suicide, which was questionable.

The autopsy report included the standard scoop: date, time of death, summary of the circumstances. Standard outlines of a body were marked to indicate damage: blows to the forehead, nose, crown. Notes explained the damage to most of his skin by the fact that the car had burst into flames. Nothing Hay discovered in Joey's autopsy—an autopsy I cursed myself for ditching—indicated poison, bullets, stab wounds or anything of the like.

We read the autopsy report twice, along with her notes, and the report from Toxicology. No surprises. I apologized as she walked me to my car. We were both weary, at the end of a week that wouldn't end.

As I sat in the driver's seat of the Caprice, I saw her size me up, along with the car. I was about Joey's height.

"Trauma to his forehead, nose, crown, right?" she asked. She tapped the spots on my face and the top of my head where he'd been hit.

It took me a moment to realize she was still working. I leaned forward, my face against the steering wheel. "Like this?" It could have accounted for the damage to his forehead and nose.

"Okay," she said.

"And the crown of his head." I leaned back. Nothing hard behind me. "Against the roof of the car when it tumbled?"

"Makes sense," she said. "The car made one arc, then hit the slope and tumbled, head over tail. He was still strapped in when he landed."

"What do you mean?" I asked. When they found Joey dead, I was drunk and distracted. I'd missed details.

"His seat belt was still on, what was left of it."

"He didn't wear one."

"What?"

Something felt very wrong. "He never wore one. Most of us don't."

"He was strapped in . . ." she insisted, and trailed off.

Hay's eyes widened and almost seemed to fill with tears as we realized the resonance of what had happened. We'd fucked up, his friend the detective and his friend the medical examiner. Three years ago, I'd laid off my suspicions about Joey's death because Miles told me to. And I was too fucked up about it to think straight. And a stupid detail, one we should have seen years ago, told us the truth. Maybe Joey had chosen his final drunken journey as the first time in his professional life he'd wear a seat belt. But another interpretation was more likely.

Joey Velez's death wasn't an accident. And it wasn't suicide.

8:00 P.M.—Mopac Expressway, Southbound

Rachel and I drove along in the cool blue of the evening, Rachel in a black evening dress, cut to highlight her cleavage and the diamond necklace my meager savings had allowed. Had the tiny pendant hung on another woman, people would have questioned my level of commitment; on Rachel, the diamond's size seemed like a point of taste, not poverty. I wore a black silk suit Rachel had bought me, blue shirt, no tie. We headed out on Bee Caves Road in the thinning evening traffic into the moneyed development of West Lake Hills and pulled into the lot at Chez Louie. As far as I knew, it was Austin's classiest

French joint. I wanted to give her a break from anything that smacked of Texan or Mexican or judicial. As I pulled into the parking lot I saw what I thought was a tan Duster pass by. If it was, it meant Serio's man was still following me. And either he was dumb enough to use the same car after I spotted him, or he didn't care whether I saw him or not. Earlier, when I was driving home from Hay's house, I thought I was being followed, but it was dark and all I could see were headlights.

I opened Rachel's door, took her hand as she stepped from the car, and offered her my arm. Inside, the bar buzzed all the way out to the entrance. "Reles for two. We have a reservation," I told the young hostess. She checked the list and the glossy map of tables, consulted a waiter and said, "It'll be ready in a few minutes. Would y'all like a drink at the bar while you wait?"

With nowhere else to stand we slipped into the edge of the bar-room and stayed at the outskirts of the crowd in the artificial dark-ness. Young couples and groups spoke animatedly. Rachel kept her back to the bar as a standard precaution, and she didn't see the TV news flash of Miles being interviewed on the APD steps that morning when he put both feet in his mouth. They froze his image to accent the bags under his eyes, the triple chin, every wrinkle and pimple, the marks of his most recent shaving incidents, and the general demeanor of a child molester. It was a shot no anchorman would have allowed of himself. They cut to the anchor in the studio, a square photo over his shoulder of Miles as villain, a tiny drop of spittle frozen in light as it flew from his mouth. I didn't have to hear the words to know that Miles had already been convicted in the court of public opinion.

"You can have a drink if you want," she said.

"No, I was . . . I'll order something at the table."

Rachel stood a couple of inches above the national average, and soon we noticed admiring stares from the other couples, Rachel in her full-lipped, feline-eyed beauty and me with my twice-broken nose and the scrape across my face from the scuffle with the GI, along with neck pain no one could see. I liked to think women saw me as hand-some, or could in spite of my ever-growing collection of scars and bumps. Maybe because of them. Men wondered what I must have

done to win over a movie star like Rachel. Rachel seemed nervous—
she kept swiveling her head, as if she were trying to find someone, or
as if she thought someone were trying to find her. I figured she was expecting me to be called away. Also, I knew it hadn't escaped Rachel,
though she'd kept quiet about it, that I'd driven her to the restaurant
in a vehicle identical to the one Joey died in.

The one that Joey was killed in.

Finally a waiter led us to an intimate semicircular booth in a dark
corner, lit, like the others, only by a small candle. We sat opposite
each other at its edges, ordered and were left alone. Candlelight and
low chatter filled the room, low enough to be canceled out.

"So." Silence.

She scanned the other tables, looked toward the exit.

I had a handful of ideas to fill the silence, apologies and promises
and more. But what I was really thinking about was how sure I was
now that Joey had been murdered. And how single I'd be if I brought
it up.

"You look great," I said. She nodded. "Listen," I started.

"No," she said, "you don't have to."

"I just—"

"It's okay," she said, all artificial poise. "The phone calls, the last
minute . . . changes. It's just the way it is."

Long silence, the kind you hear in conversations between people
who are breaking up.

She said, "Do you—"

I cut her off. "Will you marry me?"

A quiet came over the tables nearest us.

"What?" she said.

I realized what I'd said and that it was too late to back out. The
business of marrying Rachel didn't exactly make me calm. Three years
in the ground, Joey still felt like my father, and she still felt like his
wife. What's more, it didn't take much to figure out that Rachel would
have been better off without me. But I couldn't let her leave. I said, "I
think we should get married."

She flushed and turned away. "Can we buy a house?"

I opened my mouth but nothing came out, save for my throat catching.

Rachel said, "It's okay."

"No, we could—"

I stopped short. She tried to say something and cut herself off. Then we looked around the room.

"What kind of house did you have as a kid?" she asked, making conversation. The waiter came with our sodas and she sipped hers.

"We had apartments. Why?"

"Do you want a rabbi?" she asked.

"It could be a judge." Her eyes widened at the idea, and not with pleasure. "Or, whatever."

"We'll think of something," she said.

I realized she'd just said yes. We sat with that in the silence. But Rachel's mind was elsewhere.

She said, "You know Joey's dead, right?"

"Of course," I said, emphatically. But I felt my head go up and down, and side to side at the same time. If she'd been looking at me, instead of at her hands, she'd have seen right through me.

"You mean it?" she said. "Because he's dead for me."

"I mean it," I said.

She looked into my eyes to see what they gave away. She should have known better.

"I'm not Joey's wife. I'm yours."

"Absolutely."

"And you'll stick by me, no matter what."

It seemed out of character for Rachel to be so unsure, so fearful that a guy would walk out. I took her hand and looked into her eyes. "And I'll stick by you no matter what." That part I meant.

Finally she said, "Deal."

I slid around the semicircle of cushions and kissed her, awkwardly, but the second kiss took root and made up for it. For a moment we were on a raft in the Mediterranean. Everything was going to be fine.

Then I opened my eyes.

Standing over us in a sparkling gold cocktail dress, dark tan breasts ballooning out the top, with her red-tipped black hair spilling over her shoulders and what could have been her fourth tequila sunrise in her hand, was the very woman I'd shaken down that afternoon for information about my old partner Joey Velez: his hooker friend Vita.

8:15 P.M.—Brackenridge Hospital, ICU

Nan Torbett sat by her husband Jim's bed, watched him and thought of how completely all their lives had been transformed in the fall of a club.

She'd been pressed against the barricade by the crowd. Jule was crying. Nan tried to get Jim's attention, tried to alert the patrols that she was the wife of that detective, the girl was his daughter. And the patrol nearest her, irritated by demands from one too many directions, turned to her and swung. And Jim saw them and intervened.

And Jim lay in the bed, trussed, tractioned, drugged like his long-dead brother.

Nan cried out when she saw them club him. Jule screamed. And though Guy wasn't there, Nan knew later that his adult life had just been formed.

The crowd burst in every direction. Barricades toppled. Nan picked up Jule, let the girl clamp her arms and legs around her mother and wail. Two patrols, maybe including the one who'd clubbed Jim, tried to lift him. "Don't move him!" Nan screamed. "He's hurt!"

A patrol held her back.

Nan turned, chased through the bodies, looped around, saw them load Jim into the back of a blue-and-white and race off, siren blaring. It was an hour before she'd made it the few blocks to Brackenridge and identified herself, sobbing Jule in her arms. Jim had been sedated, x-rayed, tractioned. The doctor was reasonably convinced he wouldn't be paralyzed. He had no other comforting words.

Her husband had been attacked, by white cops. And he was a cop. And it didn't matter a bit.

And their baby saw it all.

8:20 P.M.—Chez Louie

"I thought I saw you!" Vita the hooker said, all chatty, a girl from the office. "I hope I'm not interrupting."

I slid back to my spot opposite Rachel. Rachel pulled out a compact and checked her lipstick.

"No," I said. "Nice to see you."

It sounded like a dismissal to me but not to Vita. It had been a whopping eight hours since I knocked on her apartment door, scared away a john and questioned her about Joey. She was pissed off and she hadn't forgotten.

She toasted her drink, "Here's come in your eye!" Then she made as if to walk away, spun on a dime and stationed herself at the table again. "You got some lipstick on you, hon," Vita said to me. "Want me to get it?"

She reached for my lips and I pulled away, barking, "No!" Rachel jolted at my voice. Then I said softly, "I got it," and wiped my mouth on a heavy cloth napkin too smooth for anything but appearances.

"Who's the lucky lady?" Vita said.

I said, "Rachel, this is . . ." I knew her name, but my mind was jumping ahead to the question of where I knew her from.

"Vita Carballo," Vita said with a special rolling of the r.

I said, "This is Rachel Velez." Outside of work, Rachel still went by her married name. But I realized too late that introducing her that way was a fatal mistake. I scanned the room for the exit sign.

They shook hands and while they were still touching, Vita said, "Velez?" Her eyes widened and she took in the two of us. "Ohhhh, like Joey Velez. I see."

Rachel caught my eye.

"Nice seeing you," I said, but Vita wasn't having any of it.

"Well, this *is* interesting. Like father like son."

Rachel straightened up suddenly. "Did you know my husband?" she asked, then surveyed Vita top to bottom. "Yes, of course you did."

Vita drew in air, shifted gears. "Look who's talking, *mamita!*" She went on to say something in a thick gutter Spanish that I couldn't quite make out, but the key word was "leftovers." It would be only seconds before Vita realized Rachel didn't speak that much Spanish. Or I hoped she didn't.

I scanned the room for a man alone and saw one about fifteen feet away, the direction Vita had come from, stuck in his booth and trying to slide under the table. "Hey," I said, "is that your date?"

Vita looked back. The guy hid his face.

"Listen," I said, "this being a business discussion, and you and I both being here with *dates*," I let the word hang for a moment, "maybe we should step into the bar."

She grimaced, turned on her heel and made clipped steps toward the front of the restaurant.

8:30 P.M.—Robertson Street

Mo and Rainbow John slouched low in the back seat of Mo's Cadillac. "Keep going, keep going," Mo said to the driver as they passed the patrol cars, still parked outside Virginia Key's house on Confederate Avenue. John watched the street signs go by. Mo sat up, leaned back, gripped his deadened crotch as if in carnal embrace and babbled. Crazier than before. Mo had that one moment of peace, whatever that was about, and lost it, plunged into the beyond of paranoia and fury.

"Black talk, back talk. Professional Uncle Tom. Kissing the collective anus of the white establishment. An aspiring white man." It didn't take too much to get that he was talking about Key again.

John had heard it all enough times to know it by heart, how he'd immigrated legally, come to America and joined the air force, and all he had to do was say, "I hate Russia," which was true. How his brothers were lost in "the struggle." How, while he was gone, his mother and father had been dragged from their home and killed, how his remaining sister had survived and turned up in a refugee camp, how desperately he tried to save her, arranging bigger and bigger drug deals at a greater risk, trying to raise cash to bribe the right people. How he'd hired Key on a dubious recommendation, a fledgling lawyer who claimed some knowledge of immigration law. How Key promised she would save his sister, get her to the United States, and took his money, much money, in cash, and promised results. And kept him waiting, and waiting, as her legal practice prospered, back burnered him in favor of easier cases, bigger money, while he stayed up all night, sending letters to Afghanistan, waiting for responses. Rainbow John could recite the stats, the broken appointments (five), the unreturned phone calls (ten), the missed deadlines (two, crucial), the nights upon nights of lost sleep, no matter what he swallowed, as he floundered in his new life, an American criminal, until finally the word came that his sister was dead and there was nothing left for him, nothing but revenge.

And when that was done, he'd be through.

But as far as John could see, the revenge list kept getting longer. Now the cop was added to it, a plan that had to end badly. They drove up the darkened side streets, Mo speaking to himself. "Bitch, bitch, bitch, you're *mine!* If only, if only, if only . . ."

"Why the cop?" John asked, the words flowing on their own power from his lips. In the silence that followed, he knew he had made a mistake.

Mo let the silence weigh in, then said, "Rainbow John. Did you speak?"

"Nothing."

"I wish to hear your thoughts."

John stalled. It was risky to question Bad Mo. But John would be doing the dirty work, now that he'd screwed up hiring Gaz. And killing a woman was bad enough. You don't go around killing cops.

"It's nothing," John said, "it's just, what do you care about a cop? He's trying to catch you. That's his job. It's just business."

Suddenly Mo was on top of him, holding John's throat with one hand and punching him with the other.

"When they knock down your door, drag your mother and father from their beds, when they kill your sister, when they steal your one chance at Paradise . . ." Mo was crying out. John tried to block the hammer blows to his head and face. All he could see was the blood in his eyes. Mo yelled, "A cop at my door is my enemy." And then Mo was holding his throat with both hands. John struggled against Mo's enormous hands, jabbed at Mo's face, but he couldn't break free. And for the life of him, he couldn't suck in a lungful of air. The last thing he heard as the blackness rolled down, was Mo crying out, "It is NOT . . . JUST . . . BUSINESS!"

8:45 P.M.—Chez Louie, Front Entrance

Past what should have been the dinner rush, the bar was packed, the entrance area crammed, and I followed Vita out to the front of the restaurant where we stood in the neons. She still held her drink.

"What the hell was that?" I said.

"You fuck my life, I fuck your life."

"How'd you know I was coming here?"

She grinned, surprised at the idea. "I didn't."

"What are you doing out here?"

She squared her jaw. "I eat."

"Go home."

"Blow me. I got more on you than you got on me."

I tried to play cool, covering how right she was, what she could do to me if she talked. I spoke low. "Were you his friend?"

"What?!"

"Were you Joey Velez's friend. I'm asking you."

She took a few steps, leaned on a car and became very interested in her drink.

"Why?" she asked. Then, "Sort of. Now and then. He was polite. And he paid."

I plucked another twenty out of my wallet to go with the two I'd given her earlier, without allowing the question of what I was paying for. She glanced at the bill and cleavaged it.

"Towards the end?" I asked.

She nodded. "He took a few calls at my place, like he was using it as a pit stop."

"Do you think he was dealing?"

She shrugged. "He didn't tell me anything. But it was the same guy, I think, who always called him. He argued. Mostly he didn't want to go somewhere and the guy needed him to go and he went."

I showed her Mo's picture again but she shook her head. "I never saw anyone. I'll tell you one thing, though. Whatever he was doing, he didn't like it."

When I looked up, the restaurant's front door was opened and Rachel stood inside, watching us. I didn't know how much she'd heard.

9:30 P.M.—1610 Confederate Avenue

Virginia Key locked her car, nodded businesslike to the cop in the blue-and-white on perpetual guard at her house, smoothed her jacket and stepped carefully up her front walk. She didn't want him to report that she had been drinking.

Inside, she closed her eyes and flipped on the light, expecting an expanse of new gold carpet, stretching around the corner and up the stairs. Instead she saw the same old one, bloodstain and all. She'd uncovered the stain, moved the smaller furniture herself, in general cleared the floor and stayed out of the house through the dinner hour for the installation. She flipped on the kitchen light, found the number and dialed.

"Don's Floors."

"This is Virginia Key. Where the hell is my carpet?"

"Sorry about that, Mrs. Key. Cops wouldn't let us go in."

She stomped out to the patrol car, cordless phone in hand. Each angry step nearly knocked her off balance. The cop rolled down the window. A young, dark-haired white man, in over his head, a clueless college boy with an education and no sense.

"Yes, ma'am."

"You kept the carpeters out this morning!"

"Huh? I've only been here since three."

"The morning shift."

"We have orders, ma'am. No one enters the house without you."

"I cleared it with your office! They had a key!"

The boy stiffened against his seat.

She asked, "Who's your supervisor?"

"Sergeant Guare, shift sergeant." He gave her the direct number and she dialed it.

"*Patrol, Guare.*"

"This is Virginia Key, you silly prick. One of your men is watching my goddamn windows and beating off. I didn't ask for your fucking police dogs around my house all day. I told your goddamned office I had carpeters coming today and now I have to spend another night in the house," she screamed, "with that *goddamn bloodstained rug!* Now, have him stay or go but stop fucking with my *life!*" She saw faces in neighbors' windows. The patrol had rolled his window up, picked up the microphone. He listened, nodded as if the radio could see him, and without comment, started the car and pulled away.

She straightened out her jacket and walked with all the dignity she could muster back into the empty house.

Now, at least, she could get some rest.

10:00 P.M.—706 East Thirty-eighth Street

I unlocked the door and let Rachel in, tossed some fresh king-size nuggets of dog food from the kitchen into the dish that fed our imaginary Doberman, hung the dog chain on the outside knob, locked the door and walked through the house, checking the doors and windows and, following instinct, the closets.

By the time I washed up, hung up my suit and shirt and reached the bedroom, Rachel was settled in and the door closed. I braced myself for the door to be locked and barricaded, for a night's sleep on the couch, a one-way ticket down bachelor lane. Rachel had been my dream girl. It was fun while it lasted.

The door wasn't barricaded and I stepped into near darkness, lights off, Rachel already in bed, blankets pulled up to her neck, head turned away. Sleep, or more likely, faking sleep. It beat the couch.

As I neared the bed, the covers flipped away as if on their own, revealing Rachel wearing the diamond pendant and nothing else, smooth skin from her lips to her toes with only a few interruptions, all in the right places. "Surprise," she said.

Before I could respond she clapped her hands around the back of my neck and pulled me down on top of her. She airlocked her mouth to mine, licked my tongue, locked our legs together. We rolled over twice and slid onto the rug. She wrestled me for top position, yanked my shorts down, then slid down and took me inside.

Suddenly all was well. She couldn't have heard too much, me talking with Vita, and do this. She couldn't be mad, worried, holding an old grudge, and act like this. Or could she? I rolled on top of her and we slammed together, building momentum.

If what Vita said was true, that Vita had been sleeping with Joey now and then, during his last days, enough for him to take calls at her place . . . I lifted Rachel to the edge of the bed and climbed on top, sliding in again like the first time, ever. She kissed my neck, squeezed me close. We had a beautiful life together. The phone could ring, I could get an emergency call from God, and I wouldn't pick it up. I wouldn't leave Rachel tonight.

But if Joey was taking those calls reluctantly, if he was being blackmailed, well, that might explain his final phone call.

Rachel sucked on my neck. I picked her up and sat her on the dresser, riding a rhythm that made us both hum. I felt the tide rising.

James Torbett was nuts over Virginia Key, that was plain. Anyone could see it except Torbett. Rachel's hum turned to a rhythmic moan as her jaw dropped and locked in the open position. She squeezed her eyes shut and cried out as I double-timed, quadrupled, and finally set paradise loose in the ultimate intimacy of fluid exchange that only monogamy allowed, the sudden revelation that whoever had Gaz go after Virginia Key in the first place hadn't given up, that the presence of Torbett and his guard was keeping the killer at bay, that it was only a matter of time before he struck. And as the last rush of love rippled through me in my helplessness and Rachel dropped tears down her cheeks and I lifted her gently and lowered her to the bed, only then carefully uncoupling but twisting together like unborn twins, rolling gently out of consciousness, and I can't tell you if I was awake or asleep, or if it was even that night or later when I knew the facts, when I could see as if I'd been there how, while I was romancing the woman I loved, Mohammed Rashid Nadiri stopped someone's lungs from pumping and scratched another name off his list.

PART THREE

LONG GONE DADDY

SUNDAY

Rubin Key was in a supermarket as big as a field, with aisles that went on forever. But the electricity went out. People came and grabbed all the food they could take but the heat was melting it all, rotting the meat and warming the juice and melting the ice cream. Rubin spooned up a half-melted dish of ice cream to quench his incredible thirst but it melted away into paste.

He had a glob of phlegm in his mouth, like a tennis ball. He tried to take it out but it stuck to his tongue. He was in a bathroom, tried to rinse it off but could only get it in pieces. He had to pee but the toilet was overflowed, filled to the top, and the bathroom was flooded. He tried to go anyway but could only squeeze out a few drops. People kept walking in.

He was in the back of a car with Jenny, Jenny looking off ahead, not worried about anything. But there was no one driving. He reached over the seat for the steering wheel but the car flew off the road. Huge arms reached up and grabbed Rubin and Jenny. One arm a mile long punched into Rubin's belly, grabbed his stomach and squeezed. He heard a high-pitched beep, another, another.

His eyes felt pasted shut. He blinked and opened them a tiny bit. His mouth felt so dry it hurt into his throat. Tubes in his nose. So dry. He tried to open his mouth to cry out, but all that came was a dry whisper.

"Mom. Mom?"

2:45 A.M.—706 East Thirty-eighth Street

A tide of milk lifted and carried me and angels sang in my ear, every cell in my body and soul resting, calm and blissful and the phone rang.

I blinked once, twice. Rachel still asleep. I reached over to lower the volume on the answering machine but I must have turned it off because the phone kept ringing until finally I picked up.

"Yeah."

"Fiesta Gardens. Now."

"Milsap? What the fuck?"

"Now."

I hung up and leaned close to Rachel's face, close enough to smell her breath, hear her breathing the controlled rhythms of consciousness. She didn't open her eyes.

"It's okay," she said, thickly, and puckered. I kissed her and found my pants.

3:00 A.M.—Brackenridge Hospital, Pediatric ICU

By the time Dr. Blair got to Rubin Key's room, the nurse had propped up his bed and was feeding him juice through a straw.

"There he is!" the doctor said as he walked in. The boy looked up and almost smiled. "I was talking to you while you slept. I told you the worst jokes! I kept thinking you would tell me to shut up, but you didn't."

The nurse said, "He went to the bathroom and had a sponge bath."

"How do you feel?" the doctor asked.

"Everything hurts."

"I know," the doctor said. Then to the nurse, "Have you called his mother?"

The nurse said, "The machine picked up."

The doctor thought about that when Rubin asked, "Is Jenny okay?"

3:15 A.M.—Fiesta Gardens

A few APD and DPS patrols stood around as a cool fog rolled off the river over the dark lagoon by the high grass where police had discovered the battered body. Its face and neck were a dark red. In spite of that I could make out bruises on the throat, likely handprints. The nose dripped crimson. And for good measure, his gut had been sliced open and his intestines unraveled but not segmented, laid out over the grass in a continuous but sloppy loop. It didn't take much to guess the subject had been beaten and strangled, killed by hand somewhere else, and laid here in the weeds before the disemboweling. The body, Milsap said, belonged to a drug dealer called Rainbow John Shaunessy. Rainbow John was a big guy. He'd been killed by someone bigger.

Ron Wachowski said, "Here's the kicker," and with a latex-gloved hand, rolled the victim's head to the side. There was a distinct mark on Rainbow John's left cheek, a broken cheekbone, I guessed, and a series of parallel lines, scabbed over. Unlike his other bruises, that one was a few days old. Ron opened a plastic basin, lifted from it the pipe he'd found at the same spot Friday morning. It was a straight eighteen inches or so of lead, grooved at both ends. Ron held it to the marks on the victim's face. "It's a match!"

"Did you find prints on the pipe?" I asked.

"Yeah," Ron said. "They were his." The chance that Rainbow John had beaten himself in the face with a pipe seemed slim. I pulled Milsap aside.

"If you have anything," I said, "I'd be glad to hear it."

"Rainbow John's as high as we got," Milsap said. "We don't know who he answers to."

"But you can guess," I said. He looked away. "Okay, I'm putting a BOLO out on him: Be On the Look Out for Mo Nadiri, stop and arrest."

"Reles, you gotta wait!"

"We got him for murder. You want him for dealing?"

"Just give me a day," Milsap pleaded.

"Did you talk to Torbett?" I asked.

"He's at Brackenridge."

"What?"

"He was at the march. He reached for his badge and some patrol figured it was a gun and cracked him on the spine."

"Why didn't you call me?"

"I just found out!"

I threw up my hands, stomped back toward my car, then turned to Milsap and said, "You've got an hour."

4:00 A.M.—706 East Thirty-eighth Street

Rachel lay in bed, wide awake, staring at the ceiling and smoking.

Sunday mornings are for lying around in your robes, sipping coffee and reading the papers, for long, leisurely breakfasts that go on until lunch. Together. Or so she'd always guessed.

Her parents gave an effective performance of togetherness, in houses on or near the campus, depending on her father's current status, hosting parties, reading the *New York Times* on Sundays in Evanston, under an oppressive silence, to show an imagined audience how sophisticated they were. And when they didn't imagine an audience, doing whatever horrible things they felt like doing. Not to be thought about.

Performing—was that what she was doing last night, using sex to pave over the rough moment at the restaurant? How long could she keep doing that? It hadn't even kept him home through the night.

And where was he now?

No news is good news, that's the police wife's creed. If Dan were dead, they'd call her, eventually. She knew that from experience. So the idea was to forget about it until he showed up or the call came. Nothing to worry about just because he got a call in the middle of the night and went out. Happens all the time.

Who was she kidding? They would never be a regular family. Sunday dinners? Mother/daughter "talks"? Rachel wasn't suited for it and neither was Dan. Dan didn't run hot and cold like Joey; he was always warm, good and warm. Or gone. Each disappearance brought with it the threat of permanence. Maybe he'd be back in an hour, maybe by dawn, maybe never. Or maybe he'd clear his head up, get a good look at her and head for the hills.

There was nothing new inside her, everything was old, but the rattle in her head kept getting worse. She'd wake up in the morning before the alarm went off, her brain spinning tales even while she was still asleep, about the importance of land ownership, the stability of a home, a safe place for your family, an investment, bullshit bullshit bullshit even if it was true. Leads to follow, calls to make, aggressive salesmanship. And the screaming ghosts of her childhood and her youth. And Dan off and gone, and always maybe dead, just enough uncertainty to drive someone like her off the wall.

That was it. She'd been with him two years plus. It was crazy enough that he was always hopping up and leaving at the ring of the phone, that one day he would surely come home in a box. On top of that, she spent all that time wondering how much he knew about her past, about the man she killed. Or what he'd learned lately. The woman in the restaurant. The voice on the phone, the man who called and knew her as Mrs. Velez. Had he spoken to Dan? Told him something? And what would Dan do with it.

It was hopeless, the matching of a murderess and a cop. And with the shifts in her life, in her body, she wouldn't even have sex to fall back on. She'd had lesser issues before and knew exactly how patient men could be. Abortions, toxic shock, the doctor telling her how unlikely it was that she'd ever have children, how it seemed like a reprieve, let her off the hook for birth control, something she'd never gotten the hang of anyway. Life was full of surprises.

But she needed to take some initiative. Up and leave before Dan made his move. Not wait to be dumped, or for all she knew, busted. The road, that was the place for her. She'd disappear, cut it off clean, start over in some other town. She had a résumé, lots of experience.

She'd have a new job in no time. She stamped out the cigarette in the ashtray by the phone, laid back and tried to get some sleep, now that a decision had been made.

But God knew where she would go. Or what she was going to do with a baby.

4:00 A.M.—Brackenridge Hospital, ICU

I pushed silently into Torbett's private room. He was trussed up, immobilized and connected to an IV drip I took for morphine. His wife slept on a padded chair facing him, her neck at an unlikely angle. She was an attractive, solidly built black woman of about forty. Tears had streaked her cheeks.

Suddenly Torbett blurted out, "A fight! A fight! A nigger and a white!"

Mrs. Torbett's eyes popped open. She looked Torbett over, saw that he was, apparently, the same as he'd been an hour back, and saw me. Though she'd been asleep seconds ago, she fixed her tired stare on me for a moment as if to say, See what you did?

Torbett babbled on. "You . . . must take the A-train . . . baby, baby, come to me, give it up, darling." Then his face twisted in a spasm of agony. "It burns, it burns." Nan rose, wet a washcloth in the sink and blotted his brow. "So cool. Make it good, Mommy, make it not hurt. Alvin?"

He settled down into what passed for sleep and Mrs. Torbett walked out into the hall. I followed.

"Who's Alvin?" I asked.

"His brother. Twenty years ago another patrol pounded Alvin on the spine with his nightstick, just like they did to Jim."

"I see."

"No you don't. I saw that bastard club my Jim."

I grabbed at a few ideas. "Is there something I can do?"

She glared fiercely toward Torbett's door. "I've been sitting here for twelve hours and there's one thought dead set in my mind. *If* Jim walks again, and God willing, if he isn't in agony all the time the way Alvin was . . ." She trailed off.

"I'm listening," I said.

"Jim takes workmen's comp, disability, whatever. Then he retires early. I don't care if he doesn't get a full pension. I don't care if I have to work three jobs. We're better off with him at home in a chair than this." She was fighting back tears.

I looked up the hall. A heavy nurse clopped out of one room on white shoes like rafts.

"What do you want me to do?" I asked.

"Back me up. Or at least don't talk him into staying. And for God's sake, don't get him excited about the case, whatever case. If you're his friend, you'll do what's good for him."

"We're not exactly friends."

"Just because he doesn't love you doesn't mean you're not his friend. He thinks you're smarter than most. And basically honest."

"But a shithead," I suggested.

She didn't say no. "We grew up in segregated Texas. Before Clarksville was paved. Can you imagine being turned away from a hospital because you were Jewish?"

I said, "Yes."

"Have you experienced it?" I didn't answer. "If you haven't experienced it, you have no idea." Then she shifted thoughts and said, "I'm going to get coffee. Stay with him in case he wakes up again."

Inside, I stood by Torbett's bed. In a few minutes his eyes snapped open, not like waking up but coming to. Sweat rolled down his face. He scanned the room. "Where is she?" he croaked. I found a Styrofoam water cup with a bent straw and he sipped feebly.

"Coffee. She'll be right back." I looked at the IV. "Morphine?" I asked.

"Nan thinks it is. Glucose. The pills are Advil. Ring for some more." I hit the nurse's bell.

"Why?"

Another jolt of pain made him squeeze his eyes shut. I could see when he opened them again that the pain hadn't stopped. He'd just decided to get used to it. It wasn't a morphine nightmare he'd been in, but sheer agony.

"She deserves a husband who isn't a junkie," he said. "Where are my pants?"

I looked around, opened some cabinets. The pants were folded on a shelf.

"Front right pocket," he said. I reached in and pulled out a piece of paper. "Open it."

I unfolded it. Bank statement. Virginia Key. "Where'd you get this?" I asked.

"From her desk."

"Was it in plain view?"

Torbett grit his teeth against the pain. "Not exactly."

Indefinite terms like "not exactly" weren't something I associated with Torbett.

He went on. "Westpark Limited in trust for Eastpark Limited. I haven't checked it out. I'm betting she's both of those companies. Hiding income."

"You think this is what someone was after?"

"Maybe," he said. "Maybe it's just why she kept us at a distance." It's the nature of secrets. A crooked businessman who's being black-mailed won't go to the police. He's afraid they'll find out about his dirty deals.

It made me think of another question but I closed the door first. "Torbett. Did you make it with her?"

He thought for a moment and shook his head. "I never touched her . . ."

"But?"

He said, "She was all I thought about."

"So you *hid* this?"

He closed his eyes, ashamed. It crossed my mind that if Nan Tor-bett was warming up to me a little, it was only because she knew someone else, a woman, was a bigger threat. The heavy nurse from the hall came in with a tiny paper cup. "Are we ready for some more Advil?"

"That'll be fine," he choked, as if he could take it or leave it. He sucked the pills out of the cup and reached for his water. When he handed the water back to the nurse he said, "Not a word to the missus. Remember our deal."

"You're a dope," she said and danced toward the door as delicately and flirtatiously as her 250 pounds would allow.

"Any leads yet?" he asked.

"Nothing for sure," I said.

He ignored the evasion.

"I'll tell you one thing," he said, and ground his teeth. "Whoever went after Virginia Key, knew her. And he was wrapped up in her. Tight."

4:30 A.M.—1610 Confederate Avenue

Virginia Key was suddenly wide awake. It was like that. She'd be asleep, turning ideas over, then suddenly conscious, have to jot something down, an idea for a speech or an interview. Or just wide awake for no reason. She sat up and reached for her robe.

She'd done well to start so young, she thought, always a positive idea on waking. Though many people started younger. Still, here she was making headlines, only a few years past the bar exam. And with two children.

That wasn't right. She had to stay busy enough not to think about it. Single mother with two children. The phrase came as naturally to her as her name. It had always been that way. She went to the bathroom and brushed her teeth.

She'd worked so hard for so long. But she'd set her sights on her goal, and she couldn't let anything sideline her. The principle had ended her marriage, thank God. But she'd learned it late, late enough to get married in the first place. Regret was a distraction, too. People who live in the past don't make it.

Foolishness all around. Nothing was personal. Not the whites who were foolish enough to fear her. Not the blacks who hated her. She was a vehicle of ideas, some dangerous ideas.

She thought how, in spite of what some people said, her emotions were genuine. They were just worn thin from four days of interviews. She didn't have the staff to support this kind of exposure. And it had come all at once. Suddenly, in one moment of outright terror, she had been thrust from the periphery into the spotlight. And already people's sympathy was slipping. Words like "ambitious" were being replaced with "opportunist." As if people had no idea what she had been through, the horror of the moment that gun went off. Both her babies shot. And she could have been killed.

Something creaked, the house settling, near the little bedroom. Jennifer's room. She'd have to go in eventually, clean it out, maybe turn it into storage. Or she'd buy a new place when Rubin got home. That would be easier on him, no empty space where Jennifer had been. Rubin knew Jennifer better than Virginia did anyway. It seemed he'd always been taking care of Jenny. And she couldn't stand him moping around all the time. She opened the door and stepped into the little bedroom.

Jenny's white dresser was spotted with her various collectibles. A rock she found particularly unusual, but Virginia didn't see why. Some leaves sealed in wax paper by the cleaning woman. Part of a tennis ball. A 1960 nickel. What did Jenny think when she collected these silly things? It was beyond Virginia. She'd never considered it before. How did Jenny see things? How did Rubin? Or anybody?

The bed was neatly made. Virginia felt dizzy and sat down on the pink coverlet. Something slid from under the pillow and touched her hip. Virginia reached for it.

It was her cameo. The hand-carved ivory silhouette, framed in gold.

She'd reported it to the police as stolen. It was the only thing the burglar took. But Jenny had taken it. Why?

And if Jenny took it, that meant nothing was stolen. Which meant the man who shot at her wasn't a thief. Jim Torbett had said as much. She'd never thought about it before.

She still had the cameo in her hand when she got back into her own bed, glanced at the phone machine and saw that the message light was flashing. She'd turned it down earlier, the reporters had been calling so much.

"Mrs. Key? Are you there? This is Hilda from Brackenridge Pediatric. Your son is awake. He seems very perky. Call right back." The machine clicked off.

Rubin was okay! Her baby would make it. She scrambled for her shoes.

And it was just then that she heard a shuffle and realized someone was in the house.

4:30 A.M.—HQ

I was making for the squad room when I saw Miles's office door open and the light on.

The room was still littered with boxes, but some of them had been sealed with packing tape. Miles stood yanking pushpins from the bulletin board and letting items drop to his desk. He surveyed them, stacked them and stuffed them into the garbage can. A whiskey bottle and a glass sat on the desk.

"Sit down, Jewboy. Have a drink," he said without breaking pace in his packing. He looked like he'd been waiting for this moment for decades.

"I'm too tired," I said. "I'd pass out."

"Never stopped me." He swigged, found a page and handed it to me.

MEMORANDUM
From: Chief C. CRONIN
To: Lt. Miles Niederwald, Homicide Division
Date: Saturday, January 19, 1991
Re: Disciplinary Hearing
Cc: Public Information

Be informed that your disciplinary hearing has been scheduled for Monday January 21 at 9:00 A.M., First Floor Auditorium. Bring any evidence you wish to present in your defense.

"Auditorium?" I asked.

He sat, dumping out the contents of his desk drawers. "Room for the press, get it? Public hangin'."

"They can't do that."

"The hell they can't. Two black kids shot. Torbett in ICU after a police clubbing. What I said on TV. They gotta throw the sharks somebody." He found a heavy black garbage bag and was shaking it open, then shoveling piles of crumpled papers into it. "The IRS can take my house, my wife can take my kids. Why shouldn't they?" He emptied his glass and filled it again.

"What are you gonna do?"

"I ain't gonna show up Monday, that's for sure."

"They'll fire you."

"I'll call in sick. See how fast I can retire. If that don't work, I'll quit, take my retirement account, pay off the IRS and get outta Dodge."

"That's crazy. Where will you go?"

He reached another glass out of his desk. It had the remnants of toothpaste on it. He poured it half full of whiskey. "My last order. Drink."

I sat and sipped. The whiskey heated a path down my throat and landed with a crash. Miles leaned back in his chair.

I said, "I hear the DA's office is looking for people."

"Yeah, and Beaumont needs a town drunk." Another silence as I looked at his glass. He saw the light in my eyes. "Whut?"

I bounced out of my seat. "The sobriety defense."

We'd seen it work in court for everything from DWI to child molesting. 'I never woulda done that to my stepdaughter, your honor. But I was drunk and I slipped. I will never drink no more.'

"I'll take you to the ER right now," I said, pacing as much as the tiny office allowed. "They put you in detox. Couple of days and you're in Oak Springs. They can't fire you while you're in rehab. You make a big show of regret, you're out in a month all bushy-tailed, saying what a great thing the department did getting you help."

He pointed to the bottle. "What about . . . ?"

"That's the point. You stop drinking!"

Miles stared at me, his eyes dead, mouth hanging open. Then he looked away. "Get those boxes," he said.

By five thirty A.M., we'd loaded the last of the boxes into his car in the building's dark, enclosed lot. On the last trip to his office, he tried to slide his nameplate off the door but it stuck and bent in half before he could peel it down. We brought it with two stuffed garbage bags and dumped them in a can by Miles's car, then stood in the echo.

I said, "Maybe if Torbett said something."

"What's he gonna say? 'Miles didn't mean nothin' against black folks. Hell, Miles *loves* black folks!' "

"You're no racist."

"Tell ya something, boy. We're all racists. We're just supposed to keep our dumb cracker-ass mouths shut." He opened the car door and dropped himself into the seat. He'd lost more weight, I realized, and his cheeks were sagging. His future did not look bright.

He started the engine, pulled back and to the right, then stopped in front of me and rolled the window down.

"Gonna catch you that A-rab?" he asked. I was guessing Jake had told him what I was up to.

"You know. I'm a Jew. It's in my blood."

He nodded and adjusted his mirrors, heading off for points unknown.

"It's in his blood to catch you."

And he drove off.

5:45 A.M.—HQ

I snapped on the light in the squad room, reached Torbett's document from my pocket wondering what it might or might not tell me, and made for the coffeepot as I noticed Jake Lund sacked out on the couch, a plaid wool jacket laid over him. He shaded his eyes and squinted at me.

"What time is it?" he asked.

"What are you doing here?" I snapped, stepping close to him.

"What do you mean?"

I slapped his cheek, just hard enough so he would know I was serious. "You're sleeping here now?"

"No."

"What's it look like?"

He was sitting up, his jacket over his lap. "Last night was the first night."

"The first?"

"All right, maybe once before."

"You have a house."

"I'm fine," he said. "It's not a big deal."

"You never leave the office!"

"This is different. I just . . ."

"What?"

"All the shit that's happened, you know? It adds up."

By now he was standing. I grabbed him by the shirt with my right hand, the Key document crunched in my left.

"Look," I said. "Miles and Torbett are out of action. It's just you and me." He looked frightened. "We don't get to hide out. We're the front lines." It was a foxhole pep talk and the realization of his responsibility wasn't doing anything to cure Jake's shell shock. I tried another angle. "We can do this. We'll nail the fucker and go out on the town. We'll get you laid, show you what the sun looks like. You'll get better, I promise, but I can't take much more here so just *fuckin' pull it together!*"

Enter Carter Serio.

I followed Jake's glance over my shoulder to Carter Serio, Internal Affairs, who couldn't have been there long, jaw dropping like he'd gotten five points for catching us in conflict. I peered into him, to cover how guilty I might look. He was holding a videocassette in one hand. I patted Jake on the shoulder and released him. With Key's document, I wiped the corners of my mouth as if I'd just finished a donut, and stuffed it into my jacket pocket, saying, "Hey, Carter, you're up early."

"Late," he said, then turned to Jake. "This man abusing you, Lund?"

If I gave Jake a warning look, Serio would have seen it and reported it. I watched Serio.

Jake said, "He was helping me stay focused." I looked at Jake. He had the glint in his eye of old times, that reality was amusing as long as he kept it at a respectable distance. I could tell he was faking—he still had that scared-little-kid look underneath—but it would do for now.

"Sure he was," Serio said. "I got the call about Torbett. That's why *I'm* here. I know how you boys watch each other's backs. Heartwarming. You should know the Fifth Floor's fixin' to sacrifice your friend Niederwald."

"Sacrifice?" Jake asked.

"The patrol who clubbed Torbett will be administratively processed and fired, quietly. Cronin figures the press needs someone and they already have Miles from that interview. If Cronin gives them the rookie too, two public discharges are worse than one. A department full of racists." Then he turned to me. "Where have you been? We called you at home. No answer, no machine."

I realized I must have turned the machine off earlier. "Why?"

"That airman you arrested," he said. "I tried to find out why he was released. Here's where I dead-ended."

He popped the video into the VCR. In a few moments, five jet fighters were making parallel lines like sheet music across a blue, blue sky. Late-night-TV quality, shoddy graphics reading "BERGSTROM— AMERICA'S HOME FRONT!"

I learned pretty quickly that Bergstrom was activated in 1942 as Del Valle Army Air Base, renamed Bergstrom after the first Austinite to die in the Second World War. I asked Serio to give me the Cliffs Notes. He fast-forwarded and said, "Department of Defense wants it closed. This guy," he froze on the face of a general, "wants it open." He hit PLAY.

The general said, *"When my father was stationed here in 1941 . . ."*

Serio paused the tape. "That is General Herbert Knobloch, who signed the release for Airman Kenneth Kemp." Knobloch was a gray-haired man in his fifties or more, born in fatigues. "This is his defense for Bergstrom. Only none of it is logical. The DOD wants to save money, and let the town buy it to make a new airport. But Knobloch's father left from Bergstrom in '44 and got shot down over the Pacific. I think when he took command of Bergstrom it was like coming home. Just a theory."

"What can you do with it?"

He said, "I can publish it in the *Chronicle* for all the good it'll do me. Thought you might be interested. And this."

He put something in my palm, a gold-framed cameo brooch, the very one, we'd been told, that was stolen from Virginia Key.

"Where'd you find it?" I asked.

He said, "In Virginia Key's cold hand."

6:15 A.M.—1610 Confederate Avenue

Virginia Ann Key, formerly Albertson, had been trampled in her home by someone wearing size thirteen shoes. Her petite torso had been smashed, irregularly. Her hips twisted to one side but her back pressed against the carpet, footprint-sized stretches of it pressed nearly flat, ribs crushed, blood spread, soft mounds of wet tissue bubbling up under the last of a thin nightgown and robe. Her features spread wide like the face of a hanged cat, sculpted in the act of vomiting blood and parts more solid than blood.

The intruder had wiped for fingerprints before he left, in spite of the more obvious bootprints in what was left of his victim. I figured he was more worried about killing the shit out of her than about whether he left a trail. The state of the body suggested a lack of emotional distance.

The techs had come and gone and left the body for the medical examiner and us. Serio took me outside the house. Milsap was waiting for us. "What's he doing here?" I whispered to Serio.

"I called him." The three of us stood in the street, facing each other as the sky began to lighten. An occasional car rolled down Robertson, along the schoolyard.

"Now," Serio said, "*we* have a problem. Virginia Key is dead, and she was under Torbett's guard."

I said, "It's not our fault some cracker patrol clubbed Torbett."

"We can't tell the press that," Serio said. "Key called off the guard so we're covered legally but not in the court of public opinion. Chief Cronin is blowing flames about this, the high-profile victim we've been watching got killed. And Miles Niederwald shoots his mouth off in front of the cameras."

"So?"

Serio squared his stance and faced me. "This would be a good time to tell me what you know."

I looked at Milsap, then gave it up and spun the whole tale.

Gaz Cruikshank had shot the Key kids, I explained. He was supposed to shoot Key. But he was no killer and he fucked up. I figured a hired hit. Gaz bought his dope from Rainbow John and John's likely boss, Bad Mo Nadiri, who fell into place as the ones most likely to hire Gaz. Nadiri, we suspected, had killed John, and now Virginia Key, and was likely going down his list, getting everyone who had ever pissed him off. And Nadiri was distributing Karachi, white heroin from Pakistan.

Milsap and Serio looked at each other.

"What?" I asked.

Milsap said, "Someone been passing around spiked white heroin on campus. Rich white kids getting sick."

Serio said, "Two college kids in the back of a BMW, making body scissors. He comes and she passes out. Then she dies."

"Thallium," Milsap said, his tongue tangling over the unfamiliar word. "Like strychnine, only different."

Serio said, "If you'd talked to each other, you'd have figured this out by now."

I pointed to Virginia Key's house. "You're saying we did this?"

Serio said, "If you did your job—"

I said, "How am I supposed to do my job if you have someone following me around?"

He looked irritated. "I haven't *had* anyone following you."

"The tan Plymouth Duster."

"I'm telling you," he said, "I haven't had anyone following you!"

Something clicked in my head. Duster following me after I was at Hay's house. I'd been on the radio, told Jake where I was. Mo could have had a police radio, bought it from a catalogue.

Ideas started to click into place. Click. Someone followed me home from Hay's house.

Click. Mo knew Joey. Joey had mentioned me to him. Mo learned I was after him. Mo found out where I lived.

Click. Mo was going down the list of everyone who had pissed him off.

Click. Mo was at my house.

Click. Rachel. Oh, God, Rachel!

6:30 A.M.—700 Tillery Street

Nearly as Narcotics sergeant Luis Fuentes could put together through the bleary light of dawn: that a bunch of white kids had gotten sick or died from white heroin, that Virginia Key's kids had been shot by a junkie, that Key herself had just been killed, that Narco had very little to show for a month of surveillance—all added up to a wee-hours phone call from Chief Cronin, and a SWAT team prepping at the shooting gallery at Tillery Street under the nominal supervisions of Fuentes, Clay and camera crews from two television stations. Someone in a face mask gave a signal and iron battering rams crashed through a boarded-up door and two boarded windows at the same moment. The SWAT team rolled into every opening wearing heavy armor. Fuentes and Clay followed in street clothes, vests underneath, through the broken doorway. A couple of armed men quickly tackled half a dozen nod-outs while the men with the battering ram charged down a staircase. Fuentes followed them down, to a brick wall with a slot in the middle. They hoisted the battering ram and crashed through the brick wall; men and women scattering at the scanning spotlights, abandoning tables of dope, scales, plastic bags. Gunfire from nowhere and Fuentes realized he was outmatched with his bulletproof vest and his Glock 23 and chased Clay and the cameraman back up the stairs as a bullet caught him in the ass, pain ripped through him, and he fell, face down on the stairs and dragged himself upward until a SWAT grabbed him and hauled him out.

Outside, as the medics were treating his wound, the SWATters and patrols on the scene cuffed the men and women, gunmen, junkies, and everything in between, two dozen in all, and piled them into vans. It would take hours of separating them, bribing, cajoling and threatening them with everything from long prison sentences to rape, to determine that most of them didn't know who Bad Mo was, and none knew where to find him.

7:00 A.M.—706 East Thirty-eighth Street

I floored it across town, lights flashing, siren blaring, whipping through intersections blind, screaming, "Please, please, please . . ."

When I pulled up, Rachel's Celica was still parked in front of the house. I unlocked the front door. The house was dark. If she was in bed I didn't want to scare her. I pushed the bedroom door open. No Rachel. A jumble of blankets. Thirty-eight in my hand, I stepped through the living room thinking, please, please, don't let me find her dead.

Kitchen. Chairs overturned, dishes on the floor, back door opened. Something sucked the air from my lungs.

Blood on the floor.

7:30 A.M.—Dreamland

Rachel saw him over her, his full weight squeezing down, Rachel struggling for breath. Then she was pulling spiders off her body, huge, long-legged, by the handful, shaking them off, running down a hallway, then outside in the bright light of Lake Michigan, running along the shore.

Two men are following her, a white and a Mexican, sunburned and greasy. Narcs. She double-times her pace and suddenly she's in Chicago at night. A darkness is after her. She runs. It's always an inch behind her. Her legs don't seem to move, a shadow creeping up on her, overtaking her, then a man, bigger than life, monstrous hands holding her down. She grabs his head and tears it off, kicks holes in his thorax. Then she's running again, running so fast her feet barely touch the ground. She lifts off and runs through the air. She's flying by sheer will, over houses, fences, trees. She can go as high as she wants, just by thinking it. But she can't think very high. She gets stuck in the trees, wrapped in the phone wires. And he's alive again, grabbing at her feet as the power lines coil around her.

Pain radiated from the back of Rachel's head, waves of agony, down her neck, to her hands behind her back. She blinked, tried to open her eyes, but she couldn't see. She was in a dark room, her wrists bound. Her mouth tasted bitter. Blood.

She'd been lying in bed, half asleep. She'd heard the back door open, relaxed back to sleep knowing Dan was home. When she opened her eyes again, a man was perched over her, on hands and knees, pinning her under the blanket. But all her thoughts of self-defense through the years, of fighting back with your last ounce of strength, all disappeared and she found herself under a huge monster of a man, with a foul smell and a flame-scarred face. She lost her breath, froze and watched her fate unfold. He peeled the blanket off her and she cringed, pulled in on herself. She'd had the same feeling before. The horror of being approached when she was most helpless, fear of what he would do, fear that fighting back would make it worse. It happened when she was young, so, she'd been told, it changed the way she saw herself, the world, men. Suddenly she felt very ugly.

The scar-faced man lifted her upright and carried her toward the back door, her feet just off the floor. And that's when, screaming and crying, her strength kicked in, and she pounded at his groin with her knee, scratched at his face, and finally, when he tried to restrain her in a bear hug, opened her mouth wide and sank her teeth into his cheek. That was the last thing she remembered.

A door opened wide and light shone on her face. She'd been in a closet. A man was looking down on her, a big silhouette, and asking, "Have you slept well?"

7:30 A.M.—706 East Thirty-eighth Street

I heard myself cry out, but it was a twisted cry, helpless, like a gurgle. I reached one hand to the top of the open back door, another on the side, and with two yanks, ripped the door off its flimsy hinges and let it topple to the floor. I picked up a chair and smashed the glass windows out of the door with it. I was still doing that a few minutes later when Carter Serio caught up with me and followed my path to the kitchen.

In an hour, Serio had alerted every law enforcement agency, including the feds, about the kidnapping. Techs took samples, dusted for prints. One thing they found for sure was a boot print, size thirteen.

Two guys from communications had set up a recorder and a tap on my phone in case Nadiri called, but he didn't. Milsap reported that Nadiri and Rachel hadn't been found at the shooting gallery on Tillery Street, or at Rainbow John's house, that Narco was "sorting through" surveillance reports, looking for locations where she might be held.

I sat on the remaining kitchen chair, like any schmuck whose wife had been kidnapped, looking at the bloodstain on the floor, while cops tracked in and out of my house. I thought of throwing them out, making demands. None of that would bring Rachel back sooner, or bring her back safe.

Once someone has you captive, in their car or their home or somewhere else, your chances of surviving are slim. And each minute they get slimmer.

I slapped my cheek. A few men stopped what they were doing. I slapped it again, harder. Serio had been standing near me. He grabbed my hands. I pulled away, grabbed all the strength I could muster and slapped my cheek again. Then I went to the sink, ran cold water and splashed it on my face. Rachel needed me. How scared I was didn't matter. If she was dead, I'd have plenty of time to deal with it. I decided to play it like she was alive.

I said to Serio, "Anything from Narco?"

"They tried the most likely spots. Nothing."

"Holding out on us?"

"I don't think so," he said. "Tillery Street, Rainbow John's house, a nightclub where Mo was spotted. Everything else is where some other dealers were seen, and no one is sure whether they're his people. But they're checking them out anyway."

I wondered how fast and how efficiently Narco was going down that list. I said, "Who do we know is connected to him, for sure?"

We both went blank for a moment. Then we clicked.

8:30 A.M.—Camelot

The scar-faced man had dragged Rachel, hands tied behind her back, out to a couch, in a shag-carpeted basement with wood paneled walls. She figured it had been decorated for the kids in 1974 by the last owner. Rachel blinked at the light and sat, leaning sideways on the end of the couch, arms behind her. He had bandaged his cheek with duct tape. Blood trickled down his chin.

She knew not to scream.

He found a bottle of rum and poured himself a glass, swigged it. "Where are my manners?" he said in a clipped accent, refilling the glass. "Would you like a drink?"

"No," she said. Then added, "Thank you."

He wiped the blood from his chin, looked at it, flashed angrily at Rachel. She had made things worse. Then he reached toward her. She drew back from him but it was no use. He wiped his bloody hand on her cheek.

"Your husband had great difficulty with you. I was unsympathetic."

"You knew my husband?"

"A fine gentleman," he said. "Would you like a drink?"

"I said no."

"Forgive me," he said, refilling his glass. "My memory is not good. Drugs and trauma."

"What do you want?" she asked.

He put his glass down and smiled.

9:00 A.M.—Bergstrom Air Force Base

With our badges and Serio's finesse, we managed to talk our way past the Bergstrom gate and into the office of a colonel named Hargaard, second in command of the base. The office had two doors besides the one we'd entered through, including one door behind the desk, adding to the possibility that we were close to General Knobloch, who had made the video about Bergstrom, who had signed the release for the airman/heroin-dealer Milsap and I busted. While we stood before the desk, waiting, Serio warned me to keep cool. The colonel came in and we showed him Nadiri's photo.

Serio said, "He's the suspect in several murders and an abduction. We have reason to believe the general crossed paths with him at some point."

"Is he air force?"

"He was. All we want is to know where we might find him."

The colonel gave a rehearsed shrug and said, "I'll see that the general gets this."

I took a breath and Serio reached a hand toward me to keep me quiet. Serio said, "We have a hostage situation. The clock is ticking, Colonel."

The colonel said, "The general is very busy."

That did it. I said, "Yeah, we don't want to bother the general. Just tell him the man in the photograph is Mohammed Rashid Nadiri, Bad Mo. He's currently responsible for most of the heroin that comes into this town, including the heroin that killed two UT students. Heroin which, incidentally, comes from Pakistan and Afghanistan. And your planes are the only ones that fly into Austin from that region that don't go through customs. We also know—"

"Reles," Serio said.

I raised my voice in case the general was listening. "We also know that the general signed a release for an airman I personally arrested bringing fifty thousand dollars out of a known venue of heroin distribution. That means either he was picking up some money he'd left there for safekeeping, or he was making a sale. Maybe the general was raising funds to buy influence, keep his base open. What do I know? I'm just a city cop." I raised the volume another notch. "But in case the general thinks I can't prove his connection, tell him I saw his videotape, 'Save Bergstrom.' He's a man who believes in the power of the image. Tell him I know a dozen TV reporters who can build a full-color story on two hints and a nod. By six o'clock tonight his face will be on TV sets across Texas, the dope-dealing general who kills college co-eds. Ask him how he thinks the base will do after that."

I turned and headed out the way we came in, when the door behind the desk opened.

9:15 A.M.—Camelot

The ugly man moved closer to Rachel. His face was clustered with pockmarks, pustules and scars. He stood huge and wide, the weight of three of her. She sat up as best she could on the couch.

"Your husband and I were the greatest of friends. We had our disagreements, of course. It began as an exchange of favors. I grew to respect and admire him, and his flexible morals." He leaned over and leered into her face.

"What . . . what do you mean?" she asked.

"He told me. Of how you met."

"Oh, God."

"Do not hold it against him. He was intoxicated, and he was growing resentful. I was his confidant."

"You?"

"As I said, he was intoxicated. I believe he felt that you had grown ungrateful, regarding the great compromises he had made for you, from the beginning. Am I incorrect?" She looked away. "I can see that I am not. That unfortunate fellow you stabbed the night you and Mr. Velez met. Velez should have known better than to involve himself with you."

"Please . . ."

"He left out a crucial piece of information that would have made the difference between self-defense and something entirely different. That anonymous attacker in your home, he was not anonymous at all."

9:30 A.M.—Ben White Boulevard, Westbound

It was midmorning. I'd been awake for seven hours. In that time we'd found two corpses—Rainbow John and Virginia Key—and were hoping not to find a third. Rachel, I hoped, was still alive, sweating for her life in a hole somewhere, waiting for a ransom demand from a guy who'd never wanted ransom before. Her best chance was that I would shake the terror out of my head and pull it together to find her, and fast.

The cool breeze whipped in the window as Serio floored it westward with the lights flashing. I radioed Dispatch to send Milsap and any patrols they had to the location Knobloch had given us, Kings Row, off West Lake Hills, in a posh development called Camelot. I asked for the SWAT team but they were stalled in the aftermath of busting Nadiri's shooting gallery. They'd come when they could. I flicked on the siren and yelled at Serio, "Faster!"

"Reles, keep your head if you want to see that woman again."

I checked my .38. Six rounds, loaded. I'd be better with my automatic, still in the lock box in what was left of my Impala in the auto shop at HQ. Shaky odds Rachel was still alive and okay, or that she was even at the address Knobloch had given us. A stab in the dark.

10:30 A.M.—Camelot

Rachel, sitting on the couch, her wrists tied behind her back, slumped over and fought tears that dripped into the folds of her nightgown. Air wheezed in and out of her lungs. Her world, past, present, future, caved in. To die now seemed the only option.

"Chin up, little slut," he said, feeling her cheek with his raw, rough hands. "I won't tell anyone. Or will I? Perhaps I can be persuaded." He cupped his crotch with one hand.

"No!"

He walked away, lifted his glass again and drained it. "Where are my manners?" he said. "Would you like a drink?"

"Yes," she said, without taking a breath. "Yes."

10:45 A.M.—Camelot

Serio and I floored it way the hell out on Bee Caves Road, through the upscale West Lake Hills, past the city limits, to an almost invisible turnoff at Kings Row, to a hidden driveway Knobloch had described. We parked on the street and put on bulletproof vests from Serio's trunk, leaving Nadiri on his honor not to shoot us in the head or the balls. I noticed a time-battered brown Oldsmobile parked two houses down, facing away from us. A head of slicked hair shifted low in the front seat. As I headed over it stopped moving. I pulled the door open. Sergeant Clay, APD Narcotics, froze in his seat, angry like a trapped coyote. The wound I'd seen on his left cheek before, I clicked, matched the one on Rainbow John's face. They'd been hit with the same lead pipe. I considered two possibilities. That he'd answered our call to Dispatch for backup. But that wouldn't explain why he was hiding from us. The other explanation was that he was there hoping to catch Nadiri himself in the aftermath of the Tillery Street bust, that he had known about the location all along and hadn't told us, while Rachel sweated for her life. My skin went hot and my heart pounded. I heard Joey's voice, a memory, but clear as a phone call, telling me, "Back off. Stay cool." And I ignored it.

Serio called, "Reles?"

I pounded Clay in the side of the head. When he tried to get up, I punched him in the ribs. Clay scrambled for his gun and I reached for mine and Serio yelled, "Freeze!" He had an automatic, and his was drawn and aimed close enough to hit either of us.

"Reles," Serio said. "Think!" My blood raced and all I could think was that the only thing that would satisfy me was ripping Clay's head off. But that wouldn't save Rachel. I'd wasted precious time.

Serio said, "Clay, get lost," and he didn't holster his automatic till Clay had drawn back to his seat and closed the door. I gave Clay a last glance before he pulled out, giving away my thoughts like a dope. He got the message and Serio could have seen it if he'd been looking. Give me a chance and I'll kill you.

When the patrols finally arrived, six of them, we rolled up the private road and parked around the house, a spread-out split level with a two-and-a-half-storey entrance topped with a steeple. There was a circular driveway and a fountain. Each patrol was armed with a handgun and a shotgun, loaded with "less-lethal" bullets, on the chance of something hitting Rachel. The downside of less-lethal bullets is that if you hit someone in the wrong spot, they're lethal. I warned the patrols to aim low.

Serio had two mobile phones, each about the size of a hand radio. He lobbed one through the front window. The glass shattered and the phone landed inside. Then we crouched behind his car. He dialed his phone and waited. I could hear the phone ring through the shattered front window. The morning's hazy light shone through the window onto a surreal cocktail party of stone nudes, expensive statues that should have classed-up the place but didn't. If Nadiri went for the phone, he knew, there was a good chance a sniper would get him. If he didn't pick up the phone it was possible he had taken Rachel out already, and maybe killed himself. It kept ringing. Serio held his receiver. I watched his face. We waited.

For ten minutes.

Serio's face shifted. He heard something on the line. He said, "This is Carter Serio, Austin Police." Then he listened and handed me the phone. "He wants to talk to you."

I took the phone, tried to think smart, and said, "This is Reles."

"Get your pigs away from my house or I will kill your woman. But I will fuck her first."

She was still alive. I could hear her crying. I wasn't sure how badly she was hurt. "Put her on," I said.

I could hear Rachel sobbing into the receiver. "Are you all right?" I asked. She sobbed louder.

She cried, *"You did this to me!"* Desperation in her throat. *"You ruined my life!"*

"We'll fix it," I said. "I swear."

"You always swear!" she screamed so I could hardly make out the words. *"You never—you break every promise . . ."*

"I'm gonna get you out of there. You're gonna be all right."

"You promised you'd be here. You promised we'd spend the weekend to—together . . ."

Nadiri took the phone from her. *"I sympathize,"* he said.

"What did you do to her?" I thought of the blood on the floor.

"Tell me, Reles," he said. *"Do you really want her back? She is a terrible mess. I will take her off your hands for nothing."*

I covered the receiver.

Serio said, "The SWAT team should be here. Stall him a few minutes."

"Don't have it," I said. I considered various entry points, but nothing that would guarantee us getting to him before he could kill Rachel. I tried to take his mind off her. "Tell me about Virginia Key."

He said, *"My brothers went the way of all warriors. My parents were killed in their beds by the Soviets. Given the chance I would have wiped out Moscow, and Washington for its part. But I still had a sister."* I heard a strain in his throat, a frustration I didn't want him getting too close to.

He went on. *"Virginia Key swore she could get my sister into the United States. A persuasive woman. I gave her much money. I don't have to tell you what I did for it. And I waited. And waited. And then the news came. It was too late."*

The driveway continued around the side of the house. I followed it past a Cadillac, two BMWs and—no surprise—a tan Plymouth Duster. He went on.

"I hold Virginia Key personally responsible for the death of my sister. I was foolish and cowardly to protect myself by sending someone else to kill her. I prayed to Allah for guidance. Then I approached her at home. I simply asked her to admit wrongdoing! I would have killed her painlessly for

that. She refused. Can you imagine? Righteousness in the face of death. From a criminal. A murderess!"

A rifle shot blasted out, echoed up in the trees and sank again. I listened to the phone. *"What the hell was that?"* he shouted.

"I don't know." I found a mute button on the receiver, hit it and ran around the back of the house. A window was shattered and a patrol looked scared, smoking shotgun in hand.

"I got him," the patrol said.

I ran to the broken window. There was a downed man inside. It wasn't Nadiri. I needed to get to Nadiri before he had a chance to think. I climbed into the broken rear window, hoping to hell Nadiri didn't have a bigger house staff. I had my .38 in one hand, the phone in the other. The lights were out, the floor carpeted. Hazy sunlight came in the windows. I stepped over the glass, past the dead, or nearly dead, man through an empty room. The front room was decorated with statues, shadows in every direction from the windows. Serio saw me. I clicked off the MUTE and spoke softly, watching my breathing.

"You knew Joey Velez," I said into the phone.

"Knew him? I killed him. What the hell was that?"

"Your guy shot one of our guys," I said, too desperately. No answer. "Nadiri?" I asked. "Nadiri?!"

"Good," he said. He didn't argue. I hoped that meant he only had one guy.

I looked down hallways in two directions. The carpet muffled my footsteps. One archway led to a room draped in cloth. Too many places for him to hide. If he was in there, I needed him to come out. Meanwhile, I needed him talking, not listening. "Yeah, good thing you killed Velez, too," I said. "I had a million reasons for killing him. Only why'd *you* do it?"

"We had a falling out. I regret it to this day. We were great friends. He used to say, six times out of ten, if you go through a victim's things, you will find pictures of the killer and the victim with their arms around each other. Is that not true, Mrs. Velez?"

I heard Rachel cry, *"Shut up! Shut up!"* An echo of her voice came from the other end of the house.

He went on. *"He had been doing me favors, small favors, for some time. Little documents, bits of evidence disappearing. In exchange for money and cocaine."* I peeked into different doorways. Television room, bedrooms. Finally a closed door I took for the basement.

"Yeah?"

"I had planned a very large transaction. I was rising, you see. I needed his assistance, his protection. He refused. We exchanged words."

I walked out to the front window, the one Serio had shattered with the phone, and saw Serio and Milsap looking dumb. I motioned them to follow me in.

"Yeah," I said, "That guy could talk your ass off."

Serio and Milsap climbed in.

Nadiri laughed. *"He was very verbose. Regardless. We had words, we fought, I struck him with a brick."*

I thought about the dents in Joey's skull that Hay had told me about. I gauged the basement door, turned the knob slowly. It wasn't locked. The house wasn't equipped as a bunker. But whoever went down those stairs first was taking a bullet.

"What about the Chevy?" I asked. Serio and Milsap flanked me.

He laughed again. *"I drove him in his car out to the cliff, pointed it toward the edge. The road was barren. I put him in the driver's seat, no small task, and I glued the gas pedal down. Then I turned on the ignition, closed the door. You will recall the position of the gear shift."*

The gear shift was on the steering column, three-on-the-tree. You could move it from the driver's side window. He put it in drive, the car burned rubber—that explained the skid marks on the road—and Joey went over the cliff. But he was already dead.

"It seemed ingenious to me at the time. Now I don't know why you didn't see through it."

"We weren't thinking straight," I said. I considered the possibilities of my rushing in on Nadiri. He could shoot me. I could run in shooting and kill Rachel. I stalled. "I was thinking," I said. "Instead of killing her, you should kill me." My breath was getting short.

"I prefer to see you in pain," he said. Then he shouted, *"You disrupted my date with PARADISE!"*

I didn't ask for details. I hit the MUTE button. "I'm going in," I whispered to Serio. "While I keep him busy, you shoot him. Milsap, the door on my signal." I handed Serio the phone. Milsap took the doorknob.

And all this time I'm thinking there has to be a smarter way, if only I could think of it. If only I had the time. But I didn't.

"Negative, Sergeant," Serio whispered. "He'll kill you. I can't allow that."

"Then I quit," I said, and nodded. Milsap yanked the door open.

In law enforcement and in the world at large, people underestimate the presence of edged weapons—knives, razors, sharpened objects— by some standards more devastating than a bullet. And if somebody is coming at you with one, you need him to be fifteen to twenty feet away to give you a chance to react, draw your weapon and fire.

I had drawn my weapon already. But he was only two feet away.

Nadiri stood in front of me on the second step down, grinning wildly. I grabbed at his wrist with my weak left as he jabbed something shiny into my thigh and I fired wildly.

11:15 A.M.—Camelot

All life is a series of fatal mistakes.

The stretched-out moment, the big boom, where everything happens in slow motion: the car going into a spin and crashing sideways against the wall, the brick that hits you over the head, the knockout punch you should have seen coming, the bullet that burns through your gut, the shot you fire in the wrong direction, the nightstick that cracks you on the spine with a prolonged *crrra-a-ck!* and gives you a chance to think, if only I had thought of that, if only I had seen that coming. And now my life will be forever different.

◆

As I fired the weapon and the blade cut into my thigh, Milsap and Serio pulled me back from the stairwell, along with Nadiri. Nadiri had clamped his free hand onto my jacket. I fired again, this time into his chest. Nadiri cried out, dark blood gushing from the bullet hole. I lost my weapon. Nadiri yanked the blade loose from my thigh. My vision went blurry. I could tell he was trying to jab me again. Serio grabbed Nadiri's wrist. Nadiri head-butted me. I wanted to lie back but if you give up, you're dead. I saw Serio try to wrest the blade from Nadiri's hand. I roared from my guts, punched Nadiri in the face with my good right, twice. He smiled, blood running down his chin.

"Do you understand?" he cried out. "I do not feel pain!"

And then Milsap got a good angle and bashed a dent into the side of Nadiri's skull with his handgun.

I said, "Rachel. Rachel."

Milsap went downstairs.

Nadiri babbled, "I will kill you like you killed my poor country."

"Why them?" Serio said. "They're not the president."

Nadiri said, "I cannot *get* to the president!" Then, gripping at the pain in his chest and the pooling blood, he screamed out to shake the building. And he died.

EPILOGUE: SUNDAY
June 30, 1991

11:00 A.M.—Barton Springs Road

Marching bands drowned the streets in the tones of John Philip Sousa. Snare drums rapped in staccato rhythms, an effective impersonation of machine-gun fire. They were followed by a procession of fully equipped, desert-camouflaged army tanks. On credit, the six-month governor had the capitol building wrapped with a yellow ribbon, six feet wide, and tied in a bow the size of a Patriot Missile. Pundits commented on the choice of the plastic ribbon, a petroleum product, as a symbol for the Gulf War.

I was stuck in traffic behind a yellow school bus packed with teenaged soldiers, cheering and celebrating their victory. The radio news said, *"The president discounted Saddam Hussein's commitment to cooperate with the United Nations, calling the Iraqi leader a liar and a cheat, who is dodging U.N. attempts to determine whether Iraq has the materials needed to construct nuclear weapons. When asked if the U.S. would be renewing military action against Iraq, the president responded that it was too early to say, but he feels the authority for such an invasion exists understanding U.N. resolutions. Meanwhile the Defense Realignment and Base Closure Commission begins meeting today in Washington. Austin's Bergstrom Air Force Base is slated for closing, the land to be developed into a new airport by the year 2000. Base commander General Herbert Knobloch will be retiring . . ."*

I killed the radio. I had joined with Serio, Milsap, Narco and the DA to put together an indictment for Knobloch, for facilitating Nadiri's import business. But we would have needed military records, cargo statements, materials we couldn't get without air force cooperation. The matter went on hold while General Knobloch retired in the hill country, west of town, the apple of his wife's devoted eye.

Debbie Kubasik, the chubby bottle-blonde from Delaware, who had been caught rolling down I-35 one morning from Dallas with traces of Karachi in her purse, was released after a week, placed on probation for possession of less than a hit of heroin and the case transferred back to her home state of Delaware. Toxicology had tested the dope and found no additives, meaning it really didn't come from Nadiri, or it came from him before he hit upon the additives idea. Or something else.

The police radio crackled. *"Homicide 8."*

I picked up the mike. "This is Homicide 8, go ahead."

"You have a call from the DA's office. I'm patching it through."

I said, "What's shaking, Miles?"

Miles, *"Boy, you wouldn't believe it. I got a buddy with the ATF. Some crazy cult outside of Waco, hoarding guns. We're driving up to sniff around. Nothin' formal. Gonna grab some beer for the ride back. Interested?"*

Ex-cops who work as investigators for the DA have a little more autonomy than cops do. Miles was now able to drink and work at the same time. I said, "Can't make it today, but keep me posted. How's the drinking going?"

"Not bad," he said. *"How's the Christ-killing?"*

A young black soldier, maybe nineteen, looked out the rear exit window of the bus in front of me and caught my eye. He dropped his smile: I wasn't a supporter of the festivities, but he couldn't guess why. Then he raised his fingers in a peace sign, a questioning look on his face. Peace. Could we agree on that?

He'd come back from the war expecting a hero's welcome, like the kids coming back from France, and later, Vietnam. Like Torbett, back on duty, with a back injury that would torment him for the foreseeable future. The kid would find out a week from now, while he was sleeping in his mother's house and looking for a job, that he'd fought to keep America exactly the way it was before he left. I peaced him back.

Torbett had come back on limited duty, on crutches, in early May. The first thing he did was to get an indictment against Virginia Key for embezzlement. Raising that kind of charge against a dead person is harder than you would think, but he used the indictment to lessen the sentence of Harold Key, Virginia Key's allegedly dead ex-husband. Torbett himself drove to Louisiana to speak for Harold Key at his parole hearing, and drove Key back to Austin to the foster home where his son Rubin had been staying since his release from the hospital. Torbett had talked to Rubin and once he was sure the release had been secured, told him his father was alive. He brought the father to Rubin, saw them look at each other, hug tenuously, saw the father cry. Torbett came back to the squad room, dropped on the floor, his back in a seizure of pain after the long car ride. Sweating and trembling, he said what cops get to say once in a great while, when they know they did something right. "It was worth it."

The night I shot Nadiri, I stumbled down the stairs on my wounded leg. Rachel was on a couch in her nightgown, crying. A bullet hole marked the wall, a foot from her head, the shot from my gun. Milsap had untied her and I tried to wrap my arms around her, make her feel safe, but she pushed me away.

Medics wrapped her in a blanket and treated her for shock. She wasn't injured. They packed my wound. Rachel didn't look at me.

The medics hoisted me up the stairs, Rachel following. My leg would need stitches if not surgery. Rachel was fine to go home, if she wanted to.

In front of the house, patrols, a fire truck and EMS packed up in the noonday light. Rachel stood in her blanket, looking down.

"I'll take you home," I said.

The medic said, "You're looking at potential nerve damage. You need to see a doctor."

"I'll be fine," Rachel said. I knew she wouldn't. But I couldn't stay with her, and I couldn't take her with me, ask her to stand around and wait in the hospital, after what she'd been through. I didn't think to have someone else stay with her. Who would I have asked? Serio? Milsap?

She told me to go and I went.

As they helped me into the ambulance, I thought about Rachel, what hell she'd been through, what I'd put her through. I thought about Joey's death, finally explained, Joey resolved and at peace. I wondered if my freedom from Joey after all these years, would be too little too late for Rachel. I'd take two weeks off immediately, take her anywhere she wanted to go. I'd quit the force if she needed me to. I listened for Joey's voice. Some words of wisdom, maybe, *"Bueno, mazel tov, amigo."* But he wasn't there.

When I got home from the hospital, Rachel was packed and gone.